Time will tell

TIME WILL TELL

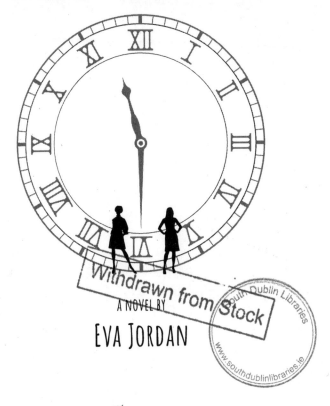

A NOVEL BY

EVA JORDAN

Urbane
PUBLICATIONS

urbanepublications.com

First published in Great Britain in 2018 by Urbane Publications Ltd
Suite 3, Brown Europe House, 33/34 Gleaming Wood Drive, Chatham, Kent ME5 8RZ
Copyright © Eva Jordan 2019

A CIP catalogue record for this book is available from the British Library.

ISBN 978-1-911583-94-3
MOBI 978-1-911583-95-0

Design and Typeset by Julie Martin
Cover by Author Design Studio

Printed and bound by 4edge UK

Urbane
PUBLICATIONS

urbanepublications.com

Mum and Dad, this one's for you.

"Time is an illusion."
– **Albert Einstein**

Contents

"Time will explain."
– Jane Austen, *Persuasion*

I stare at the four grey walls surrounding me and shiver. I'm on my own but not alone. I'm being watched. They'll be in to question me soon. But I'll stick to my side of the story. Insist it was self-defence. They've got me though. Bang to rights. Nothing I can do about it. Well, that's not true. I could do something. Tell the truth for one. But I won't.

I do what I do out of love. It's in the job description. And while I never, for one moment, imagined love would bring me here, to a place full of lies and deceit, I always knew the love for my family was like nothing else in the world. To hurt them is to hurt me, far worse in fact, and to do so leaves me with little or no choice. For when it comes to family, my love knows no law, no benevolence. It challenges everyone and everything, crushing all who stand in its path.

It's funny, though, how we kid ourselves, and one another, about our own moral compass. Of what we believe ourselves capable and not capable. It's reassuring to think we have limits, convince ourselves there are lines we would never cross, tell ourselves how civilised we are. But like our hearts, civilisation is fragile. The horrors of what we *really* are, underneath, are simply masked by a fine coat of varnish.

Scratch the surface hard enough, though, throw in the right set of circumstances, and we are all capable of anything.

Even murder.

Chapter 1

CHRISTMAS DAY
PRESENT DAY – LATE AFTERNOON

LIZZIE

Like a gun, the remote control points towards the newsreader's head. The TV dies, and her face disappears into a black hole of oblivion. A collective sound of small, inward gasps fills the air, followed by a silence both heavy and palpable. The room holds its breath. Heads turn from left to right as wide-eyed individuals, slack jawed like stranded fish gasping for air, struggle to make sense of it all.

It's Hunter Black.

Hunter Black is dead.

I should feel relief but the overriding emotion invading my thoughts is fear.

Cassie, brow creased, fist covering her mouth, stares at me. Her eyes, although fixed on my face, dart from side to side, dark lashes flickering like butterfly wings, searching for answers to unasked questions. Her skin looks pale, the ruddy glow of Christmas having all but drained from her face while mine burns, flushed with the heat of guilt and shame.

'Well. That's a surprise,' Mum says, scanning the room. 'Think I'll put the kettle on.' It's as if the ritual of drinking tea will save us all from the chaos this news promises.

I walk toward Cassie and ask her if she's okay. She shrugs. I study her face, tuck a loose piece of hair behind her ear and let my fingers rest on the soft down of her cheek. 'Yeah... course I am?' my daughter replies, her smile bright. I'd have believed her too but for the slight wobble in her voice.

'It's true.' Natasha lifts her head from her phone. 'It's all over Twitter. He's dead. Hunter Black is actually dead.'

Luke, now standing behind Cassie, places a protective arm about her shoulders. 'Good fucking riddance,' he whispers. Cassie turns to look at him, offers him a smile of sorts. His phone rings. He stares at the screen, frowns. 'Sorry. Just have to take this,' he says, kissing Cassie's cheek before loping off towards the kitchen. Cassie watches him, her expression one of surprise and something else – hurt, maybe?

'He's been dead for a couple of days, they reckon,' Natasha, my sister-in-law continues, her expression one of troubled concentration, her pixie-like features illuminated by the glow radiating from the tiny screen glued to her hand. 'In his London home, like the newsreader said. Which means...' She looks thoughtful, glances over at my brother then back towards me, a quizzical smile lifting the corners of her mouth. '...that was the same day you lot were in London wasn't it? When you all met for a drink? After Sean, Connor, Simon and Scott had been to the IndieKnot gig?' (Who'd have thought it, my brother, my son, my partner and my once arsehole of an ex-husband all going to a gig – together!).

'Yeah, it was,' Cassie replies. 'Luke and I met up with them too. And Useless,' she adds as an afterthought.

'Useless?'

Cassie grins. 'Real name, Eustace – our friend from college. He plays in a band too. Does similar sort of music to Luke. Everyone called him Useless, as a joke, because he's not, he's a brilliant guitar player. It just kind of stuck.'

'Ok-ay,' Natasha replies with a frown. 'Well, whatever, I hope you've all got your alibis sorted?' Sheepish, she glances about the room and looks at Cassie. 'You know I'm only joking, right?'

Cassie stares at her aunt, offers her a smile that doesn't reach her eyes. 'Yeah. Course,' she replies.

She's joking yet no one is laughing. Myself included. Which is strange. As a family, we've always prided ourselves on the ability to pick out the humour amongst tragedy, particularly our own tragedies. Imperative to being human, I think, to survival, even. Dad was always saying laughter is the best medicine. However, as with most things in life, it's also about timing and based on the nervous laughter of some in the room, the awkward silence of others, it seems not enough time has lapsed regarding this particular tragedy. Then again, the rape and assault of Cassie, by said dead man – a little over eighteen months ago now – is, as far as I can see, never going to be a laughing matter.

I look across at Simon, notice the quick, furtive glances he exchanges with my brother, Sean; how they both look at Connor, and how he in turn glances at me, before looking at his feet. Blink and you'd have missed it. But I didn't. So why does it make me uneasy, make the hairs on the back of my neck stand on end? Why does Natasha's chance remark have them on edge? I make a mental note to catch Simon later and talk to him. As usual he'll plead exhaustion, say whatever it is will have to wait until morning, then when morning comes, I'll roll over only to find his side of the bed empty – again. He'll be off doing other important crap. Most likely on his phone. Most likely work related? Mind you, I'm not sure I'd want to speak to me either. I haven't been a barrel of laughs of late, and despite my physical presence, mentally I've been on another planet.

Then again, fuck it, things haven't exactly been easy. It's still only a year since Dad passed away. Then there's all the police and legal crap that Cassie has needed my help with. Not to mention poor old Uncle Teddy who has deteriorated terribly since Dad left us. I remember Dad joking with him, trying to cheer Uncle Teddy up when he became annoyed or frustrated – "Oh well,

Ted," he'd say, "at least you get to meet new people every day". Or, "you don't have Alzheimer's, you have some-timers – some-timers you remember, some-timers you don't". His best Italian accent (which was almost as bad as his singing) almost always brought a smile to Uncle Teddy's face. Alzheimer's is shit, though, the gradual hollowing away of someone from the inside out; a thief of the worst kind.

Then somewhere in between all this chaos, I am supposed to be penning my next novel. Difficult when you have writer's block. When Dad first passed away, I couldn't stop writing. I found it cathartic, writing like my life depended on it, which it did in a way. Writing kept me sane, allowed me to ignore the huge gap in my heart. Now though, despite my over-crowded, muddled thoughts, I haven't been able to write another word, and each time I try, each time I sit down at my computer, I am met by nothing but a blank page and blinking cursor.

A wave of fear ambushes me, I feel nauseous, unsteady on my feet. Maybe I'm drunk – again? I am drinking far too much lately. Or maybe it's fear? Fear of losing Simon? My family? Fear of losing my mind? I take a deep breath; notice the motes of dust floating in the sunshine streaming in through the window. Life, despite outward appearances, feels difficult. I know all I need to do is keep my shit together just a bit longer – but right now that seems easier said than done.

Natasha is pressing her lips together, and looks down at her phone again. 'They've asked Honey for a comment apparently. But it says here, she's refused. Has nothing to say.'

Annoyed at Natasha for mentioning Honey, I look towards Cassie who is chewing the side of her lip; thank god Aunt Marie isn't here to defend her, which, much to my disappointment and Cassie's continual disbelief, she always does. Well, that's not strictly true, Aunt Marie doesn't exactly defend Honey, her loyalties are always with us, her family, but as one who is slightly removed, she always tries to see the bigger picture – at least, that's how it comes across – and bring the blame squarely back to the one person who deserves it – Hunter Black. Nonetheless, Honey betrayed Cassie so it's a struggle for Cassie to reconcile her great aunt's point of view, no matter how well intended it is.

Cassie doesn't respond, neither do I and thankfully Natasha makes no more mention of Honey Brown the singer, ex-best friend of my daughter.

Connor brushes past me, his face drawn, his eyes restless, shifty.

'You okay, love?' I ask.

He shrugs, looks towards the stairs. 'Getting my coat,' he mumbles.

'You going out?'

He nods. 'Jake's.'

My parental alarm bell starts to ring. I reach out and grab him, coiling my fingers around his wrist. 'How is he? Jake, I mean. How's he doing?' Connor, who doesn't look at me, shakes his arm free. I feel my thorax tighten, a bubble of self-pity well in my chest. When did the gap between my son and I get so wide?

Mum wanders back into the room and asks who wants tea and who wants coffee. I feel a hand on my shoulder and jump. Relieved, I realise it's Simon. 'You two okay?' he asks looking from me to Cassie, who is still standing behind me.

Cassie gives another shrug. 'Yeah. I suppose so. It's just… weird. I feel really weird. Suppose I should be happy, but I feel numb. Can't believe he's… dead.'

'Couldn't have happened to a nicer bloke.' Simon's voice is filled with gravitas.

'Coo-ee. Simon?' Mum calls. She is standing on tiptoes, waving a gravy-stained tea towel like a flag, a starter for ten. 'Tea? Coffee?'

'Tea, please. Thanks Ellie.' He winks at me and gives Cassie's shoulder a reassuring squeeze. 'You know where I am,' he says, coughing to clear his throat, 'if you need to talk... or whatever?'

Cassie smiles. 'Thanks, Si.'

Sean calls out to Cassie, gives her the thumbs up. Again she smiles. 'Thanks, Uncle Sean,' she says.

Sean then asks Simon if he can have a word.

I ask Cassie if she would like to go somewhere more private, to talk. She shakes her head. 'Maybe later?'

'Yes, of course. Are you sure you're okay, though?' She assures me she is then heads towards the kitchen in search of Luke.

'I'm glad he's dead.' I swing round once again, face to face with Connor. 'Serves him right.' His voice sounds choked, his words hard, angry clots.

I press my lips together, nod. I don't disagree, but I feel the need to lighten the atmosphere. 'Maybe it was Grandad,' I suggest. Connor's youthful brow creases into a frown. 'You know – like a ghost. He always said he'd watch over us when he went. Maybe he came back to haunt Black... gave him a heart attack or something?'

To my delight Connor finds this hilarious, laughs with the gusto of a five year old, the sound rippling and swelling like a stone thrown in a pond, breaking the surface tension between us. Within seconds I'm laughing along with him, our shoulders heaving, our pained expressions borne out of the sheer delight at the thought of Dad – Grandad – haunting Black, and no doubt telling him to "fack orf" in the process. It's good to see my son laugh.

Our laughter subsides and Connor, who is opening and closing his mouth, rests his chin between his fingers and thumb as if trying to realign his jaw. 'Shit, Mum – my mouth aches from so much laughing,' he says. 'You're funny sometimes, you know.'

I raise my eyebrows. He sounds surprised. Is it that long since we last laughed together? 'Almost as funny as Cassie trying to convince everyone during dinner that we all have "disposable" thumbs, eh?'

Connor rolls his eyes. 'I know, right? I mean… for god sake. How? How can she be so clever and yet so stupid at the same time?'

I cross my arms, shake my head. 'To be honest, I thought she'd grow out of it. Don't think she will though. Think we have to accept that your sister will always reign supreme as queen of malaprops and spoonerisms.'

Connor, his grin affectionate, clicks his tongue. 'Hmmm… s'pose it is easy to confuse disposable with opposable?'

'An enigma. That's what one of her teachers at a school parents' evening once told me she was.'

'Yeah? I don't doubt it!'

Or was that me… and one of my teachers?

I look at my man-child and realise I love him more now than I ever have. Despite the fact he eats me out of house and home. Despite his clumsy large hands that cause dishes to break and glasses to smash – all of their own accord. Despite his finger-tapping, pen-clicking, leg-bouncing, knuckle-knocking noises. Despite the fact he can fix a computer but can't remember how to use a washing machine. And, despite the fact that, sometimes, he gets a little pissed off with me.

I step forward. Move in closer. This time, when I place my hand on his arm, he doesn't shrug it off. I hold my breath. *Small steps, Lizzie, small steps.*

Connor looks down, kicks one foot with the other. 'Thanks for all the Christmas presents and shit,' he mumbles. 'And dinner.' He looks up again. 'It was peng.'

I smile, lean in. *Dare I ask him for "a great big bear hug"?* I open my mouth to ask just as Summer, sinuous as a cat, slopes in behind us. The moment is gone.

'Soooooo, who is it again – that's dead? Is it that man who hurt Cassie?'

Natasha looks up from her phone, studies her daughter. 'Summer, come here, please.' The intonation in her voice is warm but firm.

Summer purses her lips, slumps forward. She does as she's asked but her heavy sighing is as purposeful as her exaggerated eye rolling. I watch her saunter back to her mother. Skinny and athletic I'm in awe of the woman she'll become, half fearful too, if I'm honest. I've no idea how much she knows about Black, what Natasha and Sean have told her – as much as is appropriate for a twelve year old, I assume. *Whatever that is?*

When I turn back Connor is heading towards the door. 'Connor? You didn't say – about Jake? How is he?'

'His mum's a cow and his dad's an alchy. How do you think he's doing?'

Every time I think of Jake it's always as the chubby, cheeky-faced four year old Connor met at nursery. 'Not much of a Christmas for him, is it? Jake and his dad are more than welcome to join us, you know. I said they were welcome to have Christmas dinner with us?'

Connor rakes his hand through his sandy-coloured hair. 'I asked but Jake's dad refused. Jake would have come, I think. But he didn't, you know, want to leave his dad on his own. Not on Christmas Day.'

'No. Well, that's understandable. How are things with his Mum? Is he likely to be seeing her over Christmas?'

Connor shakes his head. His relaxed smile now thin lipped and tight. 'Nope. Her soldier boyfriend doesn't like Jake. *Apparently.*'

'Please tell me Jake at least had a Christmas dinner?'

Again Connor shakes his head. 'Uh huh. Beans on toast.'

'Really?'

'Yep.'

'Lizzie, love? Connor? Tea or coffee?' Mum interrupts, placing hot steaming mugs next to Simon and Sean at the table.

'Nothing for me, Nan,' Connor replies, 'I'm off out.'

I tell Connor to hang on a minute while I pack up leftovers for him to give to Jake and his Dad. I head towards the kitchen, pass Simon and Sean locked in muffled conversation around the large dining table now strewn with the remnants of Christmas Day dinner celebrations. A mish mash of abandoned party streamers and colourful paper hats are dotted amongst several large tubs of Roses and Quality Street. My tummy flips. I realise my old friend, nagging doubt, has reared its ugly head again. Why is Simon hell bent on talking to anyone but me?

In the kitchen I sidestep Mum who is busy stirring cups and mugs. The cutlery drawer is still open. Why does it annoy me? With a nudge of my hip it closes. I fling various cupboards and drawers open in search of plastic food containers and silver wrapping foil. Cassie and Luke come in from the garden.

'Tea? Coffee?' Mum asks them.

Cassie, her eyes red-rimmed, bows her head. Mum, who is watching her, throws me a sideways glance. Cassie reeks of cigarette smoke; I wish she would give up. Luke places his arm around her shoulders, guides her towards the living room. I watch them for a second, overcome with a huge wave of relief. I love Luke, his warmth, his intelligence, the many little ways – an encouraging word, a gentle hand, a reassuring smile – that show me how much he loves my daughter. 'Two coffees please, Ellie,' he calls across his shoulder. 'I'll be back in a minute – give you a hand.'

Mum grabs more mugs and watches me as I load up plastic containers with leftover Christmas dinner. 'Who's that lot for?'

I explain they are for Jake and his dad. 'Bloody beans on

toast, he gave that boy,' I mutter. 'For god' sake. I know his wife left him but come on... beans on toast on Christmas Day? Surely he could have made an effort for his son?'

The chinking of metal spoons against china cups ceases. 'Not everyone is as strong as you are, Lizzie. Remember that,' Mum says.

Surprised, I look up. I'm faced with my mother's back and if it wasn't for the gentle rise and fall of her shoulders, I wouldn't have known she was crying. I stop what I'm doing, go to her, rest my cheek on her back and, folding my arms around her, squeeze her. Her hair smells of lemons and limes, her clothes of cinnamon and Christmas cake. She's tiny too. Half the woman she was before Dad passed away, her bones, once soft and fleshy are now sharp and brittle. She lifts her pinny and dabs her eyes.

'Ignore me. I'm just having a moment.'

'Dad?'

She nods, gripping the sides of the worktops until her knuckles turn white. 'It still takes my breath away, Lizzie, just how much I miss him.'

I lower my head. Shrink. I wrack my brain for some words of comfort but none are forthcoming and even if they were, the lump in my throat would prevent me from saying them.

'Mum?' Connor is now hovering by the kitchen door. 'I really need to–'

Mum looks up; I look round. Connor's face drops. 'Shit, Nan, you okay?' He strides towards her, wrapping his long skinny arms around her. My heart swells.

'Course I bleedin' am.' She waves her hand to shoo him away. Undeterred, he continues to hug her.

'You'll be telling me to "fack orf" in a minute,' he says, which makes us all laugh.

I shove containers of leftovers into a large shopping bag and throw in a tin of biscuits and a packet of mince pies for good measure. Connor puts his arm around my shoulders, squeezes me. 'Thanks, Mum,' he says. 'Ugh ... what the hell is that smell?'

I look up, sniffing the air. A rather unpleasant odour hits me straight between the eyes. 'Ooh, yes. See what you mean.' It is bad, however, I can safely say I've smelled worse.

Both Connor and I look towards Freddy's dog basket in the corner.

'Freddy?' Connor calls. A rather old, rheumy-eyed cocker spaniel lifts his somewhat sleepy head. 'Was that you, Freddy?' Freddy looks at Connor, yawns, before lowering his head again, his expression one of a chastised child.

'Oh no, I bet it's the leftover turkey. I wonder who gave him that? I specifically told everyone not to give him the turkey.'

'It wasn't him.' I turn to see my rather red-faced mother stepping away. She coughs, looks down. 'Too many Brussels sprouts,' she mumbles.

Connor's laugh fills the room. 'Nice one, Nan,' he says, fanning his face with his hand. 'That's actually way worse than Robbo's farts – and that's saying something.'

Mum, who looks mortified, opens the back door to let in some fresh air. Connor, still chuckling, puts his hand up. 'Bye, Mum. Bye, Nan. Oh my god. Can't wait to tell Jake about this.' Rucksack over his shoulder, carrier bags of food swinging from each hand, I watch my son head towards the front door. I hear it slam, rattling the letterbox, despite my reminder to close it gently. And he's gone.

I look at Mum who, her face now crimson, apologises again. 'Talking of smells,' she says. 'I hope you don't mind me saying, but your hair, at least I think it's your hair, smells a little... strange? I thought maybe it was just me but Natasha mentioned it too.'

Now it's my turn to blush. I put my hand up to my head, scrape my hair to the side. 'I know. Sorry. Simon said the same thing earlier. I think it's the new shampoo and body wash I bought. It's supposed to be one of those organic ones, you know, full of natural ingredients? Think I'll go back to using the unnatural ones, full of chemicals.'

I try and join in with her laughter, then change the subject, ask her if she's heard from Aunt Marie today. She shakes her head. 'She's supposed to be popping by later, after seeing Uncle Teddy. Perhaps I should have gone with her? Teddy has really deteriorated.'

I nod. 'So I've heard. He wasn't too good last time I saw him.' I know there are arguments for and against euthanasia but with my uncle, it's sheer cruelty keeping him alive. 'Did you... erm... see Aunt Marie yesterday?' I ask.

'Yes, I did.'

'How was she?'

Mum, once again stirring mugs and cups, stops and turns to face me. *Did she notice the slight tilt in my voice?*

'Well, now you ask. She seemed a bit... off? Out of sorts.' She smirks. 'Or "out of salts" as Cassie prefers to say.' I smile. 'I put it down to the stress of Uncle Teddy. I suggested she have Christmas dinner with us, said we could visit Teddy afterwards, together.' Mum pauses for a moment, sighs. 'You know what she's like, though. Wasn't having any of it. And...' she shrugs. '...Who can blame her? I'm hardly a bag of laughs at the moment, am I? Can't believe it's been a whole year since your dad passed away, Lizzie.' Dewy-eyed, she stares at me, her head fractionally tilted. 'Do you know what the most shocking, the most unexpected thing about losing your father is?'

'What?'

'How alone I feel. I know it sounds morbid, wrong even, but we were together for so long, I didn't realise just how much I'd miss the old bugger. It's the little things I notice the most. Like his jacket slung over the back of the kitchen chair, a folded newspaper on the table next to it. Used to annoy the hell out of me. I was always moaning at him to put them away.' She pauses. 'I'd give anything to see that jacket again…'

'Oh Mum, you should have said. I never realised you were so lonely–'

'Not lonely, Lizzie. I'll never be lonely with my family around me. I'm talking about being alone. Then again, I suppose we're all alone, really? We come into this world alone and leave it the same way too, but a marriage – one that lasted as longs as ours – obscures that simple truth.'

I blink back the tears now welling up behind my eyes; feel the need to change the subject again – quickly. For both our sakes. 'What do you think about Black then?'

Mum, who has gone back to stirring cups, stops again. 'I think the world is a better place without him. You?'

'I think you're probably right.'

Mum's wrinkled eyes crease in disbelief. 'There's no probably about it, my gel! And you and I both know, if he were still here, your Dad would agree. Now, did you say you wanted tea or coffee?'

I feel my lips turn upwards into a smile. 'Yes, you're right. He would. Only he would have worded it a little more colourfully than you.'

'Hmm… wouldn't he just.'

'And thanks; I'll have a coffee please, Mum. As black and strong as it comes.'

I look out of the window, notice a blackbird perched on the branch of our silver birch tree. I remember my walk along the river with Dad not long before he passed away. "Do you know blackbirds like to sing after rain," he'd said. Just another one of his many trivial facts; no need for Google when Dad was around. Now, the blackbird tips its head, an orange-rimmed eye as black as its feathers observes me.

Is that you, Dad? And if so what do you, Salocin Lemalf, think about the death of Hunter Black?

I think of my father and of the old black and white photos of both him and my mother, and Uncle Teddy and Aunt Marie, that I have poured over, trying to remember my life in London. The years before we migrated here, before they opted for the quiet life of the Fens as opposed to the hullabaloo of the capital. Try as I might, I can recall only one single memory. It's vague and scratchy like a programme on an old TV losing its signal: Sean and I sitting in a kitchen, I think? With a man whose name and face I can't remember. He seems nice enough, unlike the man who is standing in the hallway with Mum, who is on the phone, upset... *I don't know why but I have a bad feeling in my tummy and I think it's something to do with Dad. So I run out of the kitchen and up the stairs to my bedroom. I have a bedside lamp, which Dad used as a desk lamp but gave to me when I said I was frightened of sleeping in the dark. He told me if I kept it on at night, he'd always find his way home to us. I turn it on, so he can find us, but the man, whose name and face I cannot remember, follows me, and carries me back downstairs to the kitchen...* I also think of Dad's missing finger, his insistence that it was an industrial accident at the shoe factory he worked in, but how I swear it happened *before*. In London.

Why is that part of my parents' lives so shrouded in mystery? Aunt Marie has started opening up a little just recently, but it's not enough. I need to know more, and not just to quell my curiosity, but because it's important to me, as part of my history. Mum isn't as stubborn as Dad was, though, and something tells me, if I tread carefully enough, she may be ready to talk.

Chapter 2

SALOCIN LEMALF 1945

SALOCIN

Salocin Lemalf was born on the evening of 13th December 1945, a bitterly cold day. The midwife arrived by bicycle, brushing a recent flurry of snow from her shoulders, and was more than grateful for a hot cup of tea. Several hours later, eleven minutes past eleven to be precise, the second son and last child of Wilfred and Martha Lemalf, entered the world kicking and screaming.

Martha, an avid reader with ideas above her station wanted to call him Nicolas. Wilf was having none of it. As long as there was breath in his body no son of his would be burdened with such a "pansy, poofter, shirt lifter" of a name. As a joke, Martha simply turned the letters around and convinced her ignorant husband that the name Salocin was synonymous with that of a great ancient warrior.

'He's in all the 'istory books,' she said. 'Surely you've heard of him?'

Wilf accepted this story and much to Martha's eternal amusement, their second son was christened Salocin Lemalf or, when spelled backwards, Nicolas Flamel, the name of the famous alchemist supposed to have discovered both how to turn base metals into gold and the secret to immortality.

Any show of affection by Wilf and Martha towards their sons was rare, towards each other, rarer still. Their fights were loud and physical, which wasn't unusual where they came from. Family life in the overcrowded East End of London was lived at close quarters. Aunts, uncles, cousins and grandparents all lived within a stone's throw of each other, and, as kids, Salocin and his friends ran freely among the streets. The backstreets, without cars, were perfectly safe and used as playgrounds, as were the bombsites with their 'Danger, Keep Out' signs – these much less safe, but far more alluring.

Times were tough. Folk were still reeling from another World War, following the one that had promised to be a "war to end all wars". Skilled jobs, with relatively high pay and regular hours, were ferociously guarded; kept in the family and passed from father to son. Most local men worked the docks, and whilst employment was high, wages were low, especially for unskilled casual labourers like the virtually illiterate Wilf. Dragged up, motherless, and responsible for five brothers and sisters, the brutality of Wilf's father, made the hidings Wilf dished out to his own sons seem like a walk in the park. Wilf survived, as he had always done, by diligently working both sides of the law: a charming chameleon, as capable of thieving, as he was of an honest day's work.

As a boy, Salocin often witnessed his father hanging around the gates of the East End docks, smoking and quarrelling with the others looking for work. It was a waiting game, where they played a game of puk-a-pu, or pitch and toss to while away some hours. Most were good-humoured games, never a bother playing for matchsticks or ciggies. Things got nasty, though, if they were playing for money, even just a few bob, because it was always someone's *last* few bob.

When there was no work forthcoming, Salocin, ashamed, watched Wilf trawling through old bombsites, filling bags with scrap metal in the hope of selling it on for a small profit. Stooping, eagle-eyed as if searching for treasure, Wilf didn't look out of place with the meth-swilling hobos that frequented the bits of half-fallen buildings. Or so the boys at school said who taunted Salocin, until he gave them a black eye or a split lip for their trouble. Occasionally Wilf got up when it was still very dark outside, when the stars and the moon were still awake – "the watching" he called it – and took a trip to Covent Garden, Billingsgate, or Smithfield, to see if he could find a bit of work, earn a bob or two. Sometimes, Salocin and Teddy got up too, huddling together in a corner, all wide-eyed and questioning as their father moved stealth-like, crossing the kitchen in pin steps. Boots and cap on, he'd pat his pockets, and if he were in a good mood, he'd take them with him.

Billingsgate, London's fish market, lay on the north bank of the Thames, and once visited was never forgotten. It was the smell Salocin remembered most, fishy, seaweedy; it clung to their clothes and stayed with them for days afterwards. It came from buckets of eels, slithering and sliding like snakes; baskets of grey oysters and blue mussels. There were live lobsters, their claws floundering helplessly in the air, and sackfuls of whelks and knolls of herring; white bellied turbot that shone like his grandmother's pearl necklace. It was strange to see men working in the middle of the night, setting up stalls at the same time as toffs in fancy suits – theatre-goers and the likes – were getting ready to call it a night. Now and then Wilf would pocket a shilling or two, responding to cries of "up the 'ill" which meant pushing and shoving a heavy load of precarious wooden crates, stacked on a wooden cart, up the cobbles.

Then there were the men in funny hats, Bobbins, strange black leather helmets with rectangular tops, used to balance fish baskets on their heads. Some porters could carry twelve baskets at a time, and each basket weighed a stone. "Move outta the bleedin' way! Gangway" their call if, god help you, you got in the way of these man mountains and their mission to deliver their carefully balanced cargo. When Wilf was done, if he'd had a good run, there were always jellied eels and good spirits to share on the way home.

Other times, they went to Smithfield meat market.

'This 'ere is the largest covered market in the world,' Wilf told them. 'Four hundred thousand tons of meat a year delivered from all corners of the earth.'

Teddy said the lofty roof-space reminded him of St. Paul's Cathedral. Salocin, however, hated the place. To him, the fearsome-looking men wearing white blood-splattered coats who walked among butchered animals that swung from large silver hooks, made Smithfield the stuff of nightmares. It was how he imagined a hospital operating theatre might look (little did Salocin know then, he would one day work within such close proximity of the market). Usually, Smithfield meant Wilf intended gambling money he didn't have on an unlicensed boxing match, leaving the boys hanging around outside the pub, patiently waiting for their father to raise a glass or two to any winnings, or to be a foul travelling companion home if he lost. Salocin didn't know which was worse. If his father lost, he could be scarily angry, but if he won, although happy, the celebratory drink or two at the pub afterwards usually meant hours of hanging around outside for him and Teddy. Which was fine during the summer months. With a glass of warm lemonade each and a stale sausage roll to share, they could keep themselves amused, join in the games of the other kids knocking around: tag, leapfrog, or hide and go seek. Or sometimes they'd find sticks, and with a bit of imagination, convinced themselves they were Colt-shaped, which made them Roy Rogers, while others were bow-shaped which made them Davy Crockett or Robin Hood. But during the winter months, dressed in short trousers, keeping warm was difficult. They did their best, stomped and ran around to keep the blood pumping through their thin blue veins, but it didn't take long before they could no longer feel their toes and their fingers, before everything became uncomfortably numb. The cold was like that. Had a way of burrowing through the skin, gnawing down to the bone. The young brothers never cried though. Meant a good hiding if they did. "Only sissies and girls cry," Wilf said.

Covent Garden Fruit and Vegetable Market, a stone's throw from Leicester Square, was Salocin's favourite. Everywhere he looked there were row upon row of every flower imaginable, bursting with colour. They often had funny names, too, like Busy Lizzie, or Bleeding Heart, Moth Orchid or Baby's Breath. Some flowers, like the lily, looked upright and strong, whereas others, like the Bell Flower – their flowers were shaped like tiny bells – seemed paper thin, as if made from the finest tracing paper. The long stemmed dark red roses, their petals tinged with black, looked as soft as velvet, and then there were flowers that reminded Salocin of a bright summer day: cheerful candy orange chrysanthemums and sherbet yellow daffodils.

Once, during a visit to the market, a kindly-looking stallholder approached Salocin, no more than five or six years old, and gave him a bunch of daffodils. 'Stick 'em inside yer coat.' He winked. 'Give 'em to your old mum when you get 'ome, eh? Be a nice surprise for her.'

Salocin, bursting with excitement, couldn't wait to get home and give the flowers to Martha. But instead of being happy, she scowled at him; gave him a clip round the ear and accused him of being a thief – 'just like yer bleedin' father.' Salocin tried his hardest not to cry.

Covent Garden was also, of course, famous for its fruit and veg. Salocin could soon recite it all: tomatoes from Guernsey, apples from New Zealand, Kent and Evesham, potatoes, carrots and cabbage from Norfolk, pears from Australia, oranges and lemons from South Africa, strawberries from Holland... The smell alone made his mouth water. Salocin was never quite sure what, if any, work Wilf courted at Covent Garden. After buying them a cup of tea and a fried egg sandwich to share from Arthur's café on the corner, Wilf told his sons to stay put until he got back. It was hard to make a cup of tea and a sandwich last an hour – especially when they were so hungry. Nonetheless, Salocin didn't really mind because Wilf always came back smiling, hands tucked in his pockets, whistling. If he were particularly happy, he'd sing. Wilf had a good singing voice, Salocin thought. He was an accomplished piano player too, had taught himself to play, and in turn taught Teddy; Salocin could never sit still long enough. He did teach himself to play the guitar when he was older though.

Sometimes, when Wilf came back from wherever he'd been, he'd do so smelling of roses. Which could be a worry if his mother noticed; it meant a row. 'You've been with her, encha,' Martha would shout. 'Bin with that bleedin' tart again.' Unless she had one of her headaches, of course. When she had one of those, Martha didn't care about anything or anyone, she disappeared to her bedroom, curtains drawn, for hours, maybe days, at a time.

Salocin and Teddy treasured those rare moments, alone, with their father. His trips to the markets, though, were few and far between. More often than not Wilf looked for most of his work at the docks, and when an honest day's work did present itself, usually unloading a boat, it was anything from a twelve to eighteen-hour day of unremitting manual labour. It wasn't unusual for Wilf to start work at five in the morning and finish between eight and ten o'clock at night. When the honest work dried up, though, Wilf did what he had to do.

Going as far back as Salocin could remember, the ability to fluctuate between an honest and dishonest living was imperative to his father's survival; the difference between having food on the table or not. Gang warfare and organised crime were rife where they lived and somewhere amongst it all, Wilf played his part. Salocin never knew what his father did, exactly, and although it often involved some interesting and sometimes less desirable individuals visiting their home – much to his mother's disgust – Wilf also talked of a line he was never prepared to cross. 'Never get in too deep, boys,' he told his sons. 'Bit of ducking and diving, but no more. Don't want to feel the scratch of the hangman's rope around your neck now, do yer.'

Martha hated it when Wilf was up to no good. Intelligent and well-read, she never quite forgave Wilf for deceiving her; he was not the man he had convinced her he was. Completely won over by his charm, his ability to spin a good yarn, Martha believed she had found her Mr Darcy but, within a few months of marrying him, it quickly became apparent she was instead embroiled with a cruel Heathcliff, or at least, that's how she saw it. Hard and proud, she despised Wilf's dishonest earnings, although, ironically, she never had any trouble spending them. However, Martha was determined that her sons would not follow in their father's footsteps, not if she had anything to do with it. Then perhaps, through them, she would finally elevate to her rightful position in life.

Chapter 3

PRESENT DAY
CHRISTMAS DAY – EARLY MORNING

DI KATE STEWART

DI Kate Stewart, 'Kat' to her friends, 'Boss' to her subordinates, enters the house. It's the smell that hits her first, despite the protective mask covering her nose and mouth. Using one hand to keep the mask in place, she uses the other to cradle her stomach, now constricting like a tightly wound coil, and holds her breath, closes her eyes. It's all she can do to stop herself gagging. The smell permeating the house of the deceased is almost as wretched as the man himself. Rancid. Quite unlike anything else she has ever come across – and after thirty-odd years on the force that's saying something. Puke, blood, faeces, rotting corpses, burnt flesh; she has seen and smelled the lot. She saw her first corpse just months after starting the job. A drowning. A man, swollen and blued by the water, had fallen in the Thames and was washed up a week later, some of the flesh on his face having fallen away in strips. It had quite turned her stomach at the time. She soon hardened up though; it was a case of having to.

This however, whatever the fuck *this* rotten, putrid stench is, is something else entirely. She breathes out again and braces herself as the loathsome scent clings to her flaring nostrils. A wave of nausea washes over her. She puts her hand out, steadies herself; the two cups of black coffee she'd necked on the way over now sloshing around in her otherwise empty stomach. Lowering her head, Kat concentrates on keeping her breathing slow but shallow, desperate to temper the black sea whipping up a storm inside her.

Fat chance she'll feel like eating Christmas dinner after this. Then again, who the hell is she trying to kid? She knows, despite the early hour, she'll never make it back on time. Not with this individual: his money, his celebrity status, his connections. She's already had the Home Office on the phone. They wouldn't have dragged her from her bed at this godforsaken hour on Christmas Day if it had been some junkie in a council flat. Sickening. Even in death money talks. *Fuck! Why today, though? Why Christmas Day?* She lifts her head, imagines Hannah's sulky, surly face floating in front of her like a balloon, only, like a lead balloon, Kat Stewart's heart sinks. Is Hannah even awake yet? Does she know her mother has abandoned her… again?

She sighs. How is it possible, despite having fought, apprehended and arrested some of society's worst individuals, that one word, one cursory glance, one angst-ridden flick of her daughter's shiny, long hair (straightened to within an inch of its life) can bring her out in a cold sweat? Running for the hills. Kat grins, shakes her head. *Teenagers*! On her head be it if she doesn't make it back for dinner today. And rightly so. It is Christmas Day after all. And for once, her absence would justify Hannah's creased brow and permanently painted pout. 'I don't know why you bothered having me.' she hears Hannah say, her verbose, high-pitched whining reverberating inside Kat's head like a finely-tuned pitching fork. 'You care waaaaay more for your job than you do me.'

It's not true, of course. And besides, it's still early – 5am to be precise – and while excited children all over the country are undoubtedly waking up their exhausted parents, it would be at least another couple of hours before sunrise. Everyone knows teenagers never rise before the sun. If Kat gets her shit together, she might, by the skin of her teeth, be able to slip back home, dive in the shower – god knows she'll need to wash away the foul smell that seems to cling to every fibre of her being, never mind her clothes – and all before her moody daughter realises she has gone.

'Like fuck!' she says out loud.

The brief seconds spent thinking about her daughter have given Kat enough time for her stomach to settle a little. Protective mask in place, she steps further into the sprawling hallway. Whatever the hell is causing the terrible smell, it seems to have filled the entire house.

'Fuck me,' she mumbles, more bemused than reviled when her stomach, like an agitated washing machine, whirrs and churns. What the hell is wrong with her? Is she really going to heave? She can't remember the last time she'd puked on the job – years ago, when she first started out? It's surprising how, over time, Kat has adjusted to the rotten smells that are part and parcel of the job. Never pleasant, some smells, she quickly discovered, linger in the memory as much as the visuals do, apt to blindside you on a rainy Tuesday afternoon when a vague whiff of something familiar stirs something deep within you. Reminders of some of the worst cases you'd worked on, or the ones never solved – the young woman raped and murdered, the missing child never found. Nonetheless, for the most part, when it came to odious odours, nothing much affected her these days.

But this is bad. Really fucking bad.

Clearing her throat, Kat straightens up and glances over her shoulder to see how DS York is doing. Hunched forward, his hand protecting his mouth, she sees his retreating back, and the front door slam behind him. Clearly DS York's gag reflex is working as well as hers. She feels relieved, had thought, for a moment, she was going soft. Turning back again, she walks towards the body splayed across the polished floor at the foot of the stairs.

Nice floor. Oak, I reckon. Must have cost a bloody fortune.

Forensic pathologist, George Martin, who is standing next to the body, greets DI Stewart with a cursory nod.

'How long has he been dead?' She leans forward to peer at the halo of blood surrounding the deceased's head.

'Hard to tell at the moment. At least two days.'

'Cause of death?'

'We'll know more when we get him back to the lab but his neck is broken and there's a deep wound to the back of his head. Most likely caused when he hit it on

that–' He points to the second blood covered step at the foot of the stairs '–after a fall.'

'From the top of the stairs?'

The pathologist nods. 'Judging by the trauma caused by the injury, yes.'

'A fall? Or would you say he was pushed?'

'Again, it's hard to say. He could have been pushed, or he could have lost his footing and tripped.'

'But you suspect foul play?'

'Like I said, I'll know more later, but we can't rule it out.'

Somewhat deflated, DI Stewart rolls her eyes. Why couldn't it be cut and dry? An obvious accident? Suicide, even? Would make life a damn sight fucking easier. Now though, the shit really will hit the fan. Hannah and her lead balloon once again drift into her thoughts as any hope of spending Christmas Day with her only daughter floats further away.

'And that smell?' Kat points to the body. 'Is that coming from *him*?'

'Ah… yes. Interesting, isn't it?'

'That's one way of putting it.'

'Sort of like a rotten corpse that's been stewing in a stagnant sewer for a few weeks. Pugnacious and nauseating.'

Hmm… not unlike the man himself. DI Stewart's hand flies

to her mouth. Did she really say that out loud? She coughs, clears her throat. 'Allegedly, of course,' she adds.

Pathologist George Martin stares at her. Like her, he is covered head to foot in protective clothing. Only his eyes, bright green, fringed by enviably long, dark lashes, are visible. It's hard to tell whether her sudden outburst has irritated him or if he is just indifferent. Regardless, he merely nods.

Kat has read and heard a lot about Hunter Black over the last year. Most of it vile and most of it concerning his alleged misconduct against at least ten young women, mainly while in his employment. A powerful man by all accounts; rich too, with friends in high places and low morals. American, apparently, he was one of two sons born into wealth and privilege who finished his private education by reading History at Oxford University before going on to earn a separate fortune of his own in the music industry as some bigshot record producer. It also looked, up until this point anyway, as though he was going to get away with his alleged crimes. Which didn't surprise DI Stewart. Rape cases are notoriously difficult to prove, especially against rich, self-aggrandising sociopaths like Black. And if the rumours were true, Black had been using every trick in the book, including bribery, threat and intimidation, to make sure he would not be held accountable for his actions.

'Alleged actions,' George Martin says.

Surprised, DI Kat Stewart looks up. *Shit, I really must stop talking to myself out loud.*

'First sign of madness,' the pathologist with the nice eyes, continues.

George Martin doesn't see it but Kat clamps her top lip over her bottom one. On a personal level, this is hard for her. The world, she believes is a better place without men like Black. However, on a professional level she has a job to do. If this was foul play it's up to her to understand why. God knows they won't be short of suspects though. Ten at least – for starters. She throws her head back, stares at the ceiling, and sighs. This was going to take a while.

'I'm getting too old for this shit,' she says, looking down again.

George Martin stares at her for a few seconds. She's pretty convinced he is grinning under that mask. He kneels down next to the lifeless body and Kat hears the front door open behind her. She glances over her shoulder, spots DS York who, red-eyed, his hand pressed so hard against the mask covering his mouth his knuckles have turned white, is now walking towards her.

'Boss.' He clears his throat and refuses to make eye contact with her. 'Sorry about that.'

DI Kat Stewart nods then introduces the pathologist. 'So, as I was saying, that smell – is it coming from his body? Black's body?'

George Martin shakes his head. 'No, I don't believe it is.' He points towards a large oak-panelled door, which blends perfectly with the expensive-looking polished floor. It is half open and a shaft of white light shines through from the room behind it.

'Take a look in there,' he says.

chapter 4

CHRISTMAS DAY
PRESENT DAY – LATE AFTERNOON

CASSIE

Hunter Black is dead.

Dead.

I feel... numb. Why?

I should be ecstatic, jumping up and down, fist thumping the air, ready to dance on his grave. Cremation would be better. Ashes to ashes, dust to dust, flush to flush... down the fucking toilet, where he belongs.

Gone.

Forever.

Everyone, quiet, looks at one another. Beside me, Mum tucks my hair behind my ear, touches my cheek, and asks if I'm okay? I feel my eyes widen in surprise, shrink back to being a child again. I don't know. Am I okay? I suppose I am. I shrug. 'I guess so,' I hear myself reply.

An arm, strong reassuring, folds around my shoulders. It's Luke. He leans forward, kisses the tip of my nose. I smile. Movement to the side of me finds Connor, running his hand through his hair, blowing air from his inflated cheeks. He looks agitated, offers me a tight-lipped smile. Baby Nicolas, balanced on Maisy's hip, mouth turned down, chin quivering, looks every bit as confused as me. He whimpers, quietly at first, like a faraway police siren, growing louder and whinier by the second, breaking both the silence and weird atmosphere in the room. Maisy brushes past me.

'Taking him for a nap,' she says, squeezing my shoulder. 'Good news eh, sis? Good news and good bloody riddance.' She calls to Crazee to go with her and he pauses by my side, his face reddening as he shifts from foot to foot. He opens his mouth as if to speak then seems to change his mind; fist bumps me instead before giving me the thumbs up as he leaves the room. Si, my stepdad, now standing next to Mum, also asks me if I'm okay and again I shrug my shoulders just as Uncle Sean calls out, winks, and also sticks his thumb up.

Aunt Natasha, who is bent over her phone, confirms the TV news report.

'It's all over Twitter,' she says.

Luke's phone rings and he skulks off toward the kitchen to answer it. Connor heads towards the door, Mum behind him. Nan mumbles something I don't quite catch then shuffles off, as well, to make tea for everyone. Confused, I look around, realise I'm alone. I feel weird. Everything feels weird. Hunter Black, who has caused me so much pain and suffering, my family too, is dead. So why don't I feel happy? Or relieved? Something, anything, would be good.

Wait... I *am* angry. Angry and annoyed that once a-fucking-gain *he* is at the centre of my thoughts. Today was bad enough, with it being the first year since Grandad passed away. And now this: Hunter Black overshadowing everything, taking centre stage – again. A bubble of anger, effervescent, wells in my chest, taking me by surprise. It eats away at me, making me want to scream, smash plates, get drunk... Anything that takes my thoughts away from *him*.

I decide a fag will have to do instead. I head into the kitchen, past Nan who, staring into space, is hovering by the rumbling kettle.

'Just going for a fag,' I say, unlocking the back door.

Nan's eyebrows knit together in a frown. She sighs, shakes her head. 'You should give them up, Cassie.'

Yeah. Yeah. Yeah. 'I will do, Nan. Soon.'

Luke paces back and forth at the end of the garden like a caged wild animal. Although, with his phone – *still* pressed to his ear – in one hand, and the other arm swinging back and forth, he also looks like some mad music conductor. Who the hell is he talking to? He spots me and puts his hand up.

I nod, then cup my hand around the fag hanging from the side of my mouth, waving my lighter underneath it. It hisses until an orangey blue flame jumps up and crackles, the cigarette catching light. I suck hard, close my eyes and look up; feel woozy, lightheaded. When I open my eyes again I watch the smoke billowing from my mouth disappearing into the grey sky above me. By the time I reach Luke he has finished talking on the phone, which he slips back into his jeans pocket.

I offer him a drag of my ciggie. He shakes his head then changes his mind and squinting, takes a drag.

'Who was that?' I ask.

Luke's eyes narrow and a blue grey trail of smoke wafts from the corner of his mouth. 'Just Jay.' He waves his hand in the air. 'Being a dick about the New Year's Eve set we've got planned.'

'So, is it all sorted now?'

Luke drops the half-smoked ciggie on the ground and stamps on it. My heart sinks, *I could have easy got a couple more drags out of that.* 'Hopefully,' he replies. 'C'mon, let's go in. It's bloody freezing out here. And you're shivering.'

'Luke?' I pull my hand back. 'Aren't you going to ask me how I am? How I feel about Black?'

Luke frowns. 'But I did… didn't I?' He points to the back door. 'Just a minute ago. Inside.'

'I know. But, well… that was in front of everyone. I thought, when we were alone, you'd want to know how I feel? How I really feel?'

He attempts a smile, but it doesn't meet his eyes. 'Shit. Yeah, sorry. Of course. It's just…' He sits on the seat of the old swing, its paint-peeling metal frame having seen better days, and pulls me onto his knee.

'It's just what?'

Luke, his arms wrapped around my waist, his cheek pressed against my back, squeezes me. 'I don't want to upset you,' he says. 'Personally, I think it's good news. The best.' His tone is as dark as my ex boss's name. 'Men like Black are bad. Fucking evil. And the world is now minus one less scumbag. So what? But I'm not you, am I Cassie? I know that if we could have got him there, you'd have preferred your day in court. And what with today also being the first anniversary of your grandad's… ' He knows only too well the mere mention of Grandad will set me off. I try my hardest to swallow the lump forming in my throat, control the sobs desperate to leave my mouth. 'I suppose I'm just trying to tread carefully, Cas. But… Look at me.'

I arch myself around to face him. He cradles my face in his hands, his old leather jacket creaking. I put my hand up to his eye. The cut around it looks angrier than it did earlier. He winces, moves my hand away.

'I still can't believe Useless did that to you. Are you sure you were just messing around? That it wasn't a real fight?'

'Course it wasn't a real fight.' There's a flash of impatience in his voice, like I'm a child asking too many questions. 'What on earth would me and Eustace be fighting about?' He leans in, kisses me gently on the lips. 'I love you, Cas. Always have, always will. If you want to talk about Black, Honey, the whole bloody thing, we can talk until the fucking cows come home if you like. But if you'd rather not… well, I get that too.'

I nod my head, the lump lodged in my throat now the size of a plum. 'Thanks,' I whisper, hot tears stinging my cheeks as they roll down my face. 'It's weird but I don't know how I feel about Black's death. I guess I'm relieved. But I always thought that if anything ever happened to him, I'd feel – happy, somehow? Pleased? But I don't. I just feel… numb.' I stand up, as does Luke, who then pulls me to his chest, wrapping his arms around me. And just like at the hospital, a year ago today, when baby Nicolas was born and Grandad passed away, he kisses my head and guides me into a tight circle until eventually my sobbing stops.

The back door swings open and it's Nan asking if either of us wants tea or coffee. I put my hand up. 'Coming, Nan.'

Luke laughs. 'Why do old people always want to make tea when there's a problem?'

Luke follows me into the living room, suggests I take a seat and not to worry; he just needs to make another quick phone call then he'll help my Nan and bring me a coffee. I watch him leave the room, head towards the stairs, my old bedroom. Si and Uncle Sean are still sitting at the dining table, surrounded by tubs of chocolates, half-pulled Christmas crackers and what looks like piles of coloured spaghetti, fired from the shells of party poppers. I watch them for a moment. Their voices are low, secretive, but their body language is loud and demonstrative. Chests puffed up, arms waving this way and that, I wonder what or who they are talking about. *Hunter Black – maybe?*

A hand on my shoulder makes me jump. I turn to see Summer standing behind me, cradling her yappy little pug, Sir Lancelot, or, 'Sir Barks-a-lot' as Connor prefers to call him and just plain old 'Lance' to everyone else. Summer, who's almost as tall as me now, is wearing eyeliner and mascara, and looks frighteningly older than twelve. *Don't rush to grow up*, I want to say, *it's such a scary place.*

'You okay, Cassie?' she asks.

I find my best plucky smile, nod, 'Yeah. I think so,' I reply, patting Lance on the head. He growls. I flinch. 'Not very friendly, is he?'

'Sir Lancelot, stop it.' Summer waves her finger at his big eyes set in his squashed, wrinkled face.

'How about you? How's my favourite cousin doing?'

Lance licks Summer's finger. She laughs, looks at me. 'Not so good.' She bends down to let the pug wriggle free from her arms. 'Do you know pugs originated in China, dating all the way back to the Han dynasty? And, that Marie Antoinette had a pug called Mops, and Josephine Bonaparte had a pug called Fortune?'

'They're definitely a lot of dog in a small body.' I watch the retreating back of the sturdy little dog with the huge personality as he scampers towards the kitchen, no doubt in search of food. 'And no, I knew none of those bizarre facts. Amazing what you can find on Google, eh?'

Summer chews the corner of her mouth, looks down. 'Wasn't Google that told me. It was Grandad.'

I sniff, and smile. 'Why doesn't that surprise me? There wasn't much Grandad didn't know something about, was there?'

Summer tips her head to the side and laughs, wiping away the lone tear running down her cheek.

'Come here.' I open my arms and give her a quick, tight hug. 'So, what's up then, cuz?' I ask as we pull apart.

Dragging her hand through her hair, Summer rolls her eyes and sighs. 'There's a bit of an argument going on in our WhatsApp group,' she says waving her phone from side to side.

'Really? What seems to be the problem?'

'Well, like, Amy said I called Louise fat. Which, like, I didn't coz it was actually Amy that did. But, like, she doesn't want Louise to be friends with me, so she, like, also said that Louise said I was ugly. And that I like have a big nose with a ginormous bump in it.'

She does have a nose with a bump in it, like me, like Mum, like Uncle Sean. We've all got Grandad's Roman nose.

'Which I, like, know is a lie – not like about my nose, I know I have a big nose – but it's, like, a lie that Louise said it. But now, like, Louise believes her and so does Taylor and Brittany and Olivia and Bethany–'

Oh my actual god, I'm sorry I asked. Was I ever like that? Surely, LIKE, not!

'Firstly,' I interrupt, 'it sounds like a lot of nonsense about nothing. Secondly, there is absolutely nothing wrong with you or your nose. You are beautiful just the way you are. You have the same nose as me, as Grandad, and should be proud of it. And thirdly, instead of all this silly messaging one another, where things get misunderstood, why don't you ring Louise and, you know, *like,* actually speak to her. Have a real conversation?'

Bloody hell – now I sound like Mum! What the hell is happening to me?

The wry smile from Aunt Natasha, who looks up from her phone, doesn't go unnoticed.

Summer closes her eyes, shakes her head. 'Cassie, you have no idea just how hard it is being a teenager in the twenty-first century.'

I stifle a laugh. 'Is that right?'

'Uh-huh.'

Aunt Natasha looks up again and shakes her head. She tells Summer to help Nan in the kitchen and before Summer has time to protest, threatens to take her phone off her for the rest of the evening if she doesn't do as she's told.

'Knew we shouldn't have bought her a phone,' Aunt Nat mumbles under her breath as Summer lopes off. Looking down again, Aunt Nat also says something about the police not saying much about how my ex boss died.

I wonder? Was it in pain, and fear? Like he caused me and all those other girls. And, more importantly, was he remorseful?

'I fucking doubt it.'

Nat looks up again, her forehead wrinkled. 'Sorry, did you say something, Cas?'

I shake my head; think back to the news report on TV that announced Black's death. I think of his shiny black door, now decorated with crisscrossed yellow and black crime scene tape flapping in the wind. I think of *that* night and I also think of all those months afterwards when I still worked for him, still allowed him to talk down to me. And the more I think, the more I shake. Rage and fear surge through my body like a strange cocktail of heat and ice. Even in death this arsehole haunts me.

I close my eyes, hold my breath for a count of ten and listen: the muttering of lowered voices, a car turning in the drive next door, the kettle boiling in the kitchen. I open my eyes. Breathe out. Hear the gentle chime of chinking mugs and the sound of someone's phone ringing before closing my eyes again. Rinse and repeat. Rinse and repeat. I do this a couple more times, until I am calm.

Luke is back in the room, on his phone again, texting. Nan is back too, asking again, who wants tea or coffee. Nan without Grandad still sounds wrong. I think of Grandad, his craggy face, feel a sharp tugging at my heart, wonder what he would have made of all this. I hear his voice, 'Facking good riddance! Couldn't have happened to a nicer bleedin' bloke.'

I look at Nan and in my best cockney accent I ask her for 'a nice cap o' Rosie Lee.' Clutching a bright red Christmas tea towel to her chest, Nan nods her head and smiles. I flash her the biggest smile I can manage back.

I don't give a shit. I'm done with the man. I was a few months ago, if I'm honest. Especially when it looked as though there wouldn't be enough evidence to go to trial. I would have gone, if there had been, even though I admit, I was frightened. The thought of my life laid bare, for everyone to prod and poke at; I've been judged enough. Hunter Black is gone. And he'll never be able to hurt anyone else again. That's all that matters isn't it? And now I can truly move on. *Can't I?*

I decide not to give Hunter Black another thought. At least, not today.

I tell Nan I'll give her a hand but jump when my phone rings – at the same time as a loud banging on the front door. Everyone looks up and Simon, who is still sitting at the table with Uncle Sean, stands up. 'I'll get it,' he says.

A quick glance at my phone screen and I press the accept call button and listen. I know it's Aunt Marie, recognise her voice, but I can barely make out what she is saying. High-pitched and panicky, she's not screaming but she's not far from it, either.

'What's wrong?' I ask, but she won't say. She tells me to put Mum on the phone, and as I head towards the kitchen, another loud banging on the front door makes me jump again.

Simon brushes past me. 'All right. All right,' he calls out.

Mum is still talking to Nan. 'It's for you,' I say, thrusting my phone towards her hands.

Mum looks at the phone then looks at me. 'Who is it?'

'Aunt Marie. She sounds upset. Won't tell me what's wrong. Asked for you.'

Nan, eyebrow arched, her crinkly blue eyes quizzical and steely, looks from the phone to Mum. 'Why has she asked for you, Lizzie? What on earth is the matter?'

Mum sounds agitated. 'How do I know, Mum?'

Nan bites her lip, folds her arms. I shrug. Mum lifts the phone to her ear and I notice a slight tremor in her hand. 'Hi Marie… yes, yes. It's me. Are you okay? Cassie said– What? I don't understand. Look, Marie, you need to calm down. I don't understand. Wait–'

We're all distracted by raised voices coming from the hallway. 'For what?' Simon's voice, loud and angry, drifts in, talking to whoever it is at the front door. 'What the hell is this all about?'

Mum closes her eyes for a second then opens her mouth to speak.

Nan throws her tea towel on the side, steps forward. She looks at me and I look at Mum. Simon enters the room. He looks angry, pissed off, even, drags a hand through his salt and pepper hair. Mum still has my phone pressed against one ear, her hand against the other. 'Okay. You need to keep calm, Marie. I know it is but–'

'Lizzie,' Simon interrupts, his voice sharp, demanding. Mum looks up, points to the phone, and looks away again. Simon's mouth tenses like he's angry but his eyes, darting from left to right, from me to Nan, then back to Mum, say something else.

I'm filled with a sickening panic. Is that fear I see in Si's eyes? He steps further into the kitchen and I realise there are two men standing behind him.

'Lizzie,' he says again.

Mum swings round, sighs. 'Hang on a minute, Marie.' She lowers the phone. 'What? What the hell is it?' she snaps.

'Do you know where Connor is?'

'He went to Jake's. Why?'

Simon points to the two individuals standing behind him. 'Apparently the police would like to speak to him.'

The colour drains from Mum's face. She puts the phone back to her ear and stares at the two officers. 'Marie. Listen to me. The police are here. Yes, the police. I'll call you back. Yes… No. I promise.' She places my phone on the kitchen worktop, walks up to Simon, and stares at the two police officers. 'What the hell is this all about? What on earth do you need to question my son about? Simon – what do they want?'

Simon raises his eyebrows. He looks tired, confused. 'To help them with their enquires.'

'Enquiries? Enquiries about what?'

Simon takes a deep breath. 'Hunter Black.'

chapter 5

CHRISTMAS DAY
PRESENT DAY – LATE EVENING

CONNOR

I stare at the four grey walls surrounding me and shiver. I'm on my own but not alone. If those crime programmes on TV are anything to go by. I'm being watched. I glance at my phone. Forty minutes I've been sitting here, waiting. My phone buzzes, it's another text from Jake asking me where the hell I am. Should I tell him? I decide not to, and instead tap out a quick reply explaining about Uncle Teddy. I press send and put my phone away, surprised when a lump catches in my throat. I bite the corner of my lip and look down. *Poor Uncle Teddy*.

I stare at my trainers, new for Christmas from Nan; the ones I asked for, the ones with shock absorbers. My vision blurs and my feet swim out of focus as hot tears prick the back of my eyes. I open my eyes, wide, trying not to blink. Can't let the police see me crying.

Who am I crying for, anyway? Me? Grandad? Uncle Teddy? I know who it's not for – Hunter-fucking-Black. I'm glad *he's* dead. Although, he's why I'm here, of course.

Shit. I stand up, feel my stomach fall into my arse; the floor beneath my feet feels spongy. *Trainers with shock absorbers – yeah right!* I pace the room. My armpits feel wet. I cop a sniff, pull away. Ugh. Fuck me – I have BO. How come? Could have sworn I put deodorant on today? Not that it matters. I'm in real trouble here, and there's no Grandad to the rescue this time.

Mum doesn't seem bothered either, happy to let Si bring me to the station while she went off to see Aunt Marie. Which I kind of understand. Actually… No. Fuck it. I don't understand. Why the hell isn't Mum here, fighting my corner like she's been doing for Cassie for the last fucking year? I know what happened to my sister was terrible – why else would I be here – but why is it that Mum doesn't seem to give a shit about me? I know I'm not on my own, that Si is here with me, that he'll do his best to keep Mum informed, but the bottom line is, she's my Mum. Surely she should be the one here, waiting for me – shouldn't she?

My stomach gurgles. I stop pacing the room, mid-stride, and hold my belly. I feel a familiar twinge and my arse quiver. I panic. Can't work out if it's anxiety, or the Brussels sprouts I ate earlier. I remain still, like a statue, my stomach cramping into knots. The gas builds inside me, rising like a hot-air balloon and I'm too frightened to move. Shit – what if I shit myself? I stare at the door, hoping they haven't locked it. I imagine telling the boys about this, if I ever get out of here, that is. See them: Jake, Robbo and the Rickmeister, all pissing themselves laughing. I bend forwards a little, one hand cradling my stomach, the other flapping around in the general direction of my quivering arse. *Please god don't let this be a shart!* With no further warning a huge ripping sound shoots out of my backside. I wait a few seconds, just to be sure but – thank fuck – it hasn't followed through.

Fuck me, it stinks, though. Rank, even by my standards. I wave my hand in front of my face like a fan, and walk towards the window to see if I can open it. It may be cold outside – minus one I think it said in Si's car – but this room needs fresh air. I lift the paint-peeling handle and push it, hard, but it doesn't budge. I try the other window next to it: also locked, or stuck. I'm left with no choice but to wallow in my own stinking, eggy butt fumes. I laugh. Karma? That's what Grandad would have said. I look out of the window, pressing my nose against the cold glass, to watch how it steams up. The grey sky behind it is now black, day has turned into night, and down below, the whole city is crawling with light. It's too dark to make out individual buildings, but it looks busy enough. Less traffic than usual, though, so it's eerily quiet, like a flickering TV screen with the sound turned down.

A phone rings next door. I swing round, hear a man answer it; listen to his low, deep voice. His words are muffled though, buffered by the wall between us, as if someone is speaking to me while I'm underwater, so I don't know who it is or what he's saying. I think of Simon, sitting in the waiting room down the corridor, and wonder if the police have spoken to Cassie yet? They didn't know she was staying at Mum's, said they'd planned to contact her in London and ask her to stop by one of the police stations near to where she and Luke live.

I feel my own phone vibrate in my pocket and expect to see another text from Jake but this time it's Simon asking me how it's going. I scratch the back of my head, think about telling him to go home, that I'll call a taxi when I'm done. Then again – what if they don't let me go home? What if they want to keep me in overnight – for further questioning? What if someone has set me up? I wrestle with the thought of spending Christmas night in a police cell when my phone flashes again.

I swipe the screen and read Jake's reply. He says he's sorry about Uncle Teddy but wants to let me know his uncle has been arrested and is in police custody. I look up from my phone and panic drills down into my stomach. *Fuck*. I pace the room again, chewing on non-existent fingernails. How the hell did they find him? He promised me there'd be no comeback. They must have evidence though or why else would they have arrested him? And why the hell would I be here? He must have talked. Mentioned my name. Shit. What if they arrest *me*? Shit. Shit. Shit.

I wish Grandad were here. He'd know what to do. I really miss him. Miss that craggy old face of his and how he used to tell everyone to "fack orf " whenever anyone asked him if he was okay. It was hard to tell though, sometimes, especially for strangers, because he always looked moody. Grandad said it was gravity pulling everything south, including his smile. Nan said it was just "grumpy old man syndrome." Swallowing hard, I sniff, feel tears stinging my eyes again. How can it be a whole year since he died?

The door swings open making me jump. DC's Foster and Green both enter the room. With his jaw gyrating, his cheeks bulging, DC Foster is chewing on a mouthful of something. He reminds me of a hamster. A fat hamster. And judging by the way his shirt buttons are stretching and straining across his belly, I'd say he's been eating too many burgers, or doughnuts. Maybe both. Pausing mid-chew, he sniffs the air, wrinkles his nose. DC Green, who is carrying papers and a notebook in one hand and a plastic cup in the other, steps back, as if she's just hit her head on a window or something. 'Whoa! What the hell is that–'

'Smell?' DC Foster interrupts. 'That's just what I was thinking.'

They both turn to look at me. I feel myself shrink with embarrassment, open my mouth to say something but change my mind and close it again. DC Foster wanders over to the windows, rattling the handles.

'Won't bloody open,' I hear him mumble under his breath.

DC Green coughs, puts the cup down and her hand to her mouth, throws me a narrow, sideways glance as a curtain of blonde hair falls across her face. She's quite pretty, in a stern sort of way. I wonder if she's pissed off at having to work on Christmas Day, missing her family, other half, children? Or if she lives alone, with a cat, and loves her job more than she does people and Christmas. She slams the papers on the desk, making me jump, and points to the chair opposite. I nod, pull the chair out and sit down. After a few seconds she lowers her hand away from her nose and mouth. I feel my cheeks burn.

'Coffee?' She pushes the plastic cup towards me. Even though the last cup I had was rank, I take a slurp of the muddy coloured liquid and shiver; this one's not much better. Oh well, it's hot and wet and will stop my mouth from furring up "like a badgers arse" as Grandad used to say.

DC Green takes a seat opposite me while DC Foster screws up the napkin he's used to wipe his mouth and throws it towards a small metal bin in the corner of the room. He misses, sighs, then dragging the chair out next to DC Green, sits down beside her. The chair makes a screeching noise, and DC Green stares at him, with that same sour, sucking lemons look Mum wears most of the time.

'What?' DC Foster protests, folding his arms across his chest.

DC Green shakes her head then turns back towards me. Once again she apologises for asking me to come in on Christmas Day but explains that as it concerns the death of Hunter Black, the priority is to gather as much information as quickly as possible.

'Why? Was he murdered or something?' The two DC's look at one another. 'Only nobody seems to know? Everything on the news just says he's dead. Not how or why or anything?'

DC Green says they are not at liberty to say and explains that they have a few questions to ask, mostly about my whereabouts on certain dates and times. She says I'm not under arrest and am free to leave any time. Except, I'm not though, am I? Not really. She also says she will write down all the questions I'm asked plus all my replies, which she will then read back to me. 'If you're happy with what I write, and then read back to you, and you agree that it is, to the best of your knowledge, a true statement, we will then ask you to sign it. Okay?'

I ask her why I couldn't have done all this at home? Both the officers look at one another again and mumble something else about this being a high priority case. 'It's just easier if we do all the paperwork here, at the station.' DC Green shuffles her papers again, her voice final, dismissive. She asks me if I understand and I gulp, nod my head and shift my chair forward. This time the chair doesn't make a scraping noise like DC Foster's chair did, it's more of a farting sound, not unlike the one I let rip ten minutes ago. Both DC Green and Foster look at me. I put my hand to my cheek and feel my face burn again.

'Sorry,' I say. 'Wasn't me!'

The two detectives exchange more glances. DC Green then looks back towards me, her eyebrows arched. '*What* wasn't you, Connor?' The tone of her voice is serious. 'Do you have something to tell us? Something you need to get off your chest?'

'What? No! I meant the farting noise.'

DC Green's eyebrows knit together. She looks confused. 'Sorry, what?'

'The farting noise,' I repeat. 'It was the chair, not me.'

To my surprise DC Foster throws his head back and laughs. It's hearty and guttural, reminds me of Grandad, until he starts coughing, which he then doesn't seem to be able to stop. It gets so bad, despite two hard whacks across his back by DC Green, he has to leave the room. DC Green's lips pucker. She looks thoroughly pissed off. 'We have to wait for my colleague to return,' she says. Now she's definitely sucking on lemons again.

Once DC Foster returns, with some water, the serious questions begin. They ask me if I know Vincent Brennan. 'Or, Vince "Bad Boy" Brennan as he prefers to be called,' DC Foster says, his red face breaking into a smirk.

I do know him, of course. Vince is Jake's uncle. I cross my arms, look down, sink into my chair. *Fuck.* When I look up again I find both detectives staring at me. My throat feels thick, my mouth as though it's stuffed with cotton wool. I take a quick sip of my coffee; lukewarm, it's more gross, and the only thing I want to do is spit it out again. I look around. It's not an option. Shuddering, I swallow the sickly liquid and decide to come clean.

With my head bowed, my elbows on my knees and the tips of my fingers touching, I talk. It takes a while, but I tell them everything I know.

It's a relief. A relief to tell someone.

Chapter Six

Boxing Day
PRESENT DAY – EARLY MORNING

LIZZIE

It's 4am in the morning, Boxing Day. Cassie and Connor are both home, safe and sound, as I knew they would be. They both have alibis and, no doubt, CCTV confirmation of their whereabouts on the day in question. And granted, although Connor isn't entirely innocent, his antics brought a wry smile to my face. And everyone else's for that matter. I suppose we're lucky he got off with a caution, although that said, I'm not sure what they could have charged him with, anyway? Harassment, at a push? Then there's poor Aunt Marie. Beside herself, she was. Thank god she agreed to spend the night at Mum's. Although all things considered it might have been a wiser move to have her stay with me. Oh well, at least Mum can console her. They can console one another. It's so sad to think of Uncle Teddy passing away almost a year to the day after Dad. Doesn't surprise me, though. As brothers go, they were very close. Everyone commented on how Teddy's condition deteriorated after Dad left us. I think he just gave up.

Lost in thought, I shiver, the streets deserted, the cold air snapping at my heels as my footsteps echo around me. Walking is the only thing that works for me when I can't sleep. There's something about the rhythm of it, the idea of constantly moving forward. I turn into Park Road and linger at the entrance to the Leisure Centre on the left, thinking back to a different time, the summer of 1984, when the sun shone forever and life was simple:

Ruby and I, arms linked, are eighteen, wearing short Ra-Ra skirts, big hair and earrings to match. We're tipsy after pinching some of Ruby's mum's Malibu, and are making our way to the monthly disco at "The Leisure". Drunk on life, on the heady scent of possibility, singing Cyndi Lauper's "Girls Just Want To Have Fun" from the tops of our less than harmonious voices and dancing till we drop. Despite Margaret Thatcher, despite Aids, despite the heart-wrenching pictures on the news of starving Ethiopians, despite pit closures in the north and the rise of the yuppie and greed in the south and, despite mass youth unemployment – we are happy. Happy and young and full of hope. And time. We have bags of the stuff, don't we?

Where the hell did it go then? How did I end up here, pacing the streets in the early hours of the morning, once again worrying about my family and with another funeral to arrange? God knows Aunt Marie is in no fit state to do it. Uncle Teddy is in a better place now, though, I'm convinced of that. At peace, hopefully. With Dad.

A rustling sound from the hedgerow to the side of the locked metal gates of the Leisure Centre catches my attention. Something is fidgeting. My feet are numb and I'm in half a mind to stamp some warmth back into them but I don't. I stand still, my breath steaming out in front of me, billowing like bathwater, and watch. Sure enough a blackbird, jet-black plumage, its beak as bright as polished amber, appears. He perches on top of the hedge, his head, spotlighted by the streetlamp above, is black and iridescent like a puddle of oil. With stilted head movements he watches me before breaking into sweet melodic song. Transfixed, I stand and watch. The Beatles song "Blackbird" comes to mind, as does Dad singing it badly, with Sean and I, small children, balancing on his knee, laughing. I know it's mere coincidence but I find comfort in this beautiful bird serenading me. It's easy to believe, somehow, his presence is linked to Dad. Unfortunately, though, the noise of a passing car startles my new friend and he flies off, disappears, camouflaged by the inky blue sky above.

I adjust my scarf and continue my journey. I have no planned route, I'll just keep walking until I'm too tired to think anymore. I'm thankful for the brief trip down memory lane, a brief respite from my ever-whirring mind. My head, I confess, is all over the place, my jumbled thoughts, like clothes in a washing machine. I'm a writer, my job is to fabricate fiction, and right now that's how my life feels – fabricated. I shiver again and my spine tingles. Has someone just walked across my grave? It's a bitter night, below zero. I fold my arms about myself; keep walking until the dimly lit streets give way to the bright lights of the town centre. The Buttercross comes into view, its Collyweston stone roof slightly obscured by the huge Christmas tree now taking centre stage.

I look up at the colossal swaying evergreen as an icy wind whips up around the square. A waft of pine fills my nose as the tree's huge branches rock back and forth. With gloved hands, I pull my hat down, my collar up and fasten the belt on my coat a little tighter. My twenty-minute walk has brought me to the centre of the small Fenland town that has now been my home for more years than I care to remember. And, save for the muted hum of the odd taxi passing through, the ker-chunk, ker-chunk of tyres across intermittent drains or manhole covers, all is pleasantly peaceful and quiet.

I sit down on one of the metal benches beneath the Buttercross and tip my head back. I'm met by a vast blanket of darkness, its foreboding expanse relieved by a handful of stars that, scattered moon dust, sparkle like the blinking fairy lights on our tree at home. A smile lifts the corner of my mouth.

Witching hour, Dad called this, a time when witches, demons and ghosts are at their most powerful. How fitting, considering the Fens were once regarded as disease-ridden places, rife with superstition, haunted by witches and gremlins. I shake my head. It's not an image that bears well with the sleepy little town I know. And the only gremlins present, are the ones in my head. That's the great thing about living in a small town like Great Tossen, though. It's still a relatively safe place for insomniacs like me to wander around at whatever ungodly hour. The crime rate is still negligible.

When Scott left us, it definitely made good sense for me to move back here and raise the kids, not to mention being closer to my parents who helped with childcare – Scott didn't see the need to do that. He never liked it here. 'Not exactly the epicentre of art and culture, is it?' he'd say, followed by some disparaging remarks about the local yocals having webfeet and tiny minds to match their small town mentality. I laugh. Funny how people change: Scott and Ruby are now considering buying a house here. I make a mental note to remind him of his past observations when the opportunity presents itself.

Even Simon, single parent to Maisy, living nine miles away in the city when we first met, could see the good sense of bringing the kids up here. Admittedly, everyone knows your name, likes to know your business, greets you with a running commentary about the weather, or his or her latest ailment. And yes, there are only a handful of decent restaurants, but that does include a great Thai, an award winning Indian, and the pub grub, as Dad often referred to it, isn't too bad, either. Plus a few of them host regular open mic or spoken word nights. And yes, it's also true that strangers are welcomed with caution, their badge of honour and acceptance duly earned after a stint of voluntary work: playing Santa on the annual Carol Float to raise money for charity, baking and selling cakes for the local church fetes

(Christmas and Summer), crowd and traffic control for the annual Straw Bear Festival – which takes place in January, always, undoubtedly, the coldest day of the year – or erecting the town's Christmas tree and decorations, which Simon helped to do again this year.

This time, though, without Dad.

I sniff; close my eyes for a second, and use my gloved hand to wipe away the lone tear cascading down my cheek for fear it will set and turn to ice. *Not unlike your heart this past year, eh?* Have I really become so distant, unapproachable? Connor thinks so. I'm sure Simon does too. He hasn't said as much, but I sense it in him, sense a distance between us that is growing wider. I sigh, look down at the opaque ground beneath me and rest my head in my hands. *Am I losing him? Am I really losing Simon?* I look up again, sniff again, and know I need to make amends. If I can. If it's not too late?

'Easier said than done, eh, Lizzie?' I say out loud, the heat of my words ejecting little puffs of smoke from my mouth.

Out of nowhere fatigue hits me like a blow to the head. I feel drained, physically and mentally and every bone in my body aches, too heavy to carry the weight of my troubled thoughts. Instinctively I reach for one of the scars nestling in my hair then remember I'm wearing a hat. I'm startled by footsteps behind me, and a clipping sound. I stand up, relieved to see Gary, our relatively new next-door neighbour and Sherlock Bones, their over-friendly Labrador. Gary and his lovely wife, Amra, plus their three children moved in six months ago. Loud and boisterous, they remind me of me and mine, when Maisy, Cassie and Connor were much younger. Often noisy, always polite, Simon likens them to a cross between *The Waltons* and the Gallagher family from *Shameless*. I like them a lot. We all do, much to our other neighbour, Tabitha's, annoyance.

'Hi Lizzie, it's a cold one tonight,' Gary says, as Sherlock bounds towards me. 'Or should I say this morning.' He yanks Sherlock back by the lead.

'Hi Gary. Hello Sherlock,' I say, patting his head.

Sherlock, tail wagging, looks at me, and straining at the lead, makes to jump up.

'No, Sherlock. Down, boy. I'm pretty sure Lizzie doesn't want to be licked to death by you.'

I laugh, step forward and make a fuss of the overlarge pup. Sherlock responds in kind by jumping up anyway. Almost face-to-face, his front two paws digging into my shoulders, despite my thick coat, Sherlock licks my face. I feel his hot breath and the coarseness of his pink, wet tongue on my cheeks. His boisterous energy is a far cry from poor Freddy who, with arthritic legs, is literally on his last ones.

Gary, firm but gentle grabs the playful pup by his collar, pulls him away. 'No, Sherlock,' he says. 'Sorry about that, Lizzie.'

I laugh, shake my head. 'Don't worry. It's fine. He's just young, over-excited.'

Sherlock stretches, shakes himself, and circles several times before dropping to the ground, resting his head on his paws.

'Can't sleep?' I ask.

'Sadly not,' Gary replies. Tall, with hazel eyes, floppy brown hair and sporting a couple of days' stubble, he explains, good humouredly, that despite only having three hours sleep the night before, he was struggling to nod off. 'I often wake in the middle of the night... decided to bring the pup for a walk.' He looks down at the now resting Labrador whose ears twitch. 'Get rid of some of that energy of his before the kids wake up and the whole shebang starts over again. Thankfully we're visiting family today though, so not too much to do. Except get the kids ready of course – a task in itself at the best of times.' He rolls his eyes and strokes his chin. 'One of life's mysteries, I reckon.'

'What is?' I reply, half frowning, half smiling.

'How they're up at the crack of dawn yet we still leave the house twenty minutes late!'

'Ah yes, I remember it well. Calling up the stairs a gazillion times. One shoe on, one shoe lost. A visit to the toilet before we leave. Missing shoe found, the other one now lost – later found buried in the garden by the dog. Another visit to the toilet. Mismatched socks. A meltdown on the way because of a forgotten toy. A meltdown by you because you forgot the nappies ...' Gary grins, raises his eyebrows. 'Make the most of it, though. They don't stay young for long – the kids or the dog.' Sherlock lifts his head, looks up, then yawning, lowers it again.

'Feels like it's a never ending round of noise, nappies and worry at the moment,' Gary replies.

I assure him the nappies will stop. 'At some point. Can't say the same about the noise and the worry, though. Not if my family are anything to go by!'

'Great!' he replies, dragging his hand through his hair. 'Anyway, what are you doing up and about at this ungodly hour?'

I tell him how I've always struggled with sleep. 'I thought it was because I became a light sleeper after the kids were born but now I'm thinking it's because my body is programmed for a different kind of sleep, a throwback to a different time, and something called biphasic sleep – or broken sleep.'

'Sorry? Bi – what, sleep?'

'Biphasic. Apparently we used to sleep in two segments with a period of wakefulness in between. "First sleep," or dead sleep, began around dusk and lasted for three or four hours. Then, around midnight, people woke up for a few hours and would catch up on a few jobs, housework, that sort of thing. Then "second sleep," or morning sleep began several hours after the waking period and lasted until morning. There's at least five hundred historical references to first and second sleep, going as far back as Homer's Odyssey. Chaucer mentions it in his Canterbury Tales, as does Charles Dickens in some of his works.'

Gary looks bemused and I can't make out if he thinks I'm bonkers or boring. I look down at my feet, feel my cheeks flush with embarrassment, amazed at my detachment from my current situation. That I can stand here, talking to my neighbour in the early hours of the morning, supposedly without a care in the world, as if it's the most normal thing in the world.

'Sorry ... bit boring, I know. I can go on a bit. Research you see, being a writer.'

When I look up again Gary is scratching his chin, his eyes locked together in a frown. 'No – it's actually quite interesting. I always thought I was an insomniac but this theory might explain a lot.'

'You and I are not meant for this time, Gary,' I say, purposely dramatic.

We both laugh then Gary asks me if I've heard the news about Hunter Black? If Cassie is okay? I tell him we have heard. I also tell him – because no doubt Tabitha, whose curtains were twitching, will beat me to it if I don't – about our little visit from the police yesterday evening and why they asked Connor to help them with their enquires. Which Gary finds highly amusing.

'Little bugger!' he says laughing.

'Hmm ... tell me about it.'

'And you didn't know?'

'Nope. Not a clue.'

Our laughter subsides. Gary yawns and says he should head home. 'Time for my second sleep, methinks' he adds, winking. 'Unless the kids are already awake? Which is highly probable!' He asks me if I'd like to walk back with him and Sherlock. I thank him but I'm not ready to go home just yet. Gary seems reluctant to leave me, unlike Sherlock, who now on all fours, ears up, looks extremely eager to go. 'It's not safe wandering the streets at this time of the night – or should I say morning – alone.'

I assure Gary I'm fine, that I've been doing it for years. 'Anyway, as the saying goes, it's not a life, it's an adventure.'

Gary's mouth lifts into a smile. 'One of yours?'

'Pinched it from my Dad. One of his favourites. He used to say it all the time. Especially when the shit hit the fan, as he liked to say.'

Gary nods. 'Hmm, yeah – I like it. Think I'll use that as my mantra from hereon in, especially when the kids are driving me mad.' And with that he bids me good morning and both he and Sherlock walk on and disappear out of sight.

That's the thing about Great Tossen. Yes, it may not be the epicentre of art and culture, I'll give Scott that, but there could be worse places to live. But what it undoubtedly is, generally speaking, is safe. I sometimes sense that's why Mum and Dad moved here, from London, because it felt safe. Mum has been opening up lately, reminiscing about the past, offering snippets of information I didn't know. As has Aunt Marie. There are still gaps, though, unanswered questions, things I don't understand.

And time is running out. I need to dig harder, and then surely time will tell?

Chapter 7

LONDON 1964

SALOCIN

It was fast approaching the end of 1964 and although the year had started out well for young Salocin Lemalf, the end of it looked nowhere near as promising.

Salocin was careering towards his nineteenth birthday, his brother, Teddy, his twenty-first. The average income of a man was somewhere between ten and fifteen pounds a week, the price of a loaf of bread about four pence and Beatlemania had taken the nation by storm. So much so, the newsmen considered Ringo Starr's tonsils a matter of national importance, covering his tonsillectomy with all the due diligence usually bestowed upon a royal birth.

'Facking ridiculous,' Wilf scoffed when they were watching it on the News. 'That ain't news! To think I fought in the war too. And for what?' he said, nodding at both his sons. 'You lot goin' bleedin' ga-ga over some bloke having his tonsils out. Gawd 'elp us is all I can say.'

Salocin stared up at the building, its prominent blue roller shutters down, the door carved into it, locked and bolted. He flicked his wrist, took a gander at his watch – 6am. He was too early. Good. He'd grab a drink and go over again in his head what he planned to say. It may have been the crack of dawn but London, or at least the part he was in, was alive and buzzing. Turning on his heel he headed back towards Smithfield. He was jittery, needed something strong to calm his nerves. Hands in his pockets, whistling, he turned the corner, hit by the familiar hullabaloo of the meat market. Men in white overalls, some blood-splattered, headed this way, and that, finished for the day, keen to wind down. Butchery was physical, hard graft. Salocin could see it in their exhausted eyes. The simple desire, like him, to slope off to the Hope public house on Cowcross Street, or perhaps The Cock Tavern, and whet their whistle would be strong. It was amazing what a pint or two could do, how it helped smooth out the edges of the previous night's work before the whole malarkey started again later that evening.

Salocin slipped on the white coat Mickey had given him. 'You ain't got a cat in hell's chance of getting in any pub round 'ere without one,' Mickey warned, and he found himself weaving among the jostling crowds, observing the ritual and display of the stall holders. Barrows laden with copious amounts of animal carcasses made their familiar rattling sound as the bummarees and porters pulled them down the avenues, while others, shouldering improbably large pieces of meat, shouted across to one another. Above them came the roar of the salesmen who yelled out their prices.

"Ha-a-andsome bit of beef, who's the buyer?" "Ere, this way. Nice leg of lamb, best in the market." "Ye-o-o! Ye-o-o. Ere you are guv'nor, come along, come along. Splendid bit o pork belly, you won't see betta." "Glass of nice peppermint, stave orf the chills?"

In any other part of town, these crimson-splattered white-coated men would elicit gasps of horror but here it was the norm. And some coats were grislier than others, which showed, or so Mickey had informed Salocin, the slaughter of lambs. 'You get bloodier cutting up lambs, see,' he'd said, 'because you put 'em on a block, and cut towards you. Pigs, however, are hung up, so you can cut away from yourself.'

Mickey Rosenthal wasn't a butcher but he knew what he was talking about. The man was a walking, talking encyclopaedia, for fuck sake. An educated man, self-taught, always with his nose in a book. Right from the outset, Salocin, a little in awe of this charming man, decided he liked Mickey. Liked him a lot.

An East End Jew now living in Chigwell, Mickey was a working class boy done good. In his early thirties, he was an attractive man, over six feet tall in his stocking feet, slim but well built, sporting the latest fashionable black, thick-rimmed glasses. He had an air about him, confident but not cocky, self-assured but not arrogant. He was also foreman of the Wakefield & Son Scrap Metal Yard and Salocin's boss. The big boss and owner of the yard went by the name of Georgie Wakefield, and was also Mickey's father-in-law.

Salocin pushed the pub door open and stepped in, struck by the bittersweet smell of fresh blood, stale beer and newly sprinkled sawdust. It reminded him of some trips he'd taken to Smithfield as a boy with his father.

He headed towards the bar amid a thick cloud of smoke. Freshly lit cigarettes, carefully rolled woodbines and pipes chugged by the old geezers all added to the smog. The noise levels inside the pub didn't differ much to the shouting and bawling of the outside world. Voices, some chipper, most weary, bobbed along on a sea of space-time continuum as menfolk, eagerly expecting a couple of hours' kip, swigged their pints, discussed work, 'er indoors, the football results and life in general. The sanest decision would be to walk away but Salocin found this clan of like-minded bullocks, talking bollocks, soothing. Amid the chatter, the raised voices, the clinking of glasses, and the gentle tinkling of the ivories of the old Joanna in the corner, Salocin felt strangely at ease.

'Two hundred, me and the boy done,' Salocin overheard one bleary-eyed individual saying to another, standing at the bar, his white coat stamped in varying shades of red ranging from the darkest, almost blackest red through to the brightest, pillar box red. 'Pigs mostly,' the stranger continued. 'The legs, shoulders, loins too. All done proper, like. In five minutes, mind.' The stranger's friend nodded and Salocin, taking his first sip of the pint of Guinness he'd just ordered, shuddered. A whole pig chopped up in five minutes? Didn't bear thinking about.

The landlady, voluptuous Vera, he'd heard someone call her, winked at him. 'One and ten please love,' she said, grinning, her long fingers caressing the gold heart necklace nestled between the nook of her huge bosom.

Rooting round in his pocket for some change, Salocin felt his cheeks burn. He guessed Vera was probably around the same age as his mother, despite the thick layer of face powder she wore to try and hide it. Although, with her tight-fitting sweater, short skirt and long spidery lashes, her dress sense was far less conservative than Martha's. 'Mutton dressed as lamb,' his mother would have sniffed, had she seen her.

'Be sure to come back and see us,' Vera called, her voice husky, the cackle that followed as loud as her bright red painted lips. Some of the older fellas laughed. 'Eat him for breakfast she would,' he heard someone say.

Salocin, his cheeks now crimson, pretended he hadn't heard. He slid the correct change across the bar, took another gulp of his pint and turned on his heel in search of a table. He pushed his way among the throng of men and found one tucked away in the corner of the room. He had a long day ahead of him. A pint of the black stuff would give him some energy. Maybe some Dutch courage too? Tipping his head back, eyes closed, he took another swig of Guinness. It slid down with remarkable ease, his Adam's apple bobbing up and down with each grateful mouthful.

He'd only been working at the scrap yard for a couple of weeks. It was physical hard graft and already he was wondering if he'd made a mistake. He rested his arm on the table, his chin in his hand, and let out a sigh. His mother had always said his mouth would get him into trouble one day. She'd been over the moon when he was offered an apprenticeship at Moorefield Aircraft Services. Finally, after failing the Eleven Plus and failing to get into Grammar school like older brother Teddy, Salocin had redeemed himself. Plus it also meant he'd get to work alongside aeroplanes like the ones he'd played among during his youth. However, like most things in life, reality was different to fantasy. Unlike the planes of his childhood, abandoned relics rusting among the rubble and shored up housing of old bombsites where he and his friends pretended to be pilots for fighter command, the planes he worked on as an apprentice were commissioned, working, shiny and new. Somehow, though, it wasn't the same. The rusting dinosaurs of a war he hadn't been part of, but had filled his childhood, reached out to him in a way the newer ones never did. Plus, he was sick to death of the old geezers calling him "Sally." Did they really expect him to stand there and take it? He knew they were doing it on purpose, trying to wind him up. It got worse, too. He had his suspicions why. Was sure it was the boss's son Derek, Del to his friends, Shadbrook. If the rumours were true, he paid them to do it. The reason? Sour grapes. A bruised ego because, despite being a year older than Salocin and the owner of a swanky sports car and flash suits, he still couldn't get the girl he – and probably half the other blokes at Moorefield's – wanted. The girl in question wasn't impressed and much to Derek's eternal surprise – Salocin's too, if he was being honest – she chose Salocin over Derek, and Derek had never forgiven him. However, Salocin had also been on a final warning when he lashed out at Reg, his supervisor – ugly-looking bloke, probably late thirties, narrow eyes, ratty face, dull grey complexion – after he'd asked him again, for the umpteenth time, why his parents had given him a girl's name.

'Now piss orf,' Reg had given Salocin his cards, then, his

arm outstretched, finger pointing towards the door, he was like a furious headmaster.

Constrained by a couple of other employees, Salocin had stared at Reg nursing the thick bloody lip Salocin had given him. 'Gladly,' he replied, lunging forward, only to be yanked back by the two blokes at either side of him.

Reg flinched. 'And don't bother coming back,' he added.

'As if. As if I wanna come back 'ere. End up some sad bastard like you. Doing the same job day after day, week after week, year after year. Every day the same. Fifty plus years of routine and drudgery. A nice gold watch or carriage clock in lieu of services at the end of it. Fuck that and fuck you!'

'You need to watch that temper of yours my boy,' his grandmother warned when she heard the story. 'Too much like yer bleedin' father.'

There was some truth in what she'd said, Salocin acknowledged now, because unlike Teddy he *was* quick to blow a fuse. He loved to get stuck in, especially with bullies and, thanks to Wilf, he could hold his own. As boys, Wilf had taken both his sons for boxing lessons and both had proved proper little scrappers. Salocin had even aroused the interest of a couple of dodgy managers and promoters sniffing around. Like Wilf, he was pugnacious and volatile in the ring. He could stand his ground, despite his wiry, skinny frame. However, although he could have made a small fortune out of the boy, Wilf decided that boxing, as a career, was far too dangerous for his sons. Besides which, Martha would have gone ballistic if Salocin had pursued that road. Martha was a hard woman with standards, expectations of her sons – probably to fill some void in her own life. However, regardless of Martha, even Wilf wasn't callous enough to see his son end his days as a tapper or some old 'has been' fighting in the fairground booths. Past their prime, skint and out of the limelight, there were few alternatives open to ex-boxers. Most had little choice but to endure at least ten fights a night in the fighting booths, taking and handing out their punishment for a pound a round, and when that was no longer possible, they often spent their days 'tapping' others for a drink or a few shillings. Wilf would often point out grey-haired old men to his sons, instantly recognisable as ex-boxers by their turned up, bent broken noses. Once formidable fighters but now, thanks to years of countless physical pounding, mere shadows of their former selves. Eye injuries, spine injuries, broken ribs and broken noses all left their mark and more often than not a legacy of health problems. But it was the head injuries that often reduced a hard man into a shaking incoherent spectacle. Former champions, shuffling along the road, heading for the local doss house where down and outs could get a bed for a few shillings, it was sad. They deserved better in their last days and Wilf was adamant that his sons would know how to box to defend themselves, not to earn a living.

Working as a technician had been boring, anyway. Every day like Groundhog Day. There were only so many DC generators you could wash down, take apart, reassemble and pass on to the next person. It may have been permanent, regular work, but it was also soul destroying. He didn't know what, but Salocin wanted more out of life.

'And you think the way to do that is working at a scrap metal yard, do you?' His mother had scowled, her voice thick with derision.

'Good enough for me, good enough for the boy,' Wilf had replied. Wilf had been working at a local scrap metal yard for several years now. Tired of ducking and diving he had settled into a job with regular pay and regular hours. It was hard, dirty work, but the money was good, and more importantly, it was kosher. For five and half days a week, Wilf clocked in and clocked out. He earned more than enough to give Martha her housekeeping, pay the tallyman, buy his beer and smokes, with a bit left over to boot.

And so, Salocin had his father to thank for getting him this job. God knows, Wilf rarely helped his sons but this time he'd asked his boss at the yard who asked a good friend of his running another new yard near Clerkenwell. That bloke happened to be Mickey, and the two men clicked. The following morning Salocin clocked on at the business premises of Georgie Wakefield & Son, much to the bitter disappointment of Martha and he suspected, although she hadn't said as much, Ellie – just about the prettiest girl he'd ever clapped eyes on.

Salocin, nursing his pint, and with a smile on his face, thought about Ellie, the girl he was now courting. A secretary at Moorefield, Salocin had spotted her on his first morning, although it took him a couple of months to pluck up enough courage to speak to her. He'd been parking his beloved scooter, struggling to get the kickstand to work, and quietly swearing, when his ears were drawn to the soft sound of laughter floating across the car park. Her long blonde hair, with its iridescent flecks of gold weaved among the strands, tumbled across the shoulders of the bright green coat she wore. Her aqua blue eyes, although fringed by long, black lashes were bright, and piercing, her pink lips, plump and glossy. She reminded him of Brigitte Bardot, only prettier, if that was possible, and when she'd looked at him and smiled, he couldn't quite believe his luck. He'd glanced across his shoulder, checking to see if there was anyone behind him – surely she wasn't smiling at him, was she? When he turned back, she had giggled, put her hand to her mouth. Salocin had smiled back, felt his head spin, his legs turn to jelly. Each morning, from thereon in, he looked out for her, as did she him. Before long their shy smiles turned into good morning salutations, followed by a chat on the way in to work, and soon they were meeting during tea and lunch breaks. Elle, although everyone called her Ellie, was one of five children.

'I'm the only girl though,' she'd said.

Salocin felt his eyebrows shoot into his brow. 'So... you have four brothers?' He'd imagined four protective, strapping young men and a father whose only daughter was the apple of his eye.

Ellie had laughed, waved her hand dismissively. 'Ah don't be worrying yourself about them. They won't be giving you any bother.' She'd smiled but there was a profound sadness in her eyes. 'We're just not... not close.' She'd shrugged her shoulders. 'Except Tom, that is. Me oldest brother. I like Tom. He left home years ago though. Writes every now and again. Bit of an outsider, see. Like me.' Eyes darting left to right, she had looked round, made sure no one was listening, then leaned in and whispered in his ear. He remembered feeling her hot, sweet breath on his cheek, how it had caused a stirring in his groin. 'Think he prefers boys to gels,' she'd said. 'If you know what I mean?' She'd stared at him for a few seconds, blinking, waiting for some sign of disapproval and when there was none forthcoming she'd looked relieved. 'Think my Mum has an inkling. Dad doesn't have a clue. Reckon he'd go barmy if he did. Don't bother me though. Live and let live, I say.'

Salocin also learned that Ellie loved to read. 'Don't get a look in with the telly,' she'd said. 'Not with me Dad and three brothers. So I go to me room and read... Disappear and become someone else for a while. Travel. Hope, one day, to see some places I've read about, especially Rome. I'd love to see the Colosseum. Quite fancy Blackpool, too, to see the illuminations. And Cornwall. Supposed to be lost treasure there, y'know.'

Salocin had smiled, shook his head. He *hadn't* known, but the more Ellie talked, the more he fell for her. She was beautiful. Funny too. Different to the other girls he had met, worldly and confident, yet vulnerable and naïve at the same time.

'It's true,' she said. 'Supposed to be pirate treasure, around

Dollar Cove in Perranporth. Maybe we should go there one day, look for it?'

Salocin had laughed, promised her they would, then kissed her. It was their first kiss and every bit as he'd imagined it would be. Tentative, warm and sensual. He'd kissed other girls before but this meant something. And it didn't just make his cock hard, it made his head swim and his heart swell too. This girl, this *woman*, did something, stirred something deep down inside him. And he wanted her like he'd wanted no one else in his entire life.

Like him, Ellie also loved listening to music. She often went dancing when she could afford it, with her best friend, Marie. 'Like a sister to me, she is. Don't know what I'd do without her, sometimes.'

Once they started courting they'd meet after work at a local coffee shop and at the weekends, after Salocin had scrimped and saved every penny, they went to the flicks. Salocin's favourite film that year was *Goldfinger*. Ellie preferred *The Yellow Rolls Royce*. They went dancing too; their favourite haunts were the Locarno or the Bally High in Streatham, and the Orchid Ballroom in Purley. But going out cost money and an apprentice's wage just didn't cut it, so when Mickey offered Salocin the job at the yard – a tenner a week, rising to twenty-five pounds after a probationary period, as opposed to the fiver he'd been earning – it was, for Salocin, despite his mother's words and Ellie's grave look of concern, lemon squeezy.

However, if the rumours were to be believed, businessman and owner of the yard, Georgie Wakefield was more gangster than scrap metal merchant – even Wilf had been slightly concerned when he arranged an interview for Salocin. There were rumours Georgie had connections with the Kray twins, possibly the Richardson brothers, and had purposely sought business premises alongside one of the biggest collection of slaughterhouses in the country for a reason – and not because he liked a nice piece of rump at cost. Whether the rumours were true, Wilf couldn't say, he just hoped that other stories were more accurate – namely that Georgie Wakefield was going legit and the Wakefield & Son Scrap Metal Merchants was being run by the book, leaving Wilf's conscience clear. On the day Salocin started at the yard, Wilf's advice to his youngest son was simple, 'Clock in and out when you're supposed to, keep your 'ead down, your nose clean and don't take the piss.'

Despite the outward legitimacy of Georgie Wakefield's yard, there remained rumours abound that it was just a front for his other, less lawful business ventures. Savvy, with a good head for business, it was common knowledge Georgie had been careful with the fortune he'd amassed in the fifties (from crime and prostitution rackets, Salocin heard) and how, ploughing it back into property, Georgie had gradually bought properties around London, mostly in run-down areas like Brixton and Notting Hill.

Lighting a cigarette, and taking another swig of his pint, Salocin recalled the conversation he'd recently overheard between his mother and his Aunt Flo, who, in the kitchen, the door closed, were gossiping like a couple of mother hens, as usual. Martha, clicking her tongue (and no doubt rolling her eyes) was telling Aunt Flo how Salocin had lost his job at Moorefield and was now working at Georgie Wakefield's yard. Aunt Flo then proceeded to tell Martha the rumours about how Georgie's growing property portfolio had also coincided with the mass migration of workers from the Caribbean, many of whom worked on the buses and trains but who, on their arrival, struggled to find accommodation.

'Georgie spotted an opportunity, see' Aunt Flo said. 'Most of the tenants in Georgie's properties were white working-class, had statutory protection against rent increases. So Georgie hatched a plan. Knew if he could drive his existing tenants out, he could then move the immigrants in and increase the rent prices. Launched a war of attrition, I heard. His main tactic, harassment. Started moving Toms into the adjacent flats, which were already overcrowded, and encouraged 'em all to play loud music. Then he hired local villains who used threats of violence, started killing tenants' cats and dogs, as well as cutting off electricity supplies, and having door locks removed to make 'em unsafe. Ironically, although we all know it wasn't his intention, Georgie Boy is considered a hero amongst his new tenants coz he was just one, among a mere handful, willing to offer them help. Everyone else just shunned 'em see, but Georgie saw an opportunity and made a bleedin' packet, so I heard.'

Salocin paid little interest to the rumours. People loved to gossip. His new work place looked legitimate enough, and besides, he was there for one reason and one reason only – money. And now, more than ever, he needed that money. He was saving for a ring. After that for a wedding, plus enough for a deposit on a mortgage, buy a small house – something he and Ellie could call theirs. All that would take time, and unfortunately, time was running out. Ellie, usually fit as a fiddle, had been sick during the last week or so. Mostly during the mornings, but sometimes during the evenings, too.

Salocin had no choice. He was fucked. He knew Ellie's parents wouldn't help them, and when he'd asked his own, Wilf made it quite clear there'd be nothing from them either, so he needed to ask Mickey a favour.

Would he help though?

Salocin necked the rest of his pint and headed for the yard.

He was about to find out.

chapter 8

BOXING DAY
PRESENT DAY – MORNING

CASSIE

I snap the light on and shield my eyes from the bright light that now floods the kitchen. It's 7am, not exactly early, but still pitch black outside and the house, except for the hum of the fridge and the creaking of the radiator pipes filling with hot water is, as Grandad used to say, church quiet.

I flick the switch on the kettle and notice Mum's coat hanging on the back of the chair. Damp to the touch, I realise she must have been out walking. Again. Probably couldn't sleep. Which is hardly surprising; I didn't sleep that well myself, tossing and turning all night – my pyjamas are still damp with sweat. Such weird nightmares too, filled with blue fish and *him* – Hunter Black. Still can't believe he's dead. And what's more, I can't believe Connor paid to have a stink bomb sent to him – on what turned out to be the day of his actual death, no less!

Poor Connor looked terrified when we were asked to go to the police station. Went as white as a sheep, I think the saying is. I still can't believe Mum didn't come with us. I mean, it's bad about Uncle Teddy dying and Aunt Marie needing Mum to calm her down but given how protective Mum is, I would have laid money on her going to the station with us first. I even had visions of her calling a solicitor, standing outside, waving huge white placards, shouting our innocence. But she didn't. She remained pretty calm, and Si stepped up – good old stepdad to the rescue again – and volunteered to drive us to the station and wait. And Mum agreed. Just like that. No fuss. No worry. Said we'd be fine with Si, which we were. But how could she be so sure? Until then none of us knew what Connor had done. And as he still wasn't spilling the peas at that point, how could Mum have been sure it wasn't something terrible. Weird. Then again, everyone has been acting weird since Black's death – including me, I suppose.

I feel a smile tug at the corners of my mouth. A stink bomb – because Hunter Black stinks, or should I say, stank, past tents, tense, whatever the bloody word is.

I remember when I first got offered the job to work for Black. Me. Little, naïve, inexperienced Cassie. I was like – no way. Just no fucking way. Dream come true? Course, I thought he chose me because he liked my work, my small portfolio of music production. Clearly, although I didn't know it at the time, he was looking for other attributes, though, ones that had fuck all to do with my music ability. The sad thing is, it was good fun, for a while. Before the bullying. Before he… did what he did. I've still got a pic of him and me standing next to Dezi No-A, the rapper, when we worked with him at the studio. How messed up is that? I should Photoshop Black out. Make him disappear. Obliterate him from my history, like Stalin did in Soviet Russia in the 1930s. It was during the Great Purges, I think Grandad said. Well before Photoshop, anyway.

It's funny how we react to things. Death is never like you imagine it to be, and now we have another one in the family. Poor old Uncle Teddy. A huge stroke, the doctor said. Probably for the best, Mum said. I don't feel as sad about losing him as I did about Grandad. I feel like we lost Uncle Teddy a long time ago, even before Grandad. Alzheimer's is a bitch. I don't think he recognised any of us during these last few months – not even Aunt Marie. I wonder if she'll move back to London now Uncle

Teddy has gone? She's spent a lot of time there recently. Visiting old friends, apparently.

Steam rises from the spout of the kettle and I hear the familiar click as it switches itself off. I pour boiling water on top of the brown coffee granules at the bottom of my mug, watching as they disintegrate into a hot, black frothy liquid. I reach for my coat from the rack by the door and throw it over my PJs and tap the pocket to check for the packet of fags I know I left there. I grab a ciggie from the pack and put it to my lips. The hob on the cooker hisses as I turn it on, the ignition switch *click, click, clicking,* before a ring of flame, blue and orange, bursts into life. I bend forward, being careful to keep my hair, which has grown quite a bit since I butchered it last year, out of the way and light the cigarette. I turn the gas ring off again then, coffee in one hand, my phone in the other, I head for the back door.

It looks cold out but Mum will kill me if I smoke in the house. She hates me smoking. Everyone does. Even Luke, who used to smoke, but is trying to give up, and wants me to do the same. Grandad hated me smoking, even though he did it too, when he was younger. He used to call me "Foghorn Lil from over the hill" when I was little because I was loud and noisy. Then when he discovered I smoked he changed it to "Fag Ash Lil." I should give up. Promised Grandad I would.

'Sorry, Grandad,' I shout to the wind as I step outside. 'Whoa!'

It's so windy I'm almost blown off the doorstep. My hand shakes and my coffee sloshes from side to side inside my mug. My very own storm in a mug – or is that supposed to be teacup? Shit. Some of it runs down the edge; I'm in danger of getting burnt. With my fag still hanging between my lips I stuff my phone into my pocket and cradle my mug with both hands before I scald myself. The warmth seeps through to my chilly fingers as I walk

towards the small patio table, and carefully place my mug on it.
The once-grey frame is now rusty and flaking and I swear that
green stuff growing underneath the glass top is mould. Bloody
rank is what it is, but Mum said put up or shut up, and locked
away her best table in the shed for the winter.

I perch on one of the equally worn-out chairs and pull my
phone out again while I puff on my ciggie, wait for my coffee to
cool down. My ears pick up a sound. A woman's voice, maybe?
I wait a few more seconds but the sound disappears. Nothing,
except the crackle of my burning ciggie and the wind flapping
my hair against my ears. 'Meh... whatevs,' I say out loud to no
one. I swig a mouthful of coffee, then, pulling my knees up to my
chest, I tap the twitter icon on my phone, type the letters H U...
My screen fills up with tweets about my old boss – the man who
raped me. A white sea overflowing with row upon row of black
letters and emojis. Fuck! Really? So many people mourning his
loss while others are just angry. Furious. Because, like me, they
will never have their day in court with him, get the justice they
deserve.

It's obvious Black had a lot of enemies, but he was a powerful
man and had a lot of friends too. One headline reads, *Who killed
Hunter Black?* Was he killed though? No one has actually said
how he died, and the police are not giving much away. Plenty
of knobheads speculating about what happened, though, as
usual. Everyone has an opinion these days, even if it has fuck
all to do with them. I look up, take another drag of my ciggie,
watch as the wind snatches the trail of smoke seeping from the
corner of my mouth then go back to my phone. I search for
tweets related to Honey, wonder if she had anything to do with
Black's death. I noticed on the news, that like me, the police have
already questioned some of Black's other victims – or *alleged*
victims as we are referred to – so I'm pretty sure they must have
interviewed Honey by now. Not that she had a bad word to

say about him, of course. Bitch. And yet there are those in my family who defend her. Aunt Marie, for one, is always asking me to put myself in Honey's shoes. Telling me to remember how charming, how persuasive Black is – *was*. How it can't have been an easy choice for Honey to turn her back on me and accept what Black had to offer instead. Really? I was raped, for fuck sake. Doesn't Aunt Marie get that? I'm all for seeing the bigger picture but there are some things in life you just can't forgive. I click my phone off, put it back in my pocket. I don't want to read anymore. Prefer to put the whole sorry fucking thing behind me and move on.

I place my phone on the table and stare into space as my mouth, like an old battle cannon, pushes out rapid, deliberate bursts of smoke. I still can't believe Honey betrayed me like she did, though. She was my friend. One of my best friends, I thought. How wrong was I?

I definitely hear a woman's voice again, followed by a hissing sound. I turn towards the fence and through a gap I see a flash of jet-black hair and realise someone is standing behind it.

'Psssst. Give us a drag, babe?' She waves a couple of fingers through the slit in the fence.

Her accent is similar to Nan and Grandad's, which makes me smile. I realise it's Mum and Si's new neighbour. Amra? Yeah, Amra, her husband, Gary, and their three kids. I tell her to come round.

I open the back gate for her. Like me she's also still in her PJ's but she is wearing a brightly coloured dressing gown over the top. She isn't wearing any make-up, but she's stunning all the same. Her brown eyes are huge, fringed by impossibly long lashes and her beautiful dark skin is flawless.

She flashes me a bright white smile. 'Thanks babe.' She nods towards the fence, 'The little buggers have locked me out again.' She raises her eyebrows and laughs. I get the impression that being locked out by her children is something that happens regularly. 'Cassie – is it?' I nod, pull out my packet of fags from my pocket and offer her one. 'Oh god, thanks. I really need this.' She uses my ciggie to light hers. 'Don't tell my husband, though – Gary,' she says through a cloud of smoke. 'Promised him I'd given up! Nothing wrong with the odd one from time to time, though, eh?' She winks. 'I'm Amra, by the way,' she says, scrunching her eyes tight, squinting, as smoke blows back into them. 'Your Mum's new neighbour. Neighbours from hell, she probably calls us!'

I laugh and shake my head. 'Mum loves you. Says you remind her of her. Plus she says you give Tabitha –' I point to the other side of the house.

'Yes... we've met.' Amra nods her head, smirks.

'Yeah... well, Mum says you give Tabitha someone else to focus on instead of her for a change.'

Amra throws her head back, laughs. 'Thank god the police were at your door yesterday, and not ours. I take it they were the police?' Her face is suddenly serious. 'That's what Gary said your Mum told him. Plus there's all the rumours, all the gossip circulating. Mostly on the Great Tossen Facebook group.' She looks thoughtful for a second and sighs. 'That's what comes of living in a small town I suppose, eh? Everyone knows – or thinks they know – everyone else's business. Anyway, like I said, thank god it was you lot. Tabitha would have got a petition going to get us removed if it had been us. She really doesn't like us. Especially me.'

Now it's my turn to laugh. 'She's not that bad.' I remember when she caught her husband, Mark, and me smoking pot in his shed at the bottom of the garden. It was that time Mum was attacked, still in hospital, in a coma, and I was upset, worried she'd never get better, and Mark was trying to cheer me up. I thought Tabitha would go ballistic when she found us. But she was well chilled. Even made us some sandwiches. 'Not once you get to know her,' I add.

Amra wrinkles her nose, shakes her head. 'Nope. She hates me. I think it's because I pointed out that her daughter might be autistic, same as my little 'un.'

I feel my eyes widen and I can't help the smirk that lifts the corners of my mouth. I imagine the look on Tabitha's face, know for a fact that would have gone down like a dead balloon.

'Well, it's true, for fuck' sake!' Amra continues. 'You can see it a mile off.'

I remember Mum saying a while ago she suspected Fortuna might be on the spectrum but she also said it was obvious Tabitha was in denial about it. 'And who am I to burst her bubble? She must address it – eventually,' Mum had added. Looks like Tabitha's bubble has been well and truly burst, then.

Amra asks me if our visit by the police last night had anything to do with Hunter Black. I nod, explaining how they wanted to confirm the whereabouts of both Connor and me two days before Christmas. 'Which is when they think Black snuffed it.'

Amra, sheepish, looks down. When she looks up again, she's grinning. 'I heard about Connor' she says. 'Your Mum told Gary this morning when they bumped into each other on a walk.' Then, to my surprise, she is suddenly roaring with laughter and I can't help but join in. 'Serves him right!' she adds, when she catches her breath. 'Piece of shit. Black, I mean, not Connor.' She asks me if the police have said anything about how Black died.

I shake my head. 'Uh-uh. Just said they're treating it as suspicious for now.'

'Good riddance, I say.' She says she knows what he did to me, assures me I'll be okay. 'In time,' she adds. 'And I should know. I was raped too when I was younger. By my uncle. He went to prison for it – eventually. But he caused a lot of damage and tore my family apart for a while. It's all good now, though. Like it will be for you.' And she says it in such a way, with such conviction, I believe her. 'I can see you're strong,' she continues. 'Like your Mum, like me. And I'll tell you what someone once told me – "it's not what happens to you, but how you react to it that matters". I've never forgotten those words. Not dissimilar to your mum's quote, come to think of it?'

'Which one?'

'It's not a life, it's an adventure!'

I smile and shake my head. 'That's not my Mum's quote, that's something my Grandad always used to say. He died last year, though, and now his brother, my Uncle Teddy, has just died, too.'

I feel my eyes well up and to my surprise Amra hugs me, and I let her. I feel slightly embarrassed, skanky even. I haven't even showered or cleaned my teeth yet. Amra, on the other hand, smells gorgeous – like lemons and coconuts.

A small voice coming from the gap in the fence interrupts our hug and when I turn to look I see another pair of huge brown eyes like Amra's.

'Okay,' Amra says, stubbing out her cigarette into the half-filled ashtray on the table. 'You've decided to let Mummy back in now have you?' She slips back through the gate, and glances across her shoulder. 'I'm always about, Cassie... if you ever need to talk? Or we can always just get shit-faced on gin, or Prosecco, or both? Talk bollocks for a few hours.'

And with that, Mum and Si's beautiful neighbour, who only moments ago was a stranger but now feels like an old friend, wishes me well and disappears in a puff of smoke.

Chapter 9

BOXING DAY
PRESENT DAY – LATE MORNING

CONNOR

I stare at Robbo's bruised eye and thick lip. He stares back.

'A stink bomb?' he repeats. You paid to have a stink bomb sent to Hunter Black's house?'

I grin, shrug my shoulders, take another swig of beer. 'Yeah. Why not? He stinks... stank, anyway. Thought I'd show him how much.'

The Rickmeister lowers his glass and raises his brow. 'Which just happened to be sent on the same day he was supposedly murdered?'

I hold my hands up. 'Whoa. The police are not saying Black was murdered. Just that they're treating his death as suspicious. But that's got fuck all to do with me, or the stink bomb.'

Stuffing another handful of crisps into his mouth, Robbo turns to Jake. 'And it was your uncle that made it?' he tries to say in between soggy chewed up cheese and onion bits spewing from his mouth like confetti.

Jake grimaces. 'Close your mouth, Robbo, for fuck sake.' His grimace metamorphoses into a grin, his dimpled smile stretched from ear to ear. 'Anyways, yeah, it was my uncle.' His voice is tinged with pride. 'Wanna get one for your old man?' He points to Robbo's eye.

Robbo lifts a hand to his eye and winces. 'Wouldn't stop him,' he mumbles, his smile fading.

I tip my head back and drain what's left of my pint before slamming the glass down and wiping my mouth with the back of my hand. I look round. The pub is filling up, there's the sweet scent of strong beer, and loud conversations compete with corny Christmas songs. I turn my head from left to right and notice different people nodding or pointing in our direction. News travels fast, especially in a small, gossipy town like Great Tossen.

The Rickmeister follows my gaze. 'Probably think you murdered him,' he says very matter of fact.

I shrug my shoulders, look away from the onlookers, pick up a beer mat, flick it with my finger and thumb. 'Probably. Don't give a shit if they do.'

'Nah. It's peng, I reckon.' Robbo's silly grin is now back in place. 'You might even get free beer and stuff.'

'How much was it?' the Rickmeister asks.

I look down, shifting uncomfortably in my chair. Threadbare, stained with alcohol and god knows what other shit, I wonder why the pub chose mock baroque (I think that's what Mum called it? – not Bangkok like Cassie thought) fabric to cover their chairs. Plastic would have been better, given all the spillages and stuff.

'For the stink bomb?' the Rickmeister continues. 'How much did you have to pay... Jake's uncle, I mean?'

Without looking up I snap the corner off the beer mat and a smattering of fine yellow dust settles on the table. 'A thousand...' I mumble, and despite the chatter, the loud music, I don't miss the sharp intake of breath.

'A thousand?' the Rickmeister repeats.

'... and five hundred,' I add.

'Fuck!' Robbo and the Rickmeister say in unison. 'Really?'

'Mates rates,' Jake declares proudly.

'Fifteen hundred... for a stink bomb!' the Rickmeister

shouts. 'Could have got my old chemistry books out and made a hundred for that kind of money.'

Jake sits bolt upright. 'Bloody couldn't,' he snaps. 'It's a sophisticated stink bomb. Like a...' He snaps his fingers, '... Argh what the hell is it called? Like a–'

'Malodorant,' I interrupt.

'That's it.' Jake throws his arm forward, pointing at me. 'Like a malodorant.'

Robbo looks confused, scrunches up his nose. 'A deodorant?'

Jake looks at Robbo as if *he* is a stink bomb and shakes his head. 'Duh, Robbo. Malodorant, not deod-o-bloody-rant.'

'What's one of them, then?'

'A malodorant,' I reply, 'is a chemical compound whose extreme stench acts as a temporary incapacitate attacking the olfactory and trigeminal nerves of the person introduced to it.' That's what Vinnie, Jake's uncle, told me. 'Although this particular chemical compound doesn't attack the nervous system.' I look at Jake.

Jake nods his agreement and Robbo, whose mouth hangs open, looks more confused than ever. 'Huh?' he says looking from me to Jake then back again.

'It's sort of like a chemical weapon, sort of. It works similarly, except the one Jake's uncle made doesn't attack the nervous system. It just leaves a really terrible smell that sticks to your skin, clothes, everything, and can often take weeks to get rid of.'

Robbo closes his mouth, arches his eyebrow. 'Righto. Think I've got it.' I can tell by his expression – like he's constipated – he hasn't. 'So... how did he get it into Black's house?'

I look at Jake. Bite the corner of my mouth. After my grilling by the police last night I'm not sure how much information I'm allowed to share. Mum said I'm luckier than I'll ever know that they regarded what I paid Jake's uncle to do as a prank rather than attempted conspiracy to harm Black. I suppose I am. I still don't regret it though. Just hope it offended that scumbag pig as much as he offended and hurt my family. I did shit a brick though, as Grandad used to say, when they announced his death on TV. How was I supposed to know the day Jake's uncle had the stink bomb delivered would be the day of Black's death? Talk about shitty timing.

'Tell 'em Conman,' Jake says.

I turn towards the expectant faces of Robbo and the Rickmeister then back towards Jake. I decide I will. We were both let off with a caution, so neither of us is in *real* trouble. No really. And besides, the Security Services have taken an interest in Vince's stinky invention, although, Jake and I are sworn to secrecy about that bit of information.

'Well?' Robbo says.

'Okay, I'll tell you.' I explain about my brief meeting with Jake's uncle, Vincent Brennan, a.k.a. Vince "Bad Boy" Brennan. Tall, over six feet, I reckon, skinny, like me, but wiry. You can see he works out because his chest and arms, more ink than skin, are pumped. His brown hair is long on top but almost skinhead short at the back and sides, and his bright blue eyes are unnerving. He kind of reminds me of that actor bloke from *Peaky Blinders*. Has a similar accent. Jake says Vince was always good at science, had once been offered a place at Oxford University, or Cambridge, maybe. But Jake also says his uncle messed up. Is a bit of a bad boy, in trouble with the police a few times when he was younger. He never went to uni, but he has always made money, usually illegally, and almost always with bizarre inventions he keeps coming up with. Grandad would have loved him. And that's what his stink bomb was – just another one of his curious inventions. Although to be fair, it wasn't a bomb as such, just a small device he inserted into a flower arrangement that triggered the release of a foul-smelling liquid whenever the gift card was pulled from the display.

Vince said he'd worked out a formula that was worse than any smell you could imagine and almost impossible to get rid of for a couple of weeks at least. Turns out I wasn't his first customer and Hunter Black wasn't his first recipient. Vince said it was all about supply and demand, whatever that means. And apparently a number of celebrities had been targeted, as had several MPs, which made Mum laugh – would have made Grandad laugh too. Vince had rules, though, the main one being he would never send a stink bomb to the same person more than once. That way, it would most likely be regarded as a one-off incident, less likely he'd be charged with harassment – if he were caught. He said he wouldn't be caught though – because he was too careful.

'So, how come he did then?' the Rickmeister asks, his face now a smug grin.

'Yeah – wasn't that careful, was he?' Robbo joins in.

Jake rolls his eyes and shakes his head. 'Stupid idiot got side-tracked and left his thumbprint on the device. Still, it's not all bad; he's off to London tomorrow to meet with MI5.' No sooner have the words fallen from Jake's mouth, he has clamped both his hands over his fat gob.

'No shit, Sherlock! MI5 as in James Bond and stuff?' Robbo yells.

A few people look over; shake their heads. I look at Jake and this time it's my turn to roll my eyes. 'That was supposed to be a secret,' I hiss from the corner of my mouth.

Jake shrugs his shoulders. 'Oh well, you won't tell, will you, lads?'

Robbo and the Rickmeister shake their heads, but I wonder how many people in the pub have heard anyway, whether they wanted to or not.

It answers one of my big questions though. Cause what's waaaay more troubling than the stink bomb or any of that shit, is that I can't help wondering if my stepdad and uncle had something to do with Black's death. They never made it to the IndieKnot gig in the end. Said they had somewhere else to go first, had to attend a meeting of some sort, although they wouldn't say where, or who with, just that they'd catch up with me and Dad afterwards. However, they also swore Dad and me to secrecy if they didn't make it to the gig. What was it Uncle Sean said on the train on the way to the gig? 'Don't forget, as far as everyone else is concerned, we,' he then pointed to Si and himself, 'have been at the gig with you two,' and then pointed to me and Dad, 'all night? It's important you stick to that. Okay, Connor?' So everyone, including the police, think there were four of us at that gig that afternoon, but there were in fact only two – Dad and me. Si and Uncle Sean did manage to make it to the pub later, as planned, where we met Mum, Cassie, Luke and Eustace. But it was at least thirty minutes after we got there. They made some excuse about stopping for a piss along the way, if I remember? So where the fuck were they during those missing hours – in London – and on the same day Hunter Black died? I wanted to ask Si on the way to the police station last night but it just wasn't possible with Cassie in the car.

So, what I've been wondering is, should I also tell my friends, my best mates, who probably know me better than my own Mum does right now, why I haven't slept for the last two nights? Should I ask my best friends, who I've known most of my life and who probably know me as well as I know myself – if they, like me, think my stepdad and my uncle are capable of murder? The knot in my stomach twists a little tighter and beer-flavoured bile burns my throat. I think of Si, all he's done for me – the dad I never had, at least until my real dad came back into my life. Even so, it's still Simon I turn to. And then there's Uncle Sean, who taught me how to play guitar, surf, and generally how to be peng – or cool, as he prefers to say. I once again replay his conversation with me on the train to the gig, feel sick…

I know now I can't tell my friends about Si and Uncle Sean – not because they'd deliberately tell anyone but because it's obvious these things have a way of slipping out. Wish Grandad were still here. I could tell him. I could tell Grandad anything. And he'd know what the fuck to do about it too.

'Hey, Conman!' Jake's snapping his fingers in front of me and the others are looking at me as if it's not the first time he's called my name.

'Sorry. Miles away,' I say.

Jake's asking me if I want to go back to his and smoke some puff. I shake my head. 'Can't. It's Boxing Day. Mum says she wants me home for a few hours 'cause we have another…' I raise my hands and hook my fingers into quotation marks '… "family day" planned.'

The Rickmeister rolls his eyes. 'Yeah, me too.' He lifts his glass and downs the dregs of his pint before getting up to leave. 'See you losers later.'

I invite Jake and Robbo back to mine. 'Mum won't mind,' I say, but Jake declines and Robbo says he'll go home with Jake. 'Keep him company,' he says, winking at me. I stand up; shrug my jacket on as Robbo throws his beer mat at Jake. Jake ducks and the beer mat hits the back of the head of the bloke sitting behind us. Robbo's face drops. The man stands up, turns around and is, to quote Grandad, "built like a brick shit house." Robbo looks scared. Shit, even I feel scared but Jake puts his hand up and apologises. 'Sorry, mate,' he says, offering to buy the man mountain a pint. It does the trick; man mountain accepts and sits down again. I tell the boys I'll meet them here again later this evening, and laughing, I watch as they make their way to the bar playfully pushing and shoving one another. They look more like five year olds than eighteen year olds.

I smile, grateful I have such good mates, realising how lucky

I am, but even so, I also realise how alone I am, too. Surely my bizarre thoughts say more about me than they do about what my stepdad and uncle may or may not have done? What kind of person thinks my thoughts? And I don't even have anyone to confide in. Not even Alesha. Although, I think she'd listen if I told her, might even know what to do? But what if it's not true? What if Si and Uncle Sean have nothing to do with Hunter Black's death? Besides, Grandad always said, "rule number one – trust no one."

Although... I could ask Dad, I suppose? He obviously knows more about Si and Uncle Sean's whereabouts during the time we were at the gig together than I do. I could text him; ask him to meet me, alone? Tell him he has to tell me what the fuck is going on or I'll tell Mum. I don't think my threat will work though, even though Mum is well scary at times, not judging by the look of fear he had in his eyes when Si and Uncle Sean told us to keep shtum.

I wish Grandad were still here.

Fuck, I miss you Grandad. Miss you so much. What should I do? What the fuck am I supposed to do?

Hunter Black is dead, my stepdad and uncle may be responsible and I have absolutely no one to tell.

It's a pretty shit thing when you have no one to tell.

Chapter 10

BOXING DAY
PRESENT DAY – AFTERNOON

LIZZIE

Despite recent events, Boxing Day at our house continues as planned. I'm calmer than I expected to be – Prosecco helps – but all things considered everything is running pretty smoothly. Aunt Marie is coping better than I imagined, too, which is a relief after the state I found her in yesterday evening. Having Mum around helps. As close as sisters, both women are now sailing the same boat, so to speak, only Aunt Marie, for more reasons than one, seems to have had the wind well and truly knocked out of her sails. Despite her heartbreak though, ours too, I'm pleased to see the house is once again ringing with the sound of laughter.

Mum and Aunt Marie chat about different times: when they were younger, first met Dad and Uncle Teddy, what life was like for a couple of working-class girls living in 1960s London. They have a captive audience, myself among them, and a playlist of 1960s pop music, courtesy of Cassie's Christmas gift to Mum. Everyone is fine until Love Affair's "Everlasting Love" begins to play. It's my parents' song, we all know it, and the smiles that filled the room vanish.

Music fills my ears and my head spins, drowning out all sensibility. I can't work out if it's the couple of glasses of Prosecco I've downed in quick succession or something else. Anxiety? Guilt? Stress? I put my hand to my chest, tell myself to breathe, but grief surges through me with every expelled breath, making my chest tighten. With the room still spinning I force myself to smile, try to, for appearance's sake at least, appear cogent, in control. *You've got this, Lizzie. Whatever happens, whatever the future brings, just remember you've got this.*

The song continues to play. It sounds louder. Has someone turned it up? Recent days' events and childhood memories become jumbled in my head, merging into one huge swirling ball of emotion, which like my sorrow, swells inside me like a tide of sickness. I separate from my present self and slip through time. I'm a child again, standing in the kitchen, garishly bright, all Formica worktops, mustard yellow cupboards and brash wallpaper to match. It is the 1970s and love it or loathe it, bright colours reign supreme. Dad has put the record player on in the living room. He and Mum have been arguing about money, again. The car has broken down, the TV is on the blink and there isn't enough money to fix either. Dad is trying to cheer Mum up. He swoops back into the kitchen and playfully grabs her around the waist. Wearing a gaudy flower-patterned apron that clashes with her bright orange blouse she is guarding the chip pan to fry her famous homemade chips. The memory is so real I can hear the effervescent applause as the raw sliced potatoes plunge into hot bubbling oil, the acrid smell of vinegar, the greasy taste of salt on my lips and, despite her mock protests, I see Mum laughing as Dad takes her in his arms and spins her around the kitchen. Sean is there too, about four or five years old. We grin at one another, then turn back to watch our parents. Mum is laughing so we laugh too. She scoops Sean into her arms and Dad dances with me, spinning me left, then right so that my dress twirls up. 'Remember kids,' Dad says, 'It's not a life, it's an adventure.'

Captured in the moment of a bygone era, I can't work out if I'm reminiscing or having a breakdown. Drifting – or am I drowning? – on a sea of mixed emotions, terrifying and exhilarating. I swallow hard; feel the back of my eyes prick with tears. Once again I realise just how much I miss my father, what a huge support and presence he was in my life. I remind myself it's only been a year, *no time at all*. But so much has happened since then and without Dad to advise me I flounder, the quiet pretence of coping almost too much to bear.

A hand on my shoulder makes me jump, drags me back to the present. I look up and see Simon. My rock, once upon a time. Not so much lately though. He asks me if I'm okay, but his voice, like an echo, sounds far off and distant. Overcome with exhaustion, I have to suppress the urge to grab the car keys and drive – far away – to anywhere that isn't here. Home. Only I'm not sure where home is? Anywhere that brings relief, sleep, the ability to not give a shit. I glance around the room. The faces of friends and family swim back into focus.

Running away is not an option. Whatever happens I have to keep going. Keep it all together if only for the sake of my family. I look up at Simon, bite my lip, and nod. 'I'm fine,' I reply. However, despite my best efforts not to blink, I can't help myself and the hot tears threatening to fall now burst forth like a river breaking its dam, slipping and sliding down my face. Annoyed, I turn away, wiping both cheeks with the backs of my hands. The sadness in the room is overwhelming. I don't want to be the one to add to it.

Thankfully, Cassie changes the song and Abba's 'Dancing Queen', one of Mum's favourites, plays. Sean, who catches my eye, thrusts his chin in the general direction of Connor, winks, and asks for everyone's attention. Cassie turns the music down and coughing to clear his throat, Sean declares that he has an announcement.

'Two words,' he says. 'I have just two words.'

Connor, arms folded across his chest, studies his uncle with a look of wary caution.

Sean, who looks as weary as I feel, runs a hand through his sandy-coloured hair, grins, and raises his index finger in the air like a number one. 'Two words,' he repeats. 'Stink...' He pauses to raise his middle finger alongside his index one '...and bomb.'

For a moment the room holds its breath, followed by great bursts of guttural guffawing. And like sunshine after rain, the oppressive sadness dissipates, dries up. Connor rolls his eyes and Summer, now in her formative years, takes great pleasure informing her father, in her self-aggrandizing tone all teenagers seem to have, that he actually used the word 'and' and 'stink' and 'bomb,' so did in fact use three words, not two. Her words, though, disappear, lost in a vast canyon of laughter as Connor, whose antics are the perfect antidote to grief, is once again teased without mercy.

'What did the judge say when a stink bomb was let off in court?' Luke calls out.

'We don't know. What did the judge say when a stink bomb was let off in court?' everyone replies.

'Odour in court.'

Connor groaning, takes it all in good humour. 'And you, Luke, are depriving a village of its idiot,' he shouts.

I tip my head to one side and study my son. His grin, stretching from ear to ear, lights up his whole face. I'd even go as far to say he's actually enjoying all the attention.

Unbeknownst to Connor, Simon spoke to Jake's uncle this morning, and he has agreed to reimburse Connor some of the money he paid. Especially after Simon provided him with a breakdown of what he believed his costs to make his so-called stink bomb probably were. Vincent, ever the businessman argued the toss, said his charges reflected years of research. 'Took me ages to come up with that smell,' he said. 'And there's nothing else out there to rival it. Not to mention the risk I was taking, sending it to Black.'

Simon argued that Vincent was taking the piss, not to mention he fucked up big time, resulting in an unwelcome visit by the police. 'On Christmas Day, of all days,' Simon added. 'Besides, a little birdy tells me you may have wangled yourself a nice little job out of this.' There was a long pause at the other end of the phone before Vincent, or Vince "Bad Boy" Brennan, albeit reluctantly, agreed.

Now, Simon folds his arms around me. 'He'll never live this down, you know.' He nods towards Connor.

I look up at him and smile. 'I know.' We both know this story will never die, resurrected and regurgitated at every opportune moment for years to come. 'Poor old Connor.' I close my eyes and bury my head into Simon's chest, a temporary refuge from my troubled thoughts, listening to the laughter unravelling around me. Simon holds me, kisses the top of my head and I relax, sink into him. It feels good to be held. I don't remember the last time we hugged. Or the last time we made love. Neither one of us seems to have the time, or the inclination lately. At least, that's what I keep telling myself because the alternative doesn't bear thinking about. I know I haven't been the easiest of people to live with during this past year. And god knows I've had my mind on other things, but Simon seems distant and aloof. I wonder if he's fallen out of love with me, if, god forbid, those whispered conversations on his phone are not work related but something else. It's possible. Anything is possible, given the right set of circumstances.

I hear a clicking noise; feel a mild grinding as Simon's hand massages my rigid shoulders. He tells me I've done well today, 'all things considered.'

'Mmm… I suppose. Think I can safely say Christmas is fast becoming my least favourite time of the year. Which is a shame because I used to love it.' It is then I notice baby Nicolas singing – or at least attempting to sing – 'Twinkle, Twinkle, Little Star' with Ruby's son, Andrew, and Maisy. Only he does it in that wonderful way of babies still learning to talk, all wide-eyed with wonder, pudgy hands fist thumping the air pointing to a make believe sky and stars: 'Winkle, winkle, it... all staaar... I, I, wonder ot you are. Up... bove... world... so hiiiigh! Li... diamuund in errr sky.'

Simon is watching his grandson, too. He smiles. 'I've got a feeling you'll fall in love with Christmas again soon... given time.'

I nod my head, smile. 'Hopefully.'-

We both look towards Mum and Aunt Marie, watching as one bereaved woman tries to comfort another. 'Shitty timing about Teddy, though,' Simon adds.

Mum takes Aunt Marie's hand, leads her towards the kitchen. Aunt Marie looks pale, her eyes red-rimmed from crying. I don't say it out loud but I can't help thinking it was for the best. Uncle Teddy was in a terrible way last time I visited him. Dribbling, incontinent, incapable of feeding himself; I couldn't believe the mere shell of the man he'd become was once the big, strong man I'd grown up around. Every visit was worse than the previous one and each one was heartbreakingly sad. How people call that living is beyond me. Uncle Teddy wasn't living – he was functioning. If it had been Freddy, the vet would have advised us to put him down, put him out of his suffering, out of his pain, out of all that fear and misery etched into his face.

'Almost a year to the day after your Dad, too,' Simon continues.

I bristle, take a sharp intake of breath, feel my thorax tighten as I blink back the tears again. I pull away but Simon pulls me back.

'Hey, hey... come on. You're allowed a few tears, you know? You don't have to be strong all the time.' I feel his hand beneath my chin coaxing me to look up until, face to face, our eyes lock.

He brushes my hair away from my eyes, kisses the tip of my nose – something I've noticed Luke does with Cassie. 'To be honest,' a wry smile lifts the corners of his mouth, 'I didn't appreciate just how much I'd miss the old bugger.'

I sniff. 'Hmm. He has left a gap, hasn't he?'

Simon laughs, shakes his head. 'Stink bomb... What do you think he'd have to say about that?'

I laugh. 'He'd have loved it. Laughed his bleedin' head orf,' I attempt to say in my best East End accent.

'Teddy too, I reckon?'

I nod and we both agree how much Dad and Uncle Teddy would have approved of Connor's little stunt. Our own laughter subsides and I nuzzle my head further into Simon's chest.

'You smell nice,' I mumble.

'Really?' he sounds surprised. 'Must be that new aftershave Maisy bought me for Christmas.'

I look up at him and in my best husky voice tell him he should wear it more often. 'Preferably naked.'

Simon, his hands now wrapped around my waist, pulls me closer. He looks at me with a longing I haven't seen in a while. I feel a stirring in the pit of my stomach, any distance between us diminishing. Eyebrows arched, his grin unapologetic, he leans forward and whispers into my ear. 'Are you thinking what I'm thinking?' He presses against me, I feel him harden and like a schoolgirl in the throes of first love, I succumb to the wonderful fluttering in my tummy. I glance over my shoulder, take a quick scan of the room. Simon's lips, soft and warm, press against mine.

'Eew,' Cassie, standing behind us, says. 'Aren't you a bit old for all that? At least get a room, eh?'

'Oi young lady, less of the old,' Simon says, grinning.

Cassie looks at me, wrinkling her nose. 'Ugh... gross,' she

continues, laughing. 'Anyway,' she points to Ruby, glamorous as ever in her bright red dress with her bright red lipstick to match. 'Ruby wants to know if we have any trifle for Andrew?'

Simon's phone rings. He releases me, reaches into his jeans pocket and pulls it out. 'Hello?'

'Mu-um?' Cassie continues, her tone somewhat impatient.

'What... oh, um, yes. In the fridge. The one on the top shelf. Not the one underneath, it's loaded with booze.'

Cassie lopes back towards Ruby who I notice is staring at me. 'You okay?' she mouths.

Simon, his phone to his ear, laughs and turns his back on me. 'Course I don't mind you phoning,' he says to whoever is on the other end. He reminds me of Connor when he talks to Alesha – coy, shy. I glance back towards Ruby, her look now one of concern. Maybe I should confide in her. Tell her what I've done; how I've pushed everyone away, especially Simon. How I'm becoming convinced he is having an affair. 'Yes, I'm fine,' I mouth back. I'm not though. I can feel myself sinking, my life spiralling away from me.

Simon throws his head back, laughs again. He glances across his shoulder, looks at me, and then turns away, lowering his voice to a whisper. I pretend not to care but I'm listening to every word. The only one I hear though is 'privacy.' He turns once more to face me. 'Just need to take this.' He points to his phone and rolls his eyes. 'Work.'

'Really? On Boxing Day?' I don't mean it but my voice sounds clipped, dismissive. He frowns, shrugs his shoulders and with the phone still glued to his ear, I watch as he heads out of the room.

'Lizzie, darling. Are you okay?' Ruby is holding two glasses of fizzing Prosecco. She passes me one and clinks her glass with mine. 'Cheers.'

'What are we celebrating?'

'The death of that deviant, Black, of course. Now he's gone, Cassie can really move on.'

'Let's hope so,' a voice behind us says. It's Aunt Marie. She looks tired, her pale skin as wrinkled and delicate as crepe paper.

'Oh Marie.' Ruby passes me her glass to hold as she pulls Aunt Marie into a hug, her actions both immediate and instinctive. 'I'm so sorry about Teddy,' she says with genuine warmth.

'It's for the best,' Aunt Marie replies solemnly.

'Yes. It probably is,' Ruby agrees. 'If there's anything I can do to help...' Ruby looks to me from Aunt Marie and frowns. 'You know, with the funeral and everything?'

I squeeze her shoulder, half smile. She of all people knows how hard it is to lose the man you love.

'Thanks Ruby,' Aunt Marie replies.

'You look tired,' I tell her. 'Would you like to lie down in my bedroom for a while?'

Aunt Marie looks relieved. 'Would you mind? And,' she looks from left to right, lowers her voice to a whisper, 'do you have any more of those sleeping pills?'

Before I can reply, 'Oh my actual god,' I hear Cassie squeal. 'Mum? Ruby? You too, Aunt Marie. Come and look at these photos of Nan and Grandad's wedding.'

Chapter II

LONDON 1965

SALOCIN

With the nation still mourning the loss of the great Sir Winston Churchill, Salocin and Elle's wedding a month later was, for obvious reasons, rushed. A small affair, close family, a few friends, they married on a crisp winter morning on 13th February 1965 at Hackney Register Office. Wearing her long blonde hair in an elaborate chignon, Ellie wore a beautiful blue and white knee-length dress, fully lined, with daisy detail to the bodice and sleeves that she'd bought from her local Richard shop. She was clutching a petite posy of flowers made for her by Marie, comprising white roses, blue peonies, and purple dahlias, finished with some carefully placed sprigs of gypsophila.

Nervous, cold, and chewing gum, Salocin felt his jaw drop when he saw his new wife to be. He hadn't thought it possible but Ellie looked more beautiful than ever. Swallowing hard, he pushed down the sea of emotions welling inside him. He didn't deserve her. And she didn't deserve this – a poxy register office wedding. She should have been wearing a proper wedding dress, a long white one, with bridesmaids and flowers, walking down the aisle of a church. Not because either of them was religious but because Ellie deserved the best. For now though, it was a case of beggars couldn't be choosers. Salocin made another vow, promised himself, come what may, he would make it up to Ellie, and that somehow – although he wasn't sure how yet – he would give her the life she deserved.

Salocin's hands, despite the bitter weather, were hot, clammy, prickling with heat. Not sure what to do with them he wove his fingers together and closed them as if in prayer. 'You look beautiful, Ellie,' he whispered as they waited for the Registrar to call them in.

Ellie smiled, patted her hair with one hand and clutched her posy with the other. 'Thanks. You don't look half bad yourself,' she whispered back.

Salocin, his thick, dark hair styled in a neat Caesar cut, wore the only suit he owned, a charcoal grey, three buttoned slim-fit suit, including drainpipe trousers, complete with a white, spearpoint collared shirt and skinny knitted tie. It was finished off, much to Martha's disgust, with a pair of Stetson two-tone leather slip-on shoes. Salocin didn't much care; Ellie said he looked good. That was all that mattered.

The ceremony itself was short, sealed with a polished band of gold placed on the ring finger of Ellie's left hand – Salocin promised her the engagement ring would follow soon. Back outside everyone huddled together for a few select photos, courtesy of Mickey, who had sent a photographer as his wedding gift. Unfortunately he had declined Salocin's invitation to join them at the register office citing too much work at the yard. Whether that was true, Salocin couldn't say. He had noticed that both Mickey and Georgie seemed a little jittery of late, had witnessed their furtive glances, overheard snippets of muffled conversations concerning the recent arrests of the Kray twins back in January. He also noticed that Georgie, who usually only visited the yard once or twice a week, had been showing up daily, always asking if the "Old Bill" had been sniffing around? Why he worried about a visit from the plod when the business was legit, Salocin couldn't say, but the truth was he preferred not to know. Following his father's advice, he clocked in and clocked out every day and, aside from his informal chats with Mickey over a cup of tea, or their occasional visit to the second-hand bookseller's stall on the corner of Farringdon Road during his lunch break, Salocin mostly kept his head down and himself to himself. It was no skin off his nose that Mickey couldn't make it, anyway. He liked Mickey, liked him a lot, but it wasn't like he was family or anything.

However, having said that, it wasn't family that had helped Salocin and Ellie find a place to live, it was Mickey. Ellie had said there was no point in asking her parents for help, and when Salocin had confided in his mother, pleaded to her better nature, Martha had stared at her son, her mouth twisted in… what? Judgement? Pity? Disapproval? Probably all three. 'You'll have to ask your father,' she replied. So, when the moment felt right, Salocin approached his father. Asked Wilf if, under the circumstances, they would put himself and Ellie up for a while.

'It won't be for long,' he added. 'Just until we get on our feet, save a bit of dosh to rent a place of our own?'

Wilf, unsmiling, his dark hair pressed flat against his scalp, mostly due to the cloth cap he always wore, regarded his youngest son with narrow, diligent eyes. Unlike Salocin, Wilf, with his short stunted legs, was not a tall man. He was however, a pugnacious, formidable character, still powerfully built for a man of his age. Salocin felt his arse twitch but also a glimmer of hope when he noticed a wry smile lift the corners of his father's mouth. *A smile? That was a good sign – wasn't it?* However, it went as quick as it came.

'No,' Wilf said.

Silence.

'No?' Salocin repeated. 'But… but we're desperate. Got nowhere to go.'

Wilf shook his head. 'Your mother's nerves won't take another woman living in the house. If you're old enough to get a gel pregnant, you're old enough to sort it out. You've made your bed now you'll just have to bleedin' well lie in it.'

Salocin shook himself to hear the photographer ask everyone to squeeze in, directing the parents of the bride to stand next to Ellie, the parents of the groom, next to Salocin. Ellie's father had at least tried, and wore a suit, Ellie's mother however, much to Ellie's red-faced embarrassment, wore both her work coat and work shoes.

'Dressed like a bleedin' charlady,' Salocin overheard Martha whisper to Wilf. Despite the arctic temperatures, Martha had pulled out all the stops and looked, if Salocin said so himself, rather glamorous in her smart peppermint green dress which she wore under her best coat with her best shoes and matching pillbox hat trimmed with netting and flowers, to boot. 'Ain't she got any bleedin' pride?'

One of Ellie's sisters-in-law threw confetti over the happy couple, as did Marie, which, given the icy climate, might just as well have been snowflakes. Still, although it was cold, their breath smoking as they talked, a bright winter sun warmed their faces. Like lizards, they gravitated towards it, looking skywards, basking in its limited heat, while the photographer decided where he wanted everyone to stand next. Another one of Ellie's brothers' wives, Brenda, presented them with a small fruitcake she'd baked and iced.

'I put a nice drop of brandy in it, too,' she said. 'Should help warm the cockles, eh?' she added, giggling.

There was no Reception afterwards to share the cake. Salocin and Ellie couldn't afford one and as neither set of parents was forthcoming, it was simply out of the question. Martha, however, surprised them with two nights paid bed-and-breakfast at a small guesthouse in Brighton. She'd hugged the young couple, albeit briefly, when she presented it to them, which astonished everyone, not least Salocin and Ellie.

'You're a good boy, Salocin.' Martha used her gloved hand to sweep confetti from her youngest son's shoulder. Tearful, she turned towards Ellie, tilted her head and smiled. 'Got yourself a good un 'ere, Salocin. Pretty gel, too.' Ellie blushed and Martha leaned in, lowered her voice to a whisper. 'Look after my boy, sweetheart. He's quite a sensitive little soul at 'eart.'

Ellie nodded and Salocin, trying hard to swallow the plum lodged in his throat, marvelled, as he had done frequently throughout his life, over the walking contradiction that was his mother. It was hard to reconcile her soppy words with the same woman that most times throughout his childhood appeared cold, distant. The same woman that tutted and rolled her eyes whenever he was in her presence, shooing him and his brother away from the house at every opportune moment. 'How am I supposed to get any 'ousework done with you two under me bleedin' feet all day?' she'd grumble. If they were lucky she'd pack them up with a jam sandwich each – corned beef if they were really flush – and a bottle of Tizer; tell them to bugger off and not to show their faces again until teatime. 'And cover up them legs,' she'd shout after them. 'You look like something outta bleedin' Belsen.' That always bemused Salocin. *How can I cover up me legs if you dress me in short trousers?* he'd wonder. Yet, at odd moments, like this, Martha proved she had a different, warmer side to her. Almost as if she were someone else, in fact.

With the ceremony done and dusted, Salocin and Ellie said their goodbyes and parted company with their guests. Marie was one of the last guests to leave. Standing on tiptoe, she kissed Salocin on the cheek before hugging her friend. She wore her dark hair, which matched her molten, heavy lined, brown eyes, in a Vidal Sassoon style angular bob, and a striking, short red jersey dress, including a cream Peter Pan collar and turned-back cuffs, under a heavy winter coat. 'Have fun in Brighton,' Salocin heard her whispering to Ellie. 'Don't do anything I wouldn't.' She giggled.

Salocin felt a sharp dig in the ribs, turned to see Teddy standing beside him. 'Cor blimey,' he said nodding towards Marie. 'Look at the boat race on that.'

Salocin glanced at his wife and her friend who were both still laughing and chattering. 'Marie?' he replied. 'Yeah – she's pretty enough, I suppose. Would you like me to introduce you?'

Teddy, suddenly coy, his cheeks flushed, looked down. 'Go on then,' he mumbled.

Catching the attention of the two young women, Teddy hugged his new sister-in-law. 'Welcome to the family, Ellie,' he said.

'Aww... thanks Teddy.'

Salocin looked at Ellie and winked. 'Teddy, I'd like to introduce you to Marie, Ellie's best friend.'

With his eyes fixed on Marie, Teddy pressed something into the palm of his brother's hand and gave it a firm handshake. 'Congratulations, Sal. This is for you and Ellie.' He then pulled his hand away and offered it to Marie. 'Pleased to meet you Marie. I'm Teddy. Salocin's older, better-looking brother.'

Salocin shook his head and Marie, her small hand in Teddy's large one, looked at Teddy and laughed. 'Ark at him, Elle.' She nudged her friend. 'Good manners. Good looking. And a good sense of humour, to boot. What more could a gel want, eh?'

Teddy blushed – again, as Salocin looked down, surprised to see a ten bob note. 'I can't take this, Ted. It's far too much,' he said, trying to give the money back.

Teddy waved him away, insisted Salocin keep it.
'Treat yourselves,' he said. 'Maybe a bit of posh nosh and a glass of something bubbly, eh? And I don't mean Babycham.' Turning back to face Marie, he offered her his arm. 'Can I buy you a cup of coffee?' he asked.

Marie hesitated for a few seconds; looked from Teddy to

Ellie, back to Teddy again. 'Why, thank you, sir.' She giggled, linking arms with him. 'Don't mind if I do.'

The trip to Brighton was bitterly cold. A late snow flurry had almost threatened the Brighton-bound train with cancellation, and they were lucky to make it at all. Thank god they *had* travelled by train though. Ellie had put her foot down when Salocin suggested they drive down on his scooter. It was bad enough riding pillion on a Vespa during the summer months, never mind during one of the coldest Februarys on record. Still, although Salocin wore his parka – regulation army green, practical for keeping your clothes clean and the chills out for any self-respecting Mod – and Ellie wore the beaver lamb coat she'd asked to borrow from her grandmother, they were still both rigid with cold by the time they arrived at the guesthouse. Ellie's teeth were still chattering two hours later.

The place itself was basic, but it was clean, nice enough, and the newlyweds made the most of it. It was the first time they'd shared a bed together. They'd only made love twice before, and that had been in a car Salocin had paid a friend to borrow. He hadn't got the car with that in mind, not consciously anyway, but so they could drive further out of town one night, try somewhere different for a change, but one kiss led to another, led to more. It had been awkward, fumbling, all over far too quickly, and despite the fact they'd been careful, time enough to make a baby. They agreed they hadn't wanted to be parents yet, Ellie wasn't ready and Salocin had wanted more time to save, have a proper wedding, buy a house, maybe? Ellie had panicked, later admitted to Salocin she'd thought about an abortion. That cost money, though, and was illegal, not to mention dangerous. Both she and Marie knew people, girls from school, who'd arranged back street ones and died.

So, the deed was done and here they were, married and

honeymooning in Brighton.

It was nice to lie together, to explore one another's bodies. 'Do you think we'll hurt the baby... you know, if we do it?' Ellie had asked. Except for the slight swelling of her breasts it was impossible to tell she was pregnant. Salocin said he wasn't sure and they decided not to risk it – until they kissed. Then they couldn't keep their hands off one another. With love to keep them warm, they spent the best part of both nights in a tangled maze of limbs, hot and sweaty beneath the many layers of sheets and blankets. A cooked breakfast filled them up – any sickness Ellie had been experiencing during those first early days of her pregnancy had now, thankfully, dissipated. And afterwards, they managed a couple of bracing walks along the pebbled seafront, and promised themselves a fish and chip supper by the pier.

However, on the Saturday night Salocin told Ellie to get her glad rags on. He'd booked them a table at some swanky restaurant Mickey had recommended. Although, judging by the looks on the faces of some other diners, it was obvious they were the 'wrong type' of custom. The waiter, too, regarded her with the same contempt the other diners did. He appeared horrified when Ellie insisted that all the tea in china couldn't persuade her to eat the very expensive black, slimy-looking fish eggs Salocin ordered as a starter. He regarded her with the same contempt the other diners did. They went dancing afterwards, at The Regal Ballroom, which was much nicer, full of youngsters like them. A live band played all the latest hits, and they danced until they dropped.

On Monday morning (they'd both booked half a day off work) they gathered their belongings together and made their way back to the train station, back to London and back to their first home together: a flat in Hackney, although Salocin used the word 'flat' loosely. 25C Middleton Road was more of a bedsit, two rooms including a shared bathroom, in a lofty old Victorian house – and he'd had to pay extra to have the two rooms. They used the smaller of the two rooms as a bedroom, the other, with its Yale lock on the door, brown-stained sink, and linoleum floor, as a kitchen come living room. It wasn't great, but Salocin had seen worse. And the bonus, although not much of one, was a narrow set of communal stairs in the hallway that led to a flat roof, a small, cleared area of space on an extended part of the house. It contained a makeshift washing line, and during the summer, if you were quick, you could hang your washing out to dry. The other residents were an eclectic bunch, too, especially the old man that they sometimes heard crying through the wall. But with a baby on the way and little to no money behind them, Salocin and Ellie didn't have much choice.

It was Mickey who had kindly loaned Salocin the deposit for the rent and had spoken to a friend of a friend who knew the landlady. Sparsely kitted out, what little furniture they had was all second hand. Thankfully that included an old record player given to them by one of Salocin's aunts, which they often played the few singles and LPs they had accumulated. *Meet The Beatles* was Ellie's favourite album whereas Salocin preferred the gritty, bluesy sound of The Stones and The Animals. They had a TV too, albeit a portable black and white one with a dodgy ariel that was always losing its picture – particularly annoying when whatever, or whoever, you were watching, disintegrated into a plague of flickering ants and the hiss of white noise, mid performance. A good whack on the side usually did the trick though – for a few minutes, anyway. They both enjoyed reading too, and thanks to the public library down the road there were always books on hand to escape into – and unlike the TV, books never lost the pictures they painted.

They soon discovered the flat was freezing during the winter, stifling during the summer. The small fireplace in the kitchenette-living room was boarded up so their only source of heat was a small paraffin heater, which Ellie hated, said it reeked, and that she could smell the paraffin on her clothes, in her hair, could even smell it in her dreams. She swore blind it gave her a headache. Salocin spotted and rescued a one-bar electric fire from the yard, which, after a bit of repair work he got working again. It didn't give out much heat, but was better than nothing. Huddled together on the sofa they'd long for summer which, unfortunately, due to the flat's south-facing windows, turned out to be just as unbearable as the winter months. More often than not, when the heat got too much, Salocin and Ellie would escape the stifling confines of their rooms and sit up on the roof, amongst their neighbours' washing, listening to Radio Caroline on their small transistor radio.

So, it wasn't great, could have been worse. They were grateful to have a roof over their heads, did their best to make the most of it, for now. Nonetheless, when, in time-honoured tradition, Salocin had carried his bride across the threshold, Ellie's look of disappointment didn't go unmissed.

'It's fine,' she said, trying her best to force a smile, despite the strong smell of damp that hit them head on and despite the walls, that under the light of a cold, grey Hackney morning suddenly seemed a little more stained, a little grubbier than when they'd first looked at the flat. 'We'll make it ours,' she added, her hand covering her belly. 'And at least we're together.'

Maybe they had been rash in their choice but time had been against them and they were fearful if they didn't sort something soon, they would find themselves homeless with a baby. They tried to stay upbeat – much preferred living away from home, together, even if money was tight and the flat was a bit of a dump – neither one revealing to the other just how worried, how afraid they actually were. And although their love was strong, they were also well aware, despite friends and family, that whatever happened from hereon in, it *was* now just the two of them.

Chapter 12

Boxing Day
PRESENT DAY – AFTERNOON

LIZZIE

The afternoon flies by without drama, except for when Summer loses her new phone and turns the whole living room upside down in her search for it. It takes Mum to point out that my niece actually has her phone in her hand – using it as a torch – to find it.

'God help me.' Natasha, arms folded, observes her daughter who is now posing for her umpteenth selfie with said phone.

Amused, I watch my niece. 'Teenagers, eh?'

'But that's just it – she's not one yet!'

'I blame the parents,' I reply.

Nat laughs, tilts her head a fraction, her expression one of mild fascination and slight alarm as she continues to observe the many changing faces of her daughter's quest to find the perfect pose. 'I don't know what's happened to her lately,' she says, shaking her head. 'What do you reckon her average is?'

Confused, I turn towards my sister-in-law. 'Her average, what?'

Natasha, her gaze direct, uncompromising, twists her cupid's bow of a mouth into a wry smile. 'Pics per minute. Must be a hundred? Seventy-five, at the least?'

'And the rest,' I reply to the sound of another click of Summer's phone camera, like a mechanical curtain opening and closing in quick succession, reminiscent of the old analogue camera Dad used to have.

'If she keeps this up, she won't have any thumbs left. Maybe Cassie was on to something when she mentioned disposable thumbs during dinner, yesterday.'

I laugh. 'Anyway... I thought you weren't going to let Summer have a phone yet?'

'What can I say?' Natasha replies raising the neat arc of an eyebrow. 'She pleaded her case and somehow I found myself compelled to give in.'

'Anything for a quiet life?'

'Something like that. Do you know I can actually make her angry just by saying good morning!' She sighs.

I steal a sideways glance at Cassie who, eyebrows knitted together, is staring at her own phone. 'Been there, done it and got the tee shirt.' I nod towards my own daughter.

Nat follows my gaze, then glances towards Maisy. 'Twice,' she says.

'Hmm...' I remember the first time I met my sulky, surly stepdaughter. Her determination to dislike me, her restless mischievousness that led to her getting a full leg tattoo (without permission), the Goth years, the first time she called me Mum...

I reach across, touch Nat on the arm. 'I know it's hard but try to enjoy it Nat, time passes so quickly.'

Summer, oblivious to our stares, continues pulling her many faces in her quest for the perfect selfie. There's the peace sign pose, the mouth wide open pose, the hair up pose, the hair down pose, the pouty pose, the... uh, oh... Summer looks up, see us looking at her. 'This must be the "I have caught you out and I hate you pose",' I lean over and whisper in Natasha's ear.

Summer skulks off, her backward glance, churlish, morose.

'See what I mean!'

'Give it time.' I laugh. 'Just give it time.'

Natasha faces me, her smile quizzical. 'What are we talking about, here? Two, three years?'

I look again at Cassie and Maisy now locked in passionate debate, albeit good- humoured, with their respective other halves. Natasha follows my gaze. 'You've got a short memory,' I reply. 'More like seven or eight.'

'God help me,' she says. 'No wonder most of the parents I know, drink. Another glass of Prosecco?'

'Why not?'

Natasha wanders off in search of more alcohol. I shouldn't really drink anymore, I've had far too much already, but fuck it, I need it.

I glance around the room, get a waft of cinnamon and berries from the scented candles still burning, their flickering light casting shadows about the walls. Day is giving way to night, winter's shadows creeping against the window. I shiver, grateful I have my family around me, realise how we're racing towards the end of another year. I have no idea what the future holds but if the past couple of days are anything to go by, I need to brace myself. Natasha sweeps back in, passes me a glass of wine, which, cold to the touch, is fizzing and frothing. I press the glass to my lips, take a swig, feel the bubbles dance on my tongue like popping candy, burning the back of my throat as it slides down. The sweet nectar hits the pit of my stomach then goes straight to my head. *Whoa!* Somewhat dizzy, but delightfully so, I welcome the temporary relief the alcohol brings from the myriad thoughts plaguing my worried mind.

The sweet refrain of music washes over me and I'm vaguely aware of someone calling me. 'Nat? Lizzie? C'mon…' I realise it's Sean. 'We're having a bit of a sing-song,' he says.

I turn to see my brother, Luke and Connor each holding a guitar. Sean is strumming Dad's old one, carved from the finest maple wood, weathered and worn with the scratches of time.

His expert hands strum and pluck the coarse strings, fingers, curved in many odd shapes and angles, gliding up and down the long neck of the fret board with practised ease.

Cassie positions herself on the stool in front of the piano and lifts the lid. 'Right then, what are we playing?' she asks.

Natasha, carrying her wine glass, wanders over, pulls out a chair next to Sean and drapes her arm around his broad shoulders. She touches his cheek with the many ringed fingers of her other hand and he in return smiles and kisses her. Still so in love.

I search the room for Simon, realise he's not here – again. *Where the hell is he?* Trying to quell the nagging doubt, the annoyance at the back of my mind, I search the room again; *maybe he's knelt down beside the bookcase?* My breath comes quickly, and it takes all my effort to slow it down. *Or maybe he's over by the record player, the one he bought me for Christmas last year? Or the kitchen? Yes, he's probably in the kitchen.*

My spine tingles. Someone is watching me. It's Aunt Marie. Her grey eyes, steely, unrelenting, bore into me and although she smiles, it's a forced smile, sad. There's a lingering despondency about her which, given her current state of mind, is hardly surprising. I'm worried about her. She looks none the better for her brief nap. No one else sees it but her furrowed brow speaks of a deep inner turmoil. I need to talk to her, convince her she must hold it together, to not do anything rash. I also need to find Simon. *Where the fuck is he?* But Aunt Marie comes first. I point to a chair, tell her to take a seat, and pull out the one next to her. I lean over, take her hand and hold it in mine. Like Mum, she's mere flesh and bone. Her mottled skin is transparent, her green and blue veins vivid, not unlike the tube lines of a London underground map.

'Give it time,' I whisper.

Silent tears stream down her crumpled cheeks. I squeeze her hand, my eye drawn to the beautiful sapphire at the centre of the platinum ring she wears on her right ring finger, a gift from Uncle Teddy a couple of years after they were first married. I'm not big on rings but I've always loved that one. The sapphire itself, set between an infinity symbol on each shoulder, is mesmerising, changes colour in the light, so it's possible to see splashes of the darkest midnight blue on the outer edges to the lightest, almost glacier blue in the middle. I plead with her again to trust me. Promise her everything will be okay.

Her eyes dance from left to right as everyone behind us sings along to Wham's "Last Christmas". 'I'm not so sure, Lizzie.' she whispers back.

I feel a hand on my back, hope it's Simon, can't help feeling a little disappointed when I realise it's Ruby. She looks concerned. 'Is everything okay?' she asks. 'Anything I can do to help?'

'Aunt Marie's just having a moment.'

'Well, it's hardly surprising, is it? I think you're doing marvellous. You damn well have as many bloody moments as you damn well please. But trust me,' Ruby kneels down, so she is facing Aunt Marie, takes her other hand and sandwiches it between both of hers. 'It gets better... in time. I promise.'

'That's what I keep telling her,' I say. 'And you should know. Now...' I release my Aunt's hand, pat her knee, '...what about a nice cup of tea?' The singing around us increases and it's a struggle now to hear my own voice.

I turn to head for the kitchen but Aunt Marie grips my hand. I'm surprised by her strength. Fine lines crinkle the corners of her mouth and her eyes are red, roughened from crying. 'I... I can't do this, Lizzie,' she says.

Exhaustion drapes itself around me like a heavy blanket. 'Listen.' I know impatience is creeping into my voice, 'You *will* be okay.' Aunt Marie doesn't say a word. 'Are you listening?' Glancing up, she stares at me, dewy-eyed, fearful. I feel my stomach turn. *Fuck me, I don't need this tonight.* I take a deep breath and with as much encouragement I can muster I once again reassure my Aunt that everything will be okay.'

'Time is a great healer,' Ruby adds.

'It's also the greatest killer,' Aunt Marie mumbles under her breath. She grimaces but releases me. I ask Ruby, her expression somewhat quizzical, if she'll sit with Aunt Marie while I make her a cuppa.

I also need to find Simon, wherever the hell he is.

I wander into the kitchen, fill the kettle from the tap, flick the switch and wander back out again. Connor, Sean and Luke are still strumming guitars and everyone is in full swing now, singing, of all things, Del Amitri's "Nothing Ever Happens." I laugh to myself – *if only*. I watch for a minute, smile, tap my hand against my thigh, find myself singing along. Even Aunt Marie has replaced her grimace with a smile, gently rocking back and forth. What a brilliant song – I'd forgotten how great Del Amitri are. One of Simon's favourite bands, too, if I remember rightly? *Talking of which, where the hell is he?* I head towards the hallway, arch my head at the foot of the stairs, listen. I can't hear what he's saying but I can hear the mumbled mutterings of a man's voice behind closed doors.

Being careful to sidestep the third and tenth steps, because they creak, I climb the stairs, my heart thudding hard against my chest. The man's voice, I now confirm as Simon's, is muted against our closed bedroom door. I press my ear to the door, listen, but still it's muffled. Why do I feel as though I'm doing something wrong? *Fuck this*. I press the door handle down and step into the room to be met by the back of Simon's broad shoulders. His head is back, laughing. I call his name and looking surprised, he turns to face me, running his free hand through his hair. I think how tired he looks but how handsome he still is, especially for a man of his age.

'What on earth are you doing up here?' I ask. 'Everyone is having a bit of a sing-song downstairs. Come and join us?'

Simon's brow wrinkles into a frown. 'Listen, give me a sec,' he says to the person on the other end of the phone. He stares at me, lowering his hand so his phone swings next to his thigh, his smile, tight. 'Yeah, okay, I will,' he replies. 'I have a bit of work to do here, first.'

'Really?' My voice, like earlier, is clipped. 'On Boxing Day?'

Simon offers me another tight smile but this time there's a note of impatience in his voice, as if I'm an annoying teenager or some tardy member of staff. 'Yes, Lizzie. All part and parcel of being the boss, I'm afraid. But then again you know that.'

Swallowing hard, I try to suppress the anger bubbling inside my chest. I look from Simon to his phone, back to Simon again. He raises his eyebrows, lifts his phone to his ear and nods towards the door. 'Do you mind?' The tension in his jaw is clear.

I hear a rush of blood galloping to my head. My palms prick and my tongue, like Velcro, sticks to the roof of my mouth. I'm filled with a sense of dread, a sense of panic, and suddenly everything seems too much. The room sways. I'm toppling, my world crumbling. I grab the doorframe to steady myself.

Simon lunges forward, his arm extended, his look one of confusion. He places a hand on my arm and asks me if I'm okay? I nod, wave my hand dismissively, and quietly close the door behind me. Standing in the hallway, I hover for a moment, waiting to see if Simon will follow me. When he doesn't, when he goes back to talking and laughing on the phone, I feel weighed down by an overwhelming sense of loss.

Eyes glazed, I stand at the top of the stairs staring into space. I'm not sure how long I stand there for – two minutes, ten? – before I'm interrupted by the sound of child-like laughter. I descend the stairs, slowly, purposefully, one foot in front of the other, met at the bottom by Nicolas, playing with Andrew. I don't see the oversized Lego brick on the final step and it's all I can do to stop myself yelling out in pain when I tread on it. Pulling the strangest faces to stop my screams – screams that would surely traumatise my young grandson – I lift my foot, hop and rub it until the pain dissipates. To my surprise baby Nicolas finds this highly amusing, giggling and clapping his hands together as if it was all part of some elaborate plan to make him laugh. Andrew, at five, looks less amused, asking me what I'm doing. Ruby pokes her head around the door and asks Andrew to please take Nicolas to his mummy which, taking my grandson's tiny hand gently in his, he does with no fuss whatsoever.

'He's so good with him,' I remark.

Ruby nods, says she often finds smaller children gravitate to older children, and vice versa.

I perch on the bottom step, kick the offending toy brick with my good foot, and rub my injured one with my hand.

Ruby, eyebrows arched, says she hopes I don't mind, but she's made Aunt Marie a cuppa. 'Made your Mum one too, while I was at it.'

'Shit.' I put my hand to my mouth. 'No, of course I don't mind. Thanks. I totally forgot.'

She asks me if I'm okay. 'You seem – tipsy. Have you had enough to eat today?'

I shake my head and shrug my shoulders. Tell her I've got a lot on my mind at the moment.

'Do you want to talk about it?' she replies, taking my hands in hers, pulling me to my feet.

If only, Ruby. If only I had the courage to tell you. I look up. I suppose I could tell her about Simon. I nod towards the top of the stairs and in a hushed voice tell my oldest and best friend I suspect Simon – my Simon – is having an affair. To my surprise Ruby laughs, her red-painted lips turning up in bewildered amusement.

She shakes her head. 'No,' she says, her auburn curls bouncing up and down.

I feel agitated. 'What do you mean – no? Need I remind you it's happened before with my ex-husband – now your other half?' Ruby's eyes widen in surprise. 'Sorry,' I reply, hanging my head. 'Bit below the belt.'

She smirks. 'I'm pretty certain Simon isn't having an affair.'

'But you don't know that. Do you? Not for sure? And if he isn't, why is he always skulking about, leaving the room to talk to god knows who on the phone every five fucking minutes, then? Huh? Go on… tell me that.'

Ruby shrugs her shoulders, scrapes her hair to one side. 'No, well, I don't suppose we know anyone, for sure – look at me with Harvey.' Her eyebrows shoot into her forehead. 'But from what Scott says, Simon's got a lot on at work at the moment.'

'Scott!' I scoff. I can't help myself. Can't help laugh at the irony of it all either – the fact that my ex-husband, who never paid me a penny in child maintenance, is a bona fide (and much respected, apparently) employee of my other half and now lives with, of all people, my best friend. *You couldn't make it up if you tried. No one would believe it.*

No one would believe what? Ruby asks, frowning.

Great. Good to see I'm still talking to myself – out loud.

I shake my head. 'Nothing,' I sigh. I tell her how much I appreciate her advice though; know due to years of friendship, she's being truthful, not just trying to make me feel better. However, something still tells me she's wrong. Neither do I have the courage to tell her it's probably my fault anyway, that I'm the one who has pushed Simon away. A lesser man would have given up a long time ago.

'I wouldn't blame him,' is what I do say. 'Our sex life is shit!' Actually that's a lie. We don't have a sex life. I'm too exhausted, too stressed. And the odd time we do get around to it, it's sometimes easier to fake it, make a few appropriate noises just to get it over with. 'Perhaps Simon senses that.'

Ruby laughs, rolls her eyes. 'Tell me about it, darling. I had to go to the doctor's the other day with *another* UTI.'

I wince. Put my hand up. 'You? My ex-husband? Really, Ruby.'

'I asked her why I keep getting them.' Ruby keeps talking, regardless. 'Do you know what she said?' She doesn't wait for me to reply. 'It's not uncommon for women at "your time of life". Your time of life!' She throws her hands up. 'When the fuck did that happen? One minute we are twenty-something with all the time in the world, the next we are at "*that* time of life".' She's trying to make me laugh, and it's working. 'Well, that and poor design.'

I grin, grateful for the welcome distraction from my rainstorm of thoughts. 'Poor design?'

'Yes.' She sighs. 'Apparently UTIs occur in women significantly more than men because a woman's urethra is shorter than her male counterpart's – so we're more prone to infection. Typical, isn't it. Even in matters of anatomy men get the better deal.' She looks up, thoughtful, counts on her fingers. 'So that's a lifetime of menstrual cramps, pregnancy, stretch marks, labour pain and then, just as a last laugh, there's the fucking menopause. God must have been having a right laugh when he made us, eh? Then,' Ruby nudges me, 'Get this. The doctor asked me if I was still having sex. I said I was – just! "Lucky you", she replied. "At least you're still getting some." And her advice – to help prevent the risk of further infection? To pee. Just before penetration.' I wince like an embarrassed teenager. 'Then she said it's best to pee again straight afterwards.' Ruby rolls her eyes, flicks her hair off her shoulder. 'And who said romance was dead?'

I laugh so hard it brings tears to my eyes. I'm relieved, though.

Relieved I can still laugh, despite the chaos swirling around my head. As our cackling subsides I close my eyes and take a deep breath. I ask Ruby not to repeat my concerns about Simon to anyone else.

'Of course I won't.' She raises her hand to my cheek, tenderly sweeping a curtain of fallen hair away from my face before asking me again if I'm okay. If there is anything else, other than Simon, bothering me. I shake my head, tell her I'm just tired, worn out. She opens her arms, hugs me, and again tells me not to worry about Simon. 'An-nd,' she pulls away, holding me at arms-length, studying me, 'Dare I ask how the writing is going?'

'It's not. Not at the moment.'

'So what was the meeting about you had in London with your agent a couple of days ago?'

'Nothing much,' I reply, aloof, looking away. It's hard to look your best friend in the face when you're lying. 'Just, you know, a bit of a catch up.'

'Any news? Any dishy Hollywood film producers interested in turning your books into a movie?'

'Afraid not.'

Ruby pouts, then suddenly looks thoughtful. 'Wasn't that the day Hunter Black was supposed to have died? The day Scott went to the IndieKnot gig with Connor and the others?' I nod, feel a trickle of sweat under my arms. 'You all met up for a drink later, didn't you?'

I feel agitated. Do my best to make my voice sound lucid, controlled, the same as when I'm speaking at literary festivals and book launches. 'Yes. It was. Why do you ask?'

Ruby shrugs. 'No reason. Just seems strange.' Her gaze is appraising.

Sweat forms in the small of my back and on the top of my lip. 'Strange, how?'

'Well... strange in that while you lot were out getting

bladdered, just a few streets away that poor excuse of a man was taking his last breath?'

Her words linger for a moment while I think of a suitable reply. 'Yes. I suppose,' is all I can manage.

'Anyway. Good riddance, I say. Has anyone said *how* he died yet?'

'No.' I look at the wall, the door, my hands. 'They haven't.'

'Oh, I'm sorry, Lizzie,' Ruby says, reaching for and rubbing my arm. 'I'm sure the last thing you want to be doing is talking about *him*?'

I feel my body contract, as if in labour, but my insides are hollow. Except for the alcohol that is. Guilt and shame wash over me. Ruby thinks my reluctance to talk about Black is because of all the pain and misery he's caused my family. I need to change the subject. I ask how things are with her – and Scott. 'Really, I mean?'

She bites her lip, as if she's embarrassed to talk – joking aside – about her relationship with my ex. 'We're fine,' she says. 'He's great with Andrew. Although, I am worried about him.'

'Worried?'

'That bitch of an ex-wife of his still won't let him have access to their daughter. He gets quite down about it.'

'Funny that.' Connor has appeared from nowhere, making Ruby and I jump. 'Since he was *so* bothered about seeing us when we were younger,' he says, his voice laced with sarcasm.

'Connor,' I exclaim, feeling my face flush as he skirts around us to get to the foot of the stairs. 'Don't be rude to Ruby, please.'

'I'm not,' he says, climbing the stairs two at a time, his legs long and angular like a grasshopper's. 'Just telling it how it is. He didn't give a shit about us while we were growing up – did he?' I can't argue with him. It's true. I know it and so does Ruby. 'So what is it that makes *her* – Harriet – better than us?' He pauses mid-step and turns to face us. 'Why is that? People always want what they can't have? We wanted to see him but he didn't give a shit about us. Did he?'

Ruby and I look at one another, completely taken aback by my son's sudden outburst. I thought things were better between the kids and Scott of late, any animosity by my two, buried.

'I think it's because he's learned his lesson,' Ruby replies. 'And, what he doesn't want to do, is make the same mistakes he made with you and Cassie.'

Connor shrugs his shoulders. 'Whatevs.'

Ruby sighs. 'He really is trying to make it up to you and Cas, you know, Connor? Says he feels bad for being such a knobhead. His words, not mine.'

Connor grins, looks behind us. 'Talking of which…'

We turn; see Scott loitering by the door. 'Hi,' he says, half raising his hand. 'Think we should be, erm, off in a minute. Andrew still has a bit of a cold and I think he's struggling.' His eyes flick up the stairs towards Connor. 'Oh. Hi son. Fancy going to the cinema sometime this week?'

Connor snorts, repeats the word 'son' and folds his arms across his chest. 'Dunno. Maybe.' He makes to turn away but changes his mind again. 'Did you enjoy the IndieKnot gig the other night, Dad?' he asks.

Scott smiles. 'Yes.' He straightens up. 'It was actually more enjoyable than I thought it would be.'

Connor smirks. 'And what about Simon and Uncle Sean? Do you think they enjoyed it too?'

Scott's smile disappears. He coughs to clear his throat. 'I erm, well, I think they did? Probably best to ask them, eh?'

Connor shakes his head then turns away. He mutters under his breath – *fucking adults*, if I'm not mistaken – then slams his bedroom door behind him.

Ruby and I look at Scott. 'What the hell was that all about?' I ask.

'He hates me.' Scott rubs his forehead, completely avoiding my question.

'Well that makes two of us then,' I reply. I turn to walk back towards the living room but somehow I lose my footing. My stomach lurches into my mouth as my arms flail in front of me in a desperate bid to break my fall. I feel the firm grip of a hand catching me, saving me, and straightening up I see it's him. Scott. 'Oops,' I say, embarrassed. 'Thanks for that.'

'Are you ok-aay, Lizzie?' He exchanges concerned glances with Ruby.

I look at my ex-husband. He's grown a goatee. It looks ridiculous. *Mid-life crisis*, I think. *Maybe Simon is having a mid-life crisis, too? Has found someone younger, funnier, more interested in sex... more interested in life, than me? Fuck him if he is. Thought he was better than that. Better than some sad cliché.*

'Don't you worry about me,' I reply. 'I'm abso-bloody-lutely fine.' His eyes dart towards Ruby who I catch from the corner of my eye raising and lowering an invisible glass to her mouth. I pretend not to see.

Bollocks if they think I'm pissed. Bollocks to everything.

Scott releases me.

'Oh, and don't worry about Connor,' I add. 'He'll come round – in time.'

Ruby agrees. Never one to hold back with her honesty she says Scott is reaping what he's sown. Says he should know damn well that his relationship with Cassie and Connor is better than it's ever been. But she also reminds him they're young, that they've both been through a lot. 'You can't just walk back into their lives and expect everything to be a bed of roses just because you've stuck around for a year or so. Give them time.'

Scott smiles, agrees, draws Ruby to him and plonks a kiss in the middle of her forehead. I wonder if I'll ever get used to seeing my ex and my best friend together?

Ruby, Scott and Andrew – who still calls me "Wizzie" – kiss me goodbye. Andrew has been a star, played, much to the delight and relief of Maisy and Crazee, with my grandson for hours. Nicolas cries. It's been a long day and although sorry to lose his playmate, it's also obvious just how tired he is, too. I hold him for a moment while Maisy and Crazee gather their things together, then they also make tracks to leave. Before they go, Maisy asks me where her Dad is.

Annoyed, I nod towards the hallway door. 'Upstairs,' I reply. 'Probably on the phone – again.'

Maisy frowns. 'Work?'

'I think so.'

She tuts, rolls her eyes, and asks me to tell him she said goodnight. 'Nan? We're leaving,' she says to my mother. 'Do you want a lift?'

Mum shakes her head. Says she's had one too many to drink and would prefer to walk home. Maisy looks concerned, asking her if she's sure.

'Don't worry,' I interrupt. 'I'll get Connor to walk her back.'

Maisy looks relieved. 'Okay. See you at home then, Nan?' she says.

Mum nods.

Natasha and I tidy up, collecting empty glasses and plumping up cushions. I glance across at Aunt Marie who is sitting next to my mother on the sofa. She appears to have shrunk in the last few days, the lines on her face more drawn than ever. Mum is encouraging her to stay at her house again tonight but she is also insisting they leave now so that Aunt Marie can rest.

'What about Freddy?' Mum asks, looking around. 'Where is he?'

'Probably in Connor's room,' I reply. Connor often carries him up to his room with him. 'It's not fair to walk him home,

Mum, not with his back legs playing up the way they are. Everyone's had a drink, too, so we can't drive him.'

'Should have asked Maisy and Crazee to take him with them.'

'Mum, it's fine. Let him stay here tonight and I'll drive him back to yours in the morning.'

'Are you sure?'

'Yes. Honestly. I'm sure.'

I leave Mum and Aunt Marie gathering their various bits and pieces together and ask them to wait while I fetch Connor.

'Don't be so bleedin' sorft,' Mum says. 'We're more than capable of walking back by ourselves.'

'No, Mum. I'm not arguing with you about this. It's dark, not to mention icy outside. I don't want you or Aunt Marie falling arse over tit, as Dad used to so eloquently put it.'

Mum clucks her tongue, sighs. 'I suppose you're right,' she says. 'Headstrong, like her father,' I hear her mutter to Aunt Marie as they shuffle off in search of their coats and bags. 'Right from a little baby, too. You remember, don't you, Marie?'

Chapter 13

LONDON 1965

ELLIE

Bright sunshine crept through the gaps of the flimsy curtains that hung by the window of Salocin and Ellie's bedroom. Salocin was getting ready to leave for work. Ellie felt his gentle kiss on her forehead, his hand brush her cheek.

'I'm off,' he whispered. 'I'll see you later tonight?' His voice was hesitant, almost apologetic.

Ellie raised a pale, limp hand from the sheets, half waved, half muttered goodbye. It was too much effort to lift her head even if she'd wanted to. She knew he was worried about her, but she was too exhausted to care, although she tried her best to hide it.

Salocin turned on his heel to leave but a slight snuffling sound caused him to stop. It was coming from the crib. A gift from Mickey, made from oak, and painted white with a decoupage teddy bear either end, it looked distinctly out of place alongside the other drab furniture in the flat. Ellie heard the crib rock slightly, and stiffened. She prayed Salocin would resist the urge to peek at his daughter.

Elizabeth, or as they preferred to call her, Lizzie, named after Elizabeth Bennet from Jane Austen's Pride and Prejudice, was a month old. Ellie had insisted on the name after reading the classic tale before their daughter's birth. She said Miss Bennet was an intelligent, witty and independent woman. 'A great thinker too,' she added. 'Just like our daughter will be.'

'If it *is* a girl?' Salocin had said.

Ellie had smiled. 'It is a girl.' One arm was cradling her ever-expanding belly, the other laid protectively across it. 'I don't know why, or how I know, but I do. It's definitely a girl.' Which, if she was honest, had scared Ellie a little.

On a beautiful summer morning, 9th July 1965, Ellie gave birth to Lizzie Lemalf, their first child and only daughter. Ellie had been excited about her new role as a mother. She was determined she would shower their little girl with all the love she'd never had. Ellie had never quite worked out why her mother was so dismissive of her. Why her brothers could do no wrong, she, no right. It would be many years before Ellie accepted that she had done nothing wrong. When her mother, terminally ill, asked to see her, Ellie, despite their estrangement, visited her at the hospice.

'A woman's life is nothing but sacrifice, see,' her mother had said. 'To be born into poverty is bad enough. To be born female, worse still. Life was hard when I was a young gel. You got a job, met a boy, married and settled down. If you were lucky, you'd get a good husband. Someone who worked hard, didn't blow his wages gambling or drinking. Didn't beat you or the kids and didn't treat you like a skivvy.' (Ellie's father hadn't been a gambler, however he had set ideas about the roles of men and women within marriage. He also liked a drink or two, but only on a Friday and Saturday night, and he did beat Ellie, and her mother and brothers – whenever the mood took him). 'But even a good man will wear his wife down, see? Babies coming every year. Then there's all the endless washing, cooking and cleaning, the backbreaking day-to-day drudgery of it all. And the fear? Let me tell you, the fear never leaves you, Elle. Lived on me nerves most days, I did. Always afraid. Afraid there wasn't enough money. Afraid there wasn't enough food. Afraid of being pregnant – again. Afraid of looking the wrong way, saying the wrong thing. Always afraid. Well, there's only so much you can take, see? And some women, well, they snap. I seen it with me own eyes. Change beyond all recognition, some do. It's the drink; pills, maybe. I even knew women take to their bed and feign illness – anything to keep their husbands away from 'em. So, as a daughter, well, you was just a reminder of all that. I'd had a hard enough time meself, see. Didn't have the energy to watch you go through it. Much easier to distance meself. Not to care, not to notice. Not that I'm using that as an excuse, mind. I was wrong. I know that now. I should have looked out for you, protected you. That's the trouble with women, Elle. We don't look out for one another. We'd all be a damn sight bleedin' stronger if we did.'

She had paused for a few seconds, her rheumy eyes darting from left to right, her mottled brow crumpled as if she were considering whether she should say what she was about to say next. She lowered her already quiet voice to a whisper.

'What good would I have been to you, anyway? Useless. Worthless. Good for nothing... That's what my old dad said I was. A wrong un right from when I was a little gel, he reckoned. Said it was my fault my bleedin' mother had taken to her sickbed. So to teach me a lesson he said I had to give him what she no longer could.' Her mother had paused again, tears tracing lines down her rutted cheeks, her sobs muted. 'I was only six years old...'

It was a hard story for Ellie to listen to. One she would mourn, including all the lost years she and her mother could have spent together. Thankfully, though, with forgiveness in her heart, Ellie was there the day her mother passed away, hopefully at peace, her redemption bittersweet.

However, it would be so many years before Ellie understood this, so when she gave birth to Lizzie and the love love that was supposed to be there, wasn't, Ellie panicked. She suspected there was something wrong with her, some genetic flaw passed from mother to daughter. She watched with bewildered fascination at the other mothers on the hospital ward who, oohing and aahing, genuinely appeared to dote on their babies. Ellie felt none of the longing they seemed to possess, and became evermore convinced that, just as her own mother was incapable of loving her, she too, was incapable of loving *her* daughter. She tried to hide it, knew if she said anything to the nurses, they'd probably pack her off to the loony bin, and take her little girl away. She didn't dare tell Salocin, either. What would he think of her? Knowing she didn't love their daughter.

Now, Ellie listened to Salocin, heard him whisper to their daughter, felt the knot of fury pull at her chest. Why couldn't he leave the baby alone? She'd been awake for hours last night. All Ellie wanted was a couple of hours sleep. Was that too much to ask? Under the safety of the covers Ellie clenched and unclenched her fists, digging her nails into her palms, resisting the urge to leap up and scream. She heard the quiet kiss Salocin placed on his daughter's cheek, and without another word, heard him head out their front door. He closed it quietly behind him but the familiar snuffling noises coming from the crib grew louder. Any minute now Lizzie would cry – again. Ellie's stomach fizzed and churned, the anticipation of what was about to come filling her with dread. And come it did. Wave after wave of incessant fractious crying. Ellie tried her best to ignore it, placing a pillow over her head, her hands, two balled fists, holding it in place. Anything. ANYTHING to drown out the terrible noise.

Why? *Why* was Lizzie crying again? When would it ever stop? Surely she wasn't hungry, she'd had her last feed less than an hour ago. Maybe the doctor was right, her milk was too thin? Perhaps she should give Lizzie powdered milk instead. Besides, it would be less of a stigma. Everyone knew the only mothers that nursed their babies were those who couldn't afford formula. And yes, while it was true money was tight, Salocin said they could find enough money for formula if she needed it. Ellie remembered though why she had wanted to feed her daughter herself: the impression her old neighbour, Mrs Harris, who lived three doors down from her parents' house, had made on her.

Eight children she and her husband had, girls and boys, and unlike her own mother, Mrs Harris appeared to love them all equally. Sometimes Ellie would pass her on the street, on her way to the shops, where she'd be standing on her front doorstep, simultaneously smoking and feeding one of her babies. 'Hello luvvy, ah's yerself?' she'd ask. 'Ah's about a nice cup of tea?'

Ellie liked Mrs Harris. She was a no-nonsense, down to earth, tell it how it is, sort of person, with kind eyes and a way of saying things that made you feel better about yourself. Ellie liked to pop by for a cuppa and a natter. She enjoyed talking to Mrs Harris, but she always got the impression that Mrs Harris felt sorry for her. Ellie had asked her once, outright – something she'd never have been able to do with her own mother – why she breast fed instead of bottle fed her children and Mrs Harris had simply said a mother's milk was better, full of goodness, just as nature intended. That immediately came to mind when Ellie herself found she was pregnant. Besides, Mrs Harris had made it look easy.

Ellie almost choked on the memory. What the hell did she know? Breastfeeding Lizzie was not what she had imagined it would be. Her nipples were a cracked bloody mess and no amount of Vaseline seemed to help. Was that normal? Had Mrs Harris had cracked nipples? It wasn't like Ellie had anyone to ask, either. Her mother wasn't interested, hadn't even bothered to come and see her and her new granddaughter yet. And Martha? Well, her mother-in-law just unnerved her. She'd probably tell Ellie to let the baby starve, or feed her Carnation milk like old Mrs Roberts from downstairs suggested. Said that's what the doctor told her daughter to do, what his wife had fed their children on. Didn't they have a tin in the cupboard? Ellie couldn't remember but it might be worth a look. She would try anything if it got her baby daughter to sleep for a few hours. Then, maybe if Lizzie slept, she could sleep too. Surely that was all she needed – a couple of hours proper rest and she'd be right as rain. Wouldn't she?

She lifted her head off the pillow, listening. The needy cries of her baby daughter continued. 'Please stop crying,' Ellie, herself, whimpered, her heart hammering against her chest as fear rose from her stomach, bile burning her throat. The room spun. She had an overwhelming urge to throw up. She sat up, swung her legs off the side of the bed and using what little strength she had left, willed them to move. Against all odds she made it to the kitchen sink, leaned forward, and puked. She felt her stomach expand and contract like the bellows of an accordion wrenching her forwards until, hot and shivering, her tummy was empty. She let her head, damp with sweat, flop down against her arm now resting next to the sink. Lizzie's crying continued. *Please stop. Please stop.* 'PLEASE JUST FUCKING STOP!' Ellie screamed.

Lizzie cried on.

Feeling something warm between her legs, Ellie looked down, watching as a patch of bright red blood spread across her blue nightie like ink on blotting paper. *Must have pulled more stitches.* She couldn't tell anyone, though, didn't dare. Not even the doctor. It was far too embarrassing. Would she ever heal, be normal, again? What was it the midwife said to her after a quick examination? 'Looks like a cauliflower down there.' *What had the woman meant?* Ellie was too mortified to ask. She knew what a cauliflower looked like, though. And if that's what she looked like down below… well, it didn't bear thinking about.

The birth itself had been quite traumatic, the cord was wrapped around Lizzie's neck so they used forceps and had to perform an episiotomy. Ellie did not understand what that word meant but after the ripping sound down below, she quickly discovered it was a posh word to describe cutting her from her front end to her back. Lizzie was blue when she was born. No one explained why, but they whisked her little girl away and brought her back about six hours later and by then she was pink.

In her crib, Lizzie was still crying. How long had it been now, twenty, thirty minutes? How was that possible? How could something, barely bigger than a bag of sugar, make so much noise? It was heart-wrenching to listen to, and, hanging her head in her hands, Ellie started crying too. She couldn't bear the thought of another day like yesterday. Or the one before that. Every day since she'd first come home from hospital, in fact. Endless hours stretched out before her. Where the simple task of putting one foot in front of the other required vast amounts of energy and where tending to the needs of a constantly screaming baby prodded at her sanity. She'd felt the same during her hospital stay after Lizzie was born, she just hid it a little better, glossed over it all with a smile, feigning sleep, pleading ignorance – this being her first baby, and all. At least in the hospital there had been nurses on hand if she needed them. Some were better than others, kind, reassuring, explaining it was normal to have a touch of the baby blues, promising her she'd be back to her old self in no time at all. Others, however, had been less understanding, clicked their tongues, rolled their eyes, and muttered under their breath about it being a privilege to have the time to indulge in tearful melancholy, if they caught her off guard. Either way, brisk and efficient, they all knew what to do and when.

Ellie splashed her face with cold water from the tap, slipped on a clean nightie – no point in getting dressed – and wandered over to the beautiful crib that contained her screaming daughter. Confounded, she peered in, and stared at her red-faced baby girl. Mouth wide open, eyes screwed shut, tiny fists clenched, railing at the world; Ellie felt both confused and anxious. Why was her baby so fraught? What was she, the mother, doing so wrong? She fed Lizzie, bathed her, changed her nappy like she'd been shown, but it was never enough. Maybe she was ill, in pain? Ellie placed the back of her hand across the tiny forehead of her daughter, she felt warm, but not overly so. Was it possible that this tiny bundle of life, barely four weeks old, was picking up Lizzie's resentment, sensed her guilt for not loving her like she should? She never cried for Salocin. In fact, come to think of it, it was only during the evenings, when Salocin was home, snuggled in his arms, that Lizzie was at her most content.

Ellie gently lifted Lizzie out of the crib and carried her into the other room. The place was a mess. Salocin had done his best, even folding most of the washing into a couple of neat piles. He'd washed up too, although he'd left it draining. She'd try to put it away later, if she could get Lizzie to settle. With her head resting on Ellie's shoulder, Lizzie's cries raged on, her little face now crimson. In desperation Ellie flung open the kitchen cupboard where she kept some tinned goods. Where the hell was that tin of Carnation milk? She scanned the labels, pushing tins this way and that, and still Lizzie cried. Grabbing her with both hands, Ellie thrust her daughter out in front of her. 'What? What is wrong with you? What do you want from me?' Eyes squeezed shut, Lizzie kicked and screamed, drew her legs up. Ellie's vision blurred, her gaze filming with tears. Drained, she pulled out a chair, sat down and opened her nightie. She offered her daughter her breast, still smeared with Vaseline, and watched as Lizzie greedily latched on. After a few seconds, except for the squeaky murmuring of her nursing daughter, the room was bathed in a beautiful silence. Ellie, by now more exhausted than she imagined possible, felt her eyes close, and, drifting on a sea of black velvet, welcomed the darkness like an old friend.

SALOCIN

It was still early, but the café was teeming with those in need of a well-deserved tea break. The smell of fried bacon and eggs wafted amid a thick fug of cigarette smoke as customers, men mostly, cradled mugs of steaming hot tea, despite the warm weather.

In the corner of the café a lone geezer, head in his linen draper, chugging on a woodbine, sat at Mickey's usual table. Bert, the owner of the cafe, a portly man with a round friendly face, followed Mickey's gaze. He flicked a tea towel across his shoulder and shuffled around to the front of the counter. 'Don't worry about him, Mickey' he said, coughing to clear his throat, 'That's just Stan. He don't come 'ere often. Don't know that's your table. I'll ask him to move.'

Mickey stuck his hand out, told Bert he'd do it. 'And we'll have two cups of Rosie Lee, please, Bert. Ooh, and a couple of fried egg rolls while you're at it. Salocin, you wait, bring 'em over when they're ready, yeah?'

Salocin nodded and Bert, flashing a row of crooked yellow teeth, opened his mouth to say something but clearly thought better of it, and shuffled back behind the counter. Busying himself, he turned away from Salocin, steam rising above his head as the large silver tea urn chugged and shushed like an old steam train. Bert grabbed a couple of chipped cups and sloshed tea the colour of treacle into them, all the while keeping a beady eye on Mickey. Salocin, too, watched as Mickey, who had wandered over to the table in question, took the vacant seat next to Stan, the bloke sitting on his Jack Jones. Startled, Stan looked up and stared at Mickey but Mickey, refusing to make eye contact, ignored him. Bert, now buttering a couple of bread rolls, paused, watched Mickey some more, then shaking his head and rolling his eyes, went back to the job in hand.

Salocin noticed Mickey's jaw move. He was saying something. Startled, the old geezer shot back in his seat, and stared at the back of Mickey's head, but still Mickey refused to make eye contact with him. Stan, visibly confused, shuffled in his seat, looked from left to right, then behind him. He glanced over towards the counter at Bert who, now frying a couple of hissing, bubbling eggs in a black frying pan, sighed and looked away again. Stan quickly folded his newspaper and stubbed out the cigarette he'd been smoking. Scraping his chair back, he stood up, his forehead creased in thick lines of concern, and quickly headed back towards the counter.

'All right, Stan?' Bert asked.

Stan, newspaper tucked under his arm, nodded and adjusted his cap.

'See yer next week?' Bert continued.

Stan glanced over at Mickey then quickly looked away again. 'Erm, yeah. Maybe,' came his furtive reply as, head down, he strode towards the door and left.

'Two fried eggs rolls,' Bert shouted, slamming a couple of plates down on the counter. Salocin jumped. 'You take 'em over, I'll bring the teas.'

Unsure whether he was supposed to pay, Salocin stuck his hand in his pocket, rooting around for change. 'How much?'

'No charge.' Bert's expression was world weary, his tone brisk.

Salocin carried the plates of food over, placed them on the table and sat down opposite Mickey.

Bert, behind him, carried the two cups of tea. 'Mickey,' he said, placing the rattling cups in their saucers beside the food.

Mickey, blowing smoke from the corner of his mouth, grinned his assassin's grin, and nodded. 'Thanks Bert.'

'Can I get you gentlemen anything else?'

Mickey shook his head and Bert, wiping his large hands on

his grease-stained apron, wandered back towards the counter.

Mickey laughed.

'What's so funny?' Salocin asked.

'Works every bleedin' time.'

'What does?' Salocin had a quizzical smile on his face.

Mickey reached into his jacket pocket, pulled out a packet of cigarettes, opened it, and offered the pack to Salocin, who took one.

'Thanks,' he said, placing it behind his ear for later. 'You talking about the old bloke?'

Mickey, squinting to avoid the blue smoke rising from the cigarette still hanging from the corner of his mouth, nodded. 'See the thing is, young Salocin,' he explained. 'Sometimes in life, say, when you're on the train or the bus, you may, like me, prefer to sit alone. Or, like just now, with the old geezer, you may have a preferred table you like to sit at, and sometimes, that might involve getting someone else to move. Agreed?' Salocin nodded. 'Wanna know the best way to do that?'

Salocin took a swig of hot sweet tea, feeling it scald his throat. 'Go on then. I'm all ears.'

'Words.'

'Words?'

Mickey nodded, blew a smoke ring from his mouth that wobbled then drifted away like a balloon. 'People underestimate the power of words.'

'How's that then, Mickey?'

Intrigued, Salocin watched as his boss stubbed out his cigarette in the half-filled ashtray, its orange embers sparking then fading to ash. He wore a sports jacket with an open-necked shirt. A handsome man, Salocin thought. And like him, Mickey was an East Ender born and bred but unlike Salocin, Mickey was Jewish. He was also, he said, a *persona non grata* in his parents' home for marrying a non-Jewish woman, namely Georgie's daughter, Helena. He didn't regret it though. Said his mother was stifling. Besides which, he loved Helena. 'With all me heart,' he'd once said. Like he loved Ellie, Salocin supposed, judging by the way Mickey's eyes lit up every time he mentioned his wife's name. Salocin liked Mickey. Liked him a lot, and sensed the feeling was mutual.

Their real boss though, was Georgie, of course. Mickey ran the yard, but it belonged to Georgie Wakefield: *his* name above the door, *his* gaff, and once or twice a week he liked to turn up at the yard and remind everyone of that simple fact. You couldn't miss him. A tall man, medium build, he always had a Dunhill cigarette hanging from his mouth and he always arrived in some swanky car – Jags were his favourite – always with a couple of mute heavies in tow. Unlike Mickey, Georgie Boy – as Mickey liked to call his father-in-law behind his back – was not a handsome man. He was, however, well-dressed. His suits were made to measure from Saville Row and his shoes, handmade in Italy, were cut from the finest leather, the heels of which made a particular clicking sound against the concrete. Georgie wore his thin silver-grey hair, as a comb over, parted at the side, ruler straight. He had a unique way of talking, too, especially when pronouncing his son-in-law's name. He said it slowly, emphasising the two distinct syllables, always using a somewhat higher tone on the latter one – so it sounded like a question.

'Mick-eee? Who's the new boy then Mick-eee?' he said, when he had first laid eyes on Salocin.

Mickey had sighed, rolled his eyes – the only person allowed to get away with such behaviour. 'You know who this is, Georgie, we had a conversation about him when I interviewed him, remember?'

Georgie studied Salocin, his dark eyes narrowing as he sucked hard on the cigarette hanging from his mouth. 'Remind me again please, Mick-eee.' Georgie, his beady blue eyes firmly locked on

Salocin, knew who he was. He just liked to keep everybody on his or her toes, including his trusted son-in-law.

'This is Salocin,' Mickey said. 'Wilf Lemalf's son.'

'What's he like then, Mick-eee? Is he a good boy?'

'How the fuck do I know, Georgie? What I do know is, he's a grafter, like his old man... just a lot fucking greener. Which ain't a bad thing now, is it.' It was a statement rather than a question and Georgie had chuckled.

Georgie made to leave then turned back. 'Salocin, eh? What kinda bleedin' name is that?'

Salocin had felt his face flush. He wasn't sure if Georgie was expecting him to reply but judging by the look on Mickey's face he thought better of it.

'Ah, leave it out, Georgie. He's only a young 'un,' Mickey said.

Georgie laughed again. 'He's alright encha, lad? Mind if I call you Sal?'

Salocin looked at Mickey, swallowed the lump of unease rising from his chest. There was something about Georgie Wakefield that set him on edge. Mickey nodded, as if giving Salocin permission to speak. 'Sal's fine, Georgie... I mean Mr Wakefield, sir.'

Georgie had raised his eyebrows, looked somewhat surprised. 'Sir!' he laughed. 'Boy's got manners, eh Mickey? It's just Georgie, son.' He winked at Salocin. 'Everyone calls me Georgie. And rightio – Sal, it is.' Once again he turned on his heel and made to leave.

'Don't call me Sally, though,' Salocin added, as he watched Georgie's retreating back.

Georgie stopped, turned his head in a series of stilted, almost robotic movements. 'What's that boy?' he had said, striding back towards him. Salocin gulped, felt the moisture in his mouth disappear. 'Well?' Georgie asked, his eyebrows knitting together;

by then so close, Salocin could smell the stale tobacco on his breath.

'I... the thing is... Well, I don't like it, Mr Wa... I mean, Georgie. 'Sal' is fine. So is 'Salocin'. But not Sally. I don't like no one calling me Sally.' His tone was far more measured than he felt.

Mickey stared at Salocin in disbelief, used his hand to make sawing motions across his throat behind his father-in-law's back.

'And watchu gonna do about it if I do call yer Sally?' Georgie asked.

Salocin opened his mouth to speak, about to say what he always said to anyone who called him Sally – 'I'll flatten yer. Lay yer out' – however, as the two heavies behind Georgie looked at one another, grinned and took two steps forward, Salocin clamped his mouth shut again.

'Well?' Georgie said.

Salocin glanced over Georgie's shoulder towards Mickey who, rolling his eyes and shaking his head, hit his forehead with the palm of his hand. Salocin felt his arse twitch but still he said nothing.

'What's the matter with you, boy? Cat got your bleedin' tongue. Answer me when I'm talking to yer.'

Fuck. Me and my fat gob – again. Salocin knew he had to say something, but he also knew he couldn't threaten Georgie. He didn't want to lose face either – or lose his job. He coughed, cleared his throat. 'The thing is, Georgie, if someone calls me Sally, I'll lay 'em out. But I respect you. So...' His eyes darted towards the two heavies '...I'll take one of them on instead.' Again the heavies exchanged glances 'Or... I guess I'll have to resign.'

Georgie stared at Salocin, his face thunderous. 'Resign?'

'I don't want to,' Salocin explained. 'But I got standards, Georgie. I ain't having anyone call me Sally.'

Georgie arched one of his well-groomed salt and pepper eyebrows, glanced across his shoulder. 'And you'll take on one of these – if I ask you to?' He nodded towards the two men.

'If you want?' Salocin shrugged nonchalantly, his arse still trembling.

'What? Even knowing they'll likely floor yer?'

'If that's what I've got to do, yeah. Although, if I'm honest, I'd prefer not to.'

Seconds passed, or was it minutes? Salocin found it hard to tell, and still Georgie continued to stare at him, the atmosphere as hushed as a Trappist monastery. Then, much to Salocin's surprise, and everyone else's judging by the looks on their faces, Georgie placed his arm around Salocin's shoulder, threw his head back and laughed. After a couple of seconds everyone else followed suit.

'Know what, Mick-eee?' he said, his shoulders heaving up and down. 'I do believe he would. Go on then, you cheeky little sod, fack orf back to work.'

They say ignorance is bliss and if, at the time, Salocin had known what Georgie Wakefield was capable of, he would never have dared to talk to him in such a manner. However, it's also true to say he won Georgie's respect that day and no one at the yard *ever* called Salocin "Sally".

'Hey, you with us, boy?'

Salocin realised Mickey was looking at him curiously, and let go of that momentous day. 'Come on then, Mickey.' He took a gargantuan bite out of his fried egg roll, a trickle of warm fat sliding down his chin. 'You gonna spill the beans or what?' It was the first time he'd eaten since last night and he was hungry. He'd felt sick first thing this morning, couldn't stomach the thought of breakfast. Had put it down to worry. Or lack of sleep. Probably both. 'What words did yer use to get the old geezer to move, then?'

Mickey sat back, folded his arms and grinned. He reminded Salocin of the Cheshire Cat illustrations from the Alice in Wonderland book he'd read as a child. Mickey winked, tapped the side of his nose with his finger. 'Thing is,' he said. 'You gotta choose your victim well. Someone sitting alone, but not anyone who looks a bit tasty, y'know, up for a fight. Important not to make eye contact, either, we give a lot away with our eyes. Then the rest is easy. You sit down next to them, stare straight ahead and in your most sinister voice… quietly ask if they've brought the money. When they look at you, confused, repeat it, only with more urgency. Mickey laughed. 'Works every time,' he said thumping his fist on the table.

Salocin laughed too. 'You should have seen the look on that poor bloke's face.'

'I know!'

Several onlookers glanced over, no doubt wondering what all the fuss was about, their furrowed brows marked with the same disdain they might reserve for a couple of recalcitrant schoolboys. 'Keep the bleedin' noise darn,' someone shouted, which only made them laugh harder.

'Try it,' Mickey said, when they calmed down. 'I dare you.'

Salocin took another slurp of tea. Maybe he would try it, tonight, on the bus. On his way home to Ellie and his new baby daughter – the thought of which should have lifted his heart but instead, he was ashamed to admit, made it sink.

'Come on then.' Mickey was watching him closely. 'Before you stop smiling again. Tell Uncle Mickey all about it.

Salocin sighed. When he had turned up at the yard this morning, with a face like a slapped arse, the weight of the world on his shoulders, as Mickey had put it, the older man had obviously seen that he needed to talk, in private. He invited him to chat about it over a cuppa at Bert's café round the corner. Put on the spot, Salocin stumbled to find the right words.

Ellie had changed since she'd come out of hospital, was distant, withdrawn. Lizzie was always crying too. And the flat was a mess, not that that really bothered him, it was hard to keep things tidy when there was barely enough room to swing a cat. In fact, he wouldn't give a flying fuck about the state of the place if Ellie were happy, but she wasn't. It was her apathy, both towards him and Lizzie that scared him the most. She wasn't right. He tried to talk to her about it, even goaded her, raising his voice on a couple of occasions, anything to get a response from her, but where once she would have retaliated, defended her corner, now she said nothing, her face expressionless, blank. He didn't think Lizzie was in danger or that she would come to any harm around Ellie, she loved their little girl, he was sure of it, deep down. But it was also clear she was struggling. He tried to help, he really did. He daren't tell anyone, not even Mickey, and especially not the other fellas at work, but he was even changing nappies, doing some washing. Anything to help, but it was confusing. Ellie never said, but it was almost as if she resented his help, as if by trying to ease some of the burden he was slighting her, criticising her. He was at his wits end. Didn't know what to do. Lack of sleep didn't help either. Ellie did her best, always took Lizzie into the other room for her night feeds so he could get some rest. He needed it too; it was physical hard graft working at the yard. But Lizzie never seemed to settle, kept waking every hour on the hour. Sometimes, when he was really knackered, he would drift off for a while, but most of the time he just lay there, in the dark, listening to his wife and daughter crying in the other room, wishing it would stop, and not knowing what the fuck he could do to make it better.

There was no one to talk to about it, either. No one else to ask for help. Ellie's mother wasn't interested. She hadn't even been to visit her new granddaughter yet. He had thought about asking Martha, she had at least visited Ellie in the hospital when

Lizzie was born, but they hadn't seen her again since, although to be fair, Wilf had sent word that Martha was ill, had taken to her bed with her headaches again. Maybe when she was better, Salocin could ask her. Then again, Martha might make things worse. Ellie had often said, before the baby arrived, how uncomfortable she felt around her mother-in-law, how critical she was. Salocin knew that was just his mother's way. He'd had years to get used to it. It didn't make it right, though, or her comments any easier to swallow, but the last thing Ellie needed now was tough love.

Once he got going, the words poured out of Salocin, and all the time Mickey studied him, his gaze thoughtful, appraising.

'Lizzie,' he said, when he was quite sure Salocin had finished talking. 'Lovely name. I've got three daughters myself, you know. Apple of my eye, they are. All three of them.' The corners of his mouth lifted into a smile as if a vision of them had just floated past him, like a balloon. 'Especially Laura – the youngest,' he continued. 'A real daddy's girl, she is. That smile of hers can light up a whole room,' he said proudly. 'Only nine months older than your Lizzie, too.'

Salocin nodded, thinking of his own tiny daughter. How needy and helpless she was, how much she cried all the time and how much Ellie cried too – although she did her best to hide it from him.

'Sounds like she's suffering from postnatal depression,' Mickey was matter-of-fact.

'Post nay what?'

'Postnatal depression.'

Salocin had never heard of it and waited for Mickey to explain; Mickey knew everything. Mickey reassured Salocin it wasn't unusual, the reason he knew so much about it was because Helena had suffered with it after she gave birth to their second daughter. 'She was fine with the first and third,' Mickey added. He suggested Ellie needed help, someone to take up the slack until she felt better again. He would have given Salocin time off, he said, but at the moment he really couldn't spare him.

'We're expecting a couple of big deliveries over the next few weeks,' he continued. 'And right now I need all hands on deck.'

Salocin nodded, said he understood. Taking time off was not an option, anyway. Since Ellie was home with Lizzie and they no longer had her small wage to top them up, his was their only income. Now, more than ever, Salocin needed to keep working. Besides, Salocin got the distinct impression that his presence only agitated Ellie, that somehow she believed he was judging her, which, although he never meant to, he supposed he was.

Mickey pulled a small notepad and pen from his pocket and told Salocin to make a list of those he thought he could call on. It was a small list. They went through it; mostly crossing the names back off again, until only one remained.

Mickey chucked a twenty-pound note at Salocin, told him to offer it to the person for a few days help. 'See if she can wangle a couple of days off work, just until we've had these deliveries. Then I'll see what else we can do. Might even sort a couple of days paid leave, just as long as Georgie boy doesn't get wind. But we'll cross that bridge when we come to it, eh?' He winked, pushing his chair back and standing up. 'Now come on. Chop fucking chop.'

Salocin looked at the money, then looked at Mickey. 'That's really good of you Mickey but... I can't.' He pushed the note back. 'It'll take me forever to pay you back.'

Mickey grinned, slid the money back again. 'Did I say I wanted it back, you tart? It's not a loan. It's a gift. Take it. Everyone needs a bit of a helping hand from time to time. Now, does what's-her-name have a phone? If so, you can use the office one to catch her before she leaves for work.'

'Nah, Mickey. She don't.'

'Do you know where she works then?'

'Darn the Kings Road.'

'Right. Good. Well piss orf and see if you can't catch her.'

Salocin swallowed the lump in his throat, managing a tight-lipped smile by way of thanks. Mickey would never know how grateful he was.

Chapter 14

Boxing Day
PRESENT DAY – EVENING

LIZZIE

I climb the stairs in search of Connor, surprised by the slight ripples of apprehension washing over me. However, the minute I spot the two-day-old, neatly folded pile of washing still sitting outside his room, which before that had been sitting at the foot of the stairs, my nervousness disintegrates. Annoyed I swoop down and gather the bundle in my arms. *Why the hell doesn't he just pick it up and put it away, for god sake?* I'm ready to hammer on the door but I stop myself. I hover for a moment, my heart thudding against my chest, hear Mum and Aunt Marie behind me, downstairs, gathering their things together, saying their goodbyes.

Connor, like Simon, seems so distant of late. I've always prided myself on keeping my family close, so that when the storms come, we can batten down the hatches and sit them out together. Lately though, what with Dad, and Cassie and the Hunter Black situation, everything feels broken; our crumbling unit under threat of collapse should a light breeze blow our way. Which it will. It's only a matter of time and as if on cue, the Richard Hawley song "There's a Storm a Comin" starts playing in my head.

I cough to clear my throat, and knock on Connor's door, quietly at first. No reply. I knock a little harder, this time pressing my ear to the door to listen. Again, no reply and the only sound is silence. Slightly concerned I push down on the handle, open the door. Just a fraction to start, make sure I'm not interrupting anything I shouldn't be, and peek in. Connor, sprawled across his bed has his headphones on. He is upright, his head back, resting on knitted hands, a laptop is on his knee. I push the door open wider and take a couple of steps forward. He neither hears nor sees me, his head bobbing from side to side as he continues to stare at his laptop screen, laughing, engrossed in whatever it is he is watching and listening to.

The room hangs in a fog of recently sprayed deodorant infused with the smell of stale beer, no doubt coming from the cans, crushed and deformed like abstract works of art, sitting on his bedside cabinet. There's a faint whiff of cannabis, too, although a quick glance around the room offers no incriminating evidence. I am, however, pleasantly surprised because besides the decorative beer cans, and the odd abandoned cup and plate, Connor's room is, for once, remarkably tidy. Although, to be fair, out of all three children, his room never compares to the permanent floordrobe that was Maisy's when she lived with us. The straight up-down lines on his carpet even suggest a recent guest appearance by the Hoover. My little big man is growing up. Well, either that, or he has a girl coming over?

I remain by the door, hovering, watching my son, remembering a time when the cheeky smile, not the grimaces of late, was his default response. I also remember a time, not so long ago, where great big bear hugs were the norm as opposed to the exception.

Slow down my little one, stay a while. Please?

Connor, still gazing at his laptop screen, laughs. I'm faintly aware of a rumbling noise, too. An intermittent guttural snoring. I stand on tiptoe, peer across Connor's bed and realise Freddy, his head resting on his paws, is lying beside Connor. I lift my hand into a wave. The movement catches Connor's eye. He sees me and immediately sits up, slams his laptop shut and removes his headphones. In the blink of an eye his expression changes from happy and relaxed to twitchy and uptight.

'What's wrong?' he asks.

'Nothing. Nan and Aunt Marie are going home and I wondered if you'd walk them back for me?'

'What – now?'

I nod my head. 'Please. If that's okay?'

Connor turns to look at Freddy, strokes him. 'What about Freddy?'

'I said I'd take him home tomorrow, in the car.'

'Okay. Peng. He can stay in here with me.'

I smile; walk towards him. 'Washing,' I point out, placing the pile in my hand on his chest of drawers.

'Oh yeah, sorry,' he says, head bowed. 'Didn't see it.'

'Really?' I reply, mock surprise in my voice.

He grins. I soften, walk over to his bed and reach over and pat Freddy's head that, oblivious, snores on. 'Do you remember when Nan and Grandad first brought him home? How small he was? How much you two loved to play together?'

Connor sniffs, presses the heel of his hand to his eye and looks away.

I place my hand gently on his arm. 'You okay, love?'

Connor refuses to look at me. 'Yep, fine.' But his voice is strained.

'Look, can we talk?' I risk perching on the bed next to him.

Connor swings round, his eyebrows, sandy-coloured like his hair, knit together in a frown. 'What about?' he asks, hitching himself further up the bed.

'I just want to check that you're okay? You seem... distant?'

Connor shrugs his shoulders, puffs out his cheeks. 'Yeah? Well you'd know all about that, wouldn't you?'

Connor looks away again. My heart sinks and I try a

different tactic. 'What were you watching?' I point to his laptop, his earphones swinging back and forth in his hand.

He looks at me and opens the lid of his laptop. I see Dad's face, his mischievous eyes framed by bushy white eyebrows, frozen mid-laugh. Connor pulls at the lead of his headphones and yanks it from the side of his laptop, stabbing the return button on the keyboard. To my surprise Dad springs into life. He's rapping, or should I say attempting to rap, Eminem's, 'When I'm Gone', standing in a green field, the sun, like a bright yellow orb floating on a cloudless blue sky directly behind him. An ever-growing sea of good-humoured faces has gathered around him, and somewhere in the distance there's the buzz and hum of other music. Dad lifts his head back, throws his arms forwards, points to the ground then locks both arms across his chest. The crowd cheer and clap, which only encourages him more.

'Where and when was this?' I ask. 'I can't remember.'

'The Viva Music festival. A couple of years ago, now. Before Grandad got sick.' Connor's voice is choked.

'Yes… of course it is.' I'm trying to swallow the lump forming in my throat. 'Didn't someone film him and post it on YouTube? Called it Bad Ass Grandad or something?'

Connor wipes his eyes with the backs of his hands, laughs. 'Yeah. Got a couple of million views, if I remember. Loads of comments too. Mostly about how peng he was.'

Looking down, I wipe at a non-existent mark on my jeans and swallow back the tears pricking the back of my eyes. The film footage continues to play, Dad singing verbatim.

'Do you think he's up there?' Connor raises his eyes toward the ceiling. 'You know, looking down on us?'

I look into his expectant eyes. 'Be nice to think so, wouldn't it?' I reach out to take his hand between both of mine.

'Mu-um?' His voice is almost a whisper. 'Why didn't you come to the police station with me yesterday?'

Surprised, I stare at my son, feeling myself recoil a little. 'Well, because… because I knew you'd be okay, I suppose.'

'How, though? How did you know that? The police are still not saying how Black died. And for all you knew it could have been me. Why didn't you support me like you've supported Cassie all this time?'

Connor's voice, although calm has risen in pitch and volume. I'm somewhat taken aback by his outburst, stare into his big brown eyes, and notice, like Dad's, the specs of amber in them. 'I… I…' Lost for words, I'm laughing inside at the irony. I'm a writer for fuck sake. *How can I be lost for words?* I try my best to explain. 'Look, I know this will sound feeble, and you probably won't believe me, but I knew, whatever it was you did, it couldn't have been that bad. And not only that, Aunt Marie was a real mess. I was really worried about her.'

'More worried about her than me? Your son.'

I sigh and Connor pulls his hand away. The radiator bangs, making us both jump and look up as it gurgles and fills with water.

'You do know I love you, right?'

Connor shrugs his shoulders – just as Mum calls up the stairs saying they need to get going.

'Be there in a minute, Mum,' I shout.

'I suppose,' Connor replies. 'It's just that…'

'Just what?'

'I dunno. I'm probably being childish. But it just kinda feels as though you're not really around for me.' Indignant I stare at the pile of washing on his chest of drawers. Connor follows my gaze. 'I'm not saying you don't do stuff for me. In fact, I know I should probably do more to help. And I know you're worried about Nan. Plus there's all the stuff with Cassie and Black and everything. And I know you're trying to find time to write but…' He shrugs his shoulders again.

'But what?'

'It would just be nice if you noticed me too, sometimes.'

His words sting; strike me in the solar plexus, hard. Choked, I shake my head, try and swallow my sadness. 'I'm sorry, Connor,' I reply. 'Maybe you're right. Maybe I should have gone to the police station with you. Sent someone else to help Aunt Marie? But sometimes life isn't always as black and white as it seems. Sometimes, whilst I try my best to be there – for everyone – I have to put one person before another, even my own children. Plus, I knew you'd be okay with Simon, I knew he'd look after you for me, keep me posted. And if you'd seen the state Aunt Marie was in… Well, I honestly believe you would have understood–' There *is* something else though, an allegiance to my Aunt Marie that I just can't explain to my son right now.

'That's just it,' Connor replies. 'Uncle Teddy has been ill for ages now. Aunt Marie is always saying how she lost him a long time ago. So, I know it's sad and everything, but her response just doesn't make any sense. Does it?'

I sigh and run a hand through my hair. 'Like I said, Connor, life's not always as black and white as it seems. People react differently to loss and grief – you've seen that with Grandad.'

Connor turns away, strokes Freddy. 'I know,' he mumbles. 'Sorry. Now I feel well bad.'

'No. No, you mustn't, you're not! And I'm sorry. I really am. It's just that sometimes–'

'Lizzie?' Mum calls up the stairs again, her voice now somewhat fractious.

I stand up, as does Connor, and we both look towards the door.

'Coming, Mum,' I reply.

I face my son again, put my hands on his shoulders. 'Sometimes, being a parent feels like you're being pulled in a million and one different directions. That nothing you do is right, or ever good enough. And although you do your best, sometimes, someone feels let down. It's not intentional, I promise.' I pull him into a hug, still amused at the height difference between us. 'I love you and your sisters far more than you know. Love all my family. And I'll do anything – *anything* – to love and protect you all. Do you understand that?' Stepping back I hold him at arms-length. Connor stares at me and finally nods. 'I am sorry, though,' I add. 'I promise I'll try to make more time for us.'

We head towards the door and leave Freddy on the bed, snoring.

'I'm probably gonna meet Jake and the others at the pub after I've walked Nan and Aunt Marie home,' Connor says.

'Have fun.' I rub his arm affectionately. 'And don't drink too much.'

'You can talk,' he says smirking. 'I've seen you knocking back the Prosecco today.'

Mum and Aunt Marie, swaddled in their winter coats and hats, are waiting at the foot of the stairs. 'Ah, there you are,' Mum says.

Connor grabs his coat from the rack by the stairs and I suggest he gives some thought to Scott's earlier invitation to go to the cinema with him this week. Quizzical, he raises his eyebrows. 'Meh. Maybe.'

'Look, I know he wasn't there for you and Cassie when you were little. But I also know he's really sorry about that now. He's trying, Connor, he really is. And the truth is, you can never have enough people that love and care for you.'

'Too true,' Mum says.

'I suppose.' Connor shrugs.

'No suppose about it, young man,' Mum retorts. 'It's a tough old life. We all make mistakes but everyone deserves a second chance.'

Connor chews the corner of his mouth, looks thoughtful. 'Yeah – I know. Can I... well, can I just ask you something?' He looks directly at me.

'Come on, Connor, get that coat on, love,' Mum interrupts, a note of impatience in her voice. 'I want to get Aunt Marie home and settled.'

'Yeah, sorry, Nan. Coming.' He throws his coat over his shoulders, slipping his arms through the sleeves.

'Of course,' I reply. 'Ask away.'

'Has Si or Uncle Sean said much to you about the IndieKnot gig we went to the other day?'

'No. Not much. Why do you ask? Does this have something to do with what you were asking your Dad earlier?'

Pausing for a moment Connor opens his mouth, his eyes meeting mine. 'Ah forget it. It's nothing.'

I'm confused. 'Why ask then?'

Connor runs a hand through his gelled hair, checks his reflection in the mirror hanging on the wall near the door. 'Like I said, it's nothing.'

'Connor?'

Connor pretends not to see or hear me, pats his pockets for his keys and wallet. 'Shit. Left my phone upstairs,' he says, heading back towards the stairs. Whatever he was going to ask me, he's now clearly changed his mind.

Mum and Aunt Marie are already by the front door fiddling with the lock.

'We'll walk on, Connor. You catch us up,' Mum shouts after him.

Mum and Aunt Marie wish me goodnight and I tell them I'll pop round sometime over the next couple of days to help make a start on Uncle Teddy's funeral arrangements.

'Right.' Connor reappears. 'Sees you later then. Tell Cas and Luke I'll be at The George after – if they want to join us.'

'Okay, will do. Perhaps Si and I will pop along, too?'

Connor's face drops. I laugh. Tell him not to worry, that I wouldn't dream of cramping his style. He strides towards the door, turns then pauses for a moment. 'Mu-um?' he says, scratching the back of his head. I hear the hollow trot of Mum and Aunt Marie's footsteps receding down the drive. 'I just wanted to ask…'

'Yes?' I wonder if he's changed his mind again about asking me whatever seems to be bothering him about the IndieKnot gig.

'Have you ever felt err, lost? Like you don't know where you're going or what the fuck you're supposed to be doing with your life?'

Laughing, I touch his cheek. 'All the time,' I reply. 'All the bloody time.'

Connor's eyes widen, his eyebrows shooting into his brow. I sense his relief but also his surprise, too.

'Really?' he replies. 'Even though you're, like, old and stuff?'

I tell him to bugger off, watching how, within a couple of giant paces he catches up with the shuffling bodies of Mum and Aunt Marie, muscles his way in between them, gallantly offering them an arm each. They look tiny either side of him. I smile. I've never really given it much thought before now but after talking to Mum, and thinking back to my childhood, I'm aware of the gentle but constant presence of my Aunt in my life, always there, always encouraging, but never overstepping the mark. Our bond feels stronger of late, too, especially considering Mum's recent confession – out of the blue, after we'd finished chatting about Dad the other day – that she suffered from postnatal depression when I was born and how it was Aunt Marie that helped her.

Or *rescued* her, as she put it.

Chapter 15

LONDON 1965

ELLIE

A loud hammering at the door made Ellie jump. She looked down at her sleeping daughter, her tiny mouth half open, traces of milk on her blush pink lips. She looked the most content Ellie had ever seen her. Another knock, harder, more urgent, rattled the door. Lizzie murmured, her tiny brow knitting into a frown. *Please don't wake up*, Ellie thought. She cocked her head, listened, thought she could hear a voice, a woman's voice, calling her name. She stared at her daughter, knowing if she stood up, Lizzie would wake up and the crying would start all over again. What should she do? Whoever was at the door was in no hurry to leave.

Carefully tucking her breast back into her nightie, Ellie made to stand up, slowly, hardly daring to breathe, willing whoever was at the door not to knock again, at least, not until she could lay Lizzie back in her crib. She crept across the room in pin-steps. The rat-a-tat as she passed the door immediately stopped her in her tracks. Ellie held her breath, stared at the bundle in her arms. Lizzie's eyes flickered, opened. Within seconds the sweet sound of silence was broken and Ellie's heart, like a lift with its cables cut, plummeted, dragging her further towards the depths of despair.

Angry, she yanked at the door and heaved it open.

'Marie?' she gasped, unable to keep the surprise out of her voice. Ellie stared at her friend who, wearing slim-fitting slacks and a yellow crop top, her hair fashionably back-combed, her glossy lips painted pale pink, looked quite beautiful. Like sunshine on a rainy day and everything Ellie wasn't – young, carefree and perfect. A wave of jealousy surged through her exhausted body. She caught Marie's concerned glance, the pity that flickered across her eyes as Marie took in her tired, dishevelled face, the crumpled nightie half open at the top. 'What are you doing here?' Ellie asked, stepping aside to let her friend in.

Marie brushed past her, smelling every bit as beautiful as she looked: Lily-of-the-valley talcum powder plus a splash of Estée Lauder's Youth Dew perfume, if Ellie wasn't mistaken.

Marie held up two shopping bags. 'Right,' she said, marching into the room, shrugging out of her coat. 'I have bottles and I have formula.' She placed the bags on the small Formica table Ellie and Salocin ate their meals at and hung her coat across the back of one of the two mismatched wooden chairs tucked underneath it. 'And before you protest,' she said, holding her arms out, 'Yep, come on, give Lizzie to me.' She nodded towards the still screaming bundle in Ellie's arms. 'I understand why you want to feed your little gel yourself,' she continued, as Ellie handed over her daughter. 'But sometimes you have to do what's best for you.'

Ellie opened her mouth to protest but Marie beat her to it. 'It won't kill her, El,' she said, rocking Lizzie gently in her arms. 'And unless you wanna end up in the loony bin, having that god awful electric shock treatment like my Aunt Dot, poor cow, you'll listen to me. You've got a bit of depression, is all. Ain't no shame in it. It's hard work trying to feed a baby that won't feed proper. Trying to snatch sleep with a baby that never sleeps. Tantamount to bleedin' torture if you ask me. I'd like to see a man do it. Damn sight easier to work than stuck inside with a screaming baby all day long. Most men couldn't do it. *Wouldn't* do it. And I've seen it send some women gaga. But it ain't a sign of weakness, despite what some people say. We all need a little help from time to time. Now, you run yourself a bath. Do you have any salt?' Ellie nodded, pointed to the cupboard next to the sink. 'Good. Take it with you and put a handful in your bath, it'll help with that,' she nodded, using her chin to point downwards.

Ellie followed Marie's gaze, looked down and gasped, mortified to see another red patch on her nightie. Her hands flew towards the bloody stain as she crossed and uncrossed them, trying to hide it. 'Oh no,' she mumbled, hardly daring to meet Marie's eyes.

'Have you pulled your stitches?' Ellie, eyes downcast, nodded. 'Rightio. I'll call the doctor and by the time you've had a bath and a nice little nap, he'll be here to take a look.'

'But–'

'No buts.' Marie said above Lizzie's crying. 'You might have an infection. Could get blood poising if you're not careful – I had a friend die of that. What use you gonna be to this little one if you peg it, eh?' Marie looked down at Lizzie, genuine warmth and concern pooling into her eyes as she kissed the top of the baby's head. 'Shush, shush, there, there, little gel. It's okay.'

Lizzie opened her eyes, stared at the face of the woman with the honeyed voice. She continued to cry, but it was more of a grizzle now, definitely a lot less fractious. Ellie felt her heart in her throat. Why couldn't she do that? Why did her baby hate her so much? And where the hell was the overwhelming rush of euphoria, some of the other mothers mentioned?

Marie looked up again, smiled. 'Now, you leave us two to it. A nice bath, bit of kip, you'll soon be right as rain. It won't happen over night, mind,' she warned. 'These things take time but I promise I'll be 'ere for as long as you need me.'

'But what about your job?'

Marie, who worked at a boutique clothes shop along the

Kings Road, Chelsea, shrugged. 'Had a bit of holiday due.' It was true, she did. And besides, as far as she was concerned, they owed her. She liked her job, but she was always going the extra mile, working a bit later, starting a bit earlier, sorting out the stock when new deliveries came in. And she never grumbled about it either. So she told her boss that her sister was poorly, needed some help. It wasn't much of a lie. She and Ellie were as close as sisters, closer in fact. And she didn't want the money Salocin had offered her for her help, either. Although she used some it to buy bottles and formula.

'Did Salocin put you up to this?'

Marie's eyebrows shot into her brows. 'So what if he did? He's worried about you. And like I said, we all need a bit of help sometimes. Ain't no shame in it, Ellie.'

There was genuine warmth in her friend's voice but there was also an air of finality to it. The help she offered was in good faith, from the heart. Marie expected nothing in return and for the first time in weeks Ellie felt relief. No longer drowning in despair, she spied hope on the horizon.

After scrubbing the bath with Vim – she hated the thought of sharing the same bath as her neighbours, even though as a girl she'd had to share the same tin bath, the same bathwater as her brothers – Ellie rinsed it, filled it, slipped in and closed her eyes as warm frothy bubbles enveloped her aching body. The water felt like heaven, smelled like it too. She wasn't sure if she should mix bubbles with a salt bath but she added them regardless, anything to wash away the smell of blood, sweat and tears that followed her around like a bad penny of late. The water, like an old train, steamed out in front of her, filling the bathroom in a thick fog. She slid down beneath the water until her hearing went sub-aqua, as her thoughts drifting, washing over her, transported her to another time.

She remembered a trip she and Salocin had taken to Brighton not long after they'd first courted, but unlike the sub-zero temperatures of their honeymoon, this had been a beautiful summer day. Salocin had cleaned and polished his beloved scooter, a two-tone red and white Vespa, to within an inch of its life. No mean feat considering the scores of mirrors and fog lights it contained, not to mention the chrome luggage rack and crash bars. Shone brighter than the Blackpool illuminations, she reckoned, not that she'd ever seen them. They'd met up with other Mods, some friends, others just familiar faces. But it was all about the camaraderie, all the fellas checking out each other's handiwork, discussions about what was the best – Vespa or Lambretta – many believing you were born to one or the other, same as a football team, and those stupid enough to make 'the switch' forever frowned upon. Then there'd be chat about the cut of your suit, the style of a girl's hair.

The weather that day had been perfect, filled with unbroken sunshine and a bit of a light coastal breeze. Ellie recalled the warmth of the sun on her face, Salocin's nose, with its slight bump, burning. Some of them, her included, took a dip in the sea to cool off, while older folk like her parents' generation, peered over the rails of the prom, regarding the wayward, drug taking and morally corrupt youngsters – if the papers were to be believed – with wary disdain. Rolling their eyes and clicking their tongues it wasn't unusual to hear muttered phrases of "they orta be locked up!" or "need a few years in the army mate – disgusting!" And while some of their friends popped purple hearts, not everyone did, not everyone could afford to. The Mods and Rockers riots did little to help their reputation though. Although most of the time they were little more than minor scuffles, the two groups generally avoiding one another. Salocin said he'd seen worst fights in the pubs around Smithfield. Most of the time it was a gathering of like-minded individuals, talking, listening to music, drinking coffee, and generally having a good time before it was back to the grind on Monday. A fish and chip supper followed their day on the beach and, much to Ellie's surprise, Salocin had also got them tickets to see a new up-and-coming band called The Rolling Stones who, along with a few others, were performing live at the Hippodrome. Ellie smiled – what was it her father had called The Rolling Stones when she'd been watching them on Top Of The Pops one evening? 'A bunch of greasy long-haired loafers. Won't amount to much if they keep churning out rubbish like that. I give 'em six months, twelve at the most.'

Laughing at the memory, Ellie gripped the sides of the bath and hauled herself up. She stepped out of the bath and quickly thrust a sanitary towel between her legs to stem the rivulets of blood running down them. She wrapped the bath towel across her shoulders and gently dried herself off. Was it wrong to wish for a time before her daughter was born? Before the stretch marks – that at the moment looked like the little red roads on a map – before the sleepless nights, the nappies, the endless rounds of washing? For a time when her breasts didn't swell and leak? Before her front end, which felt like it would never heal, became one long gash connected to her back end? And back to the days when she wanted Salocin inside her? Right now she couldn't imagine ever wanting him again. Oh, why did she find it so difficult to love her little girl? Why did she resent her so much? Lizzie hadn't asked to be born any more than she had.

Maybe her mother was right; maybe she was a selfish cow? Although quite why her mother called her selfish still eluded Ellie. She'd cooked, cleaned, and looked after her four brothers for as long as she could remember. It was never good enough though. Nothing Ellie did was good enough for her mother. It had been a relief to leave home. Her mother never smiled at her the way she smiled at her brothers. Never hugged her, either, like she did them, always pulling them into the crook of her ample arm. At least, though, her mother noticed her, her father barely knew she existed, treated her more like a skivvy – 'make me a cup of tea, Elle; fetch my paper, Elle; bring me my slippers, Elle; get down the shop and get me some smokes, Elle – showing little to no interest in her otherwise. She remembered a day, a couple of years ago, when one of her father's friends had commented on how beautiful Ellie was, how proud he must be to have such a lovely daughter? It had genuinely thrown her father, his expression, at first, indefinable. And then Ellie spotted it, the twitch of doubt in his eyes, the flicker of absurdity in the twist of his mouth. And it had hurt. Really hurt.

A loud banging on the door made Ellie jump. 'Just a minute,' she called out. She waited for a reply but there was none, just a shuffling along the hallway, followed by the click of a door closing. It was Ernie, the old geezer who lived in the room alongside theirs. She knew it was *him* because she could smell him – a foul mixture of alcohol, urine, sweat and stale tobacco. Sometimes, late at night, she'd hear him crying through the wall. The walls in the old Victorian house were thick, so it was more of a muffled cry, but Ellie found it both disturbing and sad. She'd never heard a man cry before, not even her brothers when her father gave them the belt for some misdemeanour or another. Some of the other residents in the flats said he was an ex P.O.W. who had survived some infamous prison in Singapore only to find, on his return home after liberation, his house gone, flattened in an air raid during the Blitz, and his wife and three children along with it. Still, despite the odious smell that followed him and their landlady's insistence that her tenants keep their respective rooms clean, Ernie was – and rightly so – tolerated. Before Lizzie was born, Ellie was less tolerant, wished Ernie would make more of an effort with his personal hygiene. Lately, since her daughter's arrival, when on some mornings it was all she could do to lift her head off the pillow, she felt that she better understood poor old Ernie.

Standing on tiptoe, Ellie pushed open the small bathroom window to let the steam out. In the hallway she gently tapped on Ernie's door, called out to say she'd finished in the bathroom then went back to her own rooms. Marie, who was rocking Lizzie back and forth in her arms, lifted her finger to her lips, nodding towards the bedroom. 'Get some sleep,' she mouthed. Ellie nodded and headed towards the cramped bedroom. The curtains were still drawn, but the bed had been re-made. She climbed in, closed her eyes, and prayed for sleep to take her.

When Ellie awoke she was aware of the gentle sound of laughter, music too, coming from the radio in the kitchen. She thought she heard a man's voice – Salocin? Surely not. Why wasn't he at work? What time was it and why was her head a little fuzzy? The fog surrounding her thoughts lifted. She remembered a visit from the doctor, a quick examination, his stern telling off for not speaking up about her nether regions. 'You have an infection,' he said, his accent posh, his tone clipped. He prescribed antibiotics plus a month's supply of 'mother's little helpers'. Ellie wasn't keen but Marie said they would help. 'Better than electric shock treatment,' she said.

Marie had made her soup, chicken; the bowl was still on the bedside dresser, empty. She'd eaten the lot and must have fallen asleep again. Anxious, she looked towards the window, light still crept in through the gaps in the curtains but it was summer, it didn't get dark until late so she had no idea what time it was. Panicking, she scrambled out of bed. She must have been asleep for hours? What would Salocin think? She imagined her mother finding out, recoiling at the shame of it. And what about Lizzie, didn't she need feeding? She couldn't hear her crying. She stuffed her feet into the slippers by her bed, scraped her hair back with a hairband and slipped her dressing gown on, heading towards the other room where the smell of something cooking hit her flaring nostrils. It smelt good. Really good. For the first time in weeks her mouth watered and her hollow stomach grumbled. She actually had an appetite. Her headache had lifted, too.

Ellie immediately noticed an improvement down below as she walked. She could hear Salocin and Marie talking, the radio playing quietly in the background – The Beatles 'With a Little Help From My Friends'. She wandered over to the pram in the corner of the room, peered in. Lizzie, with her fat rosy cheeks, a look of peaceful contentment on her face, was sound asleep. Ellie had hoped she'd feel something – something maternal – but the overriding feeling at seeing her daughter sleeping was one of relief. As she approached the kitchenette area, she noticed how tidy the room was, Salocin sitting at the table, a steaming mug of hot tea in his hand, while Marie busied herself by the cooker. They were laughing and joking, and for the briefest of moments Ellie felt a flash of jealousy surge through her. It didn't last, and Salocin, who had been about to take a sip from his mug, quickly rose to his feet to greet her, his hug as reassuring as the smile from her friend.

'Hey, sleepy,' he said, smiling, studying her face. 'You look the best I've seen you in weeks.'

Marie had been busy cooking, cleaning, feeding and changing Lizzie. She'd even managed to take her out for a walk in the pram and on top of all that she'd also made a shepherd's pie and an apple crumble. 'And I've written the instructions for making up bottles of formula,' she said, slipping into her coat, and pointing to a sheet of notepaper on the table. Marie hugged her best friend and whispered something in her ear. Something familiar. Something she had said to her earlier,

'You'll be fine,

In time,

And I'll be right behind you.'

And with a kiss and a wave Marie was gone.

Like a mantra, Ellie repeated the words, quietly to herself, *You'll be fine, in time, and I'll be right behind you.*

Good to her word, Marie turned up again the following morning. And the one after that, and the one after that. It took some time but just as Marie had predicted, Lizzie settled, Ellie felt better and, much to her astonishment, Ellie finally found herself falling in love with her small daughter.

chapter 16

Boxing Day
PRESENT DAY – LATE EVENING

LIZZIE

Cassie leans in and kisses my cheek. 'See you later, Mum,' she says, hovering by the front door with Luke. 'We're going to The George. Why don't you and Si, and Uncle Sean and Nat join us later?'

I think of Connor's face earlier, smile and tell her I'll think about it. A gust of icy wind rattles the letter-box, slips past my face into the hallway. I shiver; watch them disappear down the drive. 'Be careful,' I shout after them. 'It's a cold one tonight.' I can just about make out Cassie's hand as she throws it up and waves before I quickly close the door again. I shake my head and laugh, remembering a time, not so many years ago, when Cassie, in the throes of her angst-ridden teenage years, wouldn't have been seen dead with me in public. How times have changed.

However, less than an hour later, Cassie, much like her former teenage self, bursts back through the same front door in floods of tears.

'What is it? What's wrong?' I shout, rushing into the hallway, to be met by her retreating back as she storms up the stairs. Luke, who is hovering close by, has a bloody nose and another bruised eye to match the one Eustace gave him a couple of days ago. 'Got into a punch up,' he says, holding a blood-soaked, rapidly disintegrating tissue beneath his nose.

'I can see that.' I beckon him into the kitchen and grab some

Christmas napkins sporting a rather jolly, rosy-cheeked Santa design. 'Here.' I thrust them into his hands and I pull out a chair and tell him to take a seat, then rummage around for a carrier bag to dispose of the used bloody tissue. 'What on earth happened?'

Luke holds several napkins under his nose, his blood seeping through, obliterating all traces of the whimsical Father Christmas face. 'It was that dickhead Max Kray,' he replies. 'You remember? In Connor's year at school? Him and his older brother, Barry. Fucking imbeciles. Just like the rest of their imbecilic family.' He slams his fist on the table, making me jump. 'Sorry.' He screws the napkin he's holding, now limp and crimson, into a ball and chucks it into the carrier bag. I pass him another clean one and he looks at me. 'Thanks,' he says, his jaw twitching. 'Sorry about all this.'

I notice a vein in his neck throbbing. He's clearly furious. I'm not used to seeing Luke like this.

'They were drunk,' he continues. 'Kept pointing at Cassie and chanting, "who's the killer, who's the killer?" Fucking idiots. Hasn't she been through enough already!'

I imagine the scenario, see Cassie's face, swallow the rage pushing against my chest. Scarlet droplets of blood slip through Luke's fingers and splash onto the kitchen table. 'Sorry,' he says again, as I grab a couple more napkins and pass them to him. 'I asked them to give it a rest. We even moved to the other end of the pub but of course, they followed us. Kept mouthing off, especially Max. So...'

'Yes?'

'I swung for him.'

My eyes widen in surprise, staring at his bruised and battered face. 'Oh Luke... and now look at your poor face. Haven't you got a big gig to perform on New Year's Eve?'

He nods. 'Yep, sure have. And the sooner we get out of this

shitty little town and back to London, the better. I've always hated it here,' he adds.

I recoil a little; feel unjustifiably slighted because I still live here, still like it here. I can see the appeal of the anonymity of the city though.

I hear a sound in the doorway.

'Are they still there?' I swing round, see Simon and Sean standing behind us. 'Max and Barry, I mean?' Sean continues. 'Are they still at the pub?'

Luke shrugs, says he isn't sure. 'The bouncers got involved. We were all told to leave. Max came off worse than me though. And Barry didn't look much better, especially after Robbo, Connor's friend, had finished with him.'

'Connor was there?' I ask.

Luke nods. 'Yeah – him and his mates.'

Panic grips me. I push my chair back, stand up. 'Is he hurt too?' I look round, half expecting to see him walk through the door, a bloody mirror image of Luke. 'Where is he?'

Luke assures me Connor is fine, that after Robbo got stuck into Barry, Max and Barry legged it. Luke grins. 'Robbo surprised us all, not just Max and Barry. I always thought he was a dopey kid, wouldn't harm a fly.'

'Doesn't his Dad knock him and his mum around?' Simon is looking down at his phone, stabbing the screen with his finger.

I nod, wonder if the poor little sod just snapped, had enough. 'So, where is Connor now?'

'He's not answering his phone,' Simon says. 'It's going straight to voicemail.'

Luke assures me he's pretty sure they all went back to Jake's house.

'But... but... What if they go back to the pub? And those lads do too? You know how these things can escalate? Get out of hand. God knows we've seen enough of those true-life crime programmes that show what can happen when tempers are frayed.'

'Already on it,' Sean replies, as he and Simon disappear into the hallway.

I follow them, as does Luke. 'Should I come too?' I ask, remembering Connor's earlier comments about not being there for him.

Simon looks at me, frowns. 'You look knackered, Lizzie. Stay here. I've got my phone.' He holds it up. 'I'll call you if there's a problem.' He and Sean grab their coats hanging by the stairs.

I step forward, place a hand on his arm, wanting him to hold me. He does, but he also hesitates. It's barely noticeable, except to me, of course, but his body feels stiff, unyielding. He quickly steps away again and with a slam of the front door, Simon and my brother are gone.

Natasha wanders up behind me, stares at the front door. 'Do you think we should follow them?' she asks, before glancing at Luke. 'Ooh, nasty.' She arches an eyebrow.

I sigh, exhausted. 'Yes. I suppose we should. Give me a sec, though, will you.' I head towards the stairs. 'I want to get a warmer coat.' It's not strictly true, although I make a point of grabbing my faithful old Superdry coat. It's heavy to wear, but it's also a windbreaker so it's warm, has a big furry hood too. The main reason though, is to get my shit together, splash my face with water, take a minute to make myself look... presentable... normal. I feel sick, dizzy. Can't make out if it's the drink... or something else?

Natasha asks Luke if he can keep an eye on Summer. 'She's watching TV in the living room,' she says.

Luke agrees but insists we don't need to go. Says he's pretty sure there won't be any more trouble tonight. I tell him I could do with the fresh air, anyway.

I point upwards. 'Should I check on Cassie before I go?'

Luke shakes his head. 'I'll do it,' he says.

It's bitter outside so I'm glad of my coat but my face is stinging by the time we arrive at the pub. Natasha heaves the door open and ushers me forward with her hand. 'Ladies first,' she says laughing.

I step forward, overwhelmed by the sweet aroma of beer, the warm air on my face, blasting my skin like a hairdryer. It's busier than I thought it would be. There are no empty tables, all of them filled with rosy-faced groups of people, their charged conversations competing with the loud Christmas music playing in the background – which at the moment happens to be Wham's "Last Christmas". It's good spirited-chatter, though, nothing sinister or untoward; no raised voices or fists.

Several individuals I recognise, nod or put a hand up, while others exchange furtive glances with one another, then look away. Natasha points to the bar where Sean, sipping on a fresh, frothy-topped pint of beer, is chatting to a couple of blokes standing next to him. No sign of Simon. I look around – then spot him. My heart sinks and my breath quickens. Tucked away in a corner of the room, although still within sight of Sean, he is sitting at a table opposite a young woman. She throws her head back, laughs, turns to the side and flicks her long blonde hair. She's younger than me. Twenty years, at least. Simon, eyebrow arched, sipping his pint, appears captivated by the young woman. My head spins. I feel nauseous, bile rising from my stomach into my throat as I replay Connor's earlier comment about the IndieKnot gig? What are they all hiding? Although, when it comes to hiding things, I'm one to talk. The room spins. I can't do this right now. I have far too much other shit to deal with.

I need to get away. Fast.

A tap on the shoulder makes me jump. I spin round. Have trouble focussing. It's Natasha, talking with someone she introduces as Belinda – or did she say Linda? – who says she got my book for Christmas; loves it. She asks me if I'll sign it at some point. She seems nice, talking with a hint of northern vowels in her vernacular, and is a little plump, has frizzy short hair, a kind, wise face. I thank her; tell her I'd be more than happy to sign her book. I even suggest we meet for coffee – *what the fuck am I doing?* – and ask her to message me on Facebook. At least, I think that's what I say. My voice has receded to a faint echo so it's hard to tell. She smiles and I wonder if I'm drunk or going mad.

I glance across at Simon again. Is he frowning or just engrossed in what the young woman opposite him is saying? I tell Belinda, Linda, whatever her name is that it was lovely to meet her but I have to go, need some fresh air. I turn on my heel and leave, vaguely aware Natasha is behind me. Cold air hits me in the face, like a splash of ice-cold water. I clutch my chest, feel it bubble with pain, recent days' events pressing down on me with all the weight of a century. I think of Dad, Cassie, Black, Uncle Teddy and Aunt Marie.

Am I unravelling, having a breakdown?

Natasha calls me. She does her best to keep up with me, like a chastised child following an angry parent. 'Lizzie,' she shouts again. 'For god sake slow down, will you? What's wrong?'

'Didn't you see him?' I call across my shoulder.

'Who?'

'Simon. Sitting with that... that woman.'

Breathless, Natasha is now beside me. She looks bemused. 'Perhaps he knows her? I'm sure there's an innocent enough explanation. He's hardly going to shit on his own doorstep, is he? Especially with Sean there.'

She has a point. Then again, Sean may be my brother, but he is also just a man. Besides, who knows what bullshit Simon may have fed him? Perhaps my brother feels sorry for Simon, understands his need to find comfort in another woman?

'Look, let's go back. Find out, eh?' Natasha continues.

I stop. Turn around. Look at her. 'You go back if you like. I'm going home.'

I march home, swinging my arms, left, right, left, right. Anger keeps me warm but fatigue overwhelms me as I quietly let myself in through the front door. Natasha is no longer behind me. Weary, I pull my coat off, linger in the hallway.

Connor, the reason I went to the pub, is home. But in my grief, my anger, I realise I haven't even given him a second thought. I can hear him talking to Cassie and Luke in the living room. They haven't heard me come in so I hover by the door, listen to their conversation. Connor says he needs to talk, that he knows something that is fucking with his head.

'I didn't want to load it onto you, sis, but I don't know who else to talk to about it. And I just can't keep it to myself anymore.' He explains how Simon and Sean never made it to the IndieKnot gig, and how they swore him to secrecy about that. 'Said I wasn't to mention it to anyone. Especially Mum.'

'Ok-ay.' I hear Cassie reply. 'So, what exactly are you saying?'

'Don't you see? They didn't make it to the IndieKnot gig, but they were in London on the same day Hunter Black died. And, well, I can't help wondering if… you know, Simon and Sean had something to do with it?'

I hear Cassie gasp. 'Surely not?'

Dread hits the pit of my hollow stomach. *Not possible*, I tell myself. They could have been going to meet someone else though? A woman? Maybe? The one Simon is talking to in the pub? Common sense – or what little I appear to have left – screams at the absurdity of such a thought. Surely Sean, my own brother, wouldn't be part of something he knows would hurt me? I shake my head; I'm being ridiculous. Then again, nothing surprises me anymore. Deflated and exhausted, I feel as if I'm in some kind of surreal movie, my sleep-deprived brain longing for oblivion. I slip my shoes off and creep upstairs, heading for the sanctuary of my bed.

I think of Simon. All the years we've been together, all the tough times we've gone through, and the good. All his annoying habits like when he walks into a room, frowning because he's lost something. 'Have you seen my...' he'll say, but you can tell by the tone of his voice, it's an accusation not a question, dwindling to a mumbled, 'Oh. There it is,' when he finds what it is he's looking for, usually where *he* left it. Or how he coughs all the time to prove he's got one, or leaves his socks on the living room floor instead of putting them in the wash basket, or how he sniffs the air asking, 'Can you smell weed?' every time we go for a walk. Fucking annoying, but all part of him, nonetheless. Habits I'd miss if... if he left me. Then again. Fuck him if he does.

I'll survive. I did before – when Scott cheated then left the kids and me – so I can do it again. If I have to. But I'd rather not. Then again, Simon may just leave me anyway, when he finds out what I've been keeping from him. I suddenly feel very sad as though I'm the deceitful one. I realise I should have shared more with him. Isn't that what you're supposed to do with those you love? Dad springs to mind – perhaps if he and Mum had been honest, shared more about their past with me, I wouldn't be in this fucking mess.

I step into the small en-suite in our bedroom, look at my blotchy, red face in the mirror, wonder who the haggard woman staring back at me is. Suddenly fatigue hits with the full force of a head-on car collision. I'm too wired to sleep though, so I reach for the sleeping tablets tucked away in the back of the cupboard. The question is, do I take one or two tablets as prescribed – or the whole fucking packet?

Chucking my clothes on the floor, I slip under the duvet,

welcome the darkness like an old friend. I think of the words
Mum always says to me in times of trouble, words I now know
my Aunt Marie said to her,

'You'll be fine,

In time,

And I'll be right behind you.'

At less than six months old, I don't remember my first
Christmas, but from what Mum has told me about the dingy flat
she and Dad first lived in, I try my best to imagine it.

Chapter 17

LONDON 1965

SALOCIN

A patchwork quilt of autumnal leaves in September and October soon replaced the scorched earth of July and August, and was quickly followed by a blanket of snow in November and December.

As each month passed Salocin noticed a gradual change in Ellie. Lizzie too, was less fractious. She still cried, of course, what baby didn't? But she was thriving, and Ellie, slowly but surely, was morphing back into someone familiar, someone much more like her old self. Salocin knew he couldn't take anything for granted. Ellie's depression had scared him. He didn't tell her but he kept having a reoccurring nightmare where Lizzie was taken into care and Ellie dragged off to an asylum.

Marie, who still popped by when she could, said Ellie needed fresh air and rest. 'And make sure she eats,' she added. 'It's important to eat well. At least one square meal a day, anyway.'

Salocin promised to do his best. Sometimes, when he came in from work, knackered, he would look at Ellie's face, know it had been a bad day, and take Lizzie to the local park. She couldn't do much, she was still too little, so he mostly sat her on his knee and together they'd watch the other kids. Sometimes, if it wasn't damp, they'd sit on the grass among amidst carpet of leaves that, like confetti, fell from the surrounding trees. Lizzie, huge eyes blinking skywards, tiny fists opening and closing, squealed with delight at the simple wonder of it all. Ellie would cook while they were out, so it wasn't a proper break, but at least it gave her some time alone. And every weekend Salocin made sure they went out – as a family.

They couldn't afford much so they kept it simple: trips to the local park, a bus ride to Regent's Park. Most of the time it was the three of them but sometimes Teddy and Marie joined them. Now and again, they'd head to Spitalfields; take a stroll down Petticoat Lane ('The Lane', locals called it), which was always busy, always heaving. A market site for centuries, it was known as Hogs Lane during Tudor Times, later changed to Petticoat Lane during the 17th century. Its past, like some of its residents, was infamous and became a well-known spot for fences, many of whom would buy stolen goods from criminals before selling them on in their shops or stalls. Thus, due to some of its dubious activities, an old fable still lingered with the locals, one that suggested when entering the market, there were those deft handed enough to steal your petticoat at one end and sell it back to you at the other. At other times, Salocin would take Ellie and Lizzie down The Waste, the market on Kingsland Road a stone's throw from Dalston Junction. You name it and The Waste probably had it. Salocin relayed a story about the time, as boys, he and Teddy had made their own push-bike with parts they'd swapped with friends or scrounged from The Waste, including cow-horn handlebars and fixed rear wheels. 'Which was all good fun,' Salocin said, 'but it made riding the thing hard bleedin' work. You couldn't freewheel so the only way to keep moving was to keep peddling.'

Salocin preferred their trips to Regent's Park. Said he felt a connection, an affinity with the place. Maybe it was the wide-open spaces, the magnificent trees, he couldn't rightly say, but whatever it was, it gave him a sense of feeling grounded. He and Ellie had often wandered around the park, hand in hand, during their brief courtship. Salocin had shown her, with all the enthusiasm of an excited schoolboy, the little group of ancient fossilised tree trunks close to the waterfall in Queen Mary's Gardens, first shown to him as a boy by his father. 'Blink and you'd miss 'em,' Salocin had said. 'Millions of years old, they are.' Ellie had smiled, charmed by his childish gusto.

He had also shown her one of his favourite trees in the park, the Indian bean tree, close to Clarence Bridge on the boating lake. It was huge, with a sloping trunk and gnarly branches. Salocin said if you caught it in the right light, dusk on a typical winter's day was best, the tree had an almost gothic appeal. However come July, with its purple flecked, white and yellow blossom, it looked different, quite beautiful.

Ellie said she preferred the wide-open space of Cumberland Green on the eastern side of the park, near Holborn and St Pancras, which, close to a bend in the path near St Katherine's Gate, was also the place where two magnificent ash trees stood. She also liked the blue Atlas cedar near the Open Air Theatre. It reminded her of Christmas, especially when the branches were dusted with snow; brought to mind Charles Dickens's *A Christmas Carol*, she said.

If the weather was good, they'd take a blanket and a picnic: cheese and pickle sandwiches, ripe tomatoes, plump strawberries, a thermos of tea. Sometimes Lizzie would sleep; sometimes she would kick and wave her arms and legs, sporting bracelets of baby fat on each ankle, each wrist. Ellie too, at times, would drop off, if she'd had a difficult night with Lizzie. Sometimes they talked, or they listened to music on the small transistor radio they took with them. They liked to people watch, too. Salocin, a storyteller, would make up elaborate stories about the people they observed, their interesting jobs, places they lived, people they knew. Sometimes the stories he told were about themselves, their future, dreams of a better life, and about how one day they hoped to buy and own their own home. One with a garage for the car they'd also buy and a garden for Lizzie to play in.

Talk of more children never came up, neither one having the courage to broach the subject. Salocin wanted more. A son would be nice although he'd love another little girl. Ellie's postnatal depression had blindsided him, though – blindsided them both, leaving them cautious. Instead they talked about the news, the raging Vietnam War, the protests about it in London and America; the official opening of the Post Office Tower; the arrests of a stock clerk from Cheshire, named Ian Brady, and his girlfriend, Myra Hindley, on suspicion of the shocking murders of three children, their little bodies found buried on Saddleworth Moor; unfortunately, the announcement, in November, about the abolition of the death penalty for murder meant the child killers, referred to as the "Moors Murderers" would escape the hangman's rope.

'And what a bleedin' cryin' shame that was,' Mickey had said when they had listened to the news on the radio. Everyone at the yard agreed.

Now and again Ellie asked Salocin about work although he always did his best to put her off the subject, lest she caught wind of how isolated he felt. He didn't want to worry her, not now she was getting better. He spent most of his time sorting, grading and separating deliveries via forty gallon metal drums with their tops cut off: brass, copper, tin, zinc, gunmetal; you name it and Salocin sorted it. If only he was able to turn base metals into gold - like his namesake spelled backwards, Nicolas Flamel was alleged to have done – he and Ellie would be laughing. He didn't mind the graft, though, was never one to shy away from a bit of hard work, but it was becoming tedious. The same old thing day in, day out. No better, in fact, than the apprenticeship he had got himself fired from.

'The mornings pass quickly enough,' he told Ellie. 'There's

always a radio playing too, which helps pass the time of day. And tea, of course, to keep us all going. Liquid gold, Mickey calls it, what the entire British Empire was built on, he reckons. Well, that and slavery and oppression.'

The only problem was Salocin spent most of his time working with just one bloke, Kenny Varndale, nicknamed "hard as nails" so called because, come rain or shine, he only ever wore a tee shirt, the top half of his overalls always folded down and tied at the waist. An ex-Navy man, in his late thirties, Kenny wasn't tall, five foot six at the most, but with a bull neck and thickset jaw he was built, as his father liked to say, like a brick shithouse. Apparently he'd got into a few scrapes after leaving the Navy, done a bit of porridge, but he was straight now, happy to put his fighting years behind him and do an honest day's work for an honest day's pay. However, if push came to shove, he wasn't averse to the odd punch up, especially if a customer got lively and things got out of hand, which invariably they did if there was a disagreement over money. It didn't happen often though, and more often than not Mickey used the gift of the gab to smooth things over but when that didn't work, Kenny's presence was usually intimidation enough.

Kenny was nice enough, though, always whistling, or singing along to the radio, happy to answer any questions Salocin had, show him the ropes like Mickey asked. However, he was also a man of few words, kept himself to himself. It also felt as though Mickey was purposely keeping Salocin away from the other, more interesting aspects of the business, not to mention the other workers. They'd all made their introductions when he first started at the yard, but since then, unless it was tea break, their paths rarely crossed. Why? Salocin couldn't say.

There were other things too. Things that made little sense. Like the fact that every other week there seemed to be a security firm fitting a new alarm system at the yard, and the furtive glances everyone exchanged with one another whenever he asked why. Or the way the atmosphere crackled whenever the drivers from Babcock's – the smelters – turned up, and how Kenny disappeared, left Salocin to it, when they had a lot of deliveries at the weighbridge and Mickey said they needed his help with Joey.

Who the fuck was this illusive Joey they kept talking about, anyway? Every time someone mentioned his name it always brought to mind the only Joey he'd ever known – his Aunt Audrey's swearing budgie. The bright yellow cussing bird always spouted a few select phrases whenever someone entered the room: 'who's a pretty boy then,' and 'gurcha ya cowson,' or 'shoot the fucking Gerries,' and 'ello darling, show us ya jugs.' Salocin's Uncle Alfred swore blind it wasn't him instructing the adored little Joey in the art of talking in such a colourful fashion. He blamed it on the radio, the television, said it was most likely the neighbours' kids who you could sometimes hear blaspheming through the thinly insulated walls of their high-rise flat. Salocin's Aunt Audrey knew better though, scowled and scolded them both whenever Joey spoke.

Salocin was grateful for the job, and for all the times Mickey had helped him out – both financially and with his advice, generous to a fault in both areas – but Salocin was also restless. He wanted more out of life, and he needed more for his family – he was, after all, their provider. He'd asked Mickey to consider teaching him how to use the hydraulic crusher and work the weighbridge with the others. Mickey said he'd think about it and Salocin hoped he didn't take too long because if things didn't change soon, he'd decided, he would have to look elsewhere for work.

In December, determined to give his girls the best Christmas possible, Salocin sold his beloved Vespa, his intention being to use some of the money to buy a few extras, and put down a deposit on a ring – an engagement ring, like he'd promised Ellie. However, unbeknown to Ellie, Salocin, who had been feeling a little flush after receiving payment for his beloved bike, committed the cardinal sin of flashing his cash in the pub. Not on purpose mind; he'd got more for the scooter than he hoped for, and to celebrate he'd been treating himself to a swift half before heading to the jewellers. Stupidly he pulled the roll of cash from his back pocket to pay, and later, after patting himself down outside the jewellers shop window, red-faced, ashamed and angry, he realised his pocket had been picked.

So, despite his best intentions, it was a frugal Christmas, after all. Martha kindly invited the threesome to join her and Wilf for Christmas Day dinner, which they gratefully accepted, while Teddy, much to Martha's annoyance, had dinner with Marie and her family. They had chicken with all the trimmings followed by one of Martha's homemade Christmas puddings, which she poured brandy over and Wilf set fire to. Ellie's first mouthful found her the lucky sixpence, which she promptly washed and popped into her purse. After the Queen's speech, Salocin, Ellie and Lizzie made their way home, joined later in the evening by Teddy and Marie. Lizzie, whose eyes still lit up every time Marie entered the room, revelled in the extra attention given her by both Mee Mee (Lizzie's pronunciation) and Uncle Teddy. Hearts and bellies full, Ellie smiled. They may be poor but she was richer in love than she'd ever been.

As the evening sky faded, streaks of pink and amber replaced by deep shades of blue, Lizzie sleeping in the crook of Mee Mee's arm, all of them tipsy from the bottle of wine they shared – Mateus Rose, the height of sophistication, according to Marie – they reminisced about their childhoods. Teddy reminded Salocin about the time, thanks to his deliberate attempt to cause an explosion, Salocin almost blew the entire ceiling clean off the chemistry lab at school, and how, in order to teach him a lesson, and serve as a warning to everyone else, he was hauled up in assembly by the headmaster, and given the cane for his prank. Teddy then grabbed the beautiful new guitar he'd brought with him – his Christmas gift from Marie, which she was having to pay off in instalments – and, much to Lizzie's gummy, dribbling delight, they all indulged in a bit of a sing-song.

Afterwards, in front of the people he loved the most, Teddy, who had still not given Marie her gift, pulled a small box from his pocket, got down on one knee and asked her to marry him. With shaking hands, Marie took the tiny green box, complete with a gold clasp and intricate edging, and opened it. It creaked like an old door, and the ring, a beautiful solitaire diamond, cast brilliant sparks of silver about the room, like little pockets of sunshine glistening on water.

'Oh, my gawd! It's... it's beautiful, Teddy,' Marie squealed as he placed the ring on her finger. 'And it fits. It only bleedin' fits, El!' she gasped, turning to her friend for approval.

Ellie, her vision blurred, looked at her best friend and smiled. She couldn't be happier for her best friend, but still felt her throat constrict and hot tears prick the back of her eyes. She hated herself for the twinge of jealousy that surged through her body like a tiny jolt of electricity. She glanced at her own left hand and stared at the lone gold band she wore on her ring finger. She'd love an engagement ring like Marie's.

'I hope they're bleedin' happy tears,' Marie said, as she watched a lone tear slide down her friend's face.

Ellie took Marie's hand in hers, studied the ring that twinkled as brightly as the December stars she'd wished on late last night. 'It's beautiful, Marie,' she said. 'Just like you.' Ellie told herself to count her blessings: a man that loved her, a little girl who adored her, a roof over her head, food in her belly and, friends, good friends. A ring wasn't a priority.

The flash of disappointment that had flickered across his wife's eyes wasn't lost on Salocin. He glanced around the four dingy walls he and Ellie called home, the tiny kitchenette in one corner, the pathetic little Christmas tree in the other. Ellie had done her best to make it feel homely, had even made and hung some coloured paper chains from the walls to inject a bit of colour, a bit of Christmas cheer, into the place. But it wasn't good enough. Underneath the bright cushions, the throw that covered the threadbare sofa, the jam jars that contained sprigs of holly, and the old wine bottles, left over from special occasions, that housed half melted candles, it was nothing more than a grubby bedsit. Salocin had done his best, too, but *his* best wasn't good enough. He'd let Ellie down and he'd let Lizzie down. Now, more than ever, he knew that.

Salocin rallied and shook his brother's hand and kissed the flushed cheek of his sister-in-law to be.

'Let's really push the boat out.' Ellie produced a bottle of Blue Nun she had hidden at the back of the kitchen cupboard. 'I was saving it,' she said, wrinkling her nose, staring at Salocin. 'For New Year's Eve. May as well have it now though, eh?'

Salocin swallowed the shame lodged in his throat, pulled Ellie towards him and kissed her.

'Ah, leave it out you two, will yer,' Teddy shouted behind them.

'I love you, Elle,' Salocin whispered. 'I promise, this time next year, things will be different. Better. Much better.'

Ellie smiled, cupping her hand around her husband's chin. 'Don't you realise? They already are better. Everything got better the day I met you.'

Salocin took Ellie's hand and kissed it. Somehow, soon, he'd give his wife and daughter the life they deserved.

He didn't know how yet? *Time will tell*, he whispered to himself.

Time will tell.

Their frugal Christmas at the end of 1965 came and went, and although they barely had two pennies to rub together, Salocin had set aside enough for him and Ellie to spend a couple of hours seeing in the New Year down the Nag's Head. As pubs go, it was as rough and ready as you like but Wilf and Martha, and Teddy and Marie – if they could make it back in time from the West End show they had tickets for – were going. It was within walking distance too, which meant they wouldn't be too far away from Lizzie. Mrs Taylor, Doris, who lived in the flat below, agreed to watch Lizzie in exchange for Salocin's help to carry out a few much-needed repairs.

As it happened, though, Lizzie wouldn't settle.

'Think she's got wind,' Doris said, handing Lizzie back to Ellie. 'I'm sorry. But I can't nurse a screaming baby all night.' Doris was a short, stocky woman with frizzy grey hair, a squashed nose and stumpy arms and legs. She reminded Salocin of a bulldog, especially when she shook her head, causing the folds around her mouth to flap back and forth.

Ellie insisted Salocin go to the pub on his own. 'We'll be fine,' she said, holding their crying daughter, like she'd done on many previous occasions, over her shoulder, patting her back. 'What's the point in us both staying in?'

Salocin went, if only to appease Ellie who seemed more annoyed than pleased when he suggested they all stay in together. 'For god sake, Salocin, I'm better now,' she snapped. 'Please stop looking at me like that.'

'Like what?'

'Like I'm made of glass. Like I can't cope, can't manage. Like if I'm pushed too far, I'll shatter into a million tiny pieces. Like you're afraid of what I'm gonna do if we're…' She nodded at their still crying daughter '...left on our own for too long. It's suffocating.'

Stunned, Salocin turned on his heel and left in a pungent cloud of Old Spice – his Christmas present from Ellie – and made his way to the pub. He didn't enjoy it. Still early, the place was heaving by the time he arrived. Someone, who had clearly had too much pop, was throwing up outside and towards the back of the room there seemed to be a bit of a punch up going on. It took forever to get served, too, and the beer tasted flat, watered down.

'What's the matter with you?' Martha asked, sipping on her gin and orange. 'You got a face as long as a kite.'

That was true, but Ellie's words stung; wounded him. He was only looking out for her, wasn't he? So what if he wanted to see the New Year in with his wife and daughter. What was wrong with that?

'Don't feel too well,' Salocin lied, rubbing his belly. Necking his pint he stood up, and much to his mother's disappointment, left.

'What about Auld Lang Syne?' he heard her call behind him.

Salocin waved his hand dismissively. 'Happy New Year, Mum,' he shouted. But his words were lost, carried away on a sea of people having a good time.

He walked round the block a few times to clear his head. It was cold out, the pavements glistening, slick from a previous flurry of snow that hadn't settled. By the time he got back to the flat Lizzie was sleeping and Ellie, her legs folded underneath her, was dozing in front of a flickering TV screen, a plate containing a half-eaten slice of Christmas cake sitting lopsided beside her. Salocin woke her with a kiss and a half drunk bottle of wine he'd snatched from a table when no one was looking as he left the pub.

'You're home,' Ellie exclaimed. Unlike earlier, she sounded pleased.

'What yer watching?' He nodded towards the TV, slipping his coat off.

Ellie blinked lazily, frowning at the screen. Mick Jagger was singing. 'I think it's The New Year Starts Here,' she replied, yawning. 'I must have dozed off. The Avengers were on earlier. It was good. Think you would have enjoyed it.' She bit her lip, tucked a loose strand of hair behind her ear and looked down. 'Sorry about before,' she mumbled. 'I was being a bitch. Over-sensitive. I love that you care. But I don't want you to think that *I* don't. About Lizzie, I mean. Because, I know that's how it looked… when she was born.' Head still bowed, elbows now on her knees, her trembling fingers basket weaved together, Ellie trailed off. A fat sob took them both by surprise and Salocin realised his wife was crying. 'I'd never hurt Lizzie, you know?' she whispered. 'Never.'

'Of course you wouldn't.' Salocin put his hand under her chin and lifted it so their eyes met. 'I want you, Ellie. And Lizzie. I love being with you both. But you deserve better than this… this…' He looked up gesturing with his hands, his eyes darting left to right about the darkened room, '…this shit hole.'

Ellie's face crumpled; confused she pulled away from Salocin. 'I don't understand. What are you saying? Are you leaving me? And Lizzie?'

Now it was Salocin's turn to look confused. 'No! Of course not. Unless… you want me to?'

'Of course I don't.'

'Then what the hell are you talking about?' There was noticeable relief in Salocin's voice.

'Well, what the hell are *you* talking about?'

'I'm saying I love you, Elle. And I wanna do right by you.'

'Then shut the fuck up and kiss me, you silly fool.'

For once Lizzie slept peacefully that night, and with the TV turned down low, Salocin and Ellie snuggled up on the sofa, taking it in turns to swig from the half-finished, stolen bottle of wine. Later, lying next to Ellie in bed, her mouth partly open, the gentle rise and fall of her chest telling him his wife was sleeping soundly for a change, Salocin found he could not drift off. Ellie had admitted, after he coaxed it out of her, that she hated the flat. Couldn't stand the thought of spending another year there. She pleaded with him, more with her eyes – doleful and tearful – than with actual words, to please get them away. Then they had kissed – more passionately than they had in a long time – before falling into bed, and quite literally seeing the New Year in with a bang! They did it properly too, went all the way, which they hadn't done since before Lizzie was born. And this time it was safe. Ellie had persuaded Doctor Chapman to prescribe her the contraceptive pill, which, if he was honest, was as much of a relief to Salocin as it was to Ellie. They could barely afford to live as it was, without having another mouth to feed. Afterwards, hot and sweaty, entangled in one another's legs and arms, Salocin had stroked the soft down of Ellie's cheek, kissed the tip of her nose and promised her, as he had promised himself at Christmas, that by this time next year things would be different, better. Now though, as Ellie slept, and Salocin lay watching the shadows on the ceiling, a residual sadness encasing him, he wondered just how the fuck he was going to make that happen.

Chapter 18

December 27th
PRESENT DAY — EARLY MORNING

DI KATE STEWART

DI Kate Stewart sits behind her desk with her head in her hands. There's a knock on the door. She looks up to see DS York hovering behind the glass panel. Wearily she puts her hand out and beckons. 'Come in, Noor.'

'You, err, got a minute, boss?' He nods behind him towards his desk.

'Am I going to like it?'

'Yeah. I think so.'

She sighs. 'Okay, give me a sec.'

'Rightio, boss.' The glass in the door rattles as he leaves again and closes it behind him.

Kat raises her eyes to the ceiling. *Please god let it be something.* She had a phone call from her DS, Bob Jessup, earlier this morning. He had asked to see her, wanted an update on how the investigation is going. Unfortunately, there is nothing new to report. The investigation into the death of Hunter Black is proving to be a logistical nightmare, not least because as far as suspects are concerned they aren't short of a few. The pathologist's report states Black died from a broken neck, most likely sustained by a fall from the top of the stairs. The single blow found on the back of his head, was also undoubtedly caused when his head impacted with the second from bottom step. Whether he fell though, or was pushed, is uncertain. Black's family insist it is the latter, and because of their wealth, their connections, the Home Office are pushing for answers. This sickens DI Stewart a little. Had it been some unfortunate soul from, say, the Tulse Hill area, or the Stonebridge estate, the case would have been opened and closed within a few hours, a day tops. Verdict: accidental death.

Most of the individuals interviewed have alibis, and so far they all check out. Several witnesses have offered information about sightings of people close by or near the property on the day in question, which, with the help of CCTV, they're trying to track down. But it's painfully slow, which, in turn, adds to the tension at home. Hannah still isn't speaking to her.

'You know the drill, Kat. That lot,' Bob, had said, pointing upwards, 'want an arrest. Sooner rather than later.'

'I'm doing my best, sir,' Kat had replied.

'I know you are. Just keep me informed.'

Kat makes her way over to DS York's desk. 'What have you got then, Noor?'

DS York offers his boss a seat, points to a screen with some frozen CCTV footage of an individual standing outside Black's house on the day of his demise.

Kat squints at the screen. 'I'm surprised Black didn't sell up and move when the rape allegations against him came to light. I half expected to find him residing at some place with gated security, or an apartment like those in Chelsea Harbour with a secure, underground car park and a lift that takes you straight to your apartment. Keep the riff-raff out, so to speak.'

York shrugs his shoulders. 'Think he "liked" – he makes quotation marks with his fingers – the riff raff. Comes across as an arrogant individual, especially in some TV interviews I've watched. Seems like he had a lot of support too, despite the allegations. So perhaps he didn't feel threatened?'

Kat frowns. 'Hmm... perhaps not. Anyway, who's this?'

'Okay.' York fast forwards the footage then stops it again. 'Watch this...' They watch the individual standing outside Black's house, staring, who is then approached by another, slightly bigger individual. Both are male. They appear to be talking to one another and although there is no sound it quickly becomes apparent, given the wild hand waving and gesturing, they are shouting. The smaller of the two points to Black's house then pushes the bigger individual. Several minutes later they are fighting, rolling around on the floor. This goes on for some time before they seem to run out of steam, leaving the first individual the most battered and bruised. The second man places an arm around him and leads him away.

'Are they known to us?' Kat asks.

'Not to "us" per se, but they are to me. The first man is, anyway.'

Kat looks at her colleague and frowns. 'Explain?'

'I knew he seemed familiar but I couldn't think why for a start. Then I realised.' DS York explains about a new up-and-coming band that his teenage niece talks about all the time. 'She's been to see them perform a couple of times. Was hoping to get tickets for the New Year's Eve gig they have coming up but they've sold out. Anyway, this one,' he points to a close-up image of the first man, 'is Luke Wright, lead singer of The Flight of the Melons.'

'Flight of the what...?'

'Of the Melons. They're an indie rock/pop group.'

'And... that is significant how?'

'He's the boyfriend of Cassie Elliot. Former employee and alleged rape victim of Hunter Black.' Kat's eyes widen in surprise. 'And, get this. They are both *former* friends of Honey Brown, but from what I can gather, Honey and Cassie had some kind of altercation, some kind of falling out when Honey sided with Black after Cassie reported him. Black then made Honey a, well, a global singing star, I suppose you'd call her. Personally, I don't like much of her stuff. She's got a good enough voice but it's all a bit... poppy.'

Kat arches her brow. 'Bit of a music expert are we, York?'

York coughs to clear his throat and adjusts the button on his shirt. 'Like to think I know a bit about music, yes boss. Been to a few gigs over the years.'

Kat smirks, turns back towards the screen. 'We've interviewed both women, right?'

DS York leans back in his chair, tapping the side of his desk with his pen. 'We have. And to be fair Cassie Elliot's statement checks out. We even have some CCTV footage that confirms her movements.'

'And the singer – Honey?'

'She was at Black's house on the day in question.'

'Really?'

'But her chauffeur says he saw Black at the door when he stopped by in the afternoon to pick her up. Plus the gardener who has worked for Black for years, and was just finishing up for the day, also confirmed seeing her leave. Said he was securing everything before he left for his Christmas break and witnessed Ms Brown getting into her waiting car just as he emerged via an outside entrance down the side of the house. A neighbour of Black's, who was taking her small dog for a walk around the block, also verified that she saw Ms Brown leave just before she stopped to chat to the gardener before witnessing him get into his car and drive away.

Kat twists the side of her mouth. 'Hmm... very interesting.' She points to the screen containing the frozen image of the two persons of interest. 'What time was this?'

DS York raises his eyebrows. 'After Ms Brown and the gardener left.'

Kat stands up and folds both arms across her chest.

'What happens after they've finished fighting? Do they approach the house?'

DS York shakes his head. 'No, they appear to walk away. But we're working our way through some more CCTV to track their movements. I think we need to speak to them though, boss?'

'I don't disagree. Do we know who the other individual is?' Kat points to the larger man.

'Don't recognise him, boss. But I'm sure Mr Wright will tell us.'

'Let's hope so. Okay, get him in, and find out who the other one is. Let's see what they have to say for themselves. Good work, Noor.'

'Thanks, boss.'

Chapter 19

DECEMBER 27TH
PRESENT DAY — EARLY AFTERNOON

LIZZIE

I think I'm awake. My eyes are closed but I'm aware of light puncturing the room. I know, even before I lift my head off the pillow, I have a headache. I'm aware of voices, too. Whispering. Someone asks someone else if they think I'm awake. Is that Cassie? Am I awake? More importantly, do I want to be awake?

'M-um,' Cassie hisses, her voice a loud whisper. 'I'm leaving soon. Are you going to get up and say goodbye?'

Goodbye? Why is she leaving? Why is she here, for that matter? What the hell day is it? Then I remember. The day after Boxing Day. And so much has happened. Why? Why is life like this? Why do we drift for long periods of time where nothing much happens then, wham! Everything happens all at once. Is it a test of our resolve? I feel weary, drunk on adrenalin and fatigue, as if the last few days, the last year, in fact, has sat on my shoulders with all the weight of a century. Unwelcome memories, at first out of focus then like a fog lifting, are once again clear. My tummy flips. Why the fuck was Simon with another woman in the pub last night? Has he really fallen out of love with me?

'What time is it?' I say, or at least try to say. My tongue, which feels as rough as sandpaper, sticks to the roof of my mouth, which feels as barren as I imagine the Atacama Desert to be. I hear stifled laughter.

'It's after twelve,' Cassie says.

'Twelve? Twelve as in lunchtime, twelve?' More stifled laughter. I can't believe it. I've slept for hours! Probably the three sleeping pills I took, plus one too many glasses of Prosecco. Using the muscles behind my eyes, I try to prise them open but they're stuck, glued together, no doubt by the make-up I couldn't be bothered to remove last night. After a few seconds I manage to open them, see Cassie and Connor hovering close by. Smirking, they glance at one another, their expressions ones of mild intrigue and trepidation, as if encountering a spider for the first time, unsure whether to stay, or run. Cassie moves closer, I raise my hand, and she steps back as it thrashes about of its own accord.

'Could do with a cup of coffee,' I mumble.

Cassie smiles, says the kettle is on. 'Come downstairs and I'll make you some breakfast, too.'

I sigh. *Why can't I have a cuppa in bed? In fact, why can't I stay in bed – forever? Didn't Sue Townsend write about a woman who stayed in bed? For a year, I think it was. Bloody marvellous idea if you ask me.*

'Okay. Give me a minute and I'll be down.'

'Don't be long,' Connor adds.

They leave the room. I look at the other side of the bed. It's still made, clearly hasn't been slept in. Simon didn't come to bed. A lump forms in my throat. Perhaps he didn't even bother coming home? I think back to when Scott and I were married, how all the warning signs about his infidelity were there, but how I refused to see them. Has it happened again? Have I been so blind? So eaten up with my grief at losing Dad, of getting justice for Cassie, that I missed it? Or worse still, did I push Simon away? I don't want to get up. I don't want to do anything. Everyone thinks I'm strong but I'm not. I feel old, worn out. I'm tired of being everyone's rock. I'm too unbalanced. At least, that's how it feels - as if I walk with a permanent sensation of unbalance and a slight breeze will tip me over. And god help me if it does, for like a beetle flipped on its back, its legs thrashing and floundering, I fear I'll never recover.

I sigh. Stare at the ceiling. I will get up, of course; I have to keep going. Dad taught me that, and Mum. It's sink or swim and right now I know there are others relying on me. I promised Aunt Marie everything would be okay, said I'd look after her, help her with Uncle Teddy's funeral arrangements. And if Simon has been unfaithful, well – fuck him! I survived it once, mostly with family, good friends and cheap wine, so I'll do it again.

Besides, there's more shit yet to come.

I drag myself to the bathroom, splash my face with cold water. I look up. The face that greets me in the mirror is one of a tired old hag who, with two huge black eyes, thinks she's a member of Kiss. I barely recognise myself. I must have aged ten years during this past year, and another ten over the last couple of days. Using a make-up wipe I rub at the smudged mascara around both my eyes. I then raise an arm, turn and sniff. Recoiling, I spray deodorant under both armpits and pull my dressing gown on. I grab a hairband, tuck my feet into my slippers – a Christmas gift from Connor – and make my way downstairs using the hairband to tie my hair away from my face. I hear the kettle boiling in the kitchen, the odd muffled voice drifting through the walls, but other than that the house is quiet. Good. Hopefully everyone is out for the day. I look like something from The Walking Dead so the fewer people that see me, the better.

Filled with a quiet unease, I wonder why the kids are keen to talk. I know Cassie always likes to say goodbye before she leaves but both she and Connor appeared unusually keen to speak to me. As I reach the bottom of the stairs, it hits me like a blow to the head. Snippets of their private conversation last night intrude my thoughts and are about as welcome as a fart in spacesuit, as Dad used to say. I put my hand to my throbbing head. Maybe I should creep back upstairs to bed. Feign an illness. I don't need this, not today. Then again… *fuck it*. I take a deep breath, brace myself and push the door open.

I'm mortified. Every man, woman, child and his dog are present, including Ruby and Scott, and all eyes upon me, the only half-dressed person in the room. Resisting the urge to turn and run, I put my hand to my forehead and cough to clear my throat, then shuffle forward.

''Bout bleedin' time,' Sean shouts.

I swear he sounds more like Dad every day.

'Just catching up on your beauty sleep, weren't you, my love?' Mum says.

'Didn't work though, did it,' Connor joins in. It's nice to see him smiling for a change.

'Thanks,' I hiss at Cassie who is standing close by. 'You might have told me everyone was here.' Flustered, I put my hand to my face, feel the heat rising within me. 'I'd have got dressed if I'd known.'

'Oh Mum. Who the hell cares? Cassie replies. 'Besides, I've seen you looking worse. Way worse in fact!'

'We thought we'd let you sleep,' another voice says.

I turn around and see Simon standing behind me, smiling. His eyes bore into me, making my legs turn to jelly. Bewildered, I wonder if that look in his eyes is love, or something else? Pity, maybe? Confused, I turn away just as Cassie places a mug of steaming hot coffee on the table and Connor takes me gently by the arm towards the chair Mum has pulled out.

What the fuck is this all about? An intervention group of friends and family here to tell me they know all about my drug and alcohol addiction and that I need to put a stop to it – now! Or they'll disown me. Didn't that happen to Stephen King or something? I don't have an addiction though. Okay, not strictly true. I am partial to the odd glass or two of criminally cheap plonk and I have one addiction I suppose – writing. Not that I've done much recently. Much to my agent's disappointment.

I sit down as instructed. Sean says they have something to tell me. Something important. Cassie says I mustn't be angry.

'Yeah, don't be pissed off, Mum, please,' Connor adds. 'Me, Cas and Luke only found out this morning. So besides you, we were the last to find out.'

Oddly, their faces are all eager, happy.

Ruby starts, followed by Sean, and now and then one of the others adds the odd excitable comment here and there, thrown in like a burst of colourful confetti. Simon, ever the businessman, concludes the brief. The room falls silent and I look round, find myself floating among a sea of expectant faces.

'I… I… don't know what to say,' I mumble.

'You – lost for words? Not like you, sis,' Sean says. 'Not like you at all.'

Clapping her hands together like an over-excited child, Cassie jumps up. 'For god sake, Mum – it's bloody brilliant is what it is.'

'Yeah, c'mon, Mum, it's pretty peng,' Connor adds.

I glance at Simon, look away again. Put my hand to my face, and realise it's damp, that I'm crying, hot unashamed tears.

'Oh, please tell me they're happy tears,' Ruby says.

I smile and nod my head. They are, but they are also tears of relief as everything falls into place. I replay the whispered conversations, furtive looks and phone calls Simon insisted were work related, had to be taken behind closed doors, and suddenly, as surely as an early morning Fen mist lifts to reveal dramatic skies and far off horizons, I understand.

My happiness is uneasy though, and not least because Natasha and Sean have sold their beloved, if somewhat decrepit, farmhouse in Perranporth to help make this happen.

I turn towards my brother and his beautiful wife. 'Where

will you live?'

'With me,' Mum replies. 'Just for a while, until the business takes off and they can get a place of their own again.'

Natasha nods and Sean smiles.

'But... what do you two know about the music industry?'

'More than you realise,' Sean replies. 'We've been involved in the booking and promotion for a lot of the entertainment at several bars and pubs in Perranporth. Plus Nat has had a regular DJing spot at our local for the last year.'

My eyes widen. 'Really?'

Nat folds her arms across her chest. 'Don't sound so surprised,' she says, her eyebrow arched into a frown.

'I'm not! It's just, well, it will be so different. Your life, I mean. Not at all like your current bohemian one–'

Cassie interrupts, pointing to Luke. 'You don't have to live in a certain place to be unconventional. Most of the musicians I know are pretty bohemian.'

Palms up, like a preacher about to deliver his sermon, Sean holds his hands out and shrugs. 'Well, fuck it! In for a penny, in for a pound, as Dad used to say.'

'And what about you two?' I turn towards Maisy and Crazee. 'You have a baby to think of.'

Maisy explains that thanks to the sale of their tattoo business back in Australia they have enough money for a deposit on a house, with a fair chunk of cash left over to contribute towards the new business venture.

'We're looking at it as a long term loan, interest free, plus we'll both be working for the company,' Maisy says. 'And as I'll be doing a lot of the promotional type work, it's a win win for me because I can work from home. Which means,' she says, turning to baby Nicolas, balanced on her hip, 'I can still look after this little one.' Whereupon she lifts his tee shirt and, much to my grandson's joyous delight, blows a raspberry onto his little potbelly. His giggle is infectious and we all join in with their laughter.

I think back and remember myself as a working parent, the minefield of trying to juggle a career and small children. I glance over towards Scott. Being a single parent didn't help matters much, either. Knowing she can work and care for her child must be liberating for Maisy. It shows in her eyes, too. The relief that shines through, almost tangible.

'Ok-ay, so where will everyone else work? Do we have an office? A base?'

Simon opens his mouth to speak but Cassie beats him to it. 'We do,' she squeals, 'in London. Which is where I'll be most of the time.'

'Me too. When I've finished college,' Connor adds.

'London? How on earth can we afford London?'

Simon, who clearly sees the concern burrowing into my brow, explains that by pulling a few strings with a client he once helped out of the shit, he's wangled lower rent charges for three years on a smallish building in Kensington. 'Three years should be time enough to see where we stand,' he says. 'And who knows, I may even get a couple more years added to those three, especially if this little venture actually works.'

'It will work,' Ruby adds.

I turn around, look at my friend, take her hand in mine. 'Thank you,' I say, 'but I hope you didn't pay too much over the odds?' Ruby has bought our share of Simon's current business back (after we purchased it from her when Andy died) for slightly more than it's worth. 'Thanks to that shit bag, Harvey, last year, you've lost enough for one lifetime.'

Ruby squeezes my hand and smiles. 'You're my oldest friend, Lizzie. It feels good to help. And besides, Scott will be stepping into Simon's shoes. And if he fucks up, well, we may just be coming to you lot for a job.'

'Cheers. Thanks for the vote of confidence,' Scott pipes up, mock derision in his voice.

So, thanks to our family pulling together, pooling our various resources and assets, including a bit thrown in from Mum and Aunt Marie, we, as a family, are setting up our very own music production company and record label.

I turn back to Simon.

'And you… what do you know about the music industry?'

'My skills are transferable,' he replies. 'Plus, I've a sneaky suspicion that the world of consultancy isn't that far removed from the music industry, not when you get down to the nitty gritty business basics. And, if the other members agree,' he nods towards Luke, 'we may sign our first band, sooner rather than later?'

Luke, whose phone rings, sticks his thumb up then turns away to answer it.

'And where do I fit into this? What am I supposed to do?' I ask.

'Nothing.' Simon takes my hand and pulls me off the chair towards him. 'You, can keep yourself locked away in your writing cave and keep writing. Your words will take the publishing world by storm and our music will rock the music world.'

I look up at Simon. 'You should have told me.'

Simon closes his eyes, hangs his head. 'I know. I thought about telling you a couple of times. I should have at least checked with you. It's a huge gamble and you should have been part of that decision process. It's just that it's been a tough year. I know you were – *are* – still struggling with losing your Dad, as well as dealing with all that shit about Black…' He presses his lips together. I notice his jaw tighten, '… and what he did to Cassie and…' He looks down, coughs to clear his throat.

I lift his chin and nose-to-nose, our eyes meet. 'I thought you were having an affair.'

Simon raises his eyes. 'Really?'

'Really,' I reply.

His mouth twitches, the corners lifting into a smile. 'You may be mad, bad and dangerous to know but there's only one woman for me,' he says bending forward to kiss me.

'I haven't cleaned my teeth,' I whisper.

'I don't give a fuck,' he replies, pressing his warm soft lips against mine.

Excitable conversations continue around us. 'Sorry, who?' I think I hear Luke say. He is still on the phone, and sounds agitated but right now I am enjoying this brief interlude with my man.

'Get a room, Mum,' Connor says playfully, pushing past us, heading towards the door.

'Cheeky git,' Simon says. He nods towards the table at my half drunk, now cold cup of coffee, asks if I'd like another. I nod; resume my seat at the table. Natasha joins me.

She nudges me. 'That woman in the pub last night...' I look at her, feel my face flush '... was just some drunken stranger. Didn't even know Simon. Tried to accost the poor old thing the minute he sat down.'

Simon hears her, looks up. 'Oi – less of the old.'

'When I went back to the pub,' Natasha continues. 'After you left, went home–'

'What the fu...' Luke shouts.

Somewhat surprised everyone looks up.

'Yeah... but... why!' he continues.

Cassie taps him on the shoulder. He swings around, sees everyone staring at him. Grimacing, he sticks his thumb up, mouths the word "sorry" and heads for the back door where he continues his phone conversation outside. Cassie, who looks as confused as the rest of us, wrinkles her nose and shrugs her shoulders.

Natasha and I look at one another, a silent *what the fuck?* passing between us. 'Anyway,' she continues, 'when I went back to the pub I found Sean trying to rescue Simon.'

'Thank god,' Simon mumbles, placing a steaming mug of fresh coffee in front of me.

'Yeah, definitely a bit worse for wear that one, eh, Si?' Sean, who has now joined us, says chuckling.

'I should say so.' Simon rolls his eyes.

'I have one last question,' I say, standing up, addressing the room. 'What if it doesn't work out? What if this business venture goes tits up and everyone loses everything they put into it?'

There's a collective groan in the room before Sean declares it will be a brilliant success. 'And anyway, as a wise old man once said, "it's not a life, it's an adventure".'

Everyone, even baby Nicolas joins in cheering and the whole room fills with a merriment that has been absent from this family for far too long.

I think of Dad and smile.

'That was never his,' Mum says, pulling a chair out to sit the other side of me.

'What was never whose, Mum?' I ask.

'That saying. Your Dad pinched it – from Mickey.'

She glances at Aunt Marie and they exchange the briefest of smiles. Slowly but surely Mum is opening up but there are still huge gaps in my family history. Many of the colourful characters talked about by my father, using nicknames only, were always done so in almost comic book fashion. Mickey's name, however, cropped up a lot before Dad passed away. Georgie Wakefield's, too.

Although how much I really know is, I suspect, still censored.

Mum stands up again, asks who wants tea and who wants coffee. Aunt Marie catches my eye. She smiles but her eyes flicker. I sense both her fear and her pain. 'We need to talk,' she mouths. I nod. We have a funeral to arrange so perhaps the merriment that fills the room is disrespectful. I hope Aunt Marie doesn't think so. It's good to see everyone in such high spirits.

'Any chance of a bacon sandwich?' Crazee calls out.

I'd like to say I feel happy, hopeful even, but I don't because I have something else on my mind.

'If you help me make 'em,' Maisy replies to Crazee, grabbing bacon from the fridge.

Cassie has her nose pressed to the window, looking towards the end of the garden where Luke, still on his phone, is roaming up and down. I watch my daughter, glad she's let her hair grow again; short hair doesn't suit her. She's put on some weight, too, which is no bad thing, of course. And, despite looking slightly cross at Luke, she seems happy. I sigh; feel the weight of what I need to tell her pressing on my conscience, and my mind wanders again, imagining her reaction. I honestly have no idea how she'll react but right now I'm too afraid, too anchored, to this chair to dwell on it. I could tell her now, I suppose, but it doesn't seem right. Not when she seems so happy. She brushes past me, shaking her head, mumbling something about grabbing her bags because she and Luke need to leave soon, catch the train they have booked back to London. I catch her arm, ask her if we can meet up in London in a few days' time, before New Year's Eve.

'Erm, yeah. I suppose. Why?' Her eyes narrow. 'I'll be busy helping Luke in the run up to the band's gig, though. Can it wait?'

I shake my head. 'I've booked, well, an appointment with someone. On the twenty-ninth. Someone I'd like you to meet?'

She sighs, her voice laced with mild irritation. 'The twenty-ninth? Really? And you've only just decided to tell me about this now?' Her brown eyes open wide in disbelief.

I hang my head like a chastised child. 'Sorry. But what with

Black and the police and...' I glance at Aunt Marie '...Uncle Teddy...'

Cassie reaches down, grabs my warm hand with her cold one. I look up again. 'Of course, Mum,' she says, her eyes locking with mine. 'I'm sorry. Email me all the details and I'll be there.'

To my surprise Maisy, who has overheard our conversation, asks if she can come too. 'P-l-eee-ase,' she begs, thrusting my dribbling grandson into my arms. 'I love, love, love being a Mum but just for a few hours I'd like to know what it feels like to be me again.'

I laugh. I remember that feeling well. 'Well, it might be a bit boring. I'm not planning on doing any shopping or anything.'

'That's fine,' Maisy replies. 'Can we go for a coffee though? And cake. I dream of going for a coffee and not having to worry about heating bottles of milk or jars of food, whether they have a baby changing area, or pacifying him.' She points to Nicolas, 'because he's lost his dummy or I've given him the wrong spoon – hell hath no fury like a toddler who wants a green spoon instead of a yellow one. Or... or, he asks for a biscuit, refuses the biscuit, and then cries because I take the biscuit away. Or having to buy a change of clothes – his and mine – because, despite wearing a bib the size of a planet, he still gets food all down himself and me, and in the woman's hair sitting next to us. And then, when it's time to leave, and he's kicked his shoes off again, can someone please tell me why it takes me an hour to get them back on again but it only takes him sixteen seconds to open all the apps on my phone, delete iTunes, and call Crazee's parents in Australia?'

I look at Nicolas who, blowing bubbles, is tugging at my ears, fascinated by my earrings. Stalling for time, I kiss my grandson and pass him my earring, which, mesmerised, he rolls back and forth in his fat fingers. I'm not sure having Maisy with me is a good idea.

She looks at me, her green eyes huge, her bottom lip jutting forward. 'P-l-eee-ase,' she says again.

I sigh. Sod it. I suppose she'll find out soon enough, anyway. Everyone will.

'Yes, of course.' I reply. 'Why not?'

Suddenly the kitchen door crashes open behind us. I turn to see Connor wearing a rabbit-in-the headlights expression, his eyes red-rimmed, dewy. 'He's… he's dead,' he announces, almost choking on his words. I feel my stomach tighten.

Mum, quickly by his side, places a loving arm around my son's stooped shoulders. 'Who's dead, love?' she asks.

'Freddy,' he whispers, his voice more like that of a distressed six year old than a lanky strapping eighteen year old.

'First Grandad, then Uncle Teddy… now Freddy,' he struggles to say through muted sobs.

I wonder how it is possible for an already broken heart to keep breaking, but break again mine does. More for my son than Freddy. We'll all miss him, though. Like all the dogs in our lives Freddy has been a constant reminder of what unconditional love really is. A quote by Edith Wharton springs to mind, "My little dog – a heartbeat at my feet." That's what Freddy is – was.

As if on cue, Summer's pug, Sir Lancelot, wriggling in her arms, barks. She brings him over to Connor and we all watch in amazement as the little bundle of fur leaps from Summer's arms into his, licking his face. In between his sobs Connor smiles as Sir Lancelot does his utmost to stem the flow of my son's tears. I swallow hard, trying to dislodge the ball of pain in my throat, at once reminded of the poor demise of my first dog, Susie, a mad as a hatter golden Labrador. Dad brought her home as a surprise when Sean and I were very little. My memories of her passing are of here, living in Great Tossen, which means she must have become part of our family while we were still living in London.

Puzzlement, jostling with grief for Freddie – and Connor –

creeps through me again. Why can't I remember anything about that time?

Chapter 20

January 1966 – Into The Fold

SALOCIN

'What can I getcha?'

Salocin looked up. The landlord stood in front of him, knowing eyes either side of a long nose, his thin jaw jutting forwards.

Reaching into his pocket, Salocin pulled out his loose change. 'A pint of whatever this lot will buy,' he said. The landlord frowned, making the crevices etched into his puckered brow more pronounced. He left the change where it was, reached up for a pint glass and placed it beneath a pump.

It was Friday night and the Ship Inn was already filling up. Men mostly, although there were a few women with their husbands, glad rags underneath their overcoats, painted red lips, and hair, rigid, set thanks to copious amounts of hairspray. He should get back. Ellie would wonder where he was. But after the afternoon he'd had he needed a pint. Something to smooth out the edges of the day, even though he couldn't afford it.

'Salocin?' He felt a slap on his back, turning to see Mickey. 'Annie said she saw you wander in.'

'Alright Mickey,' Salocin replied. 'Did she now. Eyes in the back of her head that one. Don't miss a trick does old Annie – if you'll pardon the pun.'

Mickey laughed. 'She's harmless enough.'

Annie Figg first approached Salocin outside the yard a few

weeks after he'd worked there. "Give us a quid and I'll give yer a blowjob right 'ere and now," she'd said. Gobsmacked, Salocin hadn't known what to say, felt his mouth open, searching for the right words to warrant a reply but none were forthcoming. So he just stood there, gormless, staring at her worn face. He'd noticed how yellow the whites of her eyes were, not unlike her nicotine-stained fingers, and how the skin around her lips was no less puckered and pouched than the deep lines etched into her forehead. Her hair, auburn, sprinkled with flecks of grey was long and lank, hanging in matted straggles. Salocin reckoned she was probably in her early forties but her world-weary face made her look much older. "Whassa matter? Cat got your tongue?" she'd cackled, revealing a bottom row of pitted black teeth. Salocin knew about prostitutes but had never been approached by one before. He'd felt churlish, as embarrassed as a schoolboy might. He soon realised how harmless she was though, even had a bit of a laugh and joke with her. "Alright darlin'. Fank ya kindly," she'd always reply to his friendly dismissals. "You'll give in one day, mind, when that little wifey of yours stops givin' it to you. Coz she will. They all do." He didn't know Annie's back-story, wasn't sure he wanted to either, but it was obvious she'd had a hard life. So he mostly felt sorry for her. And whenever he had any loose change – which wasn't often – he gave it to her; told her to piss off and get herself a cuppa, reminding her that Georgie would kill her if he found her there. Georgie couldn't stand the prossies hanging around the yard.

'A *respectable* business ain't no place for the likes of them,' he'd once said to Salocin when he'd found him outside the yard having a bit of banter with Annie.

"That's as maybe," Annie had muttered under gin-soaked breath. "But you don't mind taking a percentage of our earnings though, do ya, Georgie boy."

Angry, Georgie had waved his arm at Annie, told her to "fack orf" as if he were shooing off some mangy, stray dog. It was a disconcerting and an ugly side of Georgie that Salocin hadn't seen before.

Now, the landlord sloshed a pint of bitter on the bar, eyeballing the pile of change still sitting there. Mickey followed his gaze. 'Same again, please, Jim.' He pulled a note from his back pocket, nodding towards Salocin's glass. 'This one's on me.'

'Right you are, Mickey,' the landlord replied, taking the note and ringing it up in the till before reaching for another pint glass.

'Thanks,' Salocin said, as he watched the deft fingers of the landlord count out Mickey's change, which he handed to Mickey along with his pint.

'You look as though you've got the bleedin' world on yer shoulders, boy,' Mickey said.

Salocin shrugged, lifted the corners of his mouth, offering Mickey a smile of sorts. He caught sight of himself in the mirror hanging behind the bar. The dark circles under his eyes corroborated just how knackered he felt. He wasn't sleeping well, and it wasn't just Lizzie's crying that kept him awake. Even on the odd night she didn't wake, he still struggled to drop off, myriad dilemmas plaguing his thoughts as he tried to figure out how the fuck he was going to get his wife and daughter out of the dingy flat. Ellie's depression, although better, reminded him of a flower without water, and he could see, despite her smiles and attempts to prove otherwise, that in the flat, she was wilting, withering away. You'd have to be blind not to see it.

'I take it you're feeling better?'

Salocin, nodded. Shifting nervously in his seat, he took a swig of his pint. He'd convinced Mickey to give him a few hours off work, said he wasn't feeling well, that he'd make up the lost time tomorrow – but instead he went looking for another job. He hated lying to Mickey, especially considering everything he'd done to help him, but the truth was he was getting restless, not to mention broke. Things could have been worse but Salocin wanted more out of life, more for his family. It was hard watching Georgie pull up at the yard in his swanky cars, wearing his flash suits, while he struggled to get enough change together for the bus ride home. He'd already given up smoking so he could give Ellie more money for food, but short of robbing a bank, he was getting desperate. So he'd gone behind Mickey's back, lined up a few interviews.

With his best suit on and his best foot forward, he'd spent the afternoon trawling one address to the next. Trouble was, either the wage was less than he was already on or he was under-qualified for those jobs that paid better. 'Go back to night school. Get a few more qualifications under your belt, then come back and see us,' some had said. Disheartened, with a bit of time to spare before his final interview of the day, Salocin wandered around the West End. One of the theatres had a chalkboard sign outside stating they were holding open auditions, and overcome with mischief, Salocin joined the queue of wannabe actors, listening to their idle chitter chatter. As the queue dwindled, it was his turn. Script thrust into his hand after feeding them some blarney about having attended RADA (he didn't exactly know what RADA was – some acting school he guessed) and repeating verbatim what he had overheard the other actors say, he auditioned for a real acting role in a real West End show. He didn't get the part but they offered him a non-speaking role, which had made him chuckle on his otherwise bleak mid-winter day. He turned it down, of course – fun, but whiled away time better spent looking for real job opportunities. Still, he had one more interview left. Maybe he'd saved the best till last?

Once inside the offices of Hubert & Hubert – an insurance company – Salocin's good mood diminished. The position he had applied for was in sales, on the telephone mostly, but again the salary was less than he was already on, although there was the opportunity to earn more on commission. Salocin had already made his mind up, anyway, had done so the minute he walked into the grey, smoke-filled offices, with its pasty-faced, chain-smoking employees and their down-turned smiles and soulless eyes. Even if it was miserably cold sometimes, he'd rather be at the yard, outside in the fresh air. Salocin played along though, listened to what Mr Jenkins, the acting manager— a ratty faced individual with silver-framed spectacles perched on the end of his rather pointed nose – had to say. And when he asked Salocin if he had any skills that made him stand out, well, it was too good an opportunity to miss.

'I do speak fluent Russian,' Salocin had replied.

'Really?' Mr Jenkins' eyes shot up towards his bushy brows.

Salocin nodded. 'Ты выглядишь как идиот,' he said in his best Russian accent, which loosely translated meant "you look like an idiot" (a phrase he'd learned from Kenny at the yard whose grandmother was supposedly Russian). How easily the lies came today, first to Mickey, then at the theatre, then to Mr Jenkins... and probably to Lizzie, when he got home.

'Well... well... that's marvellous,' Mr Jenkins had stuttered. 'Do you speak any other languages?'

Salocin had coughed, crossed his legs, then uncrossed them again. 'Bit of French, bit of German,' he lied.

'Marvellous. Just marvellous.' Mr Jenkins was almost leaping out of his seat. 'Do you mind waiting here for a moment? While I fetch my colleague,' he'd asked. 'We've been thinking about expanding the business abroad and I think you could be just the person we're looking for.'

Salocin had nodded again, wishing he were the person Mr Jenkins thought he was. If only he could speak Russian, or French or German for that matter. Salocin watched Mr Jenkins depart, then once out of sight, he jumped up and legged it, laughing all the way back to the bus stop. He couldn't wait to get back and tell Ellie about his schoolboy pranks. But then reality bit. He wasn't a schoolboy. He was an idiot – and one who'd wasted a whole afternoon fucking around. Why had Ellie ever agreed to marry him? He knew the answer to that, of course, had been thinking about it a lot just recently. What if she *hadn't* fallen pregnant? Would she have still married him? Or would she have outgrown him? Found someone who could really take care of her?

Now, faced with an expectant Mickey, Salocin came clean. 'Look, truth is, Mickey, I lied. I'm fine. I took time off to go job hunting. Sorry.' There. It was out in the open, off his chest and the relief was overwhelming.

Mickey turned towards Salocin, a look of lazy amusement on his face. 'You not happy at the yard?'

'Yeah – course I am. It's just that…'

'Just what?'

'It's not enough,' he shrugged, taking another mouthful of beer.

'I'm listening,' Mickey replied

Salocin stared at his boss, the man who had been better to him than his own father. 'I want more, Mickey,' he replied. 'A house. Nice, nothing grand, but something Ellie and I can call our own. Bought not rented. With a garden and a garage. Maybe a car to park it in? Nothing fancy, like, just something we can drive down to Brighton. Or Cornwall, maybe? Ellie's got this idea, she read somewhere, that there's supposed to be lost pirate treasure there or something.'

Mickey sniffed. 'I'd like a garage to park my car in,' he replied.

Salocin looked surprised. Mickey liked his motors almost as much as Georgie did. 'You don't have a garage?'

'I do but it's full of god knows bleedin' what. Has been since the day we moved in. Five facking years ago. Anyway, how's that young daughter of yours coming along?'

Salocin smiled. Thought of Lizzie, how her dark, knowing eyes – like his, Ellie said – watched him. The huge smile on her face that greeted him the minute he stepped through the door after work. The way she pointed at things, a spider crawling on the wall, a bird on a branch, a leaf floating on the wind. The way she called him Da-da, Ellie Mum-mum-mum, and a boiled egg a beagle. The way she curled her tiny hand around his finger, and pointed to her nose when asked.

'Sounds like my youngest, Laura,' Mickey replied. 'Apple of my eye she is. Bright as a new pin, too. Reckon she'll achieve great things one day. Become a doctor. A solicitor, perhaps? Or a politician. Maybe even make it to Number Ten.'

Salocin felt his eyebrows shoot into his brow. 'Downing Street?'

'Why not?'

'A woman – as prime minister?'

'It could happen.'

Salocin looked at his boss, saw the corners of his mouth lifting into a smile. 'Nah,' they both said in unison.

Mickey pulled a pack of cigarettes from his pocket. 'Smoke?'

Salocin took one. 'Thanks,' he said, leaning forward for a light.

Mickey took a long drag on his cigarette, a small cloud of smoke billowing from the corner of his mouth. Salocin looked down, staring at his hands. Rough, workers' hands, full of superficial cuts earned from separating metal. When he looked up again Mickey was staring at him. His steely eyes were watchful, his gaze direct, unyielding.

'You remind me of me, when I was younger,' he said. 'Hungry. Eager for more. Trying to better yourself. I get it, I really do. I like you, Salocin and I'd like it if you stuck around. Here...'

He reached into his inside coat pocket and pulled out a small brown envelope – wages. 'I was going to give you this tomorrow morning. But as you are here–'

'Another pint?' the landlord interrupted.

'Why not!' Mickey replied. 'Same again please, Jim. Salocin?'

Salocin nodded, then thanked Mickey for his wages.

'You buying this time?' Mickey turned to Salocin and asked.

Salocin looked at Mickey in disbelief. He may have just been paid but had Mickey heard a fucking word he'd just said to him? 'Erm... yeah. Course.' He scratched his head, feeling his face redden.

'That'll be two and ten please, gentlemen,' said the landlord.

Mickey looked away, sipping his pint. Fuming, Salocin ripped open the small brown envelope containing his meagre wages and handed the waiting landlord some of his hard-earned cash, then, taking his change, he sought solace in another mouthful of warm beer.

'Cheers!' Mickey swivelled round, clinking his glass against Salocin's.

'Cheers,' Salocin replied drolly. What the fuck they were celebrating was beyond him. Maybe Mickey *was* pissed off at him for taking time off to look for another job. Why did he just say he wanted Salocin to stick around, but then make him pay for drinks he knew he couldn't afford? It was all very confusing.

Mickey finished his pint, saying he had to go. 'We have guests coming to dinner.' He rolled his eyes. 'Oh, I nearly forgot... this is for you.' Once more he reached into his inside coat pocket, pulling out another brown envelope. Salocin looked at the small bulging envelope, stared at his name scrawled across it in black ink along with the words "Beer Money." Mickey told him to put it away. 'Don't open it in here,' he said glancing around.

'What is it?'

'What it says it is. Your share of the beer money. Nobody

gets any for the first year because we have to wait and see what you're like – if we can trust you. And I'm glad to say we do. Your probation period is over.'

Salocin's brow wrinkled in bewilderment. 'Trust me to what…?'

Mickey tapped the side of his nose. 'All in good time, young Salocin.' He explained that from hereon in Salocin could expect to get his wages *plus* his share of the beer money every week. Sometimes it would be more, sometimes less than was in this second envelope. 'Now, if you still want to leave, fine, it's entirely up to you, but either way, that there money is yours. The one and only thing I must insist on though is that you never mention it to Georgie boy. Not if you know what's good for you, anyway. Which I think you do.' Mickey told Salocin to take the night to consider his options. Said if he still wanted out, then fair enough, he'd give him the time off to attend interviews. 'Take tomorrow morning off too,' he continued. 'If that's your final decision. Otherwise, I expect to see you at the yard, bright and early, as usual.'

'But…' Salocin scratched his head again. 'I don't get it.'

Mickey winked and Salocin felt the hairs on the back of his neck stand on end. 'Remember this young Salocin, it's not a life, it's an adventure.'

And with that Mickey, like Cinderella's fairy godmother, was gone. Salocin was only a few minutes behind him, downing his pint because he was desperate to see the contents of the second brown envelope. He stepped outside, felt the bitterness of the North wind on his face and turned the corner. He glanced left to right, making sure no one was about, then pulled the envelope from his pocket and ripped it open. Eyes like saucers, hands shaking, he pulled out a wad of notes and counted them. A hundred quid? One hundred fucking nicker? Surely Mickey had made a mistake? Salocin looked up, half expecting to see Mickey and the others watching him from the shadows, laughing, the whole thing some elaborate joke. No one was there. He counted it again. Once, twice, three more times for luck. *One hundred pounds – my share of the beer money. Fuck me.* He didn't know what the fuck Mickey was involved in, but as long as it didn't involve killing anyone, or beating people up, Salocin was in. He looked round again, made sure no one had seen him, then tucked the money back inside the envelope. As he did, he noticed a small, handwritten note inside. He pulled it out and read it:

"Welcome to the fold", it said.

Chapter 21

1966

SALOCIN

In 1966 the Vietnam War still raged on and although Britain avoided the conflict, the streets of London bore witness to several anti-war demonstrations. It was also the year John Lennon declared that The Beatles were more popular than Jesus, which didn't go down well across the pond, particularly in the south. Salocin and Mickey were listening to it on the radio one afternoon over a cuppa. Apparently several music stations had banned The Beatles' music, while others, who said Lennon's words were sacrilege, organised bonfires, encouraging fans to burn their Beatles memorabilia. Mickey likened it to the Nazi book burnings of 1933. Said those that took part weren't really doing so in the name of religion, but that it was more to do with "blind faith".

'Which is dangerous,' he added. 'Blind faith in *anything* or *anyone* is not the path to enlightenment. Always question everything, young Salocin. Except Georgie Wakefield, that is,' he chuckled.

It was also the year Ian Brady and Myra Hindley were sentenced to life imprisonment for the Moors Murders. Ellie could barely bring herself to follow the news about the trial, she shuddered every time she saw the killers' profiles in the newspapers or on the television.

'Good fucking riddance to 'em,' Salocin had fumed when he heard the verdict, hugging his little girl just a little bit closer, a little bit longer than usual. 'Prison's too good for the likes of them. I hope they rot in there.'

However, it wasn't all bad news; 1966 was a year forever stamped in the mind of Salocin Lemalf, and not because, like for so many others, England won the World Cup. It *was* hard not to be swept away by the euphoria that gripped the nation during that glorious summer day of 30th July when England played and beat West Germany 4-2, even if, like Salocin, you weren't really a footie fan. Some likened the countrywide jubilation that followed the win to VE Day. But what made it particularly memorable was that Salocin, Ellie and little Lizzie watched the game – along with Teddy, Marie and a few friends and neighbours – from the comfort of their first house, their own house, which they'd moved into just a few weeks previously.

Still less than ten years old, Number 9 Wilmot Gardens was a modest three-bedroom semi-detached house on a small private housing estate between Harold Hill and Harold Wood. It had a bright kitchen with all the mod cons, including – much to Ellie's delight – an automatic washing machine, central heating (recently installed), its own driveway that lead to a garage, plus a garden for Lizzie to play in. Like Harold Hill it was one of several satellite towns designed to ease housing shortages of inner London, following the heavy bombing of many residential properties during the war. Only unlike Harold Hill, theirs was a private, more upmarket estate.

'Do what!' Martha had exclaimed when Salocin told his mother of their plans to move further afield. 'Essex, you say?' Her voice rose at the end of each sentence. 'Whachu wanna live in some godforsaken arse end of nowhere place like that for?' Her tone was better suited to the news her son was emigrating to Canada or Australia. 'It's miles a-bleedin'-way. We'll never see yer.' Anywhere north of Watford was too far for Martha.

'Seventeen miles from Charing Cross is hardly the other side of the world, Mum' Salocin had replied. 'And Harold Wood train station is only a mile up the road from us.'

'That's as maybe… but you needn't expect me and your father to come traipsing all the way over there for a cup of bleedin' tea and a biscuit.'

Salocin was angry at his mother's words, suppressing the urge to yell at her. How many times had she visited them at the flat anyway, popped by to see her granddaughter – once, twice maybe? Twice more than Ellie's parents, granted, but even then it had only been for half an hour or so.

I begged you, during those first couple of weeks Lizzie was first born – although Ellie knows nothing about it – to stop by a few hours while I was at work, give Ellie a chance to catch her breath, get some much-needed sleep. But what did you do when I told you Ellie was struggling? Scoff. Tell me she needed to snap out of it, pull herself together. That it was indulgent to wallow in self-pity. And yet I thought you, better than anyone, with your 'mother's little helpers' in your bedside cabinet, would understand?

Salocin said none of this. Instead he had nodded his head, smiled, like he so often did, reassuring his mother they'd still visit, regardless of the *huge* distance living in Essex would put between them.

'TV and a washing machine, eh?' Teddy said, nudging his brother. They were watching the end of the game, only minutes to go. 'Glad to see you've got your priorities right.'

Salocin looked at his brother, grinned. 'The TV was Ellie's idea.'

'Yeah – rightio!'

'It was. Said she wanted to watch *Top of the Pops* and *The Likely Lads* without losing the picture every five minutes.

'Aye, bloomin 'eck, Bob. Gotta love them Likely Lads.' Teddy's East End vowels infiltrated his shoddy attempt at a Northern accent.

'Two minutes to go, lads,' Alan, one of Salocin's neighbours swung round and said, a hint of mild irritation in his voice. Salocin and Teddy looked at one another, smiled. Alan was nice enough, Salocin thought, but took his football way too seriously.

'Think we've just been told to shut the fuck up,' Salocin whispered in his brother's ear. Teddy, whose eyebrows shot into his brow, smirked. They turned back to face the TV and as the last minutes of the game, including extra time, turned into seconds, everyone – by then gathered around the TV – watched and waited with bated breath. "They think it's all over," said the TV commentator. The final whistle blew. English fans fist punched the air. "It is now," the commentator continued. Large amounts of whooping, clapping and congratulatory backslapping filled the room, not to mention the drunken verses of "ee-aye-addio, we won the cup" sung on repeat.

Salocin took a moment to observe the unfolding commotion; watched his friends and neighbours, Teddy, and Marie, Ellie and his daughter as they snaked around the living room of *his* new home doing a celebratory conga. He could hardly believe his luck. He half expected to wake up, find himself back in the dingy flat in Shoreditch, Ellie sitting in the dark, shivering, having run out of money to feed the meter again, and discover it was all a dream. It wasn't a dream though, the house they now called home, with its centre pivot windows, sliding doors, fitted kitchen and huge shag pile rug in the living room – which caused Ellie to have a mild coronary every time someone looked like they were about to slosh their drink over it – was all *theirs*. His and Ellie's. He'd had to take out a mortgage on the property of course, so strictly speaking the bricks and mortar belonged to the bank, nonetheless, he and Ellie were the first in their respective families to buy and own their own home.

They could have stretched themselves, bought something bigger, but Mickey had advised against it. Said it had to appear

– to Georgie at least – that Salocin had bought something within his means.

'You don't want to end up like Silly Billy,' Mickey had warned.

Billy Jackson, a.k.a "Silly Billy" had been Salocin's predecessor. 'Bright young thing he was too,' Mickey said. 'Until the money went to his head. Fucking idiot turned up to work wearing gold chains, silk shirts, and flash suits. Silly bastard even bought himself a new Jag. I warned him. Told him he was being reckless, drawing too much unwanted attention to himself – and us. Young and foolish, see? "You and Georgie drive round in flash motors. Why can't I?" he'd said. Silly boy. Wanted to impress his friends, and the birds. Said if Georgie asked him how he could afford such things, he'd tell him he borrowed the money. Course, we all knew Georgie would never swallow that, and when he questioned Billy, we all closed ranks. Billy knew he was fucked. He also knew if he admitted what we'd been up to, tried to implicate us and him, Georgie would see a thieving, lying tow rag trying to save his own neck.'

'So what happened to him?' Salocin had asked.

'One day, when I got wind Georgie was on his way over to see Billy I gave him a few bob and told him to fack orf. Get as far away from London as bleedin' possible.'

'Did he?'

Mickey shrugged his shoulders. 'All I know is Billy's Jag turned up at the yard two days later, smashed to a pulp, and I ain't seen Billy since.'

Salocin shivered when Mickey told him the story of Billy Jackson, felt fingers of ice-cold dread run the length and breadth of his spine. He didn't dwell on it though, or consider what may or may not have happened to "Silly Billy", or indeed, *who* and *what* he, himself, was getting involved in, but he did have the good sense to understand Billy's was a cautionary tale.

TIME WILL TELL

Mickey ran a tight ship but as far as bosses went he was generous to a fault. All he asked in return was loyalty and discretion. It was a dog eat dog world, he said, and you either 'took or were taken, had or were had.' He had a first class analytical mind, too – a prerequisite if you were cooking the books – especially if you had several – three in Mickey's case – to cook: one for the taxman, one for Georgie, and one for Mickey. The latter two were always hidden, kept under lock and key, in a place that only Mickey had access to. Mickey said Georgie knew he gave the lads "beer money" on top of their wages, understood it was an incentive to keep his workers motivated – a bonus. What he didn't know was just *how much* "beer money" Mickey gave them. As far as Georgie was concerned the rules were simple. The yard, for all intents and purposes, was a legitimate business but it was *his* manor and part of *his* expanding empire. An empire that in the main, was built on fucking people over. He took from others, often without them realising it, and that's how he expected Mickey to run the yard too – with most of the profits, of course, going directly to Georgie. However, Georgie wasn't stupid. He knew the blokes Mickey employed on his behalf were chancers, which for most of them was all they'd ever known, often how they'd supplemented a meagre income. But like the three wise monkeys, they were also the sort of individuals that could be relied on to turn a blind eye to certain things, which was good for the many side-line businesses Georgie had going on. For instance, the various security groups that turned up every other week, and paid Georgie – rather than the other way round – to install, then dismantle a new alarm system at the yard, not unlike those fitted to various banks and vaults around the country. Georgie knew the lads would keep shtum; any robberies mentioned on the news or in the papers merely met by a few raised eyebrows, rarely, if ever, discussed.

And in return for their silence, Georgie instructed Mickey to pay them all what he considered, a good wage – a fair day's pay for an honest day's graft – plus five or ten quid extra for "beer money". That way nobody got above his station and no one took the piss. If Georgie got wind that you *were* taking the piss, you'd have to explain yourself to him and 'the chaps' – a motley looking crew of bull-necked, bent-nosed, scar-faced, pumped up individuals on the payroll, several of whom accompanied Georgie on his weekly visits to his various properties and businesses.

However, Mickey didn't see things like his father-in-law did. He preferred a meritocracy and the "beer money" he paid the lads was much more in keeping with what he believed worthy for a group of loyal, hard grafters who, come what may, turned up five and half days a week, got on with the job in hand and rarely, if ever, grumbled about it. The yard was a money-making machine, and Mickey looked at it as an opportunity to help everyone out – including himself. It was a hard slog most of the time. Salocin worked his bollocks off. They all did. Sometimes there'd be trouble too, which could make your arse twitch and your heart race, especially if a punter was cute, cottoned on to what you were up to and kicked off. It didn't happen often but when it did it was usually at the weighbridge and often involved 'Joey.' Salocin soon discovered that the illusive 'Joey' was not a *who* but a *what*. An insignificant looking but nonetheless powerful magnet placed at the back of the huge weighing scale at the entrance of the yard, which, although small enough to be hidden, was large enough to mess with the readings.

The majority of the yard's custom was clueless, happy to have a fag break, leave the lads to it, have a bit of banter. Others had an idea but didn't give a shit; merely the drivers for the company they worked for, it was of no interest to them if their boss was stupid enough to be had over. But every now and again, for the odd few, it was a big deal. No man likes to be fucked over by another, especially for money, and when the delivery was weighed, the going rate offered, the fireworks would begin: 'You cunt, you facking cunt. I know how much is there and it ain't what you lot are facking telling me. Now why don't cha put that scale right and pay me what I'm facking owed.' But if you played the game, kept your head down, and your mouth shut, Mickey could resolve any problems. He used his charm to convince an irate punter how the reading was kosher, pretending to stick his hand in his own pocket – 'just this once, mind' – and give 'em a bit extra. It rarely, if ever, became physical, although there were enough of them happy to get stuck in if it did. Mickey took a chunk more of the profits than everyone else, which nobody minded. After all, like Mickey said, most of the extra he took went towards keeping Georgie's daughter and granddaughters in their big house and helped cover the fees for the posh private schools the girls attended.

'So in a perverse, roundabout way, the money goes back to Georgie anyway,' Mickey said.

Under Mickey's guidance, the story was, Salocin had been saving for a deposit on a 'modest' house for months. Then, after passing his probationary period, Mickey had promoted Salocin, which meant he and Ellie could afford to buy furniture to fill the house.

'Remember though, it's all on the knock if Georgie asks,' Mickey said, winking.

How rapidly life had changed for the young couple in the last six months. Salocin surveyed his surroundings with quiet pride.

'Another beer?' he asked his brother as they watched the England players make their way towards the Royal Box.

Teddy held out his empty pint glass. 'Thanks. Don't mind if I do.'

'I'll get it.' Salocin turned to see Ellie, her blue eyes shining. She was wearing a purple and orange psychedelic print mini dress which, nipped in at the waist with its flared skirt and wide trumpet sleeves, left her shapely legs and décolletage gamely and – judging by the cursory glances of some in the room – enviably exposed. She tipped her head to the side, and smiled, causing her fringe to fall across one eye. Salocin stared at her, with a sudden surge of pride. How was it possible, he wondered, to be around someone so often, to know them intimately, recognise the shape of their hand, the taste of their mouth, the arc of their hip – every physical line and contour in fact – and yet still feel overwhelmed by their presence? As if every time you saw them felt like the first time all over again.

'There's two tins of Party Seven in the kitchen – want me to bring those in?' she asked him, raising an eyebrow.

Salocin nodded, resisting the urge to pull his wife into his arms and kiss her. 'You'd better bring the hammer and screwdriver, too. Think I put them in the top drawer.'

Teddy waited for Ellie to disappear then turned to his brother. 'How the fuck have you managed all this though, Sal?' His eyes darted about the room.

'Been promoted.' Salocin winked, tapped the side of his nose.

'Promoted? You sure you ain't robbed a bank or something?'

'He better not have.' Ellie was back already, carrying a can of Watney's Party Seven under each arm, a hammer in one hand and a screwdriver in the other. She gave the tools to Salocin and lowered the tins of beer onto the sideboard. 'I'll get clean glasses. And don't get none of that on my new carpet,' she shouted across her shoulder.

'C'mon then – what's your secret?' Teddy continued. 'You had a win on the pools you're not telling me about?'

Salocin shook his head, laughed. 'Hardly.'

'You know Mum and Dad think you're up to no good?'

Annoyed, Salocin looked away. 'Yeah?' He tap, tap, tapped the screwdriver with the hammer into the overlarge beer can. 'That right?' He looked up and Teddy nodded. 'Fuck,' Salocin yelled as the can slipped across the sideboard. 'Why the hell do they make these so bleedin' hard to open?'

Teddy grabbed the can, held it still for his brother.

'Thanks,' Salocin said. He tapped it again. There was a hissing sound as white froth erupted like a mini volcano from the hole he had driven into the can. 'Quick. Give us yer glass,' Salocin said as the amber liquid oozed over the edges of the can. He grabbed the glass from his brother's outstretched hand and rescued the runaway beer. 'I asked them, Mum and Dad, to come today, you know?' Teddy took the glass, staring at his younger brother. 'They declined though – as usual. So as far as I'm concerned, they can go fuck themselves.'

Teddy shrugged his shoulders, took a mouthful of beer and cringed. 'Ugh – it's warm. Must have been sitting in the sun.' Salocin rolled his eyes, poured himself a glass anyway. 'Mum really is worried about you though, Sal.'

Salocin smirked. 'Mum? Worried about me? Do me a bleedin' favour?'

'She thinks you're getting in with the 'wrong sort' of people.'

Salocin frowned. He understood his big brother was only looking out for him, but he didn't need looking after, never had. From the age of five years old onwards, Salocin had usually been the one looking out for Teddy. Teddy had always been more introvert than his younger brother, preferring to stay in – when Martha allowed it – reading his comic books and playing piano, whereas Salocin liked nothing more than being outside, playing on bombsites, setting off Molotov cocktails, and generally getting up to mischief.

'Leave it out, eh, Teddy?' Salocin said. 'England has just won the World Cup. Let's not bring the mood down.'

Marie wandered in from the kitchen with a tray of washed glasses. Her pink chiffon dress, long and floaty, complemented her sun-kissed complexion and dark hair, which, unlike Ellie's, she wore as a short, neat bob. 'Ooh look,' she said, setting the glasses down and pointing towards the TV. 'Think the Queen is about to present the cup.'

With the second tin of Party Seven now open and both cans hissing and fizzing on the sideboard, Salocin and Teddy turned to face the TV again.

'Sorry, Sal,' Teddy whispered.

Salocin waved his hand dismissively. 'Don't worry about it, Ted.'

'Nah – really. I mean it. Like you said, it ain't none of Mum and Dad's business. Or mine.'

Salocin smiled at his brother. 'Honestly. It's fine.'

'Pipe down, will yer.' It was Alan – again. Salocin and Teddy exchanged glances, grinning like a couple of school kids.

England's fans chanted – "Enger-land, Enger-land, Enger-land, Enger-land…" as – according to the commentator – a yellow-clad Queen Elizabeth handed Captain Bobby Moore the gold Jules Rimet trophy from the steps of the Royal Box. Once more the room erupted and Salocin turned to his brother and clinked glasses with him. 'Cheers!' they said in unison.

Behind them they heard a distressed child. Salocin turned to see Lizzie, red-faced and crying. Just over a year old now and walking, she stumbled forward, clutching the hand of one of the neighbour's older children.

'She ferr over,' the blonde-haired, freckle-faced girl explained.

Salocin watched as Ellie scooped down to lift their daughter into her arms. Stroking her hair, she kissed the top of her head, as Marie, concern etched into her frown, hovered behind them.

Leaving Teddy to beer-pouring duties, reminding him not to spill any on the rug, Salocin wandered over to his wife. 'She okay?' he asked, brushing his daughter's soft cheek.

'She's fine,' Ellie smiled. 'Probably just tired. Think I'll see if she'll go for a nap.'

Salocin leant forward, kissed his daughter's cheek. Lizzie, pouting but impossibly pretty, stared at him. He lifted her dress, blew a raspberry on her belly and giggling, Lizzie threw her head back to reveal a neat row of tiny white teeth. Salocin loved to see his daughter smile; hear her laugh. There was something very innocent about it. A laughter not yet tainted by life.

'Thank you,' Ellie whispered.

Surprised Salocin looked up, and nose to nose locked foreheads with his wife. 'For what?'

Ellie studied him, her gaze direct, her deep blue eyes uncompromising. 'You know what. This. All of this,' she motioned with her free hand.

'No less than you deserve,' he said. 'And if things continue as they are, well, let's just say it's onwards and upwards for us.'

Chapter 22

DECEMBER 27TH
PRESENT DAY – EARLY AFTERNOON

CASSIE

Rucksacks on our backs, Luke and I stand on the station platform, hand in hand, waiting for our train to pull in, destination Kings Cross. It's a cold day. I can see my breath; tiny puffs of white vapour billowing from my lips every time I open my mouth. Dragon's breath, Connor and I used to say, when we were little. The sun's out too, low but strong, making everything crisp and bright.

Luke squeezes my hand and winks at me. 'Good stuff, eh? Our very own record label.'

I'm still wearing the same smile I left with earlier and if I'm honest, I'm still in shock. In a good way. I can't quite get my head around it – what my family has done for me, the huge gamble they are taking. Not that the new business is just about me, or for me. It will be exactly what they said it is – a family business. Positions for everyone. Except Mum, who'll keep writing, I hope.

Grandad was right.

Luke nudges me. 'You okay?'

'Just remembering something my grandad used to say. "Out of bad comes good, Cassie. You remember that, gel,"' I say in my best cockney accent.

Luke grins, squeezes my hand again. I'm fine for a few seconds but thinking of Grandad has made me think of Freddy… and

Connor. Poor thing, haven't seen my little brother that upset since, well, since Grandad passed away. We all knew it was coming with Freddy. He could hardly walk and he was old, for a dog. Thirteen, I think? Which means Connor was only, shit, five when Nan and Grandad got him.

I remember when they first brought Freddy home. A tiny bundle of black and white fluff, so excited he peed himself. A cocker spaniel, Grandad said. A ball of constant motion is what he actually was, jumping, yapping wagging his tail. It was love at first sight for me, for everyone, in fact, but if I'm honest, I think Freddy loved Connor the most – him and Grandad, anyway. Freddy really loved Grandad, no doubt about that. And Grandad loved him right back; Freddy could always turn Grandad's grumpy face into a happy one. But Connor… Connor was Freddy's playmate. They were always rolling around the floor together, wrestling and play fighting. They grew up together. So I suppose Connor has lost a best friend… and we've all lost another part of Grandad.

The grief that comes with these thoughts, hits me, as it always does, like a head-on car collision. That's the funny thing about losing someone. Sometimes the memories of that person make you laugh, fill you up with a warm, fuzzy feeling inside. At others they can make you go from happy to heartache in nought point two seconds. It never lasts long though.

Choked, I look down, staring at my trainers, new Converse from Nan for Christmas, now sliding out of focus in a black and white blur. Desperate not to blink I open my mouth and make an O shape. It doesn't work though, and my fat tears fall, splashing onto the platform. My chest hurts too, feels tight, and heavy, pressing against me so that I struggle to breathe. But I know the drill. Take a deep breath in, then blow it back out again, slowly. And I know, just a few minutes from now, this terrible ache will pass and life will go again, as normal – until the next time. I just have to hang on. Luke nudges me, asks again if I'm okay. I look up at his worried face and do my best to smile through my tears. He forces his lips into a half smile and pulls me into him. I nuzzle my damp face against his cold leather jacket. He holds me, tight, and kisses the top of my head. Luke knows the drill now, too. I need no words. And just like that, no sooner than it arrived, my moment of sadness passes again.

A raucous, metallic shriek heralds the arrival of the train. The platform is busy but Luke and I are experienced travellers. We hover, politely, waiting for the carriages to stop, the hissing sound of the doors sliding open. Luke then strides aboard and finds us a couple of seats together. On its way down from Leeds, the train is heaving. It is only two days after Christmas, people are probably heading to Oxford Street to check out the sales. Bloody madness is what *that* is. I can't wait, *NOT,* to be stuffed into shops like sardines in a can where people stomp and rampage like wild animals, looking for that all-important bargain. You'd have thought people would have had enough of shopping by the time Christmas rolls around. God knows the Christmas displays have been up for, like, forever. And don't even get me started on the music: Christmas songs played in every shop on a continual loop until everyone has gone loopy from having to listen to them. Especially the shop assistants. Then, when the big day arrives, and no more shopping is needed – what do people do for the rest of December? More shopping! Buying crap because it's got a half price label on it from shops with signs that scream "Everything Must Go!" Which, judging by the pushing and shoving that goes on, also includes manners. I shudder. You won't catch me joining them. No way Jose.

Luke puts our rucksacks in the overhead compartment and sits down next to me. He smiles, puts his hand on my knee.

'So tell me, what the hell was all that shouting about on the phone earlier?'

Luke waves his hand in the air. 'Ah, it was just Jay. Still being a dick about the New Year's Eve set we've got planned.'

'So... it's all sorted now?'

Luke tips his head back and closes his eyes. 'Yep, all sorted,' he says.

'Oh my god,' I yell, zooming in on the picture on my phone to get a better look.

Luke jumps. 'What? What the hell is it?'

'The boots I wanted... before Christmas. You remember? The long over-the-knee ones? They've been reduced in the sales. Half price.'

Luke looks relieved. 'For god sake, Cassie, I thought it was something serious,' he says, raking his hand through his hair.

'It is serious. They'll be perfect for your New Year's Eve gig. I'm not going to the shops to collect them though. Remind me to order them online when we get home.'

Luke shakes his head and reaches across for my hand. 'You're mad, you do know that, right?'

His hands are rough, his fingertips rutted with string indentations from playing the guitar.

'Of course.' I reply. 'It runs in the family. And besides, it means I have a great mind.'

'Okay, how d'you figure that one out?'

'Something that Greek philosopher bloke said.'

'Which Greek philosopher?'

I scratch my head. Why can I never remember his name? 'Erm... the one whose name sounds like Arse Hole, no, I mean Art Stole.'

Luke, eyebrow arched, studies my face. 'Art Stole,' he repeats. 'Hmm...' he says, stroking his chin, suddenly breaking into a huge smile. 'Please don't tell me you're talking about Aristotle.'

'Bingo. That's the bloke. Aristotle.' Luke is laughing so hard he has tears in his eyes. 'It's not that funny.' I'm slightly irritated; Luke continues to laugh though, so I fold my arms, look away.

Luke nudges me. 'C'mon. What is it that arse hole Aristotle said then?'

Lips pressed together, arms still folded, I look out of the window. Watch as warehouses, shops and streets rush by in a blur of colour. 'Forget it.'

'Aww, come on now Cas, don't be a mardy bum.'

'I'm not.' I still refuse to look at him.

'Are so…'

'Ha, ha, hilarious.'

'What now?' Luke's eyes are wide, staring back at me through his reflection in the window. 'Oh… I see. "Are so" sounds like "arse hole", sounds like "Aristotle". He roars with laughter at his own joke. Idiot. Connor and his juvenile friends spring to mind. Why do men find the most stupid things funny?

I get my phone out again, swipe the screen, my finger hovering above the Facebook and Twitter icon. Nah – I decide I can't be arsed. Don't want to risk seeing anything else about my dead ex-boss. I click my phone off again and to my surprise Luke starts singing – The Arctic Monkey's 'Mardy Bum'. The woman sitting opposite us, probably about Mum's age, and the girl sitting next to her, probably about sixteen, look at us both and grin.

'When yoooou're… argumentative…' Lukes continues singing.

I swing round, look at him, then glance again at the woman and girl opposite. They are both laughing and try as I might I can't stop the corners of my mouth lifting. I try my hardest *not* to smile though. Shifting in my seat, folding then unfolding my arms, crossing then uncrossing my legs, using my top lip to press down on my bottom one, anything to fight the urge to laugh. I'd forgotten how hard it is not to laugh when you really want to.

'Now then, mardy bum…' Luke continues crooning.

Like a dam busting its waters I can't hold it in any longer. I laugh so hard my cheeks ache and I have to bend forward and hold my stomach. To my surprise the woman and her daughter opposite do the same. Luke, who loves an audience, big or small, continues singing. When he finishes, the woman opposite claps, nudging her daughter to do the same which she does, albeit reluctantly.

The woman leans forward, taps Luke's knee. 'I bet you look good on the dance floor,' she says. Her daughter, whose face is now crimson, looks mortified. Shielding her eyes with her hand, she sinks down into her seat. I smile. She reminds me of Summer... and me and Maisy when we were younger. Not that long ago, really. Although sometimes, it feels like a lifetime ago.

'Ah hah... another Arctic Monkey's song,' Luke replies. 'Classic'

Luke and the woman chat music for a few minutes while the woman's daughter remains hidden beneath her hand. My phone, which is still in my hand, vibrates. I look down and swipe the screen, see it's a text – from Honey. I sit bolt upright in my seat and Luke notices.

'You okay?' He scratches the stubble around his chin. I wonder if he'll shave that off before the New Year's Eve gig? Hope not.

'Yeah... course I am.' I point to my phone up. 'Just a text from Maisy.'

Luke nods and continues talking to the woman opposite. I stare at my phone screen, watch as it blinks back, unsure whether to open Honey's message or not? When I do, her text contains one word – one stupid word – "Hi". Hi? What the hell is that supposed to mean? Does she really expect a response? Because she's not bloody getting one.

The woman and her daughter leave the train a couple of

stops before Kings Cross, promising to look Luke and the band up when they get home.

'What did Maisy want?' Luke asks.

'Ah, you know, girl stuff,' I lie. I've learned that if you tell a boy you're talking about "girl" stuff, whether you are or not, it immediately stops them asking any more questions. He asks me, instead, how I feel about Black's death and again I shrug my shoulders.

'I'm okay-ish.' It's strange to think he's dead and I'm glad he can't hurt anyone else. But am I happy that he's dead? I don't know. Yes, I suppose I am. Is that wrong? I shiver, think of Honey. Should I tell Luke about her text? I decide not to. Not yet, anyway. I shuffle back in my seat, close my eyes. Luke asks me what the Aristotle quote was that I mentioned earlier. 'You didn't say?'

I smile. It was a quote Grandad sometimes used, one I notice Mum says a lot too. '"No great mind has ever existed without a touch of madness."'

Luke grunts then laughs. 'True.'

We travel the rest of the journey in relative silence and the gentle rocking of the train carriage makes me feel sleepy, or at least it would, if the relentless whining and creaking of the train didn't remind me of some old person moaning. I think of Grandad, how he used to moan about everything. I'd give anything to hear him moaning right now.

As we approach Kings Cross, the train slows down and the last few minutes are spent inching forward. Luke prods me then jumps up to get our rucksacks from the overhead compartment.

'I'm not coming straight home,' he declares.

Confused, I look up. 'Why?'

He runs a hand through his floppy, dark hair and takes a deep breath. 'You know I love you, Cas – more than anyone?'

Tiny alarm bells start clanging in my head. I glance out of the window behind him, noticing a lone newspaper page fluttering along the train track. 'Ye-ah. Course I do. Why?'

'Okay.' Luke holds his hand out like a stop sign and for a brief second I'm reminded of a time when we were both at junior school. How we'd walk home together and the lollipop lady would hold her hand out to the passing cars to stop them, letting us cross the road. 'So if you know I love you, you know you can trust me?'

I feel my scalp prick, my heart thud just a little bit louder, faster, unsure whether I should be concerned or pissed off. 'Luke... what the hell are you talking about?'

'Right. Well, the thing is.' He coughs, clears his throat. 'The thing is, it wasn't Jay on the phone earlier, it was Eustace–'

'Eustace? What did he want?'

'He wanted to let me know...' He blows air from his puffed cheeks, a flash of fear streaking across his eyes. 'He wanted to let me know that the police are looking for me. I have to go to the local cop shop.'

'The police? You? But why?'

'They want to talk to me about Hunter Black.'

LUKE

Luke stares at the four grey walls surrounding him and shivers. He feels so alone – even though he is being watched, being questioned, by two police officers. The woman officer, probably in her thirties, maybe younger, has blue incisive eyes. While the other one, the bloke, is probably about the same age. Has Luke heard him right though? Is his name really New York? Luke is too nervous to ask. Why the fuck does he feel so guilty? He knows he hasn't done anything wrong. Well, has had a few bad thoughts maybe, which as far as he knows still isn't illegal – yet.

Although, that said, it's probably only a matter of time before George Orwell's 1984's Thought Police are a real thing.

'So you had every intention of confronting Black?' DC Foster, the woman, asks again.

Luke looks down. 'Yes, I did.'

'Sorry, what was that?' DS York asks.

Luke looks up again. 'I said yes. I planned to knock on Black's door.'

'So why didn't you?' DC Foster asks.

Luke shifts in his chair. He's tired. He's been here much longer than expected and nerves are now giving way to frustration. 'I've told you already.' He throws up both his arms.

'Well, tell us again please,' says DS York.

'Okay.' Luke sighs, drumming his fingers on the table. 'As you know, Black raped–'

'Allegedly raped.'

Luke turns towards the woman copper, his head movements stilted, robotic almost. If she is trying to goad him it's working. He knows he has to stay calm though. '*Was* raped,' Luke continues. 'And ever since, Cassie, my girlfriend, struggles to sleep at night. Sometimes she has nightmares, talks in her sleep, although I don't tell her, and that morning, after she'd had a really bad one, I'd had enough. I just wanted to confront Black and tell him what a cu–' Luke pauses.

'Yes…?'

Luke, his elbows resting on the table, cups his chin in his hands. 'I just wanted to look him in the eye, tell him what a complete tosser he was, I suppose. Knew it wouldn't achieve anything. Stupid really. But there it is. Anyway, I told Useless, I mean, Eustace, one of my friends who'd dropped by to see me while Cas was out, what I planned to do. He convinced me it was a ridiculous idea and left shortly afterwards. However, unbeknown to me he was still hovering near the flat, talking to a neighbour, when I left ten minutes later. Although what he said made good sense, at the last minute I changed my mind again. I hopped on the tube and headed towards Chelsea.'

'Why Chelsea?' says DS York.

Luke runs a hand through his dark hair, thrusting his chin forward. 'Because that's where Black lives. *Lived*.'

'And you know that... how?' asks DC Foster.

Luke clenches his jaw, grinds his teeth. 'Because...' He offers DC Foster a tight smile. 'I had to collect a friend there once.'

'Honey Brown... the singer?'

Luke shakes his head. 'Yes. Honey Brown, the singer. But you already know this.' A note of impatience creeps into his voice.

'And what happened when you got to Black's house?'

'Really? I told you this already.'

'Tell us again, please.'

'I just stood there, for ages, staring at the front door. Eustace had a hunch I'd go there and followed me, he told me not to be an idiot. Said Black would probably enjoy being confronted, would get some kind of sick pleasure out of it. I was angry though. Haven't really been able to do anything to help Cas, and it makes me feel... useless. I was about to cross the road, head for the door, when Eustace punched me. Then we got into a fight.' Luke points to his eye. 'Although I came off worse than he did. But it was only when Eustace asked me what good I'd be to Cassie if something went wrong... if I got hurt or Black did... that I realised what a twat I was. He told me to fight back the best way I know how.'

'Which is?' DC Foster asks.

'With words and music, of course. Useless, I mean, Eustace, told me to write it all down, turn it into a song. And he's right. If things had got out of hand, and something had happened to me or Black, what good would I have been to Cassie then? She needs me and I need her. It's as simple as that. And I've told you this at least three times already. I've also told you which bars we went to afterwards and I've given you the names of all the people I spoke to. I hate Black. I'm glad he's dead, but I had nothing to do with his death. So… can I go now please?'

DC Kat Stewart, who is watching the interview in another room sits back and observes the young man. He is quite handsome, reminds her of Alex Turner from the Arctic Monkeys. She can see why her daughter likes him, even without listening to his band's music. Hannah had been well impressed when last night she peered over her daughter's shoulder, saw a photo of the band on the screen of her laptop and reeled off all the member names: Chris, Jay, Marti, and Luke. Hannah still isn't speaking to her though, isn't letting her mother off that easily for missing *another* Christmas Day. It's a step in the right direction though, a way back, maybe? Besides, Kat had actually made it back by teatime, so Hannah was being a little unfair. Then again, she's a teenager.

'I know. And we appreciate your cooperation, Mr Wright, but if you can just give us five more minutes,' DC Foster looks at DS York and nods towards the door, 'we'll be more than happy to let you go.'

Luke rolls his eyes and sighs purposefully loud as the two detectives leave the room.

DS York and DC Foster join DI Stewart, and all three stare at the screen that shows the young man in the room opposite, who is now looking at his phone, frowning.

'What do you think, Noor?' Kat asks.

'Honestly, boss? I think he's telling the truth. Him and his mate, Nowak.'

DI Stewart sighs. 'I have to agree with you.' Both Luke Wright and Eustace Nowak have seemed nervous while being interviewed but what they haven't looked is guilty. And yes, while it could be argued that Wright, boyfriend of one of Black's alleged victims, isn't without motive, he has been honest enough to admit that his purpose that day was to confront Black. What he isn't is a killer. Not of Hunter Black, anyway. York and Foster know it and so does she. Kat's been in the job too long, can't remember the last time her instinct let her down. Her gut is telling her Luke Wright is not the person they are looking for. He is not their man.

'And there's definitely no further CCTV footage of either of them near Black's house after they walk away?'

DS York shakes his head. 'No, boss. But there is some footage of the bars they went to afterwards, witnesses to back it up. Neither of them has any previous, either,' he adds. He sighs and Kat doesn't miss the note of disappointment in his voice.

'Fuck.' Kat raises her hand to the middle of her forehead and rubs it hard. 'Okay.' She sighs. 'Read back his statement to him, get him to sign it and let him go.'

'Okay, boss,' DS York replies.

'Oh... and like everyone else, get his fingerprints.'

chapter 23

December 29th
PRESENT DAY — MID MORNING

LIZZIE

Maisy, slumped in the seat opposite me, smiles. Her eyes close from time to time, the jolt of the train snapping them open again. I smile back as our heads bob rhythmically from side to side. She raises her hand to her mouth to stifle a yawn but fails. Jaw stretched, mouth wide open, she makes a strange honking noise, which for some strange reason reminds me of a hippo, not unlike the ones studied on those TV wildlife programmes. Within seconds I find I'm doing the same. We both laugh; enjoy the moment, which reminds me of a different time and place, one where I first met Maisy.

She'd have been nine or ten, her inquisitive eyes and the set of her jaw leaving little doubt whose daughter she was. She was a determined little thing, too, wilful, some said. Especially when, aged seventeen, and without permission, she got a tattoo of a tree along the length and breadth of her leg. Nonetheless, despite her confidence, her implied self-belief, it didn't take long to discover the anxious little girl beneath her tough exterior. Not unlike my own fretful daughter; both damaged by the fallout of divorce.

'Oh god. S'cuse me,' Maisy says, her nose wrinkling as she yawns for a second time. 'Didn't get much sleep last night. Think Nicolas is coming down with a cold.' She turns, shifts forward in her seat, and reaches for her bag. 'Maybe I should give Crazee another call? Just check everything's okay.' She looks at me like it's a question but we both know it isn't. She will ring regardless of what I say or think.

'Crazee's more than capable of looking after him, you know.'

She grimaces, chews the corner of her mouth. 'Yeah. But...' She pouts like she used to when she was younger.

I sigh, albeit somewhat exaggerated. 'Ring if you must. I have emails to check, anyway.'

And it's true, I do. At least ten of them are from my agent, Michelle, asking me about my plans for my next book. I don't have the heart to tell her my inclination to write has all but disappeared. I tap out a reply, explain about Uncle Teddy, ask her for some breathing space, press send, and look up again. Maisy, who has her phone pressed to one ear, her hand to the other, laughs. She looks happy, and it tugs at my heart. That's all we ever want for our children, isn't it – health and happiness? I look down at my phone again, stare at row upon row of unopened emails. My stomach flips, I don't have it in me to check any more. I don't even have the heart to read some of the fab reviews my latest book has apparently been receiving. Instead, I scroll through Twitter and Facebook, quickly wishing I hadn't.

Protests have erupted regarding another faux pas tweeted by the Trump administration; one national newspaper concludes it is only a matter of time before we are at nuclear war; the NHS is *still* in crisis; and the police announce that at present, they still have nothing to add regarding the death of Hunter Black.

My head spins. I sit back, put my phone away. Surely there's *some* good news out there? Put to good use, the Internet and social media are amazing: platform for my books, links to my readers, not to mention a universe of information on just about anything and everything. The online equivalent, if you will, of the coffeehouses I studied in history at uni. Not places like the coffeehouses of today, chains of Starbucks, Costa and Caffé

Nero, serving a wide range of preposterously named teas, coffees and smoothies. I'm talking about the English coffee houses of the seventeenth-and-eighteenth century. 'Penny Universities', so-called: the price of a cup of coffee and entry, which included an alternative to structural academic learning with patrons from all levels of society – oh, except women. However, unlike the coffeehouses of old where you could walk away and switch off from the debates of the day, the online world of today is never off. And I know, as individuals, it's up to us to censor our individual usage but surely there comes a point when so much information is *too* much information – overkill?

'Mum?'

Maisy's voice interrupts my thoughts and I look up again. 'Sorry. Miles away. Everything all right?' I nod towards the phone still in her hand.

'Yeah, all good. So, where exactly is it we are going today?' She tucks her phone back into her bag. 'Please tell me that wherever, *whatever,* it is, it involves coffee and cake?'

I smile. 'Of course. Coffee and cake are compulsory.'

The train pulls in at Finsbury Park station and shudders to a halt. The doors hiss open and weary travellers embark and disembark. A flash of neon green outside the window catches my eye. I realise it's the Police, at least three or four officers, their high visibility vests stretched over their black uniforms, roaming the platform like stray dogs.

'Ooh – wonder what they're here for?' Maisy says watching them, her head swinging left to right.

I feel the colour drain from my face, my heart hammering against my chest. 'No idea,' I reply. 'Football match?'

'Yeah, maybe.' Maisy stands up for a better look.

Whatever their business is, it's not urgent. Adrenaline gives way to relief and after several minutes the doors clunk shut again as the train rocks back into motion. Two young girls, probably about Summer's age, walk past us looking for seats. Both on their phones, one tells the other that there has been an earthquake in San Francisco.

'There's a Facebook group,' she says. 'So you can let people know you're safe. I'll mark myself as safe.'

'Why?' her friend asks. 'We're not in San Francisco.'

'Duh,' the first girl replies. 'People don't know that, though, do they?'

Maisy looks at me and rolls her eyes. I grin, open my mouth to say something but Maisy puts her hand out like a stop sign. 'Don't say it,' she says shaking her head. 'I know… Cas and I were just as bad.'

'*Were?*'-

'Aww… c'mon. Cassie's way worse than me!'

I think of my first-born, how sometimes the words that leave her mouth do so before her brain has engaged, the malaprops and spoonerisms, and can't help agree. Shifting back in my seat, I put my hand to my head. Massage it a little. Maisy asks me if I'm okay. I nod. 'Tired. Few things on my mind. Uncle Teddy's funeral, for one.' Not to mention my uneasiness about today's meeting. Or should I say, conference, as it is officially referred to.

'Do we know when it is yet?' Maisy asks, her face suddenly serious.

I shake my head. 'Not yet.'

Maisy sighs. 'It's so sad.'

I think of Uncle Teddy, how shocked I was last time I saw him, the emaciated, empty shell of a man with the sunken eyes I'd found sitting in the corner of his room. His disease riddled brain too incapacitated to register my visit. 'He's in a better place.'

'You think?'

I nod. 'Definitely.'

'Is Aunt Marie okay?'

'No. Not really... but she will be. In time.'

'Do you think she'll live in London?'

I frown. 'London? No. Why do you ask?'

Maisy shrugs. 'No reason. I just know she's been spending a lot of time there recently. I'm sure she used to meet up with Cas at least once a week?'

'Really?' I knew she was going back and forth a bit, had touched base with some old friends. Clearly, I didn't realise how much, though.

'Do you think she will, then? Live in London, I mean?'

'I don't know, Maisy.' My voice is clipped.

She looks surprised, tearful. 'Sorry. I didn't mean to–'

'No!' I shake my head. 'I'm sorry. I didn't mean to snap. I'm just so... tired, I guess. What with everything that's happened over the last couple of days.'

Maisy smiles. 'It's okay. I know. Things have been manic. I'm more than happy to help though, you know?'

I notice the slight wobble in her voice, reach forward and pat her hand. 'I know. Thank you, sweetheart.'

'It's really sad about Freddy, too,' she adds.

I think of Connor's crumpled face, my little boy gripped by grief. It is sad about Freddy but it hit Connor the hardest. He was so upset when he found Freddy on his bed, having quietly slipped away in his sleep. 'Yes. It is. We're having him cremated. Going to see if we can get permission to scatter his ashes, along with some of Uncle Teddy's, on top of Grandad's grave.'

Maisy nods, blinks back her tears. 'That's nice,' she whispers.

I sit back in my seat again, look out of the window. It's a dull day. The sky matches my inner turmoil: grey, bland and oppressive, with the odd bird, like a blur, swooping across it. The tangerine vista of earlier this morning – with its wide brush strokes of warm peach, fiery orange, and splashes of molten scarlet – has long since gone. Maisy follows my gaze, watches as desolate fields containing black barren trees – x-rays of their summer selves – blast by our window, eventually replaced by lifeless grey buildings.

'Crap weather,' she says. 'I hate winter. Can't wait for summer.'

'What – so we can all complain about the heat instead of the cold?'

'True,' she replies, grinning. 'I wonder why we do that?'

'Do what?'

'Talk about the bloody weather so much?'

I smile. 'Us Brits are a bit obsessed with it, aren't we? Wasn't it Oscar Wilde who said something about it being the last refuge of the unimaginative?' It's a rhetorical question but Maisy shrugs her shoulders anyway.

'I think people talk about the weather so they don't *really* have to talk to one another,' she suggests.

'You mean… like we're doing now?' I ask, mock askance.

Maisy fixes me with her eyes and laughs. It's a warm, full-bellied sound, and it's good to see her unwinding a little. I don't disagree with her; it's a very British thing to talk about the weather, far easier that than focus on the real issues in the world.

'Except Amra,' Maisy suggests, as if reading my mind.

I throw my head back and laugh. Tell her what Amra's reply was when I asked her if she thought it chilly the other morning. '"Fuck the weather" she said. "I heard about fuckface on the news, so quit the crap and just tell me how you are? If there's anything I can do?"' Maisy laughs, as do I. 'You have to like my neighbour's style,' I add.

Our laughter subsides as the pitter-patter of raindrops taps against the window.

'Oh great.' Maisy sighs, watching as rain streams this way and that, colliding like wasted tears. 'It's raining. And I have no hood.' She points to her rather flimsy-looking coat. 'And no brolly.'

'Good job I brought one then.' I pull a folded umbrella from my bag.

Maisy inches closer to the window, presses her nose against the glass. It immediately steams up. 'Crazee hates the winters here. I sometimes think we were mad to leave Oz.'

There's a note of nostalgia in her voice. I ask her if she's having second thoughts about living here, about investing in the "new family business". She shakes her head, reassures me she's not.

I smile, still can't believe that all the while Simon was sneaking around, trying to make this new venture happen, I thought he was cheating on me.

Maisy swings round, studies me. 'What's so funny?' she asks, wearing a look of mild bemusement.

'I... I thought your Dad was cheating on me.'

'What?' she exclaims. 'What on earth made you think that?'

I shrug, explain about the early mornings and late nights Simon was putting in, the hushed phone calls behind closed doors. The fact that Scott had cheated on me all those years ago but how I'd missed all the signs. 'So it was easy, I suppose, just to assume the worst?' Maisy both smiles and frowns at me, shakes her head.

I force another smile and look down, watch how my hands, resting in my lap, swim out of focus. 'I'm just so relieved he isn't,' I whisper.

My sobs are pitiful and quiet. I feel Maisy's arm, warm and comforting about my shoulders. 'Come here,' she says, suddenly maternal, rocking me back and forth in much the same way she does Nicolas whenever he's distressed or tired. 'You daft cow.' She lifts my chin so I am face to face with her. 'Dad would never cheat on you.'

I nod, bite my lip, feel the back of my eyes still pricking with tears, the plum lodged in my throat making it impossible to talk. She thinks my tears are about Simon – which they are, a bit – but I'm also crying because I'm worn out. Worn out and afraid.

So afraid.

CASSIE

A car door slams and I immediately open my eyes. The crack in the bedroom curtains tells me it's light out. Hurried footsteps and the sound of chattering, laughing voices, rise, fall, then fade away. I've slept in, for a change. Nice. Perhaps I really am getting better now that scumbag is dead. I roll my head across the pillow, look at Luke. He has his back to me but I can tell from the gentle rise and fall of his shoulders, the sound of his breathing, he's still zonked. I'm tempted to snuggle up but I don't want to wake him, not just yet. I roll my head back, stare at the ceiling, my eye immediately drawn to the dusty cobwebs in the far corner of the room. I make a mental note – again – to get the duster out, and laugh. I know damn well I won't. Meh, whatever. Life's too short to worry about dusting, anyway. And besides, I'd only be making some poor spider homeless.

I think about getting up to make coffee, and wonder what I should wear today. Mum said something smart. I roll my eyes. Why can't this meeting, whatever it is we're having today, wait? Until after the New Year, at least. Luke and I have still got such a lot to get sorted for his gig on New Year's Eve, and she's got to help Aunt Marie arrange Uncle Teddy's funeral. What's the bloody emergency? She still hasn't even told me who it is I'm meeting.

Luke stirs, turns over to face me but his eyes are still closed, his breathing shallow. I smile, lift one of my hands from under the duvet and wave it back and forth among the motes of dust floating in the sunshine, spotlighted through the gaps in the curtains.

'What are you doing, nutter?' Luke, sleepy-eyed, is staring at me, his voice deep, gravelly – that just woke up sound.

I drop my hand but Luke reaches out and grabs it, lifts it up again, basket weaves it with his. Inching towards me, nose-to-nose, we look into each other's eyes.

'Love you,' he says.

I know he does, but it's only in the last couple of days I've realised just how much. Part of me feels flattered that he went to Hunter Black's house to challenge him, but mostly I'm relieved. Thank god Eustace followed him, stopped him. Anything could have happened: they could have argued, got into a fight. Black could have hurt Luke, or Luke could have hurt him…and got arrested, put in prison. I know how it works; I've seen all those CSA, UB40 crime whatsit programs and read about those undercarriages of justice.

I shudder at the mere thought.

'Ditto,' I reply. 'But promise me you'll never pull a stupid stunt like going to Black's house, again? You could have really ended up in the shit if you had confronted him. What if you'd argued, got into a fight and accidently killed him? Or worse still, what if he'd killed you?'

Luke grins, his smile quizzical. 'I didn't plan to go there and kill the bloke, Cas!'

'I know you didn't. But it could have happened. By accident.' I snatch my hand from his, wave it wildly above my head. 'I mean, you hear about those sorts of things happening all the time. Ooh… I wonder if that's what happened to him. You know, with one of his other victims?'

Luke presses his finger against my lips, kisses the tip of my nose. 'I promise I'll never pull a stunt like that again – I'll speak to you first.'

I reach behind me, grab a cushion and whack him with it. An individual hit for each word; 'Don't. Be. So. Bloody. Stupid.'

Luke smirks and criss-crosses his arms in front of his face for protection. 'Okay. Enough!' he shouts playfully. I drop the cushion and he pulls me close, folds me in his arms. 'You've put on weight,' he says, running his hands down my back, squeezing my arse.

'And?' I reply, eyes narrowing.

'And it's good. I know it wasn't your fault, but you were too skinny before.'

Luke presses his lips, warm and soft against mine. I think of how gentle, how kind and funny he is. Then I think of Joe, my first boyfriend at school, and that idiot I fancied at uni. Then I think of *him*, Black. All of them wankers. If it weren't for Luke, and all the other good men who have influenced my life, like Grandad, Si, Connor, Uncle Sean, there'd be a tiny part of me thinking perhaps I deserved to be mistreated. That somehow I asked for it?

I'm glad Black's dead. But I don't want to think about him anymore. Don't want to talk to another police man, or woman, solicitor, or journalist, or ever think about that part of my life again. He's gone and that chapter of my life is over, done and dusted. The future looks good, and it's time to move on. Really move on. What's the point in living in the past?

Luke and I kiss, long and slow, neither of us seeming to care we have morning breath, haven't even cleaned our teeth yet. I'm dying for a fag and a cup of coffee, though. Luke hardens against me. I decide coffee can wait.

'Marry me, Cas,' he says.

I pull away, stare at him, and laugh – nervously. 'What? Are you mad?'

Luke's eyes, now bright and alert, flit up and down, side to side, drinking me in. 'I mean it.' He touches my cheek with his hand.

'But... why?' I'm unable to hide the surprise in my voice.

'Because I love you.'

'I love you too.'

'So let's get married.'

'But, no one gets married these days. Look at my Mum and Si, they've been together for years and they've never once talked about getting married. And look at Maisy and Crazee. They have a baby together and they're not married.'

'Doesn't mean we can't be, does it? I love you, Cas. Want all the world to know it.'

'Really?'

Luke takes my hands in his, squeezes them, tight. 'Really.'

I've never really given marriage much thought. Always hoped I'd meet someone nice, one day, maybe settle down, but I've never been one of those girls who dreamed about the big white wedding. 'What if we get married, then end up divorced, like my parents?'

Luke shrugs his shoulders. 'We won't.'

'How can you be sure?'

'Because I've loved you since we were eight years old. And I'll go on loving you till the end of time. Because we've already been through shit times together, and good times, and yet here we still are. And because time after time, if you want me, I'll always be here for you.'

'Like a stalker?' I'm laughing.

Luke rolls his eyes. 'I mean it, Cassie. And it doesn't have to be some big, fancy wedding. Or it can be if that's what you want?' He pauses, rolls onto his back, runs his hand through his floppy hair.

We lay in silence for a few minutes and I'm suddenly overcome with a lovely warm feeling inside. It starts from my heart and spreads down into my stomach, seeping into my bones.

I giggle.

Luke turns his head, looks at me. 'Sorry. Bad idea.'

'Have you got a ring?

'What?'

'A ring? Have you got a ring to go with this proposal?'

Luke pulls himself up, rests his cheek on his hand. 'No. But we can get one.' His voice is suddenly an octave higher. 'Or I can choose one on my own, if you prefer?'

Excited I sit up, too, my heart thudding in my chest. 'Okay, *we'll* choose. No! Actually, *you* choose. And I have three conditions. No! Make that four. I have four conditions you have to agree to.'

Luke scrambles to his knees. 'Name them.'

I take a deep breath. 'Okay. One, I want to wear my Aunt Natasha's white DMs. Two, I want my Mum to give me away. Three, we only invite people we really love and care for and who really love and care for us.'

Luke raises his eyebrows. 'And four?'

'Four, I buy the biggest, fuck off dress we can afford and we make it a party everyone remembers.'

'Fuck, yeah!' Luke kisses me.

He goes to the kitchen to make us coffee and for the first time in a long time, life feels like it's going in the right direction. Forwards instead of backwards and for once I feel truly happy. Thrilled.

I scan the internet on my phone for wedding dresses, wonder if I should have a huge meringue-type dress, or something slinky, slim-fitting? I think of the old photos we were all looking at the other day, of the beautiful wedding dress Aunt Marie wore when she married Uncle Teddy. In fact, I wonder if she's still got it? If it would be too insensitive to ask? I also wonder what their wedding was like? Better than poor old Nan and Grandad's by the looks of it. They got married in a Registry Office.

Chapter 24

1966 – 1970 The Halcyon Years

"Oh, I love London society! It is entirely composed now of beautiful idiots and brilliant lunatics. Just what society should be."

Oscar Wilde, *An Ideal Husband*, 1895

SALOCIN

Salocin really needed to get a shift on. He and the others were unloading some of the mono and linotype collected by the drivers who worked for Babcock Smelters. Babcock's were based in Surrey and had an exclusive contract with Fleet Street to smelt, re-cast and send back the type used by all the major newspapers. Each lorry collected and carried seven skips each, and each skip was sealed with a steel ring that had to be physically broken at the smelters. Any signs of tampering with the seals meant instant dismissal for the Babcock drivers plus the threat of criminal prosecution for theft. However, using a flat edged iron bar and a bit of muscle, Mickey and the boys found a way to spring open the other end of the skips without interfering with the seal at the front. 'It's all a matter of force and pressure, see' Mickey had explained grinning. 'And where there's a will, there's a way, eh?'

Officially, Babcock's drivers earned twenty-five quid a week but by taking a slight detour to Georgie's yard the drivers could increase their weekly income significantly. The skips were prised open, the mono and linotype skimmed from the top, then transferred to empty ammunition boxes. How much they skimmed off was down to each individual driver. 'Two hundred enough?' Mickey had asked this particular geezer who had been chugging nervously on a woodbine hanging out the side of his mouth, the smell of rolling tobacco and old wool drifting from his cabin window. 'Nah,' he'd replied, swirls of grey smoke billowing from his mouth. 'Wife wants a holiday. Add another 'undred. And put forty quid in the beer box for the boys.'

Salocin hefted the now full ammunition box off the lorry.

'C'mon along, boys, chop facking chop,' Kenny said. 'Salocin 'ere's got a wedding to go to.'

Victor looked up, surprise on his face. 'That right, Salocin?'

Victor Morris, sometimes referred to as Metal Man, was mostly an enigma. In his early forties, tall, with slate grey eyes and a head of unkempt mousy brown hair, he always wore a Donkey Jacket over his slim but wiry frame. Mickey said Victor was the only man he knew capable of sleeping – often for two to three hours at a time – whilst standing upright. Even in the pub. He'd earned the nickname, Metal Man, after almost losing his leg in an alleged road traffic accident. He sometimes complained of pain during the winter months, so as a rule Mickey had him on forklift duties most of the time. His slight disability didn't affect his output though. And when the need arose, like now, he was more than happy to get stuck in. Then again, it was a truckload of mono and linotype, which was always a big earner, so no one ever wanted to miss out when the Babcock drivers turned up – dodgy leg or not.

Victor looked at Salocin and blinked slowly, cow-like, waiting for a reply. Salocin flicked his wrist, took a gander his watch. *11.00am? Shit. Already? How the fuck did that happen?* 'Certainly is, Victor.' Salocin heaved another empty ammunition box onto the lorry. 'Teddy, my brother, is getting hitched today. Church wedding. Twelve o'clock at St James'–'

'The Great? Bethnal Green?' Victor interrupted.

'That's the one.'

'Yeah, yeah.' Victor stroked his chin. 'I know it well. Same church Reggie got married to Frances in last year.'

'Reggie?'

'Yeah – Reggie. You know. Twin brother of Ronnie.'

'The Kray twins?' Salocin asked, obvious surprise in his voice.

Bemused, Victor raised an eyebrow. 'Who else!'

'D'you know 'em then?'

Victor shrugged. 'Who doesn't?'

True, Salocin thought. Growing up in the East End you'd have to be deaf, dumb and blind to not know who the Kray twins were. Salocin didn't know the brothers *personally*, though, nor did he have any desire to. No one at the yard had said much about it but everyone knew it was Ronnie that had shot George Cornell in the Blind Beggar back in March. Rumour had it that the juke box was playing the Walker Brothers "The Sun Ain't Gonna Shine Anymore" at the time and a warning bullet which ricocheted off the ceiling, made the record stick, playing the chorus over and over again.

'Good friends with Georgie, ain't he?' Victor continued.

'Who – Reggie?' Salocin couldn't help the slight alarm in his voice.

Kenny snorted, exchanged glances with Victor, then rolled his eyes. 'Leave it out, Metal Man,' he said.

Victor grinned, carried on regardless. 'Yeah. Comes to the yard sometimes – with Georgie.'

Salocin stood up, glanced across his shoulder, half expecting to see Georgie and one half of the notorious Kray twins strolling towards them. *Fuck. What the hell have I got myself involved in?*

'Stop winding the boy up, Victor.' Kenny said, laughing.

'Don'tcha worry yourself, young Salocin. Reggie's only ever been 'ere a few times. And he's a real gent, too.'

Victor nudged Kenny. 'Bet his brother, Ron, would love to meet him, eh?' He nodded at Salocin. 'Likes young men, by all accounts.'

Kenny and Victor smirked. 'Nah,' Kenny said. 'Salocin 'ere's too old, I reckon.'

The two men laughed and embarrassed Salocin, who, cheeks burning, looked down, concentrated on filling another ammunition box.

'Anyway,' Victor continued, 'who's the lucky lady?'

Salocin looked up again. 'Lucky lady?'

'Marrying yer brother?'

'Oh. Right. Yeah. That'll be Marie. Ellie – my missus – her best friend. Ellie's a bridesmaid along with my little 'un, Lizzie. I'm best man.'

Victor's eyebrows shot into his brow. 'Really? Wotcher still doin' 'ere then?'

Chasing the money like you, you old bugger.

'Yeah. Why encha down the pub helping 'im drown his sorrows?' Harry chirped up, just as the Spencer Davis Group's "Keep on Running" started playing on the radio. 'Good advice,' he said thrusting his chin towards the wireless. 'Keep on running. That's what I do, anytime some gel mentions marriage. Don't look back neither.'

Bit of a ladies man, was Harry. Or, as Mickey put it, "always chasing a bit of strange".

'I dunno. It ain't so bad being married,' Tony added, in his gruff smoker's voice. Tony Marks, a.k.a. Ginger, mid-thirties, was a lanky git with bright blue eyes and a crop of strawberry blonde hair. 'Oi, oi. Here comes trouble,' he said, nodding towards Mickey, now making his way over from the office. It was one of a few phrases Ginger always used. "Don't talk cobblers" and "Ta, ta" a couple of other firm favourites.

Mickey clapped his hands together. 'C'mon boys,' he yelled, a note of frustration in his voice. 'We've got another three lorries behind this one. All from Babcock's. All getting twitchy. Salocin…?'

'Yes, Mickey?'

'Thanks for coming in this morning… now piss orf. You'll never make it to that bleedin' wedding otherwise.' Hitching the sleeves of his overalls up to cover his shirt, until now tied around his waist, Mickey then swapped places with Salocin. Mickey may have been the boss, spending a chunk of his time in the office, but like everyone else he was never one to shy away from a bit of physical hard graft. Especially when they were on an earner like this one. 'Oh… and Salocin? Mickey called, as Salocin sloped off. 'Don't forget the ring! Top drawer of my desk in the office. Courtesy of London's refuse workers,' he added with a wry smile.

Somewhat miffed that his beer money next week would be minus his share of the three lorry loads still waiting, Salocin stuck his thumb up and headed towards the locker room. Using the shower Mickey had recently installed, he stripped out of his work gear, and washed and changed into the shirt and suit he'd hung up this morning. Flattening his tie, he checked his reflection in the rust-corroded mirror hanging above the sink. He reached for the comb in his jacket pocket, flicked it across his head then made a quick detour to Mickey's office to collect the ring.

It may have been September, the start of autumn, but with a bright blue sky and warm gentle breeze, summer lingered. It was far too nice to catch the bus or tube. He could hail a taxi, he supposed, but if he got a move on he'd still make it – just – if he walked. He patted his jacket pockets: ring, wallet and hipflask. No fags, though. Fuck. He'd have to make a quick detour via

Reuben's on the corner. A quirky little building, triangular shaped with green painted window frames and matching door, it had been there for years, Mickey said. Always busy, too. Some customers, like Salocin, simply stopped by for a packet of fags because it was convenient. Others bought cigarettes as a front for their main purchase, always handed over and discreetly hidden in a bag. Reuben, the shop owner, a miserly rapacious individual whose grey complexion blended in with his grey shirts, didn't give a fuck either way. He knew his customers would keep coming back; keep paying his inflated prices, despite his apathetic demeanour and obvious contempt. Personally, Salocin couldn't see the appeal of pornography, then again not everyone was lucky enough to have a wife like his, he supposed. He placed his money on the counter. 'A packet of Embassy please,' he said, and Reuben, ratty eyes either side of a sharp nose, wispy grey, unkempt hair, and yellow, nicotine-stained fingers that matched his equally yellow, crooked teeth passed Salocin his usual, plus his change without so much as a word or a smile. The bell rang just as Salocin turned to leave. It was a toff in a bowler hat. Keeping his head down, he passed Salocin and made his way to the counter. Salocin laughed, shook his head. *Dirty old sod.*

Back outside Salocin couldn't help pausing in front of the street seller with the old fruit barrow full of second-hand books. Under Mickey's guidance Salocin had really got back into reading again. Mickey was one of the most well-read men Salocin had met. Knowledge was power, he said, often quoting philosophers like Aristotle and Plato, Kant or Marx. 'Why fight your way out of conflict if talking achieved better results,' Mickey argued. He loved reading fiction too, said it was just as important as non-fiction. 'People come up with good ideas through stories, see?' he said. Salocin spotted a collection of leather-bound books by Dickens, dragged his fingers across the dusty spines, the temptation to linger and browse, strong. The clanging sound of a church bell in the distance quickly brought him to his senses.

Making good headway, Salocin stopped for a minute to light a fag, drawn to a small crowd playing a card game on a makeshift cardboard table. Probably Find The Lady, Salocin thought as he flicked his lighter beneath the cigarette hanging from his mouth. Find The Lady was a three-card game otherwise known as Chase The Ace, Running The Red or Three Card Molly, and the money card, as in this instance, was usually the queen of hearts. It was also a scam. But there was always some idiot gullible enough to be taken in. He took a deep drag of his fag, rolled his eyes. The mug playing was losing hand over fist. 'One born every minute,' the old geezer wearing a flat cap, standing next to him, said. Salocin shook his head. 'Ain't that the truth?' he replied.

By the time Salocin arrived at the church, Teddy, pacing back and forth, chewing gum at an alarming speed and chain smoking, appeared frantic.

'Where the fuck you been?' he snapped.

'Yeah. Where the bleedin' hell have you been?' came a somewhat irritated woman's voice behind him. It was Martha. All dolled up in her glad rags, she looked quite glam. Salocin apologised, explained he'd had to work.

'Well, you're here now, so no worries,' Teddy replied hurriedly, obvious relief in his voice.

Martha, however, lips pursed, was less forgiving. 'Always chasing the money,' she mumbled, shooting her youngest son a look thick with disdain as, arms folded, she clicked clacked off in her kitten heels towards the church.

Agitated, Salocin bit down on his bottom lip. Why? Why did his mother have a way of getting under his skin, making him feel like everything he did was wrong?

Teddy clearly sensed his brother's annoyance, placed a hand

on his shoulder, told him to ignore her. Salocin smiled, reminded himself that today was about his brother, and sister-in-law to be – no one else.

'Nervous?' Salocin asked.

'Really.'

'Having second thoughts?'

'God, no.' Teddy took a swig of whiskey from the hipflask Salocin retrieved from his jacket pocket. He winced. 'Cor blimey. That's a bit tasty ain't it?'

'Have another,' Salocin insisted. 'It'll help calm your nerves.'

Teddy took another swig and passed it back. 'I mean, I love her. No doubt about it.' Salocin straightened his brother's tie as he talked, then concentrated on fixing his own buttonhole with the cream carnation Teddy had been holding for him. 'I just worry that...'

'That what?'

'It sounds daft, I know. But, well, I worry that I'm not good enough for Marie. That she deserves better. Does that make sense?'

Salocin smiled. 'More than you know.' He slapped his brother's back affectionately. 'Wanna take a gander at the ring?'

'Shit. Yeah. The ring. I forgot all about it.'

Teddy had spent far more than he'd budgeted for and hadn't even paid Salocin yet. Salocin knew his brother was good for the money though and was more than happy to help. 'And, come on. Let's get you inside before the bride turns up. Remember, it's not a life, it's an adventure!'

The ceremony itself passed without any hitches and the bride, who wore a fitted white column dress with lace sleeves and a long veil, looked beautiful. Ellie and Lizzie – along with three others – wore pale blue floor length Grecian style dresses with matching pillbox hats, except for Lizzie who wore a crown of daisies. *My girls*, Salocin thought, *my beautiful girls*, his heart bursting with pride. It was good to see Teddy happy, and despite his pre-ceremony nerves he hadn't stopped smiling since. The reception, for sixty people, was held in the Windsor Rooms above the local bakery, just around the corner from where Marie's parents lived, and a veritable feast was had by all. Much to Salocin's delight, it included jellied eels, cockles and winkles, plus a nice bit of salt beef.

A white iced, three-tiered wedding cake dotted with intricate handmade daises and a cake topper that simply spelled out the word "love" sat on the top table between the bride and groom. During his best man's speech, as well as welcoming his new sister-in-law into the family, Salocin did his level best to embarrass his older brother, then at the close of his speech he passed the happy couple an envelope. Inside was an itinerary, lovingly put together by Ellie, for an all-expenses paid, two week long stay in Cornwall. Marie, already slightly emotional after a couple of glasses of wine, burst into tears, swiftly followed by Ellie.

'Don't get too excited,' Salocin continued. 'The bad news is that Ellie and me are gate-crashing and will be joining you for the second week.'

Everyone cheered and while Marie clapped her hands together like an excited schoolgirl, Teddy pulled his brother into a brief, manly hug. Salocin noticed Martha roll her eyes but ignored it. He then raised a toast to the happy couple. 'And remember,' he added, 'It's not a life, it's an adventure. Cheers everyone.'

'Cheers!' the room chorused in a clink of glasses.

Then it was Teddy's turn to speak. He was much less confident than his younger sibling and noticeably ill at ease with public speaking. Taking a quick swig of his pint, his hand trembling, he pulled a crumpled piece of paper from his jacket pocket, which he then carefully unfolded and placed in front of him. Looking at Salocin, who nodded and winked at him, Teddy coughed to clear his throat, and began. As speeches go, it was brief and to the point. Mainly thanking everyone for coming, the bridesmaids for helping out, and the best man for embarrassing him, however, sensing the restlessness of his audience, he turned to Marie, took her hand in his and thanked her for helping him to believe in magic.

'Eh?' Marie stared at her new husband, her eyebrows knitting together in obvious confusion. 'Magic?'

Teddy looked towards his brother, a faint smile tugging at the corners of his lips. 'See, the thing is, when Salocin, my brother, first met his wife…' He glanced over at Ellie and smiled. Embarrassed she put her hand to her neck, looked down, her cheeks noticeably flushed. 'I asked him what it felt like to be in love. He said nothing for a few seconds but then he said one word, just one word. "Magic." Magic? I said, confused. I don't believe in magic? To which he replied, "You will when you meet her."'

Marie leapt from her chair and flung her arms about Teddy's neck. Salocin looked at Ellie who was watching her in-laws – Martha dabbing her eyes with a hankie, Wilf, arms folded across his chest, rolling his eyes. Amused she looked away and caught him staring at her. She tipped her head to one side and smiled. The one she kept just for him. The one that said "I love you".

Speeches over, the scraping of tables and chairs filled the room as they made space to clear the way for the much-anticipated knees up as a three-piece band, drummer and two guitarists, set up their instruments. The first song they played was Cliff Richard's "Congratulations". Everyone took to the floor, the atmosphere one of inebriated good cheer as the floorboards creaked and groaned in accompaniment. Salocin thought it was a miracle the floor didn't collapse. And, as the evening drew to a close, Teddy had a surprise for his new bride. Guitar in hand, he took to the front of the room and bravely serenaded his wife with the Ben E. King song "Stand By Me". Once again Marie burst into tears – along with every other woman in the room, Ellie included.

'Oh gawd. Give us yer hankie.' Ellie sniffed. 'All me bleedin' mascara's running down me face.'

Salocin smiled, pulled his wife towards him, used his thumbs, rough from manual labour, to wipe away the black streaks coursing down her face.

'He's good isn't he?' she said, obvious surprise in her voice. It was true, he was. Compared to Salocin, Teddy's singing voice was positively angelic, although both brothers were reasonably accomplished musicians.

Salocin nodded. 'Beneath that serious white collar façade beats the heart of a true musician,' he said.

'Didn't know he was so blinkin' romantic, too.' Ellie giggled. 'Why ain't you ever dedicated a song to me?'

Why hadn't he? A lot of songs reminded him of Ellie. Like the first time he laid eyes on her and The Dave Clark Five's "Glad All Over" was the song playing on the radio as he walked into work. Or how Dusty Springfield's "Wishin and Hopin" was playing on the jukebox in the café they first met at after work. Or how The Kinks "You Really Got Me" was the first song he heard after he'd kissed her goodnight. Or how The Drifters "Saturday Night at the Movies" played on a loop in his head when they went to the pictures for the first time. Or how he listened to The Beatles "She Loves You" while getting ready for their wedding day. Or Dionne Warwick's "Reach Our For Me" when she was sad after giving birth to Lizzie. But it was true; they didn't have that one *special* song.

'Because I haven't found it yet,' Salocin replied, tucking Ellie's hair behind her ear, kissing the tip of her nose. 'But I will,' he promised.'

As Christmas 1966 drew to a close Salocin brought home the biggest Christmas tree he could find.

'Oh my gawd. What on earth were you thinking?' Ellie exclaimed as she watched her husband struggling to squeeze the enormous evergreen through their narrow hallway. 'It's huge!'

Salocin winked, patted the space between his legs. 'The tree's quite big too, eh?'

Ellie laughed, flicked her husband playfully with the tea towel resting on her shoulder, the smell of chicken stew cooking in the kitchen behind her, fresh pine filling the hallway in front. 'Seriously though, why so big?'

Salocin shrugged his shoulders. 'Why not? We can afford it, can't we.' It was true. They could. Just like the oversized turkey they'd ordered for Christmas day dinner, along with the sack full of presents for Lizzie.

'A monstrosity is what it is,' Martha remarked unkindly about the tree, when she and Wilf had paid them a rare visit on Christmas morning. But Lizzie loved it, especially when Salocin lifted her onto his shoulders to place the star on top.

It was the first year Salocin and Ellie received an invitation to Georgie Wakefield's annual Christmas party. It was a big event, included many celebrities among the guest list, and this year it was taking place at the BoHo Club in Soho. It was also the first time Salocin and Ellie had left Lizzie with someone other than Marie or Martha. Luckily, the daughter of a neighbour volunteered to babysit, but naturally Ellie was a little worried. However, once they arrived at the venue which, filled with celebrities, alongside white-jacketed waiters silently moving about the room offering glasses of free Champagne from carefully balanced, silver trays, Ellie quickly forget about her daughter for a few star-struck hours. There were, of course, lots of 'ordinary people' – like them – but Ellie was sure she spotted Bobby Moore and his wife, and Cilla Black. And when Salocin nipped off to use the loo, he swore blind he saw Oliver Reed talking to Jimmy Tarbuck.

Round tables with white linen tablecloths lined the room, each containing a glass vase filled with tropical flowers – the likes of which neither Salocin nor Ellie had ever seen – as their centrepieces. There was also row upon colourful row of food platters, more akin to poetry on a plate, and glass bowls containing gold-tipped cigarettes and Cuban cigars, not to mention a few other smaller, rather discreetly placed bowls, each containing what looked like small blue triangular sweets.

'Purple hearts,' Salocin whispered, when he saw the quizzical look on Ellie's face.

Ellie got to meet Georgie too, albeit briefly, who seemed positively charming, and of course, Mickey, who introduced both her and Salocin to his beautiful wife, Helena. Tall, gamine, with huge emerald eyes, a small nose and a pink cupid's bow mouth, she wore her raven black hair in a Vidal Sassoon geometric style bob, which blended perfectly with her simple, yet elegant long black dress. She had an ethereal, almost spiritual beauty about her. She reminded Ellie of Audrey Hepburn. It was easy to see why Mickey was so proud of her. She didn't get her looks from her father though, Salocin and Ellie both agreed on that.

They danced all night and later fell into bed happy but exhausted. Unlike this time last year, life was a bit of a dream, and as they approached a new year, Salocin couldn't help thinking that the future looked bright.

Very bright indeed.

Chapter 25

DECEMBER 29TH
PRESENT DAY – EARLY AFTERNOON

LIZZIE

I sink into the plush purple sofa in the bright, airy reception area of Farringdon Court Chambers. It's an impressive building, modern, its walls, or so it appears, made entirely of glass. *Wouldn't want to keep those clean*, I say to myself – or so I think – until the receptionist, somewhat bemused, looks over his glasses toward me, a wry smile on his face. Embarrassed, I look away; replay my earlier conversation with Simon this morning, first his shock that I hadn't okayed this with Cassie – although, she doesn't have to go through with it, of course – then his hurt that until this morning, I hadn't told him either. I tried to explain my need to keep it quiet, the urgency to get the ball rolling so that when I did tell Cassie, it wouldn't feel like another mountain to climb, and the ultimate goal being some kind of justice, some kind of closure.

'You've gone about this all wrong,' Simon warned. 'You should have spoken to Cassie first.' I didn't disagree with him, his words only confirming what I already knew, twisting the tightly wound coil in my chest just a little more. 'And why didn't you tell me?' he asked. 'You used to tell me everything.'

I shrugged my shoulders and stuck my lip out, not unlike baby Nicolas. 'Probably the same reason you didn't tell me about the new business venture.'

Simon looked at me, his forehead creased, his frown fixed,

then closing his eyes, he laughed. 'Touché.' He pulled me towards him, folding me in his arms, his embrace strong, reassuring, reminding me of his faithful, constant presence.

How did I ever believe he was having an affair? He kissed the top of my head, said he loved me more now than he ever had and promised never to keep anything from me again. 'And this barrister,' he said, waving his hand like an impassioned music conductor during The Last Night of the Proms, 'is doing all this, for Cassie, for free, pro bono, you say?'

'Yes,' I nodded. Laura said–'

'You know my ex is a barrister called Laura?' Simon interrupted, grinning.

'Not Laura Noble though, is she?'

Simon scoffed, choked on the mouthful of coffee he'd just slurped. 'Noble? Hardly.' He wiped his mouth with the back of his hand. 'Definitely not my Laura.' It felt strange to hear him say *my Laura*. 'And all because of some promise made to Salocin by his old boss, Micky Rosenthal, years ago, you say?'

'Apparently so.'

'Do you know what – exactly?'

'Laura said she wasn't at liberty to say. But I'm working on it,' I'd replied.

'Oh well,' he added, with the same amused eye-rolling fondness he often applied whenever we discussed the kids, 'No doubt we'll find out just what Cassie thinks in a couple of hours' time.'

His words of comfort, reassuring arms wrapped about my shoulders, filled me with the courage I'd been lacking these past few days, eased the agonising cramp of fear that continually fizzed at the pit of my stomach. I glanced across the kitchen. The hands on our oversized wall clock told me I still had half an hour or so before Maisy and I needed to leave and catch our train to meet Cassie, and, except for the gentle hum of the fridge, the whir of the dishwasher, the house was quiet, our guests either out or enjoying a lie in.

'Simon... I... have something I need to tell you.' I took both his hands in mine, studied them. When did he start getting age spots? And when did I, for that matter?

Simon had looked at me warily, his eyes narrowing, as if sizing me up. 'Sounds serious,' he said, his scepticism making my legs wobble, the ground I stood on suddenly spongy, infirm. It was serious. *Very serious.* But I could no longer bear the weight of such a burden. Besides, if I couldn't tell Simon, couldn't trust him, of all people, then who the hell could I?

'It is serious,' I said. 'It's about Hunter Black.'

Simon had rolled his eyes, did nothing to hide the flash of disappointment dancing across them. '*Him* – again?' he replied. 'What now?'

'Lizzie.' A voice interrupts my thoughts.

I look up. Laura Noble QC stands before me. We've met on a couple of occasions now, and each time I still feel slightly intimidated. It's nothing she does particularly, more the way she speaks, the way she carries herself. Tall, with effortlessly slim legs, she is wearing a white, perfectly pressed shirt beneath her pristine navy fitted suit. About the same age as me, she is an attractive woman. Different, though, to say, Ruby's curvaceous good looks, or Natasha's hippy, almost ethereal prettiness. Laura has a different quality about her, a look that suggests an ancestry of wealth and privilege, and dare I say it, a hint of entitlement. Her make-up is minimal, skin flawless, her bright blue eyes, although creased at the corners thanks to the march of time, are big and captivating, framed by perfectly arched brows. Her nose is small and delicate and her cheekbones, like her reputation, razor sharp.

She smiles, raises one of her arched brows and scans the waiting area. 'I thought you were bringing your daughter with you today?' Her well-spoken voice is almost as thick and glossy as her dark hair.

Somewhat flustered, I stand up. 'Laura. Hi. Hello. Thanks for seeing us today.' I point towards the entrance, explain that Cassie is running slightly late. 'My other daughter is waiting for her at the coffee shop on the corner.'

Laura raises her other eyebrow. 'Other daughter?'

'Yes, that's right, stepdaughter actually. They shouldn't be too long.'

Laura holds her hand out, gestures for me to follow her. She addresses the young man sitting behind the reception desk as Markus, asks him if he will kindly show Cassie to her office when she arrives. He responds with a courteous nod and I follow Laura along the brightly lit corridor to her office. It is a huge room with panoramic views of London. An eclectic mix of historic buildings, mainly stone structures, all straight lines, clustered columns, and pointed lead windows complete with elaborate ornamentation, contrasted by new buildings like this one. A polished pebble of glass with disproportionate but geometric sleek curves so that the whole building appears to change colour with the movement and angle of the sun. Her desk, an enviably large sheet of silver polished steel contains a computer, a laptop, a landline phone and a mobile, all lined up alongside a thick, closed file of papers. To her side there is another desk housing bundles of papers, lever arch files and various hefty hardback books. Law books, I assume; where she works, spreading herself out when away from her computer. I see only one framed photo hidden behind her computer.

Laura nods towards two chairs lined up in front of her desk. 'Take a seat,' she says. 'Will your other daughter be joining us?'

'I don't see why not,' I reply. 'It's not a secret. At least, it won't be, after today.'

Laura asks me if I have actually spoken to Cassie yet.

Sheepishly, I shake my head. 'I see.' There's a slight air of irritation in her voice.

'I did wonder, well, what with Black's death and everything, if it was still possible to continue, anyway?'

Laura informs me it is but suggests it would be wise to wait for Cassie and she will explain it all then. She wanders off in search of another chair, for Maisy. My thoughts turn to Cassie. I wonder if she'll understand why I've done this. If she'll understand that it comes from a place of love or if, in fact, she thinks I've gone too far. Laura breezes back in, interrupting my thoughts, places another chair next to mine, and sits down opposite me. After a few seconds she stands up again. 'Do you think it's hot in here?' she asks, removing her jacket.

I smile. 'Hot flush?'

She looks at me askance. 'I don't know. I hadn't really considered it before.'

I mumble some garbled words about how I thought I'd started the menopause last year but how it turned out I was pregnant instead. 'Then I miscarried. Now I *am* going through the menopause – for real this time.' Laura stares at me, her expression blank. I shift uncomfortably in my chair. 'Evening primrose helps,' I suggest. 'And chewing on a few mint leaves a couple of times a day.'

'Right. Thanks,' Laura replies.

The sound of laughter echoing through the corridor breaks the awkward silence between us. 'You're such a loser,' I hear Maisy say, followed by the voice of a chattering Cassie who appears to be relaying a story about missing her bus because of a woman with a pram at the bus stop. 'It was one of those huge fuck off prams, too,' she says. 'Had a cat in it for god bloody sake.'

Squirming, I look at Laura, smile. 'Cassie,' I say, rolling my eyes, using my chin to point towards the half-open door.

'"Foghorn Lil from over the hill" my Dad used to call her.' Laura stares back at me, a slight grin lifting her lips.

'This building is–' Maisy starts to say.

'Fucking huge,' Cassie interrupts. 'What the hell is Mum up to?'

A man's voice interrupts their conversation. 'Oh. Okay, thanks,' Cassie replies. Markus, I think, pointing out Laura's office door.

Again I glance across at Laura who, except for her tight-lipped smile, remains expressionless. 'Bit loud, aren't they?' I say, my tone apologetic.

She folds her arms across her slim chest. I can't work out if she's amused, appalled or indifferent. 'I've heard worse,' she says.

Cassie and Maisy push the door open and step into the office. Laura stands up and maybe it's the way the light catches her from behind but she suddenly looks pale, flustered even?

'Oh, hi, Mum.' Cassie turns towards us, her smile turning to a wary frown as she glances over at Laura.

Maisy also looks over. She freezes, appears startled, all traces of laughter gone. 'Mum?' she says.

'Yes?' I reply.

'Mum?' she repeats.

I suddenly realise she isn't looking at me – she's looking at Laura.

CASSIE

Ignoring the weirdo on Reception, I march down the corridor, Mum's voice following me.

'Cassie,' she calls. 'Pleeease come back.' She sounds choked.

I don't want to leave, not really. But like a stroppy teenager I'm making a point so I have to go now, don't I? I barge through the glass revolving door but I can't even get that right and like an idiot I get my foot caught. Angry, I kick at it. The door shudders. I'm being childish, I know I am but I've gone too far now so I can't give in. Anyway, I'm angry, and Mum needs to know that.

Oh I don't know. What the hell? What the bloody hell! It's all just bollocks.

I somehow free my foot from the door and step outside. A cold wind whips round my ears and stings my eyes making them water – at least that's what I tell myself. The temperature has dropped, too. Winding my scarf around my neck I hug myself, suddenly aware that the pavements and roads are wet from another snow flurry. It's a sleety snow, bitter. The wind feels like a fan blasting ice-cold air on my face, my hot, flushed cheeks thawing as quickly as my anger.

Mum's voice has disappeared but I keep walking anyway. I pass the coffee shop where I met Maisy earlier and a bit further along I see the homeless girl again, the one I saw before, in the dirty blue sleeping bag. The guitar she was playing is laid on its side next to her, and there's a small pot of change on the other. Unlike earlier, though, her sleeping bag is pulled right up, her gaunt face barely visible. I continue walking, feel guilty and look over my shoulder. I've already given her what change I had. Nan's voice pops into my head, 'There but for the grace of god.' Not that Nan is religious, she just says that she and Grandad knew what it was like to struggle, especially when they were first married. 'We always had each other, though,' she always adds.

I turn back, pass the girl again and head towards the coffee shop. I push the door open and warm air hits my face like a hairdryer, the strong smell of coffee making my nostrils flare. The queue is long but I join it anyway, listening to the idle chatter of customers, the chink of spoons against cups and mugs, the gurgling and steaming of the coffee machine. I let my thoughts drift. Fuck – Laura, the barrister, is actually Maisy's mum. And Simon's ex-missus. How messed up is that? And how the fuck did Mum not realise who she was? I wonder what poor old Maisy thinks? I didn't even stop to find out.

'No,' I mumble to myself, 'it's all too much to think about right now. I'll call Maisy later, talk to her about it then.'

I pick up a pack of sandwiches; order a large latte, a small cappuccino and a couple of fudge brownies. The bored-looking shop assistant asks me if I want to eat in or take away. I tell him it's a takeaway, pay with my debit card, praying it isn't declined, and stuff the food in my bag. Carrying a drink in each hand I then head back towards the door, looking for a space to rest one of the cups so I can open the door, but a boy, about my age, gets up and opens it for me.

'Thanks.' I manage a tight-lipped smile in response to his wide-mouthed beaming one.

The door swings shut behind me. I take a few steps forward then look over my shoulder, check the boy isn't following me before heading off to find the girl in the sleeping bag. Despite the snow, she's still there. I bend down, rest the cups beside her. Her eyes are closed. She smells of sweat, and fags and booze… and… something else? I pull the sandwiches and brownies from my bag and leave them beside the latte. Going back to my bag, I rummage around inside it until I find the pack of sanitary towels I bought the other day, lift two out, stuff them back in my bag but leave the rest of the pack next to the sandwiches and the coffee. I then grab the small cappuccino and walk and walk and walk.

I stare out across the river that rises to meet the grey sky above. It's stopped snowing, but it's still bloody cold. I'm at Southbank. Not sure why? Just know I needed to get away. From Mum, and Maisy, and Laura… everyone, in fact. I need to clear my head, give myself time to calm down. A riverboat honks and I watch as it churns up the river leaving a trail of white froth behind it. The Thames is always such a murky-looking river, even during the summer, but today it sparkles, the rays of what little winter sun is left of the day bouncing off its rippling waves.

Why? Why would Mum go behind my back? Arrange everything without asking me first? I lower my head, chew on my non-existent nails. I shouldn't have shouted at her. I know she only wants the best for me, some sort of justice, some sort of closure. Sighing, I remember the look on her face, all the pain and fear etched into every line, every crevice – or was that me I saw reflected in her eyes. My heart sinks. I try to swallow the hard lump at the back of my throat. Why? Why? Why… am I such a bitch? Why do I always hurt the ones I love the most?

Ashamed, I look down. Cringe, but resist the urge to cry. I'd do anything for a hug so why did I shrug Mum off when she tried to give me one? I remember back to when she was in hospital – seems like a lifetime ago now – when she was in a coma, and we thought we might lose her. How I promised, if she'd just wake up, that I'd never ever take her for granted again.

Through blurred vision I look up, see my breath steaming in the chill evening air. I stick my gloveless hands into my pockets, then quickly pull them back out again. I feel dizzy, as if my insides are falling away, and use my hands to steady myself. When the ground stops moving, I turn away from the river. A couple of runners, two women, jog by, all tight Lycra, flushed, red faces and swinging ponytails, talking and laughing in breathless fits and starts. A few minutes later two more runners, men this time, also jog past. One of them looks at me, smiles.

'Cheer up,' he says. 'May never happen.'

Fuck off, wanker, it already has.

I walk towards an empty bench opposite and sit. The cold metal slats feel like blocks of ice against the back of my legs. I stare ahead. Look out across the river again and spot Tower Bridge on the horizon, hundreds of people, like ants, coursing across it. The light is fading fast now, the sky folding in around the city. I hate how quickly day turns to night during winter. My tummy, hollow as a cave, rumbles. I realise it's hours since I last ate. I was, of course, supposed to grab a bite with Mum and Maisy before they went home again. Before I stormed off like a childish idiot.

Why the hell did Mum think it was okay to start this shit without checking with me first? I'm glad Hunter Black is dead but I'm worn out with it all now, pissed off with his continual presence in my life and weary of the revulsion that bubbles up inside me every time I hear his name, sick of the shame that still floods through my veins because of something *he did to me*. Yes I want justice, confirmation that Hunter Black was at fault. But regardless of whether it's a criminal case or a civil one, it isn't Mum, or anyone else, that will have to stand up in court and live through it all again, is it?

Think of the shit storm it would cause. Paparazzi and reporters, death threats from online trolls again, supporters of Black, or just women haters in general, all of whom would see it as an opportunity, a valid excuse to hate me just a little bit more. Black is dead. So why, regardless of what Laura said about it still being possible to pursue a civil case against Black's estate – the purpose of which today's meeting was to reveal and discuss – would I actually want to?

Yes I understand that the purpose of a civil case for sexual assault is to sue for damages for any personal injury caused. And yes I understand, as Laura explained in her posh voice, that proof is lower in a civil case than a criminal one, is based much more on probability, whereas in a criminal case, jurors must decide beyond all seasonable doubt – reasonable doubt, whatever the bloody saying is – if the accused is guilty, which means the likely outcome of a civil case is a positive one. But what if I lose? And even if I win, I'd be suing for damages. Damages means money. So surely that sends out a message that this is simply about money? That men can keep abusing women but it's okay as long as the price is right? Because it's not. Yes the money, any money, would come in handy. I could put it into our new business, help the record label grow, but ultimately there is only ever one thing this should be about – justice – pure and simple.

Which, as I hang my head, I realise that is what Mum and Laura were talking about.

My phone buzzes in my pocket. I pull it out. It's a text. From Honey. Again?

I know you probably hate me, and rightly so. And I know you'll probably never speak to me again but… I'm sorry, Cas. So, so sorry xxx

I stare at the screen, feel numb. Does she expect me to answer? She was my best friend but she betrayed me… sold her soul to the devil in exchange for fame and fortune. Unbelievably, though, I feel myself smiling, thinking back, remembering the Honey I knew from *before* all this shit happened. Flatmates, going to gigs, sharing drunken nights out and broke ones in. And as mad as it is, I realise how much I've missed her because it's hard to hate someone that I know – have always known I suppose, deep down – is just another victim of Hunter Black. He manipulated her, did what he did – got her to the dizzy heights of fame – so she would side with him. Protect him from my *allegations*. But she would have had to pay him back, at some point, because that was the kind of man he was. It's just taken me all this time to realise it. So, and I hate to admit it, Aunt Marie was right.

I can't talk to Honey yet, though… if ever? I swipe the text away just as my phone vibrates in my hand. It's Mum calling. I should be with her, and Maisy, celebrating my engagement, looking forward to the future. Not here, on my own, my head filled with thoughts of Black, stuck in the past – again. Hot, fat tears splash onto the glass screen, my fingers hovering above it. Which icon do I select – red or green? Green or red? My head pounds and my heart throbs. Someone passes me, playing music – loud music. I recognise it straight away, it's the song Grandad always played to Connor and me when we were little, whenever we worried about things. Bob Marley's "Three Little Birds", telling me everything is gonna be all right. I laugh for real. Good timing Grandad. I press the green accept call button.

'Mum,' I whisper. 'Sorry. I'm so sorry.'

LAURA

Laura stands at the large window in her office and breathes deeply, taking a minute to enjoy the silence. It had been a shock to see Maisy again. Laura hadn't been expecting it. And if the spectacle of the last hour or so was anything to go by – best described as a firework display with an amusing variation of musical chairs thrown in to boot – neither had Maisy. Then again, with hindsight, Laura had been thoroughly naïve in believing, when Lizzie had first contacted her, she would be able to remain incognito, preserve her true identity – until she was ready.

During Laura's first, but brief meeting with Maisy, in Australia, well over a year ago, now, Laura had deliberately failed to mention the link between her own father, Mickey, and that of Maisy's stepmother's father, Salocin. Her plan being to gradually ingratiate herself back into her daughter's life, and, if it wasn't too late, make amends, earn her daughter's trust, and perhaps, one day, her love, too. Today's conference to discuss civil proceedings against Hunter Black was supposed to be with Laura's client, Cassie – if she agreed – and her mother, Lizzie. But why wouldn't Maisy come along and support her stepsister.

Maisy and Lizzie's anger towards Laura was more than

justified. She knew that. However, Laura truly hoped, in time, they would understand there had been nothing sinister in her withholding her true identity. She had merely been waiting for the right moment to come clean, explain all. Yes, perhaps, again with hindsight, Laura should have arranged for someone else to represent Cassie. But Laura had promised her father, and the conflict and desire to reconcile the deeds of the one man she had loved and respected more than any other, weighed heavily upon her. Besides, she hated Christmas, welcomed any legitimate excuse to dodge the forced celebrations and relentless feasting. So when Lizzie had contacted her, requested a conference between herself and Cassie, sooner rather than later, Laura hadn't been in the least bit perturbed to meet during the Christmas holidays.

Hugh didn't mind either. Hugh was, to quote the rather annoying American friend staying with her older sister, "a doll". He was also Laura's third husband. Her second husband, Sebastian, had been a mistake, whereas her first husband, Simon, had been the love of her life, and she his – for a while. They'd had a daughter together – Maisy. Laura's first and only child – she'd made sure of that. She was lovely, too, all things considered. Alas, though, Laura and Simon came from very different worlds. And so, not long after her twenty-eighth birthday, they parted company and divorced. John Lennon was wrong when he said love was all you needed.

Marriage came calling again, a few years later. Tall, blonde, and blue-eyed, educated at Oxford, Sebastian worked in politics. He was absolutely charming, at least, in the beginning. It didn't take long, though, for the real Sebastian to show himself. Laura had mistaken his arrogance for confidence, his conceit for good-humoured wit. Self-aggrandising, her sister had called him. Self-centred prick was what he turned out to be. He hated Laura's success, expected her to give up work, or at least only continue on a part-time basis, play the good little wife alongside his flourishing political career, as was the tradition in his family. What he really wanted, though, was control. Control over her, control over their life together, complete control over everything. Laura said, bollocks to that – her father had gone through a lot, done a lot of questionable things to ensure that she, his youngest daughter, along with her other siblings, got the education and opportunities he never had. He'd taught Laura, and her sisters, to reach for the skies, said she should never let being a woman in a man's world hold her back and she should never to let anyone, man or woman, stand in her way of success. Within eighteen months her marriage to Sebastian had ended, although she retained his name – Noble – ironic, but she liked its simplicity. There was something magnanimous, yet stolid about the name Laura Noble. From thereon in she was disinclined to share herself or her life with anyone. She threw herself into her work, called to The Bar within six months of her split with Sebastian, and had made silk by the grand old age of thirty-five.

Then along came Hugh, a friend of her brother-in-law: casual, unassuming, stout round the middle, floppy-haired, with the most perplexing green eyes. He worked for some charity or another, and the salary, if you could call it that, was appalling. Fortunately, he had inherited a 'modest cottage', as he liked to call it – "fuck off great mansion" her father, had he been alive, would have best described it – in the leafy suburbs of Surrey. Hugh was, as her father would have so eloquently put it "a good 'un" so when he proposed to her one spring afternoon from the balcony of their room in the Rome Cavaleri Hotel, boasting a hillside position in Montemario with the most outstanding panoramic view of the ancient city, it didn't feel in the least bit contrived. The word "yes" fell so easily from her lips it felt the most natural thing to say.

The wedding itself was low key, Laura wore a vintage 1960s shift dress, not unlike those her mother wore when Laura was tiny, the ones in the precious photos that now dog-eared and crumpled, she often looked upon, for her eyes only. The reception was small, close friends and family, held at Hugh's very '*modest* cottage'. There was only one person missing that day – her daughter, Maisy. But Laura knew she had to tread carefully there, couldn't go rushing in. During their last meeting, Laura had feigned casual nonchalance with Maisy, which wasn't difficult when it was part and parcel of her job. And once upon a time it wouldn't have been an act. Her fight to carve out a career for herself in a man's world had not been an easy one. But in doing so, she had become hard, had turned her back on those that needed her most.

She sighed. Hoped to god she hadn't fucked things up.

Time was all she needed. She just had to give it time.

Chapter 26

LONDON 1966–70
THE HALCYON YEARS ... CONTINUED

...merrily, merrily, merrily, merrily, life is but a dream.

SALOCIN

It is often accepted that when people look back at certain moments in their lives, they do so with a sense of dewy-eyed nostalgia, an unrealistic belief that life was better than it actually was. However, after he had been welcomed into the fold, that's exactly how life felt to Salocin and Ellie: as if the summers were always hot and long, the winters bright and crisp, and Christmases always white. It took adjustment, especially for Ellie who, so used to having to scrimp and scrape, found it hard to break the habit of watching every penny. She soon became accustomed to her new way of life though, got used to buying the best sausages for dinner, a nice bit of fillet steak for Salocin, or a new coat for Lizzie. Forgot what it felt like to wake up cold during the winter, or to have no escape from the heat during the summer, the dread at having to get another winter out of a threadbare coat, or trying to repair an old pair of shoes with a hole in them. If they wanted something they bought it, either legitimately or via the 'Dust' – otherwise known as London's refuse workers.

Mickey said if you were lucky enough to work on the 'Dust' you were made for life. Said it was one of the most sought after jobs in London, and those jammy enough to do so made more in a month than most people earned in a year. He said they ran a delivery service that had close connections with Hatton Garden, so a lot of their dosh came from jewellery.

'Who'd suspect the lowly, half-witted dustman,' Mickey said. 'But it's access all areas, see? Who else can get right of entry to those business premises closed off to everyone else without causing suspicion? A split of the profits agreed with the employees, the loot dumped in the rubbish on collection day, which the dustmen then sell on to the likes of you and me, at a massively reduced price of course, and bish, bash, bosh everyone involved gets a share, and everybody's happy.'

Mickey also explained that working on the Dust was a closed shop, that all applicants had to go on a waiting list, and even then you had to be at least third generation. He said it was a well-oiled, well-protected, moneymaking machine run by some of London's hardest families, two of which made regular visits to the yard. They came in the guise of two burly brothers, Bill and Ben Walker. 'No jokes about the flowerpot men,' Mickey warned. 'Not if you wanna keep your teeth that is.' *Twins?* Salocin thought. Both of them had the same round faces, deep set, ash grey eyes, russet, weather beaten complexions, bent noses and broad, permanently creased foreheads, so it was possible? One of the brothers however, Bill, was completely bald, whereas Ben wore a head of thick raven coloured hair fashioned into a pompadour quiff – fan of Elvis, apparently. *So maybe not twins then? Unless … Ben wore a wig?* Mickey didn't seem to know, and with Alice Bands, rough like leather and twice the size of his, Salocin knew better than to ask the brothers to find out. They did talk in unison: 'How's it going, Mickey?' they'd say in complete harmony. Or else they'd finish each other's sentences in that strange way twins often did. 'Got a couple of nice Rolexes…' Bill would start '… or some decent three piece suites…?' Ben would finish. Because it wasn't just jewellery they dealt in, you could get virtually anything from 'The Dust Delivery Service' including clothes, shoes, furniture …

'Even the dog's fucking bollocks,' Mickey added.

Salocin quickly realised that everyone was on the take though, in some form or another. 'It's about survival see?' Mickey said, highlighting how, in his humble opinion, 'most of us are born at the bottom of the scrapheap – the great unwashed, the unfed, the uneducated and, of course, always the overtaxed.' Explaining how those in charge have always exploited them that ain't, so them that ain't find their own way.'

'Do you think banks who lend people money in return for a criminal amount of interest are more honest than us? And what about those grubby politicians that charge their kids' private education, or the swimming pool for their third home, or weekly trips to Miss fucking Whiplash, to their expenses? Are they decent, honest folk? Nah, they ain't. And look at the Queen, all that money, all that land and she don't even pay any taxes! So, we've all gotta do what we've all gotta do.'

And so Salocin and Ellie did. And as long as Salocin kept under Georgie's radar, life was sweet. There were annual holidays to Cornwall, where they searched Dollar Cove for treasure, trips to Brighton for picnics by the pier, and weekend breaks – on an aeroplane – to Rome, where they explored the Colosseum and drank macchiatos by the Trevi Fountain; and to Paris, where they ate croissants, drank café au lait, and sipped Champagne on the Champs Élysées. They climbed the Eiffel Tower, too, and visited the house of Salocin's namesake – Nicolas Flamel – which they found at 52 rue de Montmorency, one of the oldest stone houses in Paris. At Christmas they always bought the biggest tree they could fit into the house and the biggest turkey they could fit into the oven.

They were generous too, always throwing parties, inviting friends, relatives and neighbours over, which always included plenty of food and alcohol. Life became a bubble, and although they were vaguely aware of life outside that bubble, it rarely affected them. They watched the news, and read the papers, of course. Applauded the Abortion Act passed in October 1967, felt somewhat repelled by Enoch Powell's Rivers of Blood speech in April 1968, were bemused by John Lennon and Yoko Ono's Bed-In for peace when they married in March 1969, and completely sickened by the news of the murder of pregnant British actress Sharon Tate the same year by the Charles Manson Family in America – especially as Sean, Salocin and Ellie's second child, was less than a year old at the time. You had to question the sanity of the person, if they had any, of those that felt justified in the murder of a pregnant woman and it had haunted Ellie for weeks.

But on the whole, life was good.

Initially they'd been cautious about having another baby, rightly concerned that Ellie might once again suffer postnatal depression like she had with Lizzie. Their fears were unfounded though, the birth itself textbook, and Ellie just fine. Despite the fact Sean, born on November 11th 1968 and weighing a whopping ten pounds, was a much larger baby than his sister had been.

'He's perfect, Elle,' Salocin said, when he first visited his wife and new baby son at the hospital.

'Handsome, like his Daddy.' Ellie watched her husband cradle their new-born son, whose head, a mass of soft white curls, peeked from one end of the blanket he was wrapped in, his tiny toes from the other. His arms punched the air in tiny, jagged motions, before the tiny fingers of his tiny hand found and curled themselves around his father's finger.

Kneeling down Salocin introduced Sean to his sister Lizzie, who up until that point had eyed her new brother with caution. 'He's very wittle,' she remarked, before gently kissing his forehead. 'I wuv my baby brother,' she declared. 'I will even share my Wice Krispies wiv him when he comes home.'

Salocin and Ellie had smiled, knowing their family was complete.

1968 also proved to be the year Salocin finally discovered and dedicated a song to Ellie – Love Affair's version of 'Everlasting Love'. 'Because that's what my love is, Elle – he only ever called her Elle when he was angry or being serious – everlasting.' Ellie had laughed, gathered up her legs and stretched out across the bed, 'their' song quietly playing in the background on the radio.

Salocin, who was getting dressed for work at the time, balancing on one leg and pulling a sock over his foot, stared at his wife. Her dress had risen up revealing her shapely thighs. She may have had two kids but she still had a cracking little figure. A few stretch marks, across her belly, her breasts, which, although she never said, he knew bothered her. Didn't bother him, though. Didn't make her any less beautiful and he still fancied the pants off her. Ellie, noticing her husband staring at her, blushed and tugged at her dress to pull it down.

'Don't,' he said, feeling his cock stiffen. He walked towards her, bent down and kissed her. She arched her neck up, her lips meeting his, soft, warm. 'God you're beautiful, Elle,' he said, as his hand on her cheek, slid down her neck, her clavicle, reached inside her dress, her bra, his fingers circling her nipple. She closed her eyes, groaned. 'How on earth did you end up with a facking idiot like me?' he whispered.

Her eyes, bright, cornflower blue, flew open. 'Luckiest gel in all of London, day I met you,' she breathed.

Salocin raised an eyebrow, twisted his mouth. 'Just London?'

'Don't be so bleedin' daft,' she said, reaching behind her for a pillow and launching it towards Salocin's head. 'You know damn well what I mean.'

Half dressed, Salocin smiled, pulled his wife to her feet and danced with her to the end of their song. 'Everlasting, Elle,' he whispered. 'Everlasting.' They would often dance and listen to 'their' song throughout their marriage.

Teddy and Marie seemed less eager to start a family. Then again, they were busy. Teddy had joined a band, with which he performed for local pubs and clubs at weekends, and Marie, promoted to Assistant Manager at the high-end clothes boutique she still worked at on the Kings Road, was enjoying having a career. They both agreed they wanted children – eventually, although, Teddy appeared keener than Marie. He loved Lizzie, his niece, with her mother's looks, her father's wit and determination, and Sean, his chubby fingered nephew who, stocky, like a tank, loved to sit on his uncle's knee, help him play guitar.

However, as the famous saying goes, nothing good lasts forever, and as they approached a new decade, a storm was coming in the guise of one very handsome, very charming man who went by the name of Frank Wakefield, son of Georgie.

'Oi, oi, here comes trouble,' Ginger had said that first afternoon Frank strolled into the yard, only unlike all the many other times Ginger had said those words, this time there was a noticeable note of concern in his voice. Frank was a good five or six years older than Salocin, and like his father and sister, he was tall. Over six foot, Salocin guessed, with fashionably long, sandy-coloured hair, bright green eyes, and a well-defined jawline. His shoulders, unlike his slim waist, were broad, pumped up, just like the rest of his sculpted physique, clearly visible beneath the shirt he wore. Like his father, he had an air about him, a confidence, with a good dose of arrogance, to boot. He whistled as he strode across the yard, one hand in his pocket, the other carrying the jacket of his flash suit slung across his shoulder.

'Oh fuck, he's out then,' Kenny mumbled.

'Out?' Salocin's forehead creased in a V. 'Outta where?'

Kenny and Ginger exchanged glances with one another.

'Wotcher, boys,' came a voice behind them. They turned to see Larry the boot, so-called because he always wore Wellington boots to hide the silver ingot he stole from the electroplating company he worked for, just around the corner. Once a month, regular as clockwork, Larry brought it to the yard to sell, claiming it made up his pension, gratuity and overtime.

'Now's not a good time, Lenny.' Kenny nodded towards the office. 'Frank's back.'

Lenny's craggy face dropped. 'Fuck.' He lifted his cap to scratch his head, exposing a mop of wiry, white hair. 'Didn't know he was out.'

'Nah, nor did we?' Ginger replied.

'Okay, thanks boys,' he said, turning on his heel. 'Tell Mickey I'll pop by tomorrow.'

'Outta where?' Salocin asked again.

Kenny glanced towards the office, lowered his voice. 'Prison… or the loony bin,' he said. 'Nobody's sure which, and if you've got any fucking sense in your head, you won't ask.'

From that moment there was an uneasiness about the yard, as if they had all been performers in a play, a Shakespearean play, a divine comedy. A comedy that would, however, turn out to be a tragedy.

Salocin put his hand to his cheek, felt the patter of rain against his skin. *There's a storm coming,* he thought.

He looked up. And is if on cue, a charcoal sky rumbled overhead.

Chapter 27

LONDON 1971

SALOCIN

Nationally, 1971 marked the beginning of big changes including a new decimal currency, and new postcodes. There was also public anxiety about terrorism, street violence, and strikes, not to mention flares, platform shoes, sideburns and thick bushy moustaches reminiscent of storybook magicians. The world was changing, the optimism of the 1960s fast dissolving, and empires crumbling, including the British one.

Georgie Wakefield's empire was changing too, but far from collapsing, it appeared to be, like the man himself, going from strength to strength. 'Remember, good or bad, nothing ever stays the same,' Mickey had once said to Salocin. And it was true. Despite the fact Georgie's business empire was flourishing, the halcyon days at the yard were ending. What was also chillingly obvious, was Georgie Wakefield appeared to be untouchable. He had everyone in his pocket: traffic wardens, Old Bill, MPs, judges, barristers, Lords; you name it. There was always someone, somewhere, watching his back. It had taken a lot of hard work to get there, hard work and money. Money allowed you to live by different rules to most people. Old money, new money, it made no odds. All that mattered was how much you had – and as far as Georgie was concerned too much was never enough.

Therefore, by 1971 Georgie was on a massive clean-up mission. That didn't mean he'd gone soft – he was still just as likely to order a pair of cement boots and a swim in the Thames for anyone who didn't tow the line. And there were still plenty of loyal hanger-ons willing to do his bidding. It was just that now he wanted everything to run legit – or at least *look* like it did. There were rumours he had spies in the yard that he'd paid – or at least promised to pay – inordinate sums of money to certain individuals in exchange for information. How true the rumours were, no one knew, but it made everyone edgy, jumpy. The laughter and camaraderie once shared among Salocin and his workmates was gradually replaced by fear and suspicion. Everyone was fucked. Salocin knew it and so did the others. Even Mickey. He'd said as much over a pint.

Mickey rarely talked shop at the yard anymore, said he was worried the phones were tapped, and there was one person in particular who would love to see the back of him. Not to mention the fact Georgie was getting involved in things he wanted no part of. So Mickey had invested some of his money in art, first edition books, plus a couple of business premises. Said he had a plan. Hoped, eventually, to break away from Georgie, and when he did, he wanted Salocin with him.

'Course, it won't be for a while yet,' Mickey added.

Salocin felt honoured but he couldn't imagine Georgie ever letting Mickey go. Mickey had turned the yard into a successful, profitable business and Georgie wanted to keep it that way. However, the one person that would love to see Georgie shot of Mickey was Georgie's son, Frank.

Frank despised Mickey, said his sister could have done far better for herself than marrying some dodgy East End Jew. Not that Frank really gave a shit about his sister. Frank didn't give a shit about anyone except himself... and Georgie. Frank was afraid of Georgie. Not of the man, per se, but of what he had to lose if he got on the wrong side of his father, because Frank was a ponce, enjoying the particular lifestyle of a good-time boy who liked the finer things in life: sharp suits, flash cars, fast women.

Boys too, if the rumours were true, not to mention gambling and drugs. But Frank was taking his playboy lifestyle too far. Happy to spend his father's fortune but none too keen to work for it, he was proving to be a real problem for Georgie, who told Mickey that Frank was becoming a fucking liability.

There were rumours Frank had killed one of the prostitutes he liked to visit. High on blow, as usual, he'd supposedly pushed her head into the pillow while shagging her from behind and accidently suffocated her. Poor cow. No one knew if it was true, but if it was, Salocin couldn't help wonder if Frank had done it on purpose or if he was just too out of his fucking head to realise what he'd done. And where was her body? There was no mention of her or the incident in the news. Salocin had a few ideas – remembered overhearing some muted conversations between Georgie and his cronies about freezers and car crushers – but it just didn't bear thinking about. And if Mickey knew, he wasn't saying. Besides, Salocin didn't want to know. He hadn't signed up for that shit.

The ducking and diving he could live with. Ripping someone off who was probably ripping someone else off was fine. It didn't make it right of course, but Salocin had seen and heard it all over the years: bent coppers, dodgy politicians, corrupt judges, coked up bankers. It was a joke. At school they had taught him to respect his betters: the knobs, the toffs, the establishment, but from where Salocin was standing they were the biggest bunch of reprobates around. The very same people – *respectable* people – in positions of power, responsibility, that made up or preached about the rules that society must live by, while they happily twisted or broke every single one. So, like Mickey said, it was a 'have or be had, take or be taken' world. Salocin could live with his crimes. However, knocking people off and the disposing of their bodies was something else entirely, something Salocin – and Mickey – wanted no part of. And this was why Georgie wanted Frank working at the yard, to instil a bit of normality, a bit of decent work ethic into his wayward son's lifestyle.

'And there's nothing like a bit of hard graft to do that eh, Mick-eee?' Georgie had said.

Having Frank around really put the cat among the pigeons. No one at the yard liked or trusted him. He, in turn, thought he was above everyone else, too good to get his hands dirty, spending most of his time *pretending* to help in the office or otherwise swanning about the yard annoying the fuck out of everyone. Which also meant, unless Mickey said otherwise, all deals were off, leaving everyone's weekly takings at an all-time low – with moods to match. If they were careful, they could still call on 'Joey' from time to time, and when the drivers from the smelters came in, Mickey would try to lure Frank over to the car crusher – the only piece of machinery he would agree to work on – and everyone else got on with the job in hand.

Regardless of Frank's unwelcome presence, the thrill of the job was wearing thin for Salocin. He'd kidded himself for long enough that the money he made on the side harmed no one; that, like Mickey had said when he first welcomed him into the fold, it was a dog eat dog world. Nonetheless, on a pleasant autumnal afternoon when Frank was being particularly *unpleasant*, Salocin slipped away from the yard for an hour to have his lunch at Regent's Park. He needed time away, time to gather his thoughts, time to make sense of the private insanities rattling around inside his head.

He sat down on a park bench and picked at the cheese and pickle sandwich he'd bought from the vendor on the corner. He didn't have much of an appetite though, ended up feeding it to the pigeons that, softly cooing, head-butting the air as they walked, had quickly gathered around him. When they had finished, Salocin watched as the pigeons moved to the next bench along. A young woman, with a mop of bright red hair, head bent forward, sat with another, much older, grey-haired woman who, somewhat alarmed to find themselves surrounded by a gang of hungry pigeons, waved her hand to shoo them away.

'Go on. Bugger orf,' she shouted, as the startled birds flapped their wings and temporarily took flight.

The younger woman also looked up, squinting. Her eyes were red, possibly roughened from crying. Blinking, she held her head towards the sky and watched as the harassed birds dispersed. After a few seconds she turned her attention to a small child, a boy, standing several feet away, and called out to him. 'Alfie,' she said. The child, probably slightly older than Sean but younger than Lizzie, was throwing, with the same abandoned glee that only children possess, handfuls of crisp leaves from the thick carpet at his feet.

'Alfie?' the woman called again, more urgency in her voice. The small child, his smile fading, turned abruptly to face his mother. 'Don't go off. Do you 'ear me. Stay close.'

Smiling again, the small boy nodded his head furiously before once again swooping down to gather more leaves which, like his laughter, rose into the air with wild abandon. The young woman, his mother, Salocin guessed, watched him for a moment, smiled, then clearly upset, looked away again. She looked at the older woman sitting opposite her, then, delicate as a piece of paper, Salocin witnessed her fold and crumple. The older woman pulled the younger woman into a hug, stroked her hair.

Intrigued, Salocin shifted along the end of the bench, cocked his head to one side, listening. His hearing had always been good, something he'd often put to good use at the yard. It was none of his damn business what the two women were discussing, of course, but for some reason he couldn't put his finger on, he felt compelled to listen. It didn't take long to get the gist. The younger woman had recently lost her husband, which meant it was reasonable to assume the young lad had lost his father.

The young woman's engagement ring had become too big for her finger, was always falling off. She left it at a well-respected jeweller in Hatton Garden to have the ring downsized but the jewellers had been robbed. The shop's insurance covered the cost of a replacement ring. 'But it ain't *my* ring, is it?' the young woman sobbed. 'It ain't the ring my Dave worked his bollocks off to save for. The one he got down on bended knee with on Tower Bridge and proposed with. He's gorn and the ring he bought me has gorn too.'

It was a sobering moment for young Salocin. The first time he made a human connection to some of the dodgy dealings he had made use of over the years. It caused him to consider the second diamond ring he bought for Ellie a couple of years back, wondered if that too, like the woman sitting on the bench next to his, also had its own story. He didn't know her so it was stupid but he was almost as bereft as she clearly was. He looked up, noticed a gulp of swallows overhead, black dots against a pink and orange sky. His scalp prickled and the familiar knot of fear that plagued him of late rose up, snaking its way from his chest into his throat. He'd read a book recently, *Middlemarch* by George Elliot, and there was a sentence that had stayed with him,

"What loneliness is lonelier than mistrust."

He knew, deep down, it was time to get out. Working at the yard wasn't what it used to be. And it was all very well Georgie talking about cleaning up but as far as Salocin could see, things were just getting messier. Mickey had done his best to keep Salocin and the others away from the nasty shit that seemed to be going on of late but surely, anyone with any common sense could see it was only a matter of time before Salocin, the others too, if they stuck around, were dragged into a life they didn't want. One that, perhaps, took the lives of others, which is what he suspected Mickey was now involved in.

No one discussed it but everyone knew there was a room at the back of the yard, locked and off limits. Rumour suggested it was used for torture. Men, bound and gagged, supposedly held on trial, punishments meted out, anything from beatings, pulling teeth, electric shock treatment to the hacking off of fingers. Salocin had only dared venture there once. About nine or ten months ago, after work, when he was looking for Mickey, and before gossip about the mock trials had really started circulating. He found him, covered in blood, which, much to Salocin's relief was animal blood. Mickey had taken order of a recently slaughtered cow from someone at Smithfield and was supposedly practising his butchering skills. Why? Salocin didn't have the bottle to ask and as Mickey was keeping shtum, Salocin didn't push it. Mickey invited Salocin in though, to see for himself. And there on a huge wooden block lay the half-slaughtered cow; the air acrid with the smell of fresh blood.

Intrigued, Salocin watched for a while as Mickey, wearing a blood-stained apron, cigarette hanging from the side of his mouth, grunting, sliced and chopped the carcass, turning it into sirloin, rump, best rib, brisket, shin, silverside, and chuck. Concentrating on the job in hand, Mickey didn't really talk much but when he did, it appeared to be in riddles, not dissimilar to the incoherent ramblings of a coked up Frank. Mostly, he talked of lines. How you should never cross them, the difficulty in coming back if you did. When he'd done, Mickey wrapped a couple of bits of sirloin in sheets of white greaseproof paper and passed them to Salocin. 'Here. Take 'em home. Enjoy,' he said. 'Oh, and Salocin,' he added, wiping his sweat-stained brow with his blood-stained arm, 'Don't come down here again. Ever. You got that?'

On his way home Salocin binned the package. He'd lost his appetite and was convinced Mickey had lost something that night, too. Instead of his plucky, confident self, he had seemed drawn. The intelligence behind his eyes remained, but he also looked furtive, trapped, his once bright, mischievous eyes thereafter, dull, lifeless. Salocin had felt very low that evening when he got home, carried with him the quiet sense of unease.

It was the small things he concentrated on though. The small things that swelled his heart, gave him some much needed relief, much needed comfort: the jangle of his keys in the front door; the outline of the kids through the bevelled glass dashing down the hallway – arms wide open, gleeful shouts of 'Dad-eeeeee' as he stepped across the threshold; Ellie, smiling, behind them, the crackle and swish of her dress against her nylon tights; the dog, tongue out, tail wagging, barking; the smell of stew, freshly baked apple pie, the clinking of wine glasses, the whistle of the kettle; the hum of the fridge; the rattle of a saucepan lid. Home, a place of forgiveness and redemption.

Later that evening, Salocin put the kids to bed with a story – making sure to leave his desk lamp on, the one he had transferred to Lizzie's bedroom after her admission she was afraid to sleep in the dark because of the monsters.

'What monsters?' he'd asked.

Lizzie, quite a studious little girl, pushed out her bottom lip, shook her head, her curls bouncing wildly. 'The ones that take you away, Daddy.' She sniffed, sitting bolt upright, hugging herself. 'The ones in my dreams.'

'I think you've been reading too many books.' He laughed, pointing to the half- hidden one under her blankets.

'No,' she quipped in the same determined voice as Ellie, her eyes darting skittishly about his face. 'I keep thinking... that... you're... not coming home, Daddy.' Her fearful eyes were lucid pools of tears.

Salocin hugged his daughter, found her fears unnerving, but promised her that as long as she kept that small light on, he would always come home, always find her.

Salocin confided in Ellie, even though Lizzie made him promise not to, and they both agreed to keep an eye on her. She was clearly anxious about something – either that or she was picking up on her father's unease. Salocin also talked about his concerns for Mickey, and the conversation of the young women he'd overheard in the park. 'There's change coming, Ellie,' he said. 'And it ain't for the better. I want out but I'm not sure Georgie, or Mickey, will let me go.'

That was when Ellie mentioned the idea of moving to Australia. 'Ten pound Poms,' she said.

'Ten pound, what?'

'It's the nickname for the Assisted Passage Migration Scheme. Adults travel for a tenner each and the kids go free. The rest is subsidised by the Australian government. We could sell the house, the car, everything we own, and because they pay most of our passage, we could use every penny we have to buy a house there and start again. I can't see Mickey or Georgie looking for us in Australia, can you?'

'What's the catch?'

'What do you mean?'

'If we take the subsidised passage rather than pay our own way – what's the catch?'

Ellie's eyes widened in mock surprise. 'There ain't one.' She grinned.

'Ell-eee,' Salocin replied. 'Don't kid a kidder.'

Coy, she looked down, a curtain of blonde hair falling across her face. Salocin moved closer to his wife. She looked up again, one of her pale blue eyes visible, the other concealed by her hair. Smiling, Salocin reached out and tucked her hair behind her ear; let his fingers linger on her cheek. She sighed, leaned into his hand. 'It's two years,' she said.

'Two years?'

Ellie nodded. 'Yeah. That's how long we'd be obliged to stay, otherwise we'd have to refund the cost of the assisted passage plus our fare home.'

'And you'd be happy to do that? Take the kids, leave London, family, everything we know and start again?'

Ellie shrugged. 'I hardly see my family and the only time we see your parents is if *we* make the effort. Martha's always saying we live in the back of bleedin' beyond – at least if we move to Australia she'll be justified in her whinging.'

Salocin grinned. 'What about Teddy and Marie?'

Ellie's smile faded. 'I'd miss 'em both terrible,' she admitted. 'They'd be the only ones though. And you never know, they might come with us? I mentioned it to Marie the other day, and she said, if Teddy was up for it, she'd give it some real thought. Although 'cause she's really close to her mum it would be much harder for her.'

Salocin, brow creased, leaned back against the sofa and took another sip of the rum and coke Ellie had made him. Looking into space he crunched on a piece of ice, swirling the contents of the tumbler with the gentle rocking motion of his hand. 'What if we don't like it there?'

'I don't see why we wouldn't. It's summer all year long!'

'What about all the creepy crawlies? Don't they have spiders and snakes and things?'

'Can't be any worse than some of the snakes you have to mix with here.'

'Ain't that the truth?' Salocin took another swig of rum. 'Seriously though, Elle, two years is a fucking long time if we're miserable.' Ellie laughed. 'What's so funny?'

'Whinging Pom,' she replied.

'You what?' Salocin said.

'I read somewhere that that's where that Aussie phrase "whinging Poms" comes from. It's the name they gave to the

Brits that didn't like it in Oz. The ones who spent most of their time complaining until the two years was up and they could get back to Blighty.'

'So, people didn't like it? Have come back?'

Ellie rolled her eyes. 'Yes, of course. But honestly, love, I'm sure we wouldn't have to wait that long if we wanted to come back.' She pointed upwards. 'We've still got a drawer full of your unopened wage packets upstairs. Plus...' She lifted her left hand, twisted the rock on her ring finger, '...We can always sell this?' She stared at the huge diamond, titled her hand so it caught the light, sparkled.

'Really? I thought you loved that ring?'

'I do. It's beautiful. But I love the first ring you bought me just as much, more so in fact...'

She tailed off. Tears filled her eyes and Salocin took her hand in his. 'It's okay, I get it.'

She nodded. 'Sorry.' She quickly wiped her tears with the back of her hand. 'But I was just thinking about that poor gel in the park. Got me wondering if this...' she rotated her hand with the ring on '...has its own story, too?'

Salocin squeezed her hand and finished his drink. 'Fuck it,' he said, crunching on another mouthful of ice. 'Let's do it.'

Ellie was surprised, recoiled a little. 'Really?'

'Abso-fucking-lutely. Let's talk to Teddy and Marie and put the wheels in motion. Not a word to anyone else, mind. I don't want Mickey or Georgie getting wind of this.'

Chapter 28

London – December 1971

SALOCIN

Salocin switched off the lights and the engine, let the car coast up the drive. He needed to sneak into the house, past Ellie, past the kids, and – somehow – past the dog, all to get the painting upstairs. Or… maybe he should hide it in the shed? Or the loft? Then again, they were too obvious. What about taking it to Teddy and Marie's house, or better still, his parents? No. This was his problem. He couldn't drag them into it. Wilf would tell him to sling his hook, anyway. He'd warned both his sons years ago to never bring trouble or the Old Bill to his doorstep. Said he would kill them if they did. He'd meant it, too. *Fuck!* He needed more time. The one thing he didn't have. *Fuck. Fuck. Bollocks and fuck!* He had no choice. He'd take it upstairs, for now; hide it somewhere in the bedroom, or maybe one of the kid's bedrooms. *Fuck, no!* What the hell was he thinking? He gripped the steering wheel, watched as his knuckles turned white. What the hell had he done? How could he put his family in so much danger? A familiar feeling of panic washed over him, and his breath, coming quickly, made him gasp. He concentrated on slowing it down, knew he couldn't think straight if he was panicking. He closed his eyes, counted to ten then released the steering wheel. A mixture of hope and defeat replaced the adrenalin pumping through him. He'd hide the painting upstairs for now, and try to think of a better hiding place while he got ready.

He could do without Georgie's annual Christmas bash, if he was honest. Which was a shame because he and Ellie had loved them in the early days. However, the last party had seemed less about sparkle and glamour and more about buffoons and idiots. D-list celebrities looking for a leg up had replaced most of the A-listers – many of whom, after several tabloid executions of friends and colleagues now distanced themselves from the more infamous, less salubrious characters they knew – and were only interested in who you were and what you could do for them. Once they'd established the answer was no one and nothing on both counts, they were quick to move on, leaving a pungent cloud of indifference behind them. A number of other guests: coked up gangsters, drunken politicians, businessmen, bankers – most of whom came without their wives – were only interested in getting off their faces, relying on friends in high places should they get into trouble. Which meant that where Georgie's parties were once fun, full of polite conversation, interesting individuals, they were now an awkward mix of normal people like Salocin and Ellie, and drunken, drugged-up idiots who shared an innate sense of grandiose entitlement. Ellie was propositioned a number of times last year, and after the second attempt, Salocin made sure he didn't leave her side. He knew she wasn't keen on going again, and after today's commotion at the yard, neither was he. In fact, he was fucking terrified. However, he also knew it would draw unwanted attention if he didn't go. And at least this year, Ellie would have Marie for company.

Stealth-like, his arse twitching, he stepped out of the car, glanced up and down the street and gently closed the door, grimacing as it clicked shut. Then, taking pin steps, he walked to the back of the car. Again he looked left and right, checking up the street for anything, *anyone,* suspicious, before quietly releasing the boot. With his heart thudding hard against his chest, he reached in and lifted out the small painting wrapped in the white sheet and carefully clicked the boot shut again. He carried the painting under his arm and managed, against all odds, to open the front door with no one hearing him. Once inside the hallway he crept past the living room, the door slightly ajar. He could see Ellie and Lizzie trimming the Christmas tree he'd brought home yesterday and Sean, lying on the sofa, his little face flushed, mouth wide open, who appeared to be fast asleep.

'Wait till Daddy sees this,' Lizzie squealed, clapping her hands together excitedly.

Shit. What had he done? He'd give anything to go back in time. Twenty-four hours would do it. Back to this time yesterday when any ideas of stealing the painting had been just that – thoughts. He was as surprised as the others when Old Bill raided the yard this afternoon. A gang of eight led by, of all fucking people, DI Jim Wiley of Vice. Notoriously bent and fucking vicious it was safe to say he was suitably pissed off when he discovered that whatever it was he was looking for at the yard had disappeared. It was a set-up, obviously someone had tipped him off, and it didn't take a lot of working out who. Frank, supposedly manning the office for Mickey who was taking his wife to a hospital appointment, hadn't looked in the least bit perturbed when the fuzz turned up. In fact, he looked positively smug. It didn't last long.

Riding the forklift, along with DI Wiley, they went straight up to the rack of shelving where Mickey had secretly placed the painting several days earlier, and it was obvious, even from a distance, just how quickly the blood had drained from Frank's face. He was positively ashen.

Feeling a dig in his ribs, Salocin had turned to see Kenny, wide-eyed, staring at him. 'What the fuck is that all about?' he muttered under his breath.

Salocin, who had felt his knees quiver, the horror and

incredulity at what he had done finally sinking in, had stuck his hands in his pockets and shrugged. 'Fucked if I know.'

'I'll 'ave yer. I'll 'ave the facking lot of yer. Do you 'ear me!'

Salocin and Kenny turned in disbelief and watched as DI Jim Wiley shook the cage of the now descending forklift like a rabid, wild animal.

'Something to do with Mickey, d'ya reckon?' Kenny had folded his arms across his chest, chewing the corner of his mouth.

Salocin, fear wedged tight in his chest shrugged again. 'I honestly don't know, Kenny.'

Salocin and Kenny watched in morbid fascination as Wiley paced the descending cage of the forklift. 'He's gonna go ballistic as soon as he gets outta that cage,' Kenny said. 'You know that, right? Might even arrest us all.'

Salocin closed his eyes for a second, felt his head spin, wishing Kenny would shut the fuck up. Thank god he'd had the good sense to park his car – where the sought after package was now stowed in the boot – a couple of streets away. Mickey knew Frank, the lazy fucker, wouldn't turn up at the yard until mid-morning at the earliest, so he had given Salocin a set of keys and asked him to open the yard. Salocin, who mostly travelled into work by train and tube had, that morning, driven his car for a change. He'd arrived extra early too, and it would have been so easy to start the forklift, take the package down that way but he couldn't afford for anyone to hear. Georgie had eyes and ears everywhere. That's why Salocin had spent the previous afternoon fashioning together a long pole, with a hook on the end, made of aluminium tubes that came apart. No one had been suspicious either. Why would they? He was, to all intents and purposes, gathering and sorting the aluminium tubes left behind by the alarm fitters. He was, however, also practicing what his mentor, Mickey, preached: namely hiding what he was doing in plain sight. Mickey had relayed the story about Harry Parks who, among other things, had made a living out of stealing and selling original street name plaques.

'But he did so in plain sight, see,' Mickey explained. 'Climbed a ladder pulled from his work van, unscrewed the plaques from the wall and stole them in broad daylight. He dressed the part, though. Workman, "sent by the council, guvnor", he'd reply if asked what he was up to, "replacing all the street signs in this area with new ones." People believed him too. Cool as a bleedin' cucumber, old Harry,' Mickey had said chuckling.

So, except for the hook, which Salocin took home with him, as he'd made it himself and may have raised a few eyebrows if noticed, he hid the rest of the adapted aluminium tubes in one of the forty-gallon metal drums. In other words, in plain sight.

Then, after opening the yard the following morning and putting the kettle on, Salocin had taken his extending aluminium pole, plus hook, to the storage racks, where a couple of days earlier he'd seen Mickey, late one evening, when he clearly thought no one else was about, hide something in the rafters. It was at least twenty-five feet up but with a careful bit of manoeuvring Salocin located the package, wrapped in a sheet inside a cloth bag, and hooked it onto his pole before carefully lowering it down.

When he unwrapped it, and was presented with a small oil painting, he had been pretty underwhelmed. It depicted a weather-beaten, pipe-smoking old man in the middle of a wide-open field, tending to a horse and wagon. It wasn't Salocin's cup of tea and he had no idea what it was worth but unlike Mickey, Salocin didn't know a lot about art. Knowing Mickey, it had to be worth a bob or two. In fact, now he came to think about it, hadn't Ginger commented about a story in the paper about some toff offering a reward for a stolen painting?

Fuck knows.

He'd stared at the painting, wondering why Mickey hadn't

told him about it. They'd grown close over the years and Mickey had confided in Salocin a lot – trusted him. Thought of him like a brother, he'd once said, and Salocin had done likewise. So something wasn't right about this. Then again, things hadn't been right at the yard for a while, especially with Frank working there.

Salocin stood, in two minds, about taking the picture, unsure what he'd do with it if he did take it. He'd be in Australia soon, so if worst came to the worst he could always sell it there, couldn't he? He looked around; time was ticking and he needed to make a decision before the others turned up. He thought of Mickey, the man who had mentored him, taken him under his wing, educated him about life, and wavered for a few seconds, guilty, then took it anyway. Stuffing it inside his overalls, Salocin had walked out of the yard and locked it in the boot of his car, then went back to work – making a quick pit stop at Reuben's along the way to buy a packet of fags, should anyone have seen him leaving the yard and asked why.

Self-preservation, he told himself, *self-preservation*.

But, as DI Wiley yelled, and began smashing up the place, the gravity of what he had done finally sank in. Wiley had ordered his men to gather everyone together, including Frank, who no longer looked white, but grey. Some of the officers grabbed a couple of discarded iron bars each, swishing them above everyone's heads so they made a loud whooshing sound when they got too close. Salocin noticed Frank, his mouth twitching, eyeballing him. But as much as his legs shook inside his overalls, his breath caught in his throat, and his mind created scenarios too hideous to consider, Salocin imagined a veneer encasing him, a hard impenetrable varnish that would not give the game away. And as much as he now disliked him, Salocin also prayed Georgie would turn up. He suspected this visit from Old Bill was nothing to do with Georgie, and everything to do with Frank.

And Frank knew, as did everybody else, if Georgie found out that the police had paid a visit to the yard without an invitation, or without his prior knowledge, son or no son, there would be fucking hell to pay.

DI Wiley rifled through one of the large metal drums containing scrap yet to be sorted – the same one in which Salocin had hidden his hook. He swallowed hard, felt his arse quiver again. If Wiley found it, Salocin knew it would pique his curiosity because although strewn among several scrap odds and sods, Salocin had made the hook especially, and although Wiley was bent, he was still a copper. Which meant he was a nosey fucker, noticed when things weren't right. Salocin had meant to hide the hook in his car with the painting, but like a fucking idiot he'd forgotten it. *Sloppy*, he told himself, *fucking sloppy*. He'd become complacent, taken his eye off the ball for a second and it might just prove to be his downfall.

Salocin watched as DI Wiley lifted an item from the drum, examined it, then tossed it to the floor. Perversely he reminded Salocin of his baby son, Sean, the way he enthusiastically searched his toy box, dumping everything either side of him until he found the toy he was looking for. Wiley did this for several minutes while the rest of his men, their smirks and smiles as menacing as their silence, circled Salocin and the others like sharks about to embark on a feeding frenzy. Wiley pulled out one of the aluminium tubes Salocin had used for his makeshift pole, held it up for inspection then threw it aside. He did this once, twice, three more times. Salocin felt a rush of blood to his head, heard the whooshing sound it made between his ears, his eyes darting towards the office, towards the entrance to the yard – also the main exit – the fight-or-flight reflex kicking in. He pressed his fingers into the palms of his hands, still stuffed in the pockets of his overalls, prickling with sweat. He took comfort in the pain his nails, what few he had, caused as they pressed into the soft skin of his damp palms. It helped him focus, reminded him to keep his shit together – after all, no one knew for sure who had taken the painting.

Bored with the contents of that drum, and much to Salocin's relief, DI Wiley strutted over to another one containing crowbars and such, used as leverage when moving some of the more heavy equipment about the yard. 'Aha,' he said, pulling one out. 'That's more like it.' He looked at Frank, tapped the bar back and forth in his hand while one of the larger coppers grinned, cracked his knuckles, and bounced up and down on his toes.

'Right then,' Wiley said. 'Which one of you cunts is gonna tell me where my package from the racks has gorn?'

Everyone turned to look at one another, genuine confusion etched into their faces.

'Package? What bleedin' package?' Kenny asked.

DI Wiley turned to look at him, his head movement slow, stilted, eyes glinting. He walked towards Kenny who immediately straightened up, thrust his chest forward, one eye on Wiley, the other on the crowbar the copper was still tapping against his hand.

Masticating the gum in his mouth at an alarming speed, Kenny then folded his large arms across his chest, his clearly defined muscles taught beneath his tee shirt.

'You don't like me, do yer, boy?' Wiley was inches away from Kenny, eyeballing him, when the phone in the office trilled. Distracted, Wiley looked away. 'Get that will yer, Francesca,' he said to Frank, 'there's a good gel.'

Frank opened his mouth to speak, object, maybe? Then closed it again, having clearly thought better of it. Head down, Salocin watched as Frank headed towards the office just as Wiley swung round and smashed the crowbar on the ground causing a mini tornado of dust. Startled, everyone took a large intake of breath, and stepped backwards. The other coppers had laughed so hard it was a wonder they didn't piss themselves.

'Now,' Wiley said, 'I'll ask again. Which one of you ladies knows the whereabouts of my package?'

Salocin tried to swallow but his mouth was dry as if stuffed with cotton wool. Something bright caught his eye. He noticed one of Wiley's cronies, his mouth twisted, leering, spinning a pair of handcuffs in his hand. He knew, judging by the fearful faces of the others, that he had to say something, had to placate DI Wiley, somehow.

'Look, like Kenny said, nobody 'ere knows anything about your package.' Salocin spoke with such gravitas he even believed himself – almost.

DI Wiley cocked his head, looked at Salocin. 'Well, well, well. Sally has spoken, 'as she?'

Salocin felt a shot of anger surge through his body, sank his top teeth into his bottom lip to stop himself saying something he *may later rely on in court.*

'It's true,' Ginger piped up. 'Ain't no one 'ere knows what the bleedin' 'ell you're talking about.'

'Shut yer facking mouth, sweetheart,' DI Wiley shouted. 'You interrupt me again and I'll cut yer facking Jacobs off. You 'ear me?'

Ginger flinched, nodded, just as Frank appeared from the office. His walk was brusque, his forehead wrinkled in concern. He looked afraid and annoyed all at once. 'That was Dad... I mean Georgie,' he said.

'And?' DI Wiley asked.

Frank coughed, adjusted the collar of his shirt. 'And, well, I tried to stall him but–'

'But what?' Wiley walked towards him, dragging the iron bar he still held in his hand behind him.

'See, the thing is, Jim... He's on his way over.'

'When?'

'Now.'

DI Wiley clenched his fist, then, quiet for a moment, raised his hand to stroke his jaw before going ballistic. Using both hands he threw the crowbar around as if it were a golf club, swinging it this way and that. At one point Salocin saw the glint of the metal rod coming towards him but ducked as it narrowly missed his head. If they weren't Old Bill, Salocin would have taken his chances, laid into the whole fucking lot of them. He was sure some of the others felt the same too, especially Kenny and Harry.

A loud crunching noise interrupted his thoughts. Salocin spun round, relieved to see the crowbar lying on the floor beside one of the forty-gallon drums. DI Wiley had clearly smashed it against the drum and dropped it. Breathless, Wiley yanked at his collar and straightened his jacket. 'You've got a week,' he said, his voice laced with menace. 'One facking week. And if my package ain't returned to Francesca, 'ere, by then…' He waved his finger in Frank's direction 'I'll 'ave the facking lot of yer.'

The phone in the hallway begin to trill, dragging Salocin back to his present predicament. Hovering in the hallway at the top of the stairs, he shot into the bedroom and stuffed the painting at the back of Ellie's wardrobe behind her long evening dresses before making his way back along the unlit landing. He heard Lizzie race towards the phone to answer it.

'Ha-wow – is vat you Dad-eee?'

Sometimes, if Salocin was running late, Mickey would let Salocin call home from the office phone so he could let Ellie and the kids know, and more often than not, Lizzie would answer.

'Oh!' Lizzie continued. A ripple of confusion lifting her little voice. 'Hello Uncle Mickey. Where's Dad-eee?' Salocin hovered in the shadows, listening, and although his heart was in his mouth when he realised Mickey was looking for him, he couldn't help but smile as he listened to his young daughter talking. 'Nope… not home yet.' There was a pause. 'Yes he is!'

Lizzie giggled. 'Okay... I will. But... guess what, Uncle Mickey? I've been decabating the kissmass tree!' She lowered her voice to a whisper. 'But shhhhh... it's a su-pise. Uh-huh. Yep,' she continued. 'Erm... Mummy helped a vittle bit. Not much, though. Sean? No! He felled asleep... on the sofa like a great big lazybones!' Salocin quietly chuckled to himself. 'Yep... yep... uh-huh. Okay... Mu-um? Mum-mee? Uncle Mickey wants to talk to you.'

Lizzie dropped the receiver onto the small table by the front door, and Salocin heard it make a clonking noise as Lizzie ran back into the living room. Then came Ellie's voice, honeyed, warm.

'Hello Mickey... no... not yet. Is anything wrong? Actually... no. Salocin may have to go on his own tonight. Sean has a temperature, doesn't seem at all well? Exactly... just what we need for Christmas! Shall I get Salocin to call you when he gets in? No. Okay... if you're sure?' Ellie said goodbye, hung the phone up then looked up as Salocin switched on the landing light.

'Salocin! Oh my god, you scared the hell out of me,' she yelled, putting her hand to her chest. 'I didn't hear you come in?'

'Sorry. Didn't mean to scare you. Needed a slash so I just went straight upstairs.'

'You just missed Mickey.' Ellie pointed behind her. 'On the phone.'

'Really? What did he want?'

'Dad-eee!' Lizzie's angelic face appeared at the bottom of the stairs next to her mother.

'There she is.' Salocin descended the stairs and scooped Lizzie into his arms.

'He was just checking if we were still going to the Christmas do tonight?'

'I've got a su-pise for you Dad-eee,' Lizzie giggled, planting a kiss on Salocin's cheek.

Salocin returned his daughter's kiss then leaned across and kissed Ellie too. 'Have you now?' he replied to Lizzie.

'I said you might have to go without me.' Ellie continued. 'Sean has a bit of a temperature, has been a bit grizzly for the last hour or so.

Salocin frowned. 'Do we need to call a doctor?'

Ellie shook her head. 'No, I don't think so. It's only bit of a cold but it's not fair to expect Rachel to watch him.' Rachel was a rather sullen looking fifteen year old, and daughter of a neighbour, who occasionally babysat for Salocin and Ellie. 'I'll call her. Tell her not to bother coming over. You okay going on your own?'

'I'd rather stay home with you.' Salocin said, blowing a raspberry on Lizzie's cheek. Lizzie giggled.

'So stay home then?'

'Can't. I need to talk to Mickey.'

Ellie threw her husband a sideways glance. 'Problem?'

Salocin shrugged his shoulders. 'Maybe.' He nodded at Lizzie. 'Talk to you about it later. And besides, Teddy's band are playing tonight so–'

'Shit.' Ellie's hand flew to her mouth.

Lizzie took a sharp intake of breath and turning to Salocin, she pointed to her mother. 'Om-err. Mummy said a swear word.'

'Marie. I forgot all about Marie. This is the first time she's been able to go to one of Georgie's parties but she's only going because she knows I'll be there.'

Salocin nodded towards the phone. 'There's still time to let her know. Ring her, before you call Rachel, and Lizzie here can show me her surprise, eh?'

Lizzie cradled Salocin's cheeks in her small, soft hands. 'Oh yes Dad-eee. You are going to be so supised!'

chapter 29

DECEMBER 29TH
PRESENT DAY – MID MORNING

LIZZIE

Mum looks as weary as I feel. 'There you go,' she says, placing two mugs of steaming hot tea on the kitchen table and pushing one towards me. 'That'll warm your cockles. What the entire British Empire was built on – apparently.'

I smile. 'Dad?' I reply, taking a sip.

Mum nods. 'Always a caveat to what followed next, "more like slavery, greed, and corruption – like all empires"' she says, mimicking Dad's grouchy voice.

'You missed off the first two words.'

Mum frowns. 'Which two?'

'Fack orf.'

Mum throws her head back and laughs. It's a delightful sound, and one that swells my heart.

'Maisy not about?' I'm suddenly aware how quiet the house is.

Mum says she and Crazee have gone out for a bit of fresh air. 'Taken Nicolas to the park, I think? Said they might look at a few furniture shops, too. It's only a couple of weeks now until they move into their own house. I'll miss them, you know, especially baby Nicolas.' She smiles, tries to keep her voice perky, but it's the slight wobble that ruins her façade.

I place my hand on top of hers, squeeze it, and remind her that they are only moving down the road. 'Hardly Australia.'

'No – thank gawd!'

Aunt Marie shuffles in and looks at Mum. She says she heard us laughing and asks what was so funny? Swaddled in a thick, fluffy dressing grown, her unkempt hair is sticking up at various odd angles, her face blotchy and red. She pulls out a chair and joins us.

Without asking, Mum gets up again, flicks the switch on the kettle. 'Tea?' She's already spooning sugar into a mug.

Blinking, mole-like, Aunt Marie nods and says thanks, as I explain the reason for our unruly laughter. Staring into space, her eyes glaze over but the corners of her mouth lift into a smile. 'What we gonna do without them, Ellie?' she whispers. A lone tear runs down her crumpled cheek – followed by another, then another. She places her head in her hands, her shoulders rising and falling in time with her muted sobs. I look at Mum who, tea towel in hand, holds her hands out, her look one of somnolent concern. I hitch my chair along the floor next to Aunt Marie's and fold my arms around her, giving her a tight, reassuring squeeze. It's like hugging a bird. Her frame, like Mum's, is frail and bony. I stroke her head as if she were a child and tell her to shush. Her lank hair feels oily against the palm of my hand.

Mum makes and butters a couple of slices of toast, and between us we coax Aunt Marie to eat. It's almost too painful to watch, however, slowly but surely, she finishes both slices. Up on her feet again, Mum takes Aunt Marie's plate and our mugs and loads them into the dishwasher. I look towards the window; stare at the motes of dust floating in a shaft of sunlight bathing the kitchen in a warm yellow glow. My eyes flit towards the old clock on the wall, the one I remember Dad attempting to hang, swearing like a trouper after hammering his thumb, instead of the hook, by mistake. I also spot the cactus, erect in its bright orange pot, still in situ on the windowsill, a birthday gift to Dad from Cassie a couple of years ago. She said she bought it because, like him, it was prickly. As always, he took it in good humour.

I ask Mum, who is still vociferously stacking the dishwasher, if she needs help, she shakes her head, waves her hand in the air. I look away again, my eye drawn to the photo on the fridge, one of many of Dad, his arm around Connor, both wearing identical back-to-front baseball caps, both beaming. It's still very painful but I can look at that photo now and smile – a little – which is more than I could do this time last year.

The caw of a crow at the back of the house interrupts my thoughts. My eyes flit back towards Mum who, still hovering by the dishwasher, turns and pushes it closed with her hip.

'So, how did it all go yesterday?' she asks, once again re-joining us at the table. 'With Cassie and the barrister?'

I sigh; raise my eyes to the ceiling. 'Hasn't Maisy told you?'

Mum shakes her head. 'No, she was very quiet when she got home yesterday. Didn't say much at all really, except that she'd let you fill me in.'

'Great,' I mutter under my breath. 'Is it hot in here?' My cheeks are burning, my underarms uncomfortably moist. I stand up, fighting to pull my jumper over my head which, full of static, sparkles and crackles.

'Hot flush?' Mum asks.

I nod, pick up the discarded magazine at the end of the table – which I notice is the local lifestyle one I write a monthly column for – and wave it front of my face like a makeshift fan. I swear, if scientists could capture and bottle the heat radiating from me right now they would have enough warmth to heat an entire hospital wing.

I sit down again. 'When the fuck do they stop?'

'I still get them,' Mum says drolly.

'Gawd 'elp me,' I say, in my best cockney accent, which makes both Mum and Aunt Marie laugh.

'Well?' Mum says, a note of impatience in her voice. 'Tell us about yesterday then?'

I sigh, place the magazine back on the table and use my hand to massage my aching forehead.

'Pfft – what a carry on – Dad would have laughed his socks off. "Like a game of bleedin' musical chairs," he would have called it. Lots of standing up, sitting down, then standing back up again. Felt like I was in some random sitcom at one point.' I realise now, though, how funny it was, how thinking about it makes me laugh out loud. Yesterday, however, amid the raised voices, flushed angry faces and finger pointing – lots of finger pointing in fact – it was a different story. 'Well, it all started with Maisy–'

'Maisy?' Mum and Aunt Marie say in unison.

I explain that Laura, the barrister I appointed on Cassie's behalf, is in fact Maisy's mother – birth mother – and therefore Simon's first wife, but whom until now I had never met. I pause for a moment, wonder again how or why she abandoned her daughter, both emotionally and physically, as well as financially. She's no different to Scott of course, who did exactly the same to Cassie and Connor but I can't help feeling resentful, especially when I think of all those years Simon and I struggled, how much easier life might have been if our respective exes had taken their fair share of the responsibility of *their* children. I don't say this of course, what's the point? Besides, at the moment, I have other questions I need answers to.

'She is also, as it turns out, the youngest daughter of one Mickey Rosenthal...' I let that nugget of information hover in the air for a moment. As I suspected though, Mum and Aunt Marie say nothing, merely exchange concerned glances with one another. I continue to explain that because Laura practises Law under another name – the surname of her *second* ex-husband – I never made the connection to Maisy. 'Why would I?'

'But... but... she must have known who you were?' Mum says. 'Simon's other half? Maisy's stepmum?'

'She did. Although quite when she planned to tell me – if at all – is anyone's guess?' I tell them how scarily angry Maisy became. 'Haven't seen her that angry since, well, since she was a teenager! Glad it wasn't me in the firing line this time though.'

I tell them that once Maisy had calmed down, reassured with promises of a full explanation at a later date, we then moved on to Cassie, which of course was the whole purpose of our visit. I also explain that the real reason Laura will represent Cassie for free is to honour some historical debt of gratitude between Laura's father, Mickey Rosenthal, and Dad. Once again Mum and Aunt Marie glance at one another before lowering their heads, reminding me of a couple of chastised dogs caught doing something they shouldn't have been doing.

'And,' I continue. 'Right now I have no bloody idea what this "debt of gratitude" – whatever the hell that means – actually is? Laura said she's not at liberty to say.'

Mum, sheepish, tight-lipped, looks up again, as does Aunt Marie. 'And neither, so it appears, is anyone else?' Silence. I shake my head, sigh.

When Dad gave me the card with Laura's name and telephone number scribbled on it, he simply said, if he'd passed away and things looked like they were going tits up with Black, I was to call it, tell them I was Salocin's girl. Which I did. But he never said anything else. Never mentioned anything about some "debt of gratitude"? So when I did make that call, and Laura introduced herself, I just assumed, at first, she was just a barrister. A good one of course, but one that Dad had tracked down and specialised in rape cases, and was willing to help us – for a nominal fee. What I didn't know, until I met with her in person for the first time, was that she was a link to my past, to Dad? That her father, Mickey, owed a debt of gratitude to my father, and because of that link she is offering her services free of charge? What she won't elaborate on is, why?

Somewhat irritated I continue to explain that Laura and I agreed, should Cassie ask, that we will say that the reason she is not charging us for her services is because she was recommended to me as someone who does a small percentage of pro bono work for rape victims (which she does actually do anyway).

'What I didn't expect,' I continue, 'is the fireworks that followed when I explained to Cassie that I had instructed Laura on her behalf to start civil proceedings against Black.'

I'd seen it in her face, of course, even before I'd finished speaking, even as Laura explained it all. Quiet throughout, the signs were all there: the refusal to meet my eye, the tension around her mouth, the jiggling up and down of her left leg, her hand spread-eagled across it in a bid to stop it moving; all indicators of Cassie's bubbling anger.

'I had my suspicions, I suppose, deep down,' I confess. 'Thought there was an outside chance she wouldn't want to do it, might be a *little* annoyed, a *little* pissed off, but I underestimated just how much. All she wanted to do was to put the whole thing behind her and move on. She said that by instructing Laura on her behalf, without checking with her first, was a betrayal. So, that was my first mistake.' I pause for a minute. Take a deep breath, and blow it back out of my puffed cheeks. 'Going to Black's house was my second.' I add.

'What?' Mum exclaims, her brow knitting into a frown.

Aunt Marie looks at me, a flicker of unease in her eyes.

'Which is also why the police were waiting for me when I got home yesterday evening–'

'The police?' Mum's eyebrows shoot up into her already perplexed brow.

I rub my eye with the heel of my hand and sigh. 'Yes, just

what I needed when I got home.' Thank god Simon was with me, though, that I'd talked to him that morning, told him everything I'd done, everything that had happened. 'They asked me if I'd be willing to accompany them to the police station to answer a few questions. Explain to them why they believed they had CCTV footage of me, albeit in a disguise of sorts, hovering outside Black's front door on the day of his death.' Apparently one of the officers who came to the house on Christmas Day evening to speak to Connor, recognised me, despite my baseball cap and baggy jeans.

Aunt Marie lets out a small inward gasp, covers her open mouth with her hand, whereas Mum just looks confused. 'What?' she says again. 'Why on earth would you do that?'

I shrug my shoulders like a petulant child. 'Because late afternoon, the day before I planned to go to London to see my agent–'

'Michelle?' Mum asks.

'Yes, Mum,' I reply. 'I received a phone call from the solicitor working with Laura and myself, and we agreed it would be a good idea to book a conference between Laura and Cassie sometime between Christmas and New Year–'

'What do you mean, a conference?' Mum interrupts – again.

'It's the same as a meeting.' I try to keep the growing impatience out of my voice. 'But when you meet with a barrister it's called conference.'

'I see.'

'She said, as long as Cassie was on board, they were good to get the ball rolling. And I felt relieved. Like it was the first time in a long time I could see hope, spy justice on the horizon. And as stupid as it now seems, I wanted to tell Black for myself. Wanted to see his face, his reaction. Let him know that plans were afoot and even though he thought he'd got away with his crimes, he was about to find out he hadn't. So I still went to

London as planned but I cancelled my meeting with my agent and instead went to Black's house. Waited for him there.'

'But why the disguise?' Mum asks.

'Because at that point Cassie didn't know, hadn't actually agreed to any of it. So I didn't want Black to recognise me – not that he would! – in case he had me arrested for harassment or something. I told him to prepare himself for a shit storm, though.' I pause for a moment, sigh. 'Ridiculous behaviour for a grown woman, don't you think?' To my surprise Mum says yes and Aunt Marie says no.

'So, were the police happy with your explanation?' Aunt Marie asks.

'They seemed happy enough,' I reply. 'Asked if I would sign a statement confirming everything I'd said was true, and if I'd be happy to give them my finger prints, which they said was routine, something they were asking everyone they questioned to do.'

'And did you – give them your fingerprints?' Aunt Marie's dark eyes widen.

'Of course. Why wouldn't I? There wasn't any reason not to.'

'Surely, even if Cassie comes round to this, this… civil case against Black, there is no case now he's dead?' Mum asks.

I tell them what Laura told me, namely that if the defendant – which would be Hunter Black in this case – dies before the case goes to court, then yes, the case can still go ahead, but it will be against his estate if there is sufficient money in it. However, I also explain that the case now becomes one under the Law Reform (Miscellaneous Provisions) Act which has significant limitations. 'Makes the procedure a lot more difficult but, nonetheless, Laura says it is still possible.'

Mum nods, whereas Aunt Marie stares straight ahead, says nothing. Both women look thoughtful as if trying to digest everything I've just told them. The sound of a key in the front door interrupts our moment of silence. The letterbox rattles followed by a scrape and a hiss as the door eventually opens. Maisy walks in carrying Nicolas, followed by Crazee who, spotting us, puts his hand up. 'G'day,' he says, smiling. It's at that moment I realise how often Crazee – laid back, easy and unassuming – smiles. How much light he carries with him whenever he steps into a room. How good he is for Maisy and my grandson. A keeper, as Cassie would say.

'Look. Look who it is?' Maisy, arm outstretched pointing to me, says to Nicolas. He follows her finger and spots me, offering me the biggest of smiles. 'Nan, Nan, Nan,' he replies, his chubby fingers grasping chunks of air as he wriggles in his mother's arms, desperate to break free.

'Okay, okay, okay,' Maisy says laughing, carefully lowering her precious cargo to the ground. And he's off! As soon as his feet hit the ground he races, albeit slightly wobbly, barrelling into my legs.

'Gay – bit – beg – ug!' he declares.

I laugh, swooping him up in my arms, smothering his head in kisses. 'That's right,' I reply, 'Great – big – bear – hug!' I think of Connor, wonder when it was, exactly, he no longer felt the need to give me bear hugs. And when exactly, I stopped noticing. 'Treasure this time,' I say, my eyes meeting Maisy's. 'While he's still young. It's a cliché but time passes so fast.'

Mum looks on and sighs. 'Too fast,' she adds, slightly tearful. She sniffs, stands up and turns to Maisy. 'Anyway, sounds like you had an interesting day, yesterday?'

Maisy looks at me and raises her eyebrows. 'That's one way of putting it,' she replies. 'I'm just back from talking to Dad about it all, actually.'

'Oh?' I reply. 'I didn't know you'd planned to pop by.'

'I hadn't. We were out shopping plus I knew you'd be here and, and... I just felt the need to speak to Dad... alone.' She explains that while she was there, Laura phoned; that all three of them had a real heart to heart about everything. 'We've arranged to meet up some time next week, just the three of us. If you don't mind?' she adds.

I cough to clear my throat, smile, as expected, and feel a maddening prickle at the back of my eyes. 'Course I don't mind,' I lie. Hot dread flares inside me – either that or I'm having another hot flush. I'm angry with myself because I should be happy for my stepdaughter, encourage her to have a relationship with her natural mother but if I'm honest, part of me is pissed off. I'm the one that, alongside Simon, brought Maisy up. I nursed her when she was ill, went to all her parents' evenings, encouraged her with her studies, dried her tears when she cried, supported her, sided with her against her Dad when she got her whole leg tattooed – without permission! And it's me that guided her through, what felt like, the never ending, angst-ridden, teenage years. I did that. ME! So why does this woman, this Laura – successful, rich, and well-spoken – think she can simply swan back into *my* daughter's life now the hard work is done? Because she abso-bloody-lutely can't. She will, though. It's inevitable. I swallow hard; do my best to push down the anger pressing against my chest, chastise myself. I'm being ridiculous. Selfish, in fact. I know Maisy. And although we've had our fair share of problems over the years I also know I love her. And I'm pretty sure she loves me too – at least, I hope she does.

Maisy, arms outstretched, bends down to take my grandson – technically Laura's grandson – from me, her hair falling across her face as she does. She then leans forwards and kisses the side of my cheek and says something. Six words in fact – well, seven I suppose, one of them is a contraction, so it sounds like six words – but six little words so powerful that, like the calm that surely follows every storm, I am once at ease.

'Thanks Mum,' she says, 'I knew you'd understand.'

Crazee offers to put Nicolas down for a nap and Maisy lopes off to the living room to catch up on a bit of "Christmas TV crap" as she so eloquently puts it.

When I'm convinced both Maisy and Crazee are out of earshot, I turn to Mum and Aunt Marie and ask which one of them will explain to me the relationship between Dad and Mickey Rosenthal. Aunt Marie has clearly decided to play dirty though, and pulling a crumpled piece of paper from her dressing gown pocket she asks me if I've heard about possible dates for Uncle Teddy's funeral yet. She stares at me, her dark eyes now two grey limpid pools of tears, the lines around them much deeper than usual, no doubt roughened by crying and probably dehydrated from lack of sleep. My heart softens and I realise, along with everything else, it's easy to lose sight of the fact that this poor woman, my aunt, has just lost her husband. With sad resignation I tell her I have heard from the crematorium.

'They've offered two dates. The earliest is 6th January, but it's late, 4pm. Or they can do the 10th at 1.30pm?'

Mum clicks her tongue. 'Ridiculous amount of time to wait.'

Aunt Marie flattens the piece of paper in her hand on the table, the light catching the brilliant blue of the beautiful sapphire and diamond ring she always wears on her right hand. 'Okay. Let's do the 10th,' she says. 'It's dark by 4pm and I don't want to send my Teddy into the darkness. It doesn't seem right.' She passes me the sheet of paper. Scrawled across it are the handwritten names of three songs she says wants played at Uncle Teddy's service. I read them aloud: "Stand By Me" by Ben E. King'–'

'Because he did,' she interrupts.

"These Are The Days of our Lives" by Queen, and "Here Comes The Sun" by George Harrison.' I look up at my beautiful Aunt. 'Perfect,' I whisper, and there's nothing I can do to stem the flow of tears now streaming down my face.

'I don't want it to be sad,' she says.

'No, let's make it a celebration.'

Pressing her lips together, Aunt Marie nods through her tears, and when I glance across at Mum, I see her shoulders heaving up and down, her head cradled in her hands. I grab the box of tissues I know will be in the top drawer and after we all dry our eyes and blow our noses, I convince Aunt Marie to take a shower.

I hadn't noticed until now but she is holding my gloves, studying them with morbid fascination. She stands up and places the gloves back on the table beside me.

'Do you know you have a hole in one of your gloves?' she says. 'In one of the fingers?'

My tummy performs a tiny somersault. 'Yes. Yes, I do,' I reply gravely. Today was the first day I'd worn them again since before Christmas and that was when I noticed the hole. How long it's been there, I couldn't say. I showed Simon, but he told me not to worry about it.

Mum looks at me, then at Aunt Marie, her mouth twisting into an amused smile. 'Oh for goodness sake you two, it's only a hole…'

I pick the gloves up – woollen with yellow and grey stripes – turn them over in my hands and lay them back down again.

'I'll buy you a new pair, if you like?' Mum continues. 'Bound to be plenty on offer in the Christmas sales.'

'They're the ones you and Dad bought me a couple of years ago.'

'Oh. I see,' Mum replies, as if that is explanation enough for my sudden moroseness. 'Then I'll fix them for you. Repair the hole. Now, c'mon,' her voice is brisk, 'enough with the long faces. Marie, have your shower and I'll pop the kettle on again.'

Aunt Marie throws me a sideways glance then shuffles off as Mum makes another cuppa.

I watch her for a moment, afraid to say what I'm about to, knowing that I need to. 'Mum, I need to ask you something?'

'What?' She flings open the cupboard door above her head. 'Fancy a biscuit? I've got Jaffa Cakes.'

'Mum?' I say again, my voice laced with trepidation. 'I know what happened to Aunt Marie – Mee Mee. I *know*.'

Startled, Mum swings round, looks at me. 'I haven't heard you call her Mee Mee in years.'

'I don't remember it, if I'm honest. Aunt Marie told me that's what I used to call her when I was little.'

The radiator makes a loud banging noise making us both jump. Mum turns away again.

'So. Like I said… I know.'

'Know what?' Mum sniffs.

'Mum? Pleeease. You know what I'm talking about. But now I need to know the rest.' I stand up; scraping the chair behind me, I walk towards her. Blinking fast she throws her eyes to the ceiling. I place my hands on her shoulders. 'C'mon, Mum. She looks down again, her tired eyes meeting mine.

'Isn't it about time?' I say.

Chapter 30

London – December 1971

GEORGIE WAKEFIELD'S CHRISTMAS PARTY

MARIE

Marie glanced towards the door again, and flicked her wrist to check the time on her watch; a gift from Teddy last Christmas, she loved her Rolex. It was genuine, too, and unusual, with a blue face to match the sapphire in the ring he'd bought her the year before – the reason he had chosen it, he said. Well, that and the fact that Salocin had sourced it for Teddy at a "reasonable price", a small, insignificant detail both she and Teddy were happy to overlook.

It was nine o'clock. Ellie had said they'd be here by eight, eight-thirty at the latest and she wished they'd hurry up. It was the first time she'd been to one of Georgie Wakefield's famous – or should that be infamous – Christmas parties and if she was honest, she felt a little out of her depth. Teddy's band, like a lot of bands, had been desperate to secure the Christmas gig for the party because not only was it well paid, it was also usually well attended, often by celebrities and famous people – so there was the added possibility it might just give the band the leg up they needed, get someone in the industry to notice them. Teddy didn't mind the day job of course, but music was his passion, and although Marie laughed at him, he still had dreams of making it. So, thanks to Salocin, who had asked Mickey, who had asked Georgie, it was Teddy's band that got the gig this year.

Georgie had one stipulation though, that the band played music for everyone, 'the odd rhumba, tango, jitterbug, stuff for the oldies as well as all that modern racket,' he said. Teddy, who was keen to make an impression, said he'd do his best.

Arriving early with the band, Teddy had secured a seat for Marie at a table by the stage, next to where the band would be playing. Which was fine when they had been setting up, it meant Marie could hover backstage, help out, but once they played, Teddy had to leave Marie to it. Now mid-way through their first set, Marie sat at the table, twiddling her thumbs, with no one to talk to, at least, no one she knew. She recognised a few people from the telly: singers, actors, a game show host, models, a couple of footballers. There was also a scruffy-looking bloke taking photos too, mostly of tall – very tall – young women. Marie couldn't be sure but she thought he looked a bit like David Bailey. That's who she'd tell the girls at work it was, anyway.

It was strange being in a room full of people you felt as though you knew but were, in fact, complete strangers. The power of celebrity, she supposed. None of them knew who she was. Nor, she supposed, would they want to, at least, not judging by some of the bitchy looks she kept getting. From women mostly, especially older women. Glamorous older women, mind, who, despite their advancing years, happily showed off their bronzed décolletages beneath their long evening dresses, flaunting their coiffed hair, buffed nails, and crimson lips. Marie wasn't sure whether she pitied or admired their attempts to cling to their youth, a bit of both, if she was honest. Marie, herself, had a thick skin though, a prerequisite when you worked in retail like she did. So, unperturbed, she met their steely glares with a smile. A smile, she often found, could disarm even the most stony-faced individual. And even if they didn't return her smile, she still preferred their looks of disdain to the stolen glances of their older, greying, pot-bellied husbands. Men, in Marie's experience, needed no encouragement at all, especially those who regarded you as inferior to them. Men who undressed you with their eyes and had the utmost confidence that, had their wives not been with them and they had propositioned you, you would – either because of their charm, title, wealth, profession, or whatever – succumb to their advances, despite their crumpled faces, bad teeth, Brillo pad wiry hair and ruddy, thread-veined complexions. Marie wondered if all men were born with an innate sense of self-belief? Teddy had it, despite feeling nervous about performing sometimes, and despite being one of the kindest, most supportive men she could have ever hoped to marry, he still had bags more confidence than she did.

Marie looked over again towards the stage. Teddy, playing his guitar, caught her eye, nodded and smiled then looked towards the entrance. Marie swung round, hoping to see Ellie – she had news, and she was desperate to share it with her best friend – but still there was no sign of her. Or Salocin. Where the hell were they? Marie was actually worrying now. What if they'd had an accident? Teddy would say she was overreacting but why else would they be so late? They were never late for anything.

A passing waiter, wearing a crisp white jacket and gloves to match offered her a glass of Champagne from the silver tray he was holding. Tempted, she stared at the effervescent yellow bubbles fizzing and frothing in their elegant flutes but thought better of it, shook her head, and instead asked where she could find a phone. The waiter pointed towards the main door, said to ask at Reception. She headed towards the door, stealing another quick look across her shoulder at Teddy who, strumming his guitar, completely immersed in the job in hand, was well and truly lost in music. Smoothing down the fabric of the elegant black playsuit she wore, Marie weaved her way among the jostling crowds and headed towards the entrance.

She nodded, smiled politely at the odd few people she thought she might vaguely know, glared at those she believed responsible for groping her arse – the gauntlet most young women walking anywhere on their own among crowds had to run. She swore blind she'd swing for the next git that tried it – whoever he was.

A couple of tall fellers to her left caught her eye. She was pretty convinced one of them was Mickey. She'd only met him a couple of times, and even then it was brief, so it was hard to say. Good-looking, he had the same build as Mickey, wore glasses too, but instead of the thick-rimmed pair he'd sported last time they met, this bloke wore a tinted, much thinner framed pair. He had bushy sideburns too, a bit like Teddy and Salocin, whereas before Mickey had been clean-shaven. He had the same mannerisms as Mickey though, the same expressive hands as he talked, the same charming smile, and air of confidence. It must be him, which meant the tall woman by his side was his wife? Head back, she was laughing, her long auburn hair tumbling down her back, a flash of her long, lean legs exposed every now again through the thigh high slits of green, floor length dress. If this was Helena, she was striking. Ellie had said as much. Marie knew who the older bloke standing with them was, of course, the one with the slightly droopy eyelids and the thin greying hair. He'd introduced himself earlier, when the band were setting up. He wasn't a particularly handsome man, but he had an air about him, a presence that was impossible not to notice. It was, the host of the party himself, as well as Mickey's father-in-law and Salocin's boss: Georgie Wakefield.

Lost in thought, Marie jumped when she felt a hand on her shoulder. It was Salocin. He looked drawn, his complexion grey. He spotted Mickey and waved, who in return waved back.

'Oh my gawd, Salocin.' Marie craned her neck, looking for her sister-in-law. 'Where the hell have you been? I was getting worried.'

'Sorry, Marie. Ellie's not coming.'

Disappointment flashed across her eyes. 'Oh? Why's that, then?'

'Sean's not well. Got a temperature.'

Concerned, she raised her eyebrows. 'Ahh no, poor little fellar. Nothing serious, is it?' She prayed he couldn't hear the disappointment in her voice.

Salocin shook his head. He reached inside his jacket pocket and took out a packet of fags and a lighter. 'Don't think so. Bit of a cold. But Ellie doesn't want to risk leaving him with the babysitter. She tried to ring you. Didn't get any reply though. Assumed you must have left already. Want one?' He offered her the packet of cigarettes and when Marie declined, Salocin looked surprised. 'Giving up?' he asked, glancing towards the stage.

Marie shrugged her shoulders. 'Maybe. Ellie keeps telling me I should.'

Salocin grinned, lit the cigarette now hanging from his mouth and blew a ring of blue smoke into the air. 'Yeah, me too,' he said. 'Don't sound bad, do they?' he added, jutting his chin forwards towards the stage where his brother and the band were still playing.

Marie smiled, tipped her head to one side, and studied her husband. 'Somewhere inside that accountant's body is a frustrated rock star dying to be let loose on the world,' she said, watching his fingers glide up and down the strings of his guitar.

'Maybe he could do it full time, you know? When you come over and join us in Oz?'

Marie bit her lip, looked down. 'I'm… I'm not sure I can do it, Salocin,' she said.

'Well, no. Not straight away. Ellie said you were thinking about coming over in a year or two?'

Marie looked up again, locked eyes with Salocin's drawn, tired ones, and shook her head slowly. 'No, Salocin. I've talked it through with Teddy and I don't think I can do it – full stop.

Don't think I can go all that way and leave my family. I don't mind a fresh start somewhere here. In this country. Just not, well, just not the other side of the world.'

Salocin held her gaze. 'Oh. Oh, I see,' he replied quietly.

'Are you and Ellie still set on going, then?'

Salocin blew another small puff of smoke from the corner of his mouth, his eyes darting nervously towards his boss and Mickey. 'Keep yer bleedin' voice down,' he said. 'Yeah. We should complete on the sale of the house next month, then we plan to rent somewhere until we sail in March.'

'March?' Surprise lifted Marie's voice. 'I... I didn't realise you were leaving so soon?'

'Oi, oi,' Salocin mumbled, smoothing down his hair. 'Here comes trouble.' He'd spotted Mickey walking towards them.

Had Salocin even heard her, Marie wondered? Did he realise how upset she was? She didn't want to go to Australia, but she didn't want them to go either. Had he not heard the distress in her voice? Evidently not, she thought, as he reached out and grabbed two glasses of Champagne from the tray of a passing waiter, sinking them both in quick succession. Marie couldn't put her finger on why exactly but Salocin seemed different tonight. Edgy. Preoccupied.

'Salocin?' She gently squeezed his arm. 'Is everything okay?' She followed his gaze; saw him staring at a startlingly handsome young man who was now standing opposite Georgie.

Probably six or seven years older than Salocin, he was tall with a slim waist and broad shoulders. He had a well-defined jawline, and his mop of fashionably longish hair was a dirty blonde colour. He tipped his head back, laughed, which, even above the music, the noise and the chatter, Marie could hear. It was a jubilant laugh, exposing a row of perfectly straight, perfectly white teeth behind a pair of plump, pink lips and unlike Teddy – Salocin too – his nose was perfectly straight, not a bump in sight. The suit he wore, slate grey, teamed up with a wide-collared, bright orange shirt beneath it, fitted him perfectly, hugging every line, every contour of his body.

The man spotted her looking at him, smiled, and winked. Feeling her cheeks burn, she realised she was blushing and glanced away again. When she looked back, he was still staring at her, smiling. She laughed, giddy as a schoolgirl, surprised by the wave of excitement suddenly ambushing all her senses. Wildly, she imagined him naked... then, glancing at Teddy, stopped, guilty. What on earth had got into her? Why she would even think of another man in such a way? Concentrating her gaze on her husband, who was still playing his heart out on stage, Marie kept her back to the handsome stranger. She'd never be unfaithful to Teddy. She knew that. But it did no harm to look now and again, did it? Window-shopping, her mother called it. 'Men do it all the bleedin' time,' she'd once said. 'You mark my words. Married or not. See a pretty gel and it's all they can do not to look. Ain't no harm in it. But sometimes men have to understand that we like to look at something pretty too. After all, we may be women, but we ain't bleedin' saints.'

Salocin looked at Marie then the two empty glasses in his hand. 'Shit, sorry,' he said. 'I assumed you had a drink. The mother of all fuck-ups. According to Mickey at least, anyway.'

Marie frowned. 'Sorry?'

'Assumption,' Salocin replied. 'Mickey says you should never assume anything without checking all the facts first.'

Marie nodded but would later wish she'd followed her brother-in-law's advice.

'Salocin,' a voice said behind them. They turned to see Mickey.

'Mickey,' Salocin replied, 'You remember my sister-in-law, Marie?'

Mickey nodded. 'Of course I do.' He placed a kiss on each of her cheeks. 'So lovely to see you again, Marie.' He nodded over towards the stage. 'Very good, aren't they?'

Marie blushed with pride. 'I think so,' she said, stealing another affectionate glance at Teddy. Her Teddy.

Mickey asked Salocin if he could have a word. 'In private?' he added. 'Only don't make it obvious in front of Georgie boy.'

'Of course.' Salocin loosened his shirt collar.

'Marie, let me introduce you to my wife, Helena.' Mickey guided her towards the beautiful woman in the emerald green dress who was now standing next to the equally beautiful man who had winked at her.

Helena, as friendly as she was beautiful, greeted Salocin with all the warmth of an old friend. However, the man in the grey suit and orange shirt was much less receptive.

'Frank,' Salocin said, his voice clipped.

'Sal,' the grey-suited man replied, a flash of arrogance in his eyes.

Mickey nudged Salocin, asked him if he'd got a minute.

'Won't be long,' Salocin said.

'Oh err... okay.' Marie replied.

Salocin, who looked as unsettled as she felt, stuffed some scrunched up notes into her hand. 'Here, take this,' he said. 'I'll be as quick as I can. But if you have enough, get bored, use it to get yourself a cab home. Or go back to ours, if you prefer? I'm sure Ellie would love the company.'

Marie nodded, offered him a smile of sorts. 'Thanks. I think I might.'

'I'm sorry about all this, Marie,' Salocin added. 'It hasn't really turned out to be the night you were hoping for, has it?'

Marie sighed, held up her hands. 'Oh well, best laid plans and all that, eh?'

'C'mon Salocin,' Mickey urged.

Salocin smiled at Mickey's retreating back. 'Look, I really

have to go but if you're not here by the time I get back I'll know you've gone home?' Marie nodded. 'Oh, and by the way,' he added, his voice a whisper. 'Stay well away from him.' He nodded towards the good-looking suited and booted bloke. 'He's trouble. Real trouble.'

SALOCIN

'I heard about Wiley and his merry men turning up at the yard today,' Mickey said, as they settled at a table in the corner of a pub down the road. It was busy, smoke-filled, full of work-weary people, eyes bright, chattering, some – getting into the festive spirit – wearing brightly-coloured paper hats, scarves of glittery tinsel.

Salocin nodded, took a swig of whiskey and placed his jacket over the back of his chair. How the fuck was he going to explain?

Mickey leaned forward, looked left to right and over his shoulder. 'I take it you've got it?' His voice was low, quiet. 'The thing they were looking for?' Again Salocin nodded. Mickey sat back, placed a hand to his chest, relief flooding his face. 'Thank fuck for that,' he mumbled. 'So what happened? How did you know Wiley would turn up?'

Salocin gulped, felt the whiskey burn his throat. 'I overheard Frank talking to him on the phone in the office,' he lied.

Mickey smirked, slammed his fist on the table. 'Knew it,' he said. 'I facking knew it. You ain't earned the nickname Silent Salocin for nothing.' Salocin looked surprised. *Silent Salocin?* 'Arrogant fuck, that Frank is,' Mickey continued. 'All the ambition of his father but none of the brains. Which makes him dangerous. Really dangerous. Reckon he has a plan to get us all locked up.' Salocin's eyes widened. 'Well, not you lot, perhaps. But me. And definitely a few others. Those in charge at some of Georgie's other businesses. Then, once we're out of the way, I think he hopes to usurp his old man. Take over. With the help of Wiley and his cronies, of course.'

'Really?' Salocin was surprised. 'He'd do that – to Georgie?'

'No doubt about it,' Mickey dragged on the cigarette hanging from his mouth. 'Not that old Georgie boy would believe a word of it, of course. Doesn't seem to matter how many times his blue-eyed boy fucks up, he still bails him out.'

It was true, he did. By the time Georgie had arrived at the yard earlier that day, Wiley had gone. He would have known about the Old Bill's visit though. And he wouldn't have been pleased. Georgie didn't like Wiley, and the feeling was mutual, but both men, working from the same side of the track so to speak, tolerated one another. So god knows what cock and bull story Frank had fed his old man, but there was a noticeable atmosphere in the yard, which like the weather, had turned distinctly frosty.

Mickey looked thoughtful for a moment, an elegant plume of grey smoke rising from the cigarette resting between his fingers. 'I can't believe he and Helena are brother and sister, you know? It's almost as if, when they were born, everything good about Georgie passed to Helena and everything bad, to Frank. I said as much to her on the way to the hospital this morning.'

Hospital. Fuck. Of course. 'Shit. Sorry, Mickey.' Salocin hit his forehead with the heel of his hand. 'I completely forgot. How did things go… with Helena?'

Quiet for a moment, Mickey stubbed out the cigarette he'd been smoking and stared as the bright orange sparks disintegrated to ash. 'Doc says she has a lump in her breast.'

'Fuck. I'm sorry to hear that, Mickey. Is she… I mean will she be okay?'

Mickey shrugged his shoulders, refused to look at Salocin. 'Don't know. They're talking about operating to remove it, the breast I mean. Beside herself, she is. Although, you wouldn't know it to look at her tonight, would you?'

Salocin looked down, shook his head, remembering how, not less than twenty minutes ago, and as gracious as ever, Helena had greeted him like an old friend. Asking after Ellie and the kids, despite only ever having met Ellie a handful of times, genuine warmth in her concerned reply when Salocin had explained about Sean.

'Nah. I never would,' Salocin mumbled. 'Does... does Georgie know?'

'Not yet. Neither does anyone else. And I'd like it to stay that way for now.'

'Of course.'

'Did you look at it?' Mickey said. Salocin looked up. 'The painting – did you look at it?'

'Erm, yeah. Course I did!'

'Whatcha think?'

'Not a bleedin' lot if I'm honest.'

Mickey laughed.

'Stolen?' Salocin lowered his voice again. Mickey replied with a slight nod. 'Valuable?' Again, another nod. 'How though... did you know I was the one who'd taken it?'

Mickey took another swig of malt whiskey – it was always malt if Mickey was buying, the elixir of life he called it. 'Because, Salocin, me old china, you don't miss a facking trick. You're my eyes and ears when I ain't around. And if there's one person I've been able to count on all these years it's you, young Salocin.'

And yet I still haven't told you about my plans to emigrate. Salocin felt ashamed, a knot of fear and betrayal fizzing in the pit of his stomach. He was curious, though, why Mickey hadn't mentioned the painting.

'I'm sorry I didn't tell you about it,' Mickey said, as if reading his mind. 'I would have, eventually. It was a stupid facking place to hide it, anyway. Don't know what the hell I was thinking?

But maybe that's just it, I wasn't thinking. What with Frank.'
He waved his hand dismissively. 'Plus all this shit with Georgie
boy. And now, Helena...' He ran a hand through his thick
curly hair and sighed. Squinting he took his tinted glasses off,
revealing the dark circles and heavy bags under his eyes. Child-
like, he rubbed his eyes with his fist in much the same way Sean
did when he was tired. When he'd finished Mickey stared at
Salocin, blinking. 'Fuck me, I'm tired,' he said. 'When did life
get so facking hard?'

They reminisced for a few minutes. Talked about the early
days when Salocin first came into the fold. Laughed about the
time a local news reporter came to the yard to interview Georgie
and Mickey, write a piece about the place for the paper, and all
the while outside, out of sight, the Babcock drivers were queuing
up – what a scoop it would have been, had the reporter got
wind of it. Or the time Mickey let Salocin use the yard van, the
large transit one, to take some of his family down to Kent for
a wedding. How they'd loaded it with a couple of old sofas so
some of his older relatives had something comfy to sit on, but
how the sofas kept rolling backwards every time they went up a
hill, careering forwards again when they went down it.

'Like something outta *The Benny Hill Show* it was,' Salocin
said, Mickey now laughing so hard he had to hold his stomach.
It was good to see him laugh. Salocin couldn't remember the last
time he'd seen Mickey happy.

'So where is it now?' Mickey asked after a bit. 'The painting
I mean? Somewhere safe, I trust?'

Salocin nodded, explained how he'd taken it home, hidden it
in one of his wardrobes for now.

Mickey said it was a rare seventeenth century painting by
a rather obscure artist who'd died a pauper but whose work
in recent years had become popular with collectors. He didn't
say how he knew about it or how he'd acquired it. Nor did he

say how much it was actually worth. And although curious, if he was really honest, Salocin didn't want to know. He'd learnt, especially during recent years, that sometimes ignorance was bliss. He wished now he'd never taken the bloody thing and yet, in doing so, he may just have saved Mickey from going to prison.

Mickey said people – ruthless people – were looking for the painting. 'Not to mention Wiley, of course,' he added. Who was, according to rumour, as ruthless as any gangster. 'And fuck knows what Frank has told Georgie about it – if anything. Old Georgie boy hasn't said a word about it so I'm fucked if I'm gonna mention it.' Mickey crossed his legs, uncrossed them – crossed his arms instead. 'Best thing to do is lie low for a couple of days,' he said. 'Leave the painting where it is for now.'

Salocin shook his head. 'I dunno, Mickey. I don't wanna put Ellie and the kids at risk?'

Mickey looked at him, stroked his chin. 'Of course not,' he replied. 'I understand. But I just need a bit more time to think this through. Sort this shit out. Give me twenty-four hours and I promise I'll get it shifted. Now, c'mon.' He slapped his knees with both hands, standing up. 'We need to get back. Georgie will get suspicious if he notices I've gone. I'll go first. You follow in five minutes.'

Salocin slipped his jacket back on, necked the dregs of his glass and watched as Mickey headed towards the door. It was raining. You could see it lashing against the pavement outside as Mickey opened the door. After giving him a few minutes grace, Salocin followed him, the slick ground, spongy beneath his feet. It wasn't too much alcohol that was making it difficult to walk though, even though he'd already had his fair share. No, it was the pain in his stomach. The uneasy, agonising cramp of fear that had taken root and wouldn't leave.

FRANK

Tommy Harris was an alcoholic and a drug addict and even though he was a dirty, lying tow-rag he was a good man to call on. Why? Because when he needed it, he'd sell his own grandmother to get his next fix. He wasn't fussy either, he'd take anything as payment: money, fags, booze, stolen goods, prescription drugs, illegal drugs, anything that would help him escape, take him away from reality for a while. Although quite what Tommy's reality was, Frank didn't know, and nor did he want to. He didn't give a shit. As far as Frank was concerned, Tommy was just another lowlife scumbag to call on when he needed him.

Tommy finished telling Frank about the conversation he'd overheard between the two blokes in the pub, the ones Frank had told Tommy to follow. By way of thanks, Frank waved a pony in his face.

Tommy grabbed the money. 'Fanks, Frank,' he said. 'Any chance of a few bob more, what with it nearly being Christmas an' all?'

Frank smirked, raising his eyebrows. You had to admire the audacity of the man. 'You cheeky fucker,' he replied, as he stuck his hand in his pocket, pulled out another tenner and stuck it in Tommy's hand.

'Gawd bless yer, Frank.' Tommy said. 'You're a good man.'

'Not if I've got anything to do with it,' Frank replied. 'Now go on, fack orf.'

Tommy scuttled off and Frank headed back to the party. He was buzzing after the two lines of coke he'd just sniffed. He was also, after earlier events at the yard today, extremely pissed off, especially now he knew who had fucked things up for him.

So now it was time to party. Have a bit of fun – quickly, though, before Mickey and Salocin got back.

MARIE

'Cheer up Twinkle Toes, it may never happen!'

Marie turned, smiled. 'Sorry,' she said, 'It's just that I was so looking forward to tonight and well...' She sighed, and turned to look out of the window again which, opaque, had steamed up. Using a circular motion with her gloved hand she wiped it, peering up at the inky blue sky, the stars, like iridescent dots, twinkling, as the bright street lights and pre-Christmas shop fronts of London passed her by in a blurred haze of speed.

'Well, what?' His voice was soft, like silk, a low baritone, caressing the back of her head, her neck.

She shivered, feeling her skin pucker. She'd forgotten, until she left the party, just how cold it was outside. A recent snow flurry had promised a white Christmas – then gone as quickly as it had arrived. Not that it was cold in the car, not now they'd been driving for a few minutes, giving the engine enough time to heat the fan now blowing hot air onto her cold face.

Marie turned to look at him again, felt her hand go to her chest, the familiar flutter in her tummy she'd experienced earlier. There was no denying it, this man was strikingly handsome. His hands were expertly gripping the steering wheel, hands, she was ashamed to admit, she kept imagining on her body, caressing, fondling, cupping her. She looked down, bit her bottom lip, wiped a piece of fluff from her coat. She thought of Teddy. How disappointed he had been she was leaving and, how his disappointment had irritated her. It wasn't like she hadn't seen him and the band play a thousand times before. And as much as she loved watching her husband perform, as opulent and as grand the setting for the party was, filled to the brim with an eclectic mix of several hundred weird and wonderful people, she was lonely.

It wasn't Ellie's fault she couldn't make it, of course, and if Salocin had been around, perhaps he could have introduced her to some other guests. Helena, stunningly beautiful, was nice enough, however as she was the daughter of the host of the party, it was clearly her job to mingle. Marie got that. Helena had left her in the capable hands of a few friends she'd introduced her to, but once Helena had disappeared, pleasantries exchanged, there was little else to say to one another. It had been a mistake to come, Marie thought. Initially dazzled by the razzle, the preliminary excitement had now worn off and she was disappointed; Ellie had made it sound so much fun, too, which, in all fairness, with Salocin by her side, it probably was.

She stole a sideways glance at him again, noticed a look of lazy amusement cross his face. Was he laughing at her? As handsome as he was, and as flattered as she had been that he'd helped her, accepting a lift from him was also another mistake. She should have thanked him but declined. What would she have thought if Teddy had offered a young woman a lift in his car – just the two of them? She should have waited for the cab Reception ordered, or better still she should have walked, hailed one along the way, or caught the bus, even. There had been enough time. But it was cold outside; the pavements slick with intermittent rain and sleet were a health hazard when you were wearing heels. And as she had stood there, on the steps of the hotel, hugging herself, coat collar up, trying to keep warm and no sign of the taxi, he had pulled up, out of the blue, right in front of her. The engine of his swanky sports car, quietly, impressively grumbling.

'Jump in,' he called through the passenger window, leaning across to speak to her. 'Engine's running, heater's on.' He revved the engine. 'Soon have you home.' It was tempting. She'd thanked him, said no at first, but he was insistent. 'I don't bite,' he had said, laughing. And unlike the icy temperature, her resolve cracked, thawed.

He revved the engine a couple more times and, partly

embarrassed, partly impressed, she noticed the admiring looks it drew from hotel staff and guests alike. Oh sod it, what harm could it do? Salocin had warned her off, though, earlier, told her to steer clear of him. And, his sister had too, come to think of it. What was it she'd said? 'Don't be taken in by his charm, he can be very beguiling.' Surely there were worse things than being charming though? He'd been a perfect gentleman to her, one of the few people at the party to take any real notice, show any real interest in her.

She remembered Ellie mentioning Frank once, a while back, saying how handsome he was, but how much Salocin disliked him. Marie had been quite amused at the time because Ellie, like a teenager experiencing her first crush, had seemed somewhat awestruck, all the baggage of being a wife and stay at home mum to two small children having slipped, albeit temporarily, uncharacteristically, away. So surely, if Ellie thought he was okay, he must be? Marie trusted Ellie. She had a good heart – too good, sometimes – always tried to see the best in everyone, but she was still a good judge of character, knew who to steer clear of and who, despite outward appearances, deserved a chance.

So really, when all was said and done, what was the harm in accepting a lift from a handsome man who'd offered to take her home in a warm car with no real agenda other than some polite conversation?

'Most of the women at that party are just a pretentious bunch of gold diggers.' He interrupted her thoughts. 'Only interested in what I can do for them, rather than showing any real interest in me.'

Marie was baffled that such a good-looking, successful man, struggled in affairs of the heart, but then again, like Ellie always said, appearances could be deceiving. 'All the good women, like you,' he stared at her, 'are all gone, all spoken for.'

Marie blushed, flattered. The party had been full of beautiful

women, including models and actresses – admittedly some
lesser known ones, but beautiful nonetheless. And yet, this
handsome man singled her out. Her, a nobody, just an East End
girl who made the best of herself. Not that Marie thought she
was ugly or anything. Her figure wasn't bad, less curvy than
Ellie's but she had a long, shapely pair of legs, and dark eyes,
which complimented her dark hair and Mediterranean skin –
her mother reckoned they had Italian blood on her side of the
family – and if she applied enough slap she did, at times, look
quite pretty. Teddy adored her, said he was a goner the moment
he clapped eyes on her. 'Stole my heart, you did, gel,' he'd said,
'and now I don't think I'll ever get it back again.' She smiled
at the memory. Falling in love had been a much slower process
for Marie. She had fancied Teddy, course she had. Enjoyed his
company, too, liked that he was a musician and an accountant
but unlike him, it had taken her a little longer to fall in love.
However, when she realised she loved him, it was with all her
heart, all-consuming, and their lovemaking, although a little
clumsy at first, had turned into something quite wonderful,
something deeply passionate.

So why was she here, in a car with a man she barely knew,
imagining him naked, doing things to her that only Teddy did.
She felt a flurry of panic in her tummy, sat bolt upright, turned
away towards the passenger seat window again. She shouldn't
have accepted the lift. It was wrong on every level. She knew
it and so, she suspected, did he. Maybe she should ask him to
pull over, let her out so she could hail a cab. If worst came to
the worst she could always walk back to her parents' house,
sleep on their couch for the night. They'd pretend to be annoyed
because it was late, but secretly they'd be pleased, and her mum
would make her an Ovaltine and they'd chat while she drank
it. Or she could ask to use their phone, ring the hotel, leave a
message for Teddy and ask him to pick her up after the gig.

His voice interrupted her thoughts again. 'You okay? You've gone very quiet?'

'Oh it's nothing,' she replied. 'Things haven't gone to plan, is all.'

'Best laid plans and all that.' He flashed her his pearly whites, eyes, quite green.

Marie nodded. 'Look,' She shuffled forward in her seat, 'If you don't mind I think I'd prefer–'

'I've got an idea,' he interrupted. 'Why don't I take a drive along Regent Street? We can look at the Christmas decorations and afterwards we can go to this little café I know, tucked away, around the corner – does the best hot chocolate in town? Then, once we've cheered you up and warmed you up, I'll drive you home. How does that sound?'

Marie wasn't sure, but it sounded tempting. After all, as she'd already said, the evening hadn't gone at all as planned. And it was cold outside. Did she really want to bite her nose off to spite her face?

'Yeah… okay then,' she replied. 'Thanks, Frank. I'd love to.'

'Good gel,' he said, winking at her. 'You know it makes sense.'

Of course it did. And after all, it was cold outside.

chapter 31

LONDON – DECEMBER 1971

AFTER... GEORGIE WAKEFIELD'S CHRISTMAS PARTY

"I have known a vast quantity of nonsense talked about bad men not looking you in the face. Don't trust that conventional idea. Dishonesty will stare honesty out of countenance, any day in the week, if there is anything to be got by it."

Charles Dickens, *Hunted Down*

MARIE

She would like to have said it was quick, a moment that had taken them both by surprise. That somehow, she had led him astray, had sent him the wrong message, the wrong signals. That it was her fault, and he had misinterpreted her intentions, took no to mean yes, but when the deed was done, was remorseful. Such remorse would make his actions more palatable, a mistake – on both their parts – she could scrub away in the shower, lock away in the back of her mind and never think of again. That wouldn't have made it okay, or any more acceptable, but, if that's the way the end of her evening had played out, Marie believed, on some subconscious level, she could have buried her assailant's violation of her.

She was wrong of course, because regardless of how much, or how little violence is involved, rape is rape.

And that's not how it played out, anyway. Frank Wakefield, as it turned out, was a violent psychopath and misogynist. The rape was brutal, the violence involved, despite her upbringing in

London's East End, shocking. It was slow and torturous. Blunt force trauma was used, as were knives, pliers, teeth, rope and various implements designed to penetrate and rupture.

By the time Frank had finished with her, Marie knew she would die. The taste and smell of her blood was overwhelming; the pain, like nothing she had ever experienced, or imagined. She tried hard to fight back – at first – but Frank was so high, so frenzied, it would have been near on impossible for a grown man to fight him off, never mind a woman who was half his weight and size. Crawling on her hands and knees she made one last-ditch attempt to drag herself across the floor but it was so wet, so slippery, it was impossible.

Where the hell had all the water come from?

She quickly realised, as Frank watched her, goaded her, laughed at her attempts to get away, it wasn't water. It was blood. Her blood. Warm to the touch, metallic on the tongue, the fight in her not yet gone, she threw one arm in front of the other and inch by inch tried to heave her broken body across the floor. She heard the cruel taunts of her torturer but somehow she blocked them out and instead imagined wings on her back – huge white ones – lifting her, carrying her to safety, carrying her home. But there were no wings and there was no escape. And as she continued inching across the floor, slipping in and out of consciousness, *his* hands gripped around her throat, Marie finally stopped fighting and succumbed to the darkness, all her strength swirling and draining away like water down a plughole. Frank was screaming at her but her hearing, sub-aqua, meant she couldn't understand him. The muffled sound strangely brought to mind trips to Cornwall with Teddy, and Salocin and Ellie and the children; picnics on the beach, frolicking in the sea together, swimming, drifting.

She was drifting again, now, upwards, away from her body. She thought of her parents, her brothers and sisters and of

Teddy – her Teddy. What would he think when her mutilated body was discovered – *if* it was discovered? And finally, as the darkness engulfed her, pressing down on her like a huge, heavy blanket, she thought of the baby that had been growing inside her – the news she had been so desperate to share with Ellie, her Christmas gift to Teddy.

Poor little thing never stood a chance.

ELLIE

Ellie waited up for Salocin, any frost between them, regarding the stolen painting, significantly thawed. She was still angry with him, though, despite his conversation with Mickey – who said he'd sort it, which was something she supposed. They weren't out of the woods just yet though.

'I just don't understand why you would do that, Salocin? Put me, the kids, all of us in danger?' Ellie said. 'You've heard the rumours about Georgie. What he does to men that screw him over? It's up to Mickey if he wants to try his luck with his father-in-law. Chances are, given that he's the father of Georgie's granddaughters, the consequences will be a lot less dire for him than they would be for you? I understand that it's time to get out, that it was fun while it lasted and you're just trying to make sure that we'll have enough money behind us to make a new start. But we've made a bit of profit on the sale of the house. Plus there's still all your unopened wage packets–'

'Where are they?' Salocin interrupted. 'My wage packets, I mean?'

'Still in the top drawer of the chest of drawers in our room – why?'

'I think we should move them tomorrow. Just in case we get a visit from Old Bill or Georgie boy.'

Ellie's eyebrows shot up. 'Really?' Her voice was an octave

higher, clipped. 'You think they'll come here – to the house?'

'Highly unlikely,' Salocin sounded quiet, reassuring. 'I just think it's better to be safe than sorry. How's Sean?'

He knows how Sean is. It was the first question he had asked when he got home. *Diversionary tactics*, Ellie thought. The game Salocin liked to play when he's backed into a corner, or when he didn't want to discuss something further, or if he didn't want to worry her. Exhausted, she swallowed her annoyance. She couldn't be bothered to argue any more tonight. Instead she thought of her now sleeping son, compact, chubby-kneed, grasping hands, big brown eyes, inquisitive like his father's. 'He's sleeping,' she replied. 'He's been a bit grizzly. But he's okay, I think. At least his temperature has broke. I did the right thing not going to the party tonight, though.'

Salocin got up from the armchair and joined Ellie on the sofa. She tucked her legs up underneath her but Salocin gently pulled them out again. Reluctantly, she allowed him. He laid them across his lap, massaged her feet. 'I'm sorry Elle,' he said. 'I know I've fucked up. Stealing the painting, bringing it here. But I guess, well, I guess I let curiosity got the better of me.'

'Yeah? Well we all know how that worked out for the cat!'

A faint smile flickered across his face, any tension between them now shrivelling like a burst balloon. 'It's hard to explain what it's like at the yard at the moment,' he said. 'Sinking ship and every man for himself comes to mind. But I'll sort it, Elle. I promise you that.'

Ellie smiled, reached for his hand. 'I know you will,' she said. She asked him how the evening went; if Georgie seemed suspicious; if Frank had said much. Who was there and who wasn't; what the food was like; whether the guests liked Teddy's band; what Helena was wearing, and finally, if Marie had had a good time?

It saddened her to hear the news about Helena. She'd only

met her a couple of times but there was something pure, something ethereal about her, one of those people that gave out a lot of light, Ellie thought, bit like Marie. Talking of which, she was surprised to hear her sister-in-law had gone home early. Why hadn't she phoned? Then again, she knew how much Marie had been looking forward to the party, had talked of nothing else for the past week. Maybe she was annoyed with Ellie? She'd be surprised if so, Marie wasn't like that. Maybe she was unwell and had gone straight to bed? It was possible. The nasty cold Sean had was doing the rounds; half of Lizzie's class at school had been off with it before they broke up for Christmas.

'Did she seem okay? Not unwell or anything?'

Salocin shrugged. 'Seemed fine to me. Not that I saw her for long. I introduced her to Helena, told her to steer clear of that scumbag, Frank, who was lurking around, then shoved some bangers and mash in her hand. I told her I had to have a quick word with Mickey, that I wouldn't be long, but to use the cash to get a taxi home if she got bored. Things took a little longer than planned with Mickey – but then again, after the showdown at the yard earlier today, I didn't know what the fuck to expect? So I had to tread lightly, see, not rush things. When I got back to the party, Marie had gone. And later, in between sets, Teddy confirmed she had said her goodbyes and was going to Reception to book a taxi home. I assumed she might have come here? Or phoned you?'

Ellie frowned. 'The phone hasn't rung once all evening.' She felt slightly uneasy, her mind whirring. 'Maybe she's mad at me?'

Salocin frowned, his lips pursed in amusement. 'Who, Marie?'

'No. Not her style is it?' Salocin shook his head. 'Maybe I should call her?'

'Now? What if she's sleeping? It's really late, love.'

'I suppose so. I'll call her in the morning, then. First thing,' Ellie said, just as the phone trilled in the hallway.

Salocin and Ellie looked at one another. They both stood up and rushed to answer it. Salocin got there first. He whispered so as not wake the children but he wasn't on the phone long. 'That was Teddy,' he said, replacing the receiver in its cradle. 'Marie isn't home.'

'What? What do you mean?' Ellie's stomach tightened in anticipation.

Salocin frowned, stroked his chin. 'Teddy said Marie isn't home. Not at her parents' house either. He's on his way over here, asked me if I'll help him look for her.'

Before Teddy and Salocin drove back to the hotel where the party had been, Teddy gave Ellie their address book, asking her to ring round all their friends and anyone else she could think of. Thirty or so phone calls later and Ellie feared the worst. There was nothing else for it, she'd have to start ringing round all the hospitals in London. The second hospital she called, The London Hospital on Whitechapel Road, confirmed that someone similar to Marie's description had been brought in several hours ago.

'Is… is she all right?' Ellie asked.

'I'm not at liberty to say over the phone,' came the curt reply.

'Please? I'm her sister,' Ellie pleaded.

There was a pause. Then the voice on the end of the phone, now a whisper, spoke again. 'You didn't hear this from me,' she said, 'but she's currently undergoing emergency surgery. They think she'll be okay but I suggest you get your skates on.' There was a click as she hung up.

Ellie dropped the phone, reaching out towards the wall to steady herself, her heart hammering thick and fast against her chest. Why? Why was Marie having emergency surgery? What the hell had happened to her? She closed her eyes, took a few deep breaths, waited for the panic rising within her to settle. Should she phone Marie's parents – or should she wait and see? As a parent herself, she knew the answer; she would phone them. She then wrote a note for Salocin and Teddy, which she left on the kitchen table, and bundled the children into the car and headed towards Whitechapel. Thank god, Salocin had taught her to drive – she passed her test first time, too. Being able to drive with two little ones was a godsend.

'There, there, shush, shush,' she whispered covering Lizzie and Sean with a blanket, as she lay them on the backseat of the car. 'We're going for a little drive.'

'But it's der middle of der night, Mummy,' Lizzie said sleepily, using her two tiny fists to rub her eyes.

Ellie hated waking them both, especially Sean, who had, literally, been sleeping like a baby, but waiting wasn't an option.

SALOCIN

The institutional linoleum covering the floor of the hospital corridor made a squeaking sound underfoot. Salocin stuck his hand out, and grabbed his brother by the arm, which was all he could do to hold him back. 'Slow down, Ted. A few more minutes won't make any difference.'

'Easy for you to say,' Teddy snapped.

They turned the corner, as instructed, spotting the signs up ahead for the ICU ward.

'Intensive care? What the fuck happened to her, Sal, to end up in intensive care?'

Salocin reached for Teddy's arm again, squeezed it. As they drew closer it quickly became clear there were several bodies milling around outside, including a couple of uniformed coppers. There was a row of plastic chairs lined up against the wall where Ellie sat, Sean cradled in her arms, sleeping, and Lizzie, also sound out, curled up on the chair next to her. On the other side of Ellie sat Marie's mother, Winnie, her head forward, elbows resting on her knees, hands cradling her chin. Salocin felt his guts turn like the drum of a washing machine. Even from this distance, despite being unable to see Winnie's face, he could see the anguish etched onto Ellie's gentle features and straight away, he knew it was worse than he had hoped and as bad as he had feared.

Teddy, like an angry bull, headed straight for the double doors where he assumed his wife was. A mild scuffle broke out as Len, Marie's father, and Dave, one of Marie's brothers, held him back.

'She's a mess, Ted,' Len said, his voice strained. 'Doc's in with her at the moment. Asked us to wait outside. Said she'll answer any questions when she comes out again.'

Salocin approached one of the uniformed coppers and asked him what they knew. Teddy followed him, standing behind his younger brother, his breath hot on Salocin's neck. The copper, nice enough, considering he was Old Bill, explained that from the limited information Marie could give them, someone had attacked her while hailing a cab. 'We've got people looking into it,' he said.

Mrs Thompson, the consultant, was a tall woman with short, cropped mousy brown hair, a sharp nose, thin mouth and alert, violet eyes. She spoke like a BBC newsreader, crisp, clear and concise but she also had a warmth, a noticeable kindness to her tone. 'Now, Mr Lemalf,' she said, with some gravitas.

'It's Teddy. Call me Teddy.'

Mrs Thompson paused for a moment, looked at Teddy. 'Very well – Teddy. I'm afraid your wife has suffered severe trauma, both to the head and the abdomen. We've operated and the good news is, she'll live. However...' She drew breath '...unfortunately she has lost the baby. And, I'm afraid, it's highly unlikely she'll be able to conceive again.' The silence among them all was shattered by a collective intake of breath, for although Mrs Thompson was addressing only Teddy, everyone else was close by, listening. 'Do you have any other children?' Mrs Thompson continued.

Teddy, devoid of words, mouth wide open, merely shook his head. 'I... I... didn't...'

'Ah. I see,' Mrs Thompson replied. 'You didn't know she was pregnant?' Again, Teddy shook his head. 'Oh dear, I really am very sorry Mr – Teddy. Look, I can see this is all a bit of a shock.' There was genuine pathos in her voice. 'Why don't you sit with your wife for a moment. Not for long, mind. She's very weak and needs lots of bed rest during the next few days. I've prescribed her a mild sedative to help her sleep. Then I strongly recommended you go home, all of you.' She looked up, then, addressing everyone else, before turning back to Teddy. She laid her hand on top of both of his, which he held in his lap. 'And if you think of any more questions, you can ask me this afternoon during visiting hours when I pop down to check on your wife's progress. How does that sound?'

Teddy, nodded, stood up. 'But... how... What?' he stuttered.

Mrs Thompson gently patted his arm. 'Like I said, get some rest. You can ask me this afternoon. Oh, and Teddy, your wife is a real fighter,' she added, as she reached the door. 'Not everyone would have had the strength to hang on like she did. She must love you very much. You should be proud of her.'

Teddy coughed, cleared his throat. 'Thanks, Doc,' he said, with a slight wobble in his voice. 'I am.'

Mrs Thompson nodded. 'Until this afternoon, then.'

Teddy went in first, followed by Salocin – Salocin having already asked Ellie to make sure no one interrupted them for at least ten minutes. Winnie was about to follow but Len held her back, shook his head. 'In a minute, love' Salocin heard him mutter. Deflated, Winnie sat down again, smiled, and then sobbed as Lizzie who, bleary-eyed, having just woken up, crawled onto her knee and hugged her.

Salocin was shocked when he saw Marie. He knew the woman lying beneath the crisp white sheets of the hospital bed was his sister-in-law because, although barely a whisper, he recognised her voice. However, that was the only thing about her that was recognisable. Her face, bruised and swollen, was a map of violence. Each cut, each bruise, like the countries on a map of the world, a different shape, a different colour, whilst her hair, stiff like cardboard, was a matted mass of congealed blood interspersed with the odd patch of white, exposing her bare scalp, doubtless where her hair had been torn from her head. Around her neck she wore a choker of deep purple and claret red bruises not dissimilar to the ones that ran the length and breadth of both arms. When she spoke her voice was hoarse, her lips fat and bloodied, the whites of her eyes bloodshot.

Teddy tried to hug his wife, gently, but it was near on impossible; she winced every time he got close. He pulled out a chair and sat down beside her, held her hand in his, studied it, as if it were something delicate, a Fabergé Egg that must be handled with care. 'Who the fuck did this to you?' he finally said, his voice choked, his words hard, angry clots. 'Did you see? See who it was?'

Marie flinched, pulled her hand away from his, and looked down. She shivered. 'Water please?' she said, looking up again, pointing to the glass at the side of the bed. Teddy reached for the glass and held it to his wife's mouth. She moved forwards and somehow knocked the entire contents of the glass over the bed.

'Shit. Not a problem.' Teddy leapt up, wiping the spillage with the swift brushstroke of his hand.

Marie lifted her chin, pointed it in the general direction of the door behind them. 'Ask the nurse for some more, please. I'm so thirsty.' Teddy exchanged glances with Salocin. 'Please, Teddy,' she pleaded.

'Course, love.' Teddy touched her cheek, wiping away the silent tears rolling down them. 'Anything for my gel,' he said winking. 'Back in a minute.' He smiled, unable to disguise the tremor in his voice.

Salocin watched his brother leave then took his place on the chair beside the bed. 'I'm so sorry, Marie,' he said, placing his hand on top of hers. When Marie turned to look at him, his eye was drawn to her cracked, bloody lips, her bruised eyes, one of them so swollen she could not open it.

'I know who it was,' she whispered, a lone tear running down her cheek.

'Tell me.'

Marie made Salocin swear – on her life, and Ellie's and the kids – that he wouldn't tell Teddy. 'Or the old Bill.' Her eyes flitting towards the door.

Salocin nodded. 'I promise.'

'I'm scared, Salocin. So scared. Thought I was a goner. You were right. I should have listened to you.' She began to sob. 'How could I have been so stupid. It's all my fault... Why didn't I listen? Why!' Her shoulders shook, her sobbing, like a throaty cataract, grew more ugly.

Salocin lifted Marie's hand, and cupped it in both of his. He implored her to look at him, tell him who it was. 'Teddy will be back in a minute. We're running out of time. I need you tell me what happened and I need you to tell me now.'

Marie looked at her brother-in-law and immediately stopped crying. With one eye on the door, she spoke quickly and quietly. She offered an abridged version of events – and for that Salocin was truly grateful. His overactive mind easily filled in all the gaps. It sounded as though, for all intents and purposes, Frank had been a perfect gentleman. True to his word they had taken a drive down Regent Street to see the Christmas lights and decorations, before stopping off at a beautiful little Italian style café where he drank coffee and she, hot chocolate. On the way home Frank said he needed to make a quick pit stop at the yard, as he needed to collect something. When they parked up, he asked her to accompany him inside, said it could take a few minutes for him to find what it was he was looking for.

Marie paused, held her head in her hands. 'I believed him, too,' she mumbled.

She continued to explain how Frank led her to a room at the far end of the yard. Salocin's blood ran cold, a mixture of revulsion and fury coursing through his veins. 'And then... and then... I just never saw it coming.' She raised her hand to her mouth to stifle her grief. 'I could feel myself going,' she continued. 'Like I was floating away and then suddenly, well, it was like a miracle. Reckon she was my guardian angel or something.'

Confused, Salocin frowned. '*She?* I don't understand? *Who* was your guardian angel?'

'That's just it,' Marie replied. 'I don't know who she was, but she saved me.' Marie explained that as Frank had his hands gripped around her neck, she heard a woman's voice screaming at her to run. 'I had me eyes shut, see. And when I opened them, I could see Frank rolling around on the floor, swearing and shouting, holding his head.' Through her bloody, blurred vision Marie said she could also just about make out a woman screaming at her to run. 'She was holding something in her hand, smashed it down on Frank's back. God knows how, but somehow my mind convinced my legs to move, to walk, to run. "What about you?" I called out to whoever she was but again she just told me to leg it. Said she'd be okay. So I ran and ran and ran until I collapsed. Next thing I remember is waking up here... in hospital.'

Later it would come to light that it was Annie Figg who had saved Marie. She had been good friends with the girl Frank had "accidently" suffocated, and rumour had it, Georgie had ordered some of his cronies to dispose of the body. Annie had gone to the police to tell them what she'd heard but with no body and no proof, they told her to sling her hook. Several months later, on that fateful evening, she happened to be passing the yard and recognised Frank's car parked outside. She crept in and thought she heard screaming. Convinced it was Frank hurting another girl, she went in to find out.

That was the last night Annie was ever seen again.

The door swung open and with a jug of water in one hand, an empty glass in the other, Teddy walked back in. 'Water,' he said, filling the glass and passing it to Marie. She took the glass, her hand shaking a little, and holding it against her dry, bloody lips, took a sip. Salocin stood up, moved out of the way so Teddy could resume his seat next to Marie. 'Everything, err, okay?' He glanced at both his wife and brother.

Salocin smiled, although it was more of a grimace. 'It will be,' he replied. 'Listen, Teddy,' he said. 'I've had a good chat with Marie, about what little she remembers...' Marie shot Salocin a concerned sideways glance '...and if it's all the same to you I'd like to nip off. Put some feelers out. See if we can't find out who did this, eh?'

Teddy nodded, scraped his chair back, stood up. 'Yeah – okay. Good idea. I'll come with you?'

Salocin put his hand up. 'Nah – you'll only slow me down. You should stay here – with Marie.'

Marie smiled, took her husband's hand.

'If you're sure?'

'Good man. You know it makes sense. Do you want me to phone Mum and Dad? Let them know about Marie?'

Teddy looked at his wife, silently asking her permission.

Marie released Teddy's hand, looked away. Teddy shook his head. 'Nah – it's okay. I'll call them a bit later.'

Salocin headed towards the door, promising them both he'd stay in touch.

Marie looked up, no doubt aroused by the harshness of his voice, the twitching of his jaw, the vein, throbbing in the side of his neck. '*Please* be careful, Salocin,' she called, holding a fist to her mouth, her voice still a croaky whisper. Don't do anything… anything rash.'

Salocin glanced across his shoulder, offered Marie a smile of sorts and left the room. Spinning the same yarn to Ellie that he'd just fed his brother, Salocin secretly applauded his ability to hide the murderous rage now surging within him. To the outside world he was just a normal man going about his business but unbeknownst to them, a permanent red mist has descended upon him, igniting a lethal white heat from within, any common sense quite gone. And, despite his veneer of civility, he was now someone different. Someone base; primal, animalistic, firing only on his reptilian brain. He was on a mission without a thought or care for the consequences.

He was dangerous, and he was about to cross a line and when he did, he knew there would be no turning back.

chapter 32

LONDON – DECEMBER 1971

RETRIBUTION

SALOCIN

He wasn't sure where he'd find Frank but his starting point had to be the yard. Leaving the warmth of the hospital, Salocin pushed open the door and stepped out into the stark December morning. It was 6am and bitterly cold. With the Christmas party the night before, Mickey had, as usual, given everyone the day off, regardless of whether they attended or not. Normally, Salocin would be at home nursing a hangover, Ellie's warm body curled up next to his, Lizzie and Sean threatening to break the peace at any moment. He would moan of course, pretend to be grumpy, stick his head under the covers when they came rushing in and climbing into bed with them, their infantile chants of "wake up, wake up" stuck on repeat like a broken record. Until, giggling with delight, Lizzie would pull the covers off his face, smooth his forehead with her soft, pudgy hand and beg him to tell her a story. Whereas Sean, wide-eyed and alert, would watch his sister, and marvel at her mastery of manipulation.

Not this morning though. This morning Salocin had murder on his mind.

Should he walk to the yard or take the tube? The walk, about fifty minutes from here, would give him more time to think, calm down, whereas the tube ride was about ten minutes. It was an easy choice. He turned right onto East Mount Street, left onto Whitechapel Road, and ducked down on the underground. Mickey once said to him that although described by The Times in 1862 as an "insult to common sense" he reckoned the London Underground was one of the greatest engineering feats of modern times. And although early, still dark out in fact, the train he rode, rocking rhythmically from side to side as it sped along, was already filling up with bleary eyed commuters on their way to work.

Ten minutes later, Salocin emerged from the depths of London's basement to find morning had well and truly broken, the sun just rising above a colourless winter day, cold and windblown, the pavements slick with sleet. Head down, avoiding the hullabaloo of Smithfield, which was now winding down for the day, he headed for Clerkenwell. Thankfully, he still had the set of keys to the yard that Mickey had given him to unlock the place yesterday, had forgotten to give them back last night.

There was no sign of the Old Bill, either, which didn't surprise him, especially as Marie had been too scared to tell the police where the assault had *actually* taken place. Some passers-by close to a pub called the Magpie and Stump, a good couple of miles from the yard, had found her. How the hell she had got there in her state was beyond miraculous. Mickey said people used to watch the hangings outside Newgate Prison from that pub. Salocin would love to watch a certain someone swing from the hangman's rope over a pint. And there'd be no fucking last pint, as was tradition, for that condemned bastard.

As expected, there were no cars about, either, so he was surprised to find the place already unlocked. Cautious, Salocin entered the yard through the partially open door, each step he traced long, silent, doing his very best to avoid drawing attention to himself. The yard itself, both indoors and out, appeared to be empty, eerily quiet. Keeping his wits about him, he headed towards the room at the far end of the place. As he drew closer, he could see a shaft of light emanating through a slight crack in the door. Holding his breath, he pushed the door, gently, and there before him, his back to him, stood Frank Wakefield who, leant over a mop and bucket, appeared to be mopping up bloodstains from the floor. The cunt was whistling too, Bing Crosby's 'Busy Doing Nothing' if he wasn't mistaken? And dancing. Shuffling side to side, throwing the mop handle this way and that, as if it were a person, a dance partner. The rage simmering in Salocin's chest, rose now like a demon, black, soulless, deadly, with a life force all of its own.

Knowing Frank was unaware of his presence, Salocin studied him for a moment; watched as he washed the blood – Marie's, no doubt – away, with no more concern or compassion than if it had been an oil stain. With his breathing shallow, his heart hammering loud and slow between his ears, Salocin took a step forward, then stopped again, as Frank, resting the mop against the bucket, turned sideways and swaggered, cowboy-style, towards a large desk in the far corner of the room. *Cocky cunt*, Salocin thought. The desk itself, which contained three drawers, an antique banker's reading lamp and a black Bakelite telephone, was otherwise empty. Still whistling, Frank reached down, opened one of the drawers and retrieved a half drunk bottle of Scotch and a single glass tumbler. Unscrewing the lid of the bottle he poured a shot into the glass, then lifting it to his mouth, he downed it in one gulp. Reaching into his trouser pocket he then pulled out a package, tipping its contents onto the desktop. *Coke*, Salocin thought, as he watched Frank make a neat line of white powder and snort it up his nose. He then poured himself another Scotch, and sniffing loudly, swigged it back in one.

'That's more like it,' he shouted, slamming the glass down onto the desk and glancing across his shoulder. 'You gonna stand there all day, Sally boy, or what?'

Startled, Salocin took a step back. Frank had known he was there all along, then? Which seemed to amuse him, make him smile that charming smile of his, his face a picture of cordial benevolence. 'Encha been home yet? You're still wearing your suit?'

'Nah,' Salocin lied. 'Me and some of the others fancied a bit of an all-nighter, went to a couple of clubs in Soho.'

Frank arched an eyebrow, lifted the bottle of Scotch. 'Drink?'

Salocin nodded, walked towards him. Frank reached into the drawer of the desk and pulled out another glass. 'So you ain't been home yet, then?' he asked as he poured a shot into both glasses, passing one to Salocin.

Salocin took the glass, shook his head, grinned. 'Nah. Ain't worth it now. Her indoors will have a right bleedin' strop on. Thought it best to come into work for a couple of hours. Give her time to calm down and me time to think of a way to make it up to her.'

Frank, whose rigid shoulders had deflated somewhat, laughed. Quick as a flash Salocin reached for the bottle of Scotch and slammed it with all of his might across Frank's head. Stunned, Frank staggered backwards, one hand reaching blindly behind him, the other cradling his head, staring in disbelief at the blood on his hand when he pulled it away.

'She was pregnant, you cunt.' Salocin lunged towards him with the now broken bottle. He swung, again, for Frank's head but this time Frank ducked, jabbed something into Salocin's side. Salocin felt nothing except a warm creeping sensation beneath his shirt. Then he noticed the blade in Frank's hand, covered in blood – his blood he assumed? Without looking down Salocin put his hand inside his jacket, felt his shirt, soaking wet. The smell wafting towards him, was strong, metallic, like water from a rusty tap, filling his flaring nostrils.

Frank had stabbed him. No doubt about it.

He didn't know how bad it was but he didn't care. He'd kill the sick bastard if it was the last thing he did. The beast within him, dark and brooding, had now well and truly awoken. Like a superhero he had the strength of a thousand mere mortal men and he intended to use it. If he died trying, so be it. Rapid-fire thoughts surged through him. Everything was ruined now anyway. Every time he looked at his brother or his sister-in-law from now on, he knew he'd always blame himself for what happened to Marie. And as for Ellie, well, she'd always deserved better than some common barrow boy from the East End, because, dress it up how you like, that's all he was really – a chancer who took from others with no thought or consideration for his victims. And he didn't mean the fuck off big companies and corporations who, unbeknownst to the great unwashed, used every trick in the book to dodge their taxes, fiddle their expenses – as far as Salocin was concerned they could go fuck themselves – Salocin was talking about the little people, like the woman in the park. Honest, hard-working people who cared, people who tried to make a difference by example, not by doing the same as the crooks – the legal ones and the illegal ones. Nah – Ellie and the kids would be better off without him. Salocin knew Georgie wouldn't hurt them because unlike the psycho scumbag standing in front of him, Georgie was old school, didn't believe in hurting women and children, not like the new breed of gangster emerging. So, as far as Salocin was concerned, he had nothing to lose; he didn't care if his life ended here, just so long as he killed Frank first.

Again Salocin lunged towards Frank, his movements deft, concentrated, nimble as a ballroom dancer. Before Frank realised how it had happened Salocin had him pinned up against the wall, one arm tightly wound around Frank's neck, the other holding Frank's twisted arm behind his back. Frank, now coughing and spluttering, tried to break free, prompting Salocin to press harder, crushing Frank's windpipe. Salocin could feel the veins in Frank's neck throbbing against his arm. He thought of Marie's bloody, bruised face and took great pleasure in yanking Frank's hand, still holding the knife he had stabbed Salocin with, further up into his back, twisting and turning it like a corkscrew. There was a snapping sound, bones breaking, the clatter of metal hitting concrete as Frank finally dropped the knife. Frank, unable to scream due to Salocin's grip around his throat, began thrashing his one free hand about in a desperate bid to break free.

'Now you know what it feels like you psycho, good-for-nothing piece of shit,' Salocin whispered into Frank's ear before sinking his teeth into it.

Salocin didn't hear the door open, the footsteps behind him. Suddenly there was a searing pain in the back of his head.

He fell to the floor and everything went black.

ELLIE

Ellie held onto her sister-in-law's hand, watching as Teddy, forlorn, glanced over his shoulder. 'Are you sure you want me to go?' he asked his wife. Marie nodded, told him she needed some rest.

'Don't worry, Ted, I'll stay with her for a few more minutes,' Ellie said, using the same honeyed reassuring voice she used with the children whenever they were upset or afraid. 'She'll be fine.' She turned to look at her sister-in-law, gently squeezing the fingers of her hand. 'She's safe now,' she added, trying not to cry.

Teddy sighed, put up his hand and left.

When Marie was quite sure he had gone, the tears came, spilling down her face, splashing onto the crisp white sheets that covered her bruised and battered body. Her sobs were muted but her pain, physical, emotional, and raw, was etched into every curve, every line of her face. 'I'm scared, Ellie,' she whispered.

Ellie blinked away the tears forming behind her own eyes, swallowed the pain lodged in her throat. Having grown up in the East End she was no stranger to violence, had witnessed men fighting in the street, heard the domestic disputes of her neighbours, felt the back of her father's hand if she had stepped out of line. This though – the bloody, beaten body of her sister-in-law, her best friend – was something else, caused by something dark and depraved. Something terrifying. 'Of course you are,' Ellie replied. 'But you're okay now. Safe.' She placed her hands on top of Marie's, her eye immediately drawn to the blood-stained sapphire ring Teddy had bought her a couple of years ago. 'And I'm sure, once Salocin puts the word about, we'll soon find the bastard that did this to you. Georgie and Mickey know people, Marie. They'll flush him out, you mark my words.'

Marie, her skin unnaturally pale, as if her spirit and her body had been beaten and crushed, sobbed again, her hands trembling. 'No,' she said, 'you don't understand. I've done something stupid. Something terrible.'

Ellie, confused, frowned. 'What on earth are you talking about? I don't understand?'

Marie threw her a sideways glance. 'You can't tell anyone,' she said, 'but I know who did this to me.'

'You know?'

'And now I'm afraid he'll do something stupid,' Marie continued. 'I've never seen so much anger in a man's eyes before.' Her voice verged on hysteria. 'I just thought… if I told him… he might tell Mickey… who might tell Georgie.

'Told who, what?'

Marie wasn't listening, just kept rambling on. 'But I was wrong. Underestimated his reaction.'

Ellie put her hand to the back of her head, felt her neck prickle as she struggled to make sense of her sister-in-law's garbled words. The bed shook as Marie's body trembled and convulsed. Concerned, Ellie stood up just as Marie threw up. 'It was Frank, Ellie,' she said wiping her mouth with the back of her hand. 'It was Frank did this to me.'

Eyebrows arched, Ellie stepped away from the bed. 'Frank?' she exclaimed, pacing the room left to right, searching for something to clean up the mess. 'What do you mean?' She flung open the drawers of a cabinet beside the bed. *Nothing. Not even a towel.*

'I told Salocin,' Marie whispered.

Ellie stopped what she was doing, looked at her sister-in-law, and felt the blood in her veins turn to ice. 'You told Salocin?' Marie nodded, looked down as the full force of her confession hit Ellie right between the eyes. 'Oh my god,' she said, raising her hand to her mouth. 'Salocin will kill him.' It was true. Ellie knew her husband better than he knew himself. Knew what he was capable of, what every person, perhaps – given the right circumstances – was capable of. 'Does Teddy know?' she asked, her voice unintentionally curt.

Panicked, Marie looked up again. 'No! Please don't tell him.'

Ellie felt her chest constrict then swell with anger. It was misplaced anger, but Salocin was in danger. She knew it and so did Marie – now. Ellie's anger quickly dissipated, though. Marie was a mess. She hadn't intended to put Salocin at risk. Calling one of the nurses for help, Ellie gently kissed Marie's forehead, told her not to worry. 'I've got this,' she said soothingly. 'You concentrate on getting better and I'll be back to see you later.'

Marie grabbed Ellie's hand. 'I'm so sorry, Ellie,' she said, her face damp with tears.

Ellie forced herself to smile, patted Marie's hand. 'You ain't got nothing to be sorry about. Nothing at all. Do you hear me? This ain't your fault. And you will get over this – in time.

Remember what you once told me? "You'll be fine. In time. And I'll be right behind you." And I am – right behind you, Marie. I promise.'

And with that Ellie left the room leaving a rather stern-faced looking nurse pulling vomit-covered sheets from the bed. She hated leaving Marie, she really did. She looked so tiny, so vulnerable, like a broken doll savaged by a dog. It was heart-breaking. But right now her priority was her husband. She needed to find Salocin before it was too late. Before he did something he might regret.

She thanked Marie's mother for watching the children, and with Sean balanced on her hip, and Lizzie by her side, holding her hand, she headed towards the car park. Bundling them both into the back she jumped into the driver's seat and reversed the car out of its parking space. She wasn't sure where she was going but the yard seemed like a good starting point.

A car blared its horn as she pulled out in front of it. 'Mind where yer going you silly cow,' the driver, a man wearing a tan leather jacket and gold rimmed sunglasses, called out of his window. Ellie put her hand up in apology. 'Facking women drivers,' she heard him add.

Ellie didn't give a shit, and putting her foot down, she sped away. She had to find Salocin before it was too late. But not with the kids in tow. If she'd thought it through properly, she could have asked Marie's mum to watch them for a bit longer, or asked Teddy to mind them. Then again, they were in shock, didn't need the hassle, plus it may have aroused their suspicions, had them wondering, without good cause, why she needed them watched. There was no point going to her parents so the only place she could think of was Wilf and Martha's.

'Where are we going now, Mummy?' Lizzie asked.

Ellie looked at her daughter's reflection in the rear-view mirror. She was pouting, her little forehead wrinkled in a confused frown. 'To see Nanna and Grandad,' Ellie replied. 'Won't that be fun?' She flicked the indicator.

Lizzie shook her head causing the curls of her hair to bounce, crossed both her chubby arms. 'No!' she said. 'I want to go home to Daddy.'

Ellie, her stomach a jittery jumble of nerves, ignored her daughter's surly face, took a left and headed for her in-laws.

'Fack orf,' Wilf said.

Ellie looked at her father-in-law in disbelief. Thank god she'd had the good sense to leave the kids in the car. 'Did you not hear what I said?' she said, her voice several octaves higher. 'I think Salocin has gone after Frank. He nearly killed Marie last night. It's a wonder she's still alive!'

Martha, her face barely visible behind her husband's broad shoulders, hovered in the background. Ellie cocked her head to the side, looked at her mother-in-law. 'Martha?' she pleaded. Martha twisted her mouth to one side, looked away in sad resignation.

'I told him,' Wilf continued, 'facking years ago. Never bring the Old Bill or trouble to my door. Yer on yer own if you do.' His eyes were grey, steely cold, his voice tinged with self-righteous sanctimony.

'But he hasn't,' Ellie hissed. 'I'm simply asking you to watch your grandchildren,' she swung round, pointed to the parked car, 'while I try to find out what the fuck is going on – before it's too late!' Her voice quivered and just for a split second, the air thick with anticipation, Ellie sensed Wilf's hesitation. However, once again and to her utter disbelief, he shook his head and quietly closed the door in her face. Ellie felt her shoulders shake and, despite her muted sobs, the tears rolled down her face. She stared at the door of her in-laws house, its peeling paint and the gold Yale lock, not dissimilar to the one that had been on the flat all those years ago.

Sniffing, she took a deep breath and used both her hands to wipe away her tears before turning round to face the car and her children again. They had been up for hours now, were probably tired, getting hungry, she reasoned. It wasn't fair to keep dragging them around London, especially as Sean hadn't been well. She looked up at the sky, grey, oppressive, noticed the neat row of terraced houses opposite, the chimney stacks cluttered with TV aerials. *Fuck. What the hell should I do?* The temptation to scream was overwhelming. She didn't of course, knew she needed to keep calm, make a plan. Taking the kids to the yard was out of the question, far too dangerous. She'd drive them home, looking for a telephone box along the way, hope to god she wasn't too late. Then she'd see if one of the neighbours would sit with them.

Ellie didn't see the car parked up the road as she pulled into their drive, or the two individuals that jumped out and walked behind her and the children as she headed towards the front door.

Not until it was too late to do anything about it.

SALOCIN

Salocin jumped, woken by the sound of a gunshot – at least, that's what it sounded like. Soaked in sweat, he'd been dreaming – he was in a forest and up ahead, Ellie and the children were trying to escape a couple of hunters with guns. To the left of him, partially buried in a shallow grave, he saw Marie and to his right, lying face up, was the bloody body of his brother, Teddy. It was only as his eyes focused properly that Salocin realised the ground beneath him was not woodland but concrete and the only bodies present were those milling about, laughing and joking. He lifted his head, winced at the glare of the artificial light, felt a searing pain shoot from the back of his head to his left eye. He tried to move his arms but they were tied tight behind the chair he was sitting on. Remembering the knife in Frank's hand, he looked down, noticed the bloodstain on his shirt, which appeared dry, dark red. *Hopefully, just a flesh wound then? Nothing serious.*

'Oi, Georgie. Looks like Sleeping Beauty's awake,' someone called.

Salocin didn't recognise the voice. He turned, tried to see who it was but instead noticed Frank, some distance away, glaring at him. He was also sitting on a chair, one arm swinging by his side, the other lying limply in his lap. He made to stand up but a hand on his shoulder pushed him back down again.

Georgie.

'I facking told you to stay put,' he ordered, and Frank, scowling like a child, a spoilt brat who couldn't have his own way, sat down again. 'You've caused me enough grief for one night.' Georgie then turned to face Salocin.

'Salocin,' he said, as if greeting an old friend. 'I'm very disappointed in you, young man.' He headed towards the desk that earlier, except for a lamp and a telephone, had been empty but now contained, Salocin noticed with great alarm, several knives, meat cleavers and other butchering utensils, a sort of makeshift surgeon's table. Salocin tried to swallow, felt his tongue stick to the roof of his mouth, his arse quiver. Was this it? How his life would end? Tortured, dismembered, thrown on the scrap heap? His wife a widow, his children fatherless? And for what? Angry, he glanced again at Frank, remembered Marie's bruised and battered face. The murderous rage that had brought him here, was still present, still pulsing through his veins, but as Georgie picked up a knife, used a cloth to wipe fresh blood from the blade, Salocin congratulated himself on being a prize mug, an emotional fuckwit who, when the chips were down, had allowed his anger to rule his head. Mickey, his mentor and role model, had taught him many things over the past few years, dished out many poignant sayings and quotes, offered many nuggets of wisdom. The one that immediately sprang to mind was "don't make decisions when you're angry." Salocin lowered his head, laughed quietly to himself. *What a cunt.* He'd always believed he was a better man than the likes of Georgie and his cronies – yes, he was a chancer, yes, he'd made his money ducking and diving, but he didn't kill and torture people like they did – and yet, here he was.

'Right. I understand you may have something that belongs to me?' Georgie said.

Salocin frowned. *Fuck! The painting. He'd forgotten all about it.* He needed to warn Ellie and the kids not to go back to the house. *But how?* Nervously, Salocin looked across at Frank, met by his malevolent grin. Smug, Frank rolled a wet, pink tongue across his bottom lip. His eyes, dark and menacing, reminded Salocin of a snake.

Salocin turned to Georgie, but nodded towards Frank. 'You know he had Old Bill 'ere yesterday?'

Frank's face dropped but Salocin had nothing to lose now. He'd already cast his eye about the room and with only one door, both entrance and exit, no windows, and a room full of blokes more than willing, or at least, too scared not to do Georgie's bidding, he was fucked. He was scared, too, more than he'd been in a long time. Scared of the pain he knew was coming and scared of leaving Ellie and the kids behind. What kind of man put his emotions above the safety of his family? Even Wilf had had the good sense not to fall into that trap. Anger had fuelled him, and although he did his best to hold onto that emotion, it was fear that was in the driving seat now. *Fuck* – how he wished to god his hands were free to calm his jittery leg. 'Crawling all over the bleedin' yard they were.' Salocin used his best matter-of-fact voice.

Georgie looked at Salocin, threw his son a sideways glance.

'Yeah, I know.' His tone was tinged with the impatience of a frustrated father addressing a disobliging child. 'Seems though, according to my son, it's my son-in-law that has been up to no good.'

'You what,' Salocin shouted in disbelief. 'Are you having a laugh? The only one round 'ere, up to no good is him.' He used his chin to point to Frank. 'Only you're too stupid to see it – or admit it.'

The room fell silent, all eyes upon Georgie, waiting to see how he would deal with the disrespectful little upstart bad-mouthing him and his son. Salocin felt his guts turn over, not sure if he wanted to puke or shit himself. *Fuck it!* Why didn't he think before he opened his fat gob? Why didn't he think full stop?

He shouldn't have come here. As bad as it was with Marie, she was alive and she was safe. He should have gone straight to Mickey. Mickey would have known what to do, even if it meant waiting a while. Then again, time was running out. He and Ellie had made plans to do a bunk to Oz, plans Mickey knew nothing about. Nevertheless, everyone knew Frank was a wanker, a liability, a self-entitled scumbag who relied on his father's reputation and connections to do whatever the fuck he wanted to do. But blood was blood at the end of the day and if you had half an ounce of sense, you didn't talk to the boss the way Salocin had just talked to Georgie.

From the corner of his eye, Salocin noticed Georgie nod his head slightly. He didn't notice the man mountain on his other side – the bloke with the huge shoulders, the bull neck, fists the size of a joint of ham – at least, not until one of those fists pummelled the side of Salocin's face. Salocin heard a cracking sound, felt his jaw move, his mouth fill with blood and several teeth dislodge. Trying to open his mouth, move his jaw, he felt the blood run down his chin.

Georgie went back to the desk and picked up a pair of bolt cutters. 'Bring him to me,' he instructed.

Man mountain wiped the back of his fist, streaked with Salocin's blood, on his jacket, then grunting, bent down, and shoved both his hands under the chair Salocin was tied to. He lifted and carried it towards the desk. Desperate, Salocin tried to break free, twisting his head left to right, studying the faces of the other men in the room. There were six of them, eight if you included Georgie and Frank. He recognised one or two, had seen them on the odd occasion accompanying Georgie at the yard, but the others were strangers and it was obvious by their blank expressions, none of them gave a shit about him. The room crackled with apprehension and not for the first time, Salocin felt his heart thud against his chest.

'See that?' Georgie pointed to the phone which was in fact a speakerphone, 'I'm expecting a phone call any minute. One you might just be interested in.'

ELLIE

Ellie, jumped, shocked by the sharp pain between her shoulder blades. She spun round, surprised to find the cause of the pain had been the hand of one of two individuals. Men, strangers, a look of menace about them, had crept up behind her, one of whom had nudged her in the back. Nervous but somewhat pissed off, Ellie opened her mouth to say something but the smaller of the two men put a finger to his lips, sneering.

'Who are you?' Lizzie, who was clutching her mother's hand, looked up and asked.

The younger, taller man, probably in his early thirties, with longish red hair, sideburns to match, broad shoulders, a squashed nose and cauliflower ears, looked at Lizzie, offered her a smile, of sorts, whereas the other man, shorter, wider, more squat, with slicked back hair, bushy eyebrows and copper flecked deep-set eyes, was less convivial. Ignoring Lizzie, he stared at Ellie who was holding Sean against her hip with one hand, clutching the front door keys in her other.

'Open it,' he ordered, glancing at Sean and Lizzie, 'then no one gets hurt.'

Ellie, aware that Lizzie, wide-eyed, bewildered, was watching her, kept her voice low, almost sing-song in its delivery. 'And why would I do that?' she asked, her eyes flitting towards her parked car on the drive, her neighbours' windows across the road, their curtains still drawn.

'Because,' he brought his face so close to hers she could smell the tobacco on his breath, 'my boss has something…' he smiled, although it was more of a leer '…or should I say *someone* close to your heart.'

Ellie took a sharp intake of breath. *Salocin*, she thought.

The stranger drew away, ruffled Sean's unruly hair.

Sean flinched, scowled – his little forehead knitting into a frown. 'No,' he said, raising one of his pudgy hands to swat the stranger's hand away.

'Leave my bruver alone,' Lizzie added, using one of her balled fists to hit the stranger's leg.

The stranger looked down, laughed. 'Feisty little bitch,' he said clamping his large hand around Lizzie's small one and yanking it back.

Lizzie's eyes filled with tears. 'Ow-err,' she wailed in a short, sharp sob.

'Get your fucking hands off her,' Ellie yelled, stabbing the stranger's hand with her keys.

Again the stranger laughed, releasing Lizzie's small arm. It was red, marked with his fingerprints where he'd gripped her too tight.

As it fell to her side, Lizzie used her other free hand to lift and nurse her injured arm, burying her head in Ellie's dress. 'Where's Daddy? I want my Daddy,' she mumbled.

'For fuck sake, Jeff,' the younger of the two men said. 'Leave it out. She's only a kid.'

Smarting at his companion's comments, Jeff snatched the keys from Lizzie's hand and jangled them in the lock of the front door. 'In. Now,' he said, shoving Ellie so hard in the back she almost tripped over the step. Once inside he ordered Ellie and the children into the living room, told them to sit on the sofa and not to move, informing the other, younger man to watch them while he went from room to room ransacking the place.

After ten minutes or so, both the children began to whine, complaining they were hungry. Reluctantly, their guardian, who Ellie discovered went by the name of Les, agreed to let Ellie make both the kids some breakfast. 'Just some cereal,' Ellie said. They traipsed into the kitchen together and Ellie seated the children at the small breakfast table, pouring them each a bowl of Rice Krispies. Lizzie reached for the jug of milk, poured some onto the cereal and putting her ear to the bowl, listened for the snap, crackle and pop. She giggled, poured some milk into Sean's bowl, and copying his big sister, he did the same.

Ellie marvelled at the ability of her children to be frightened to death one minute but relaxed enough to eat and smile the next. Ellie's nerves were too frazzled to eat but she could murder a cup of tea. Again, somewhat reluctantly, Les agreed. He stood guard behind the children, watching her as she filled the kettle with water – it was a Russell Hobbs, state-of-the-art kettle that switched itself off, another kitchen must-have gadget they really didn't need – and flicked the switch. She grabbed two cups from the cupboard above her head, pulled open a drawer for some spoons – glancing at the black handled bread knife – before nudging it shut again with her hip. Spooning dried tea leaves into her favourite chipped teapot, she couldn't say the thought of throwing boiling hot water across Les' face hadn't crossed her mind, nor had grabbing a knife and sticking him with it – then she could grab the children and make a run for it. But what if she missed? Or tripped? Burned or stabbed herself, or one of the kids instead? No. It was too dangerous. She had to keep calm. Think. Wait for an opportunity to present itself.

Pouring two cups of tea, Ellie sat down at the table with the children to drink hers whereas Les remained standing with his.

'Got any biscuits?' he asked.

'Rich Tea? Ellie pointed to a barrel decorated with bright orange flowers beside the kettle.

'Well, well, well,' Jeff, the other bloke said, as he strutted into the kitchen. 'If we ain't all playing 'appy families.' His voice dripped with sarcasm. He stabbed Les in the chest with his finger. 'Thought I told you lot to stay in the living room.'

'Aw, c'mon Jeff.' Les almost spilt his tea. 'They was hungry. They're only little uns.'

'I don't care if they're bleedin' starving to death. We're 'ere to do a job and you do as your told. Got it?'

Les put his tea down, and nodded like a chastised child.

Ellie kept looking at the cupboard behind them; the one she knew contained her large, cast iron frying pan.

'You,' Jeff said, pointing at her. 'Into the hallway – NOW. You and me is gonna make a little phone call.'

Lizzie immediately leapt up from her chair and threw herself at her mother, coiling each hand, each foot around her, clinging, like ivy to a wall. It was all Ellie could do to convince her young daughter to let go. 'C'mon, I need you to be a big, brave girl,' she said, touching her cheek. 'Can you do that for me?'

Lizzie pouted, nodding her head back and forth in that exaggerated way children often do, and as Jeff walked on ahead, Les winked at Ellie. 'They'll be okay,' he mouthed. All the while

Lizzie, her big brown eyes, innocent, questioning, followed her as she left the room. Ellie shuddered, felt the weight of her daughter's stare bore into her, found her total trust unnerving.

In the hallway, as she passed the door, Ellie noticed the living room had been completely trashed. The Christmas tree lay on its side, ornaments ripped from its branches, the lava lamp Sean loved to stare at, beside it, smashed, its watery contents having leaked all over the geometric style rug she and Salocin had picked up from Camden Market a couple of years ago. Their beloved books, with their ripped pages and broken spines, lay scattered about the floor, as did a decapitated Tiny Tears doll and crushed Etch-a-sketch. It was more than unsettling. And no doubt there would be tears later, when the children saw their broken toys, but it was all immaterial – if that was all that got broken today, she would be happy. Material things could be replaced, Salocin and the children couldn't.

Jeff picked up the phone, stuck his fat, clumsy finger into the plastic dial and turned it several times. Ellie heard the familiar purr of the ringtone, then a clicking sound as someone, a man, answered the call.

'Georgie?' Jeff said. 'Yeah, it's me. Nah, searched the whole bleedin' 'ouse… Nah, I ain't. Yeah, she's 'ere.' Jeff thrust the receiver in front of Ellie's face. 'For you,' he said, grinning.

Bracing herself, Ellie took the phone from his hand. She coughed, cleared her throat, and tucked the curtain of hair that had fallen across her face, behind her ear. 'Hello,' she said.

'That you, Ellie,' came Georgie's voice.

'Yes,' said Ellie. *Course it fucking is!*

SALOCIN

'That you, Ellie?' Georgie said.

Alarmed, Salocin looked up. Georgie had put the call on

loudspeaker. 'Elle,' he shouted. 'You okay?'

'Salocin?' came Ellie's concerned reply. 'Where the hell are you? And yeah, me and the kids are fine but there's a couple of blokes here, at the house.' Salocin felt the blood drain from his face. 'I don't know what the hell they want…' There was a pause '…but one of 'em's made a right bleedin' mess of the place.' Her voice was filled with quiet bravado.

Knowing she was trying not to show it, Salocin could still hear the trepidation in her voice, the slight lilt, the tremor as she talked. Like grainy old film footage he imagined the kids crying, cowering, wondering who the big horrible men were and where Daddy – who was supposed to protect them – was. He could also see Ellie, purposely keeping her voice light, skating over the fear, doing her best to stay calm for the kids. *Fuuuuuuck!* Once again Salocin felt the familiar rush of rage resurface. Red, hot blood surging through his veins, flaming his insides. He looked up, noticed the slight flare of Georgie's nostrils, his steely stare – the spider watching the fly – as he repeatedly opened and closed the bolt cutters in his hand. *How the fuck had it all come to this?* Mesmerised, Salocin watched as Georgie opened and closed, opened and closed the cutters; he felt an irrepressible urge to yell at Georgie to stop it. The cutters made a squeaking sound, like a rusty hinge on an old wooden gate, and the more Georgie opened and closed the cutters the louder, more annoying the noise became.

'Sorry about that Ellie,' Georgie interrupted, laying the cutters back down again. 'Pity you didn't make it to the party last night. Salocin said your boy – Sean, is it? – was poorly?'

Ellie bristled, Salocin could hear it in her voice. 'It was just a cold,' she replied, a layer of resentment anchoring her voice.

'Good, good, glad to hear it.' Georgie's voice was purposely soft, the cat playing with the mouse. 'See, the thing is, Ellie, I had to send a couple of my men over to look for something.

Something that belongs to me. Something...' he stared at Salocin, cocked his head, birdlike '...I believe your husband stole from me. Him and that two faced son-in-law of mine, that is.'

There was a brief pause. 'I don't know what you're talking about, Georgie,' Ellie replied.

Georgie smiled. 'That's as maybe,' he said. 'But Salocin does. Now...' He nodded towards two men standing behind Salocin, ordered them to untie him.

Salocin panicked, the fight-or-flight reflex well and truly kicking in. 'Look, Georgie.' He glanced from left to right, desperate to discover a way out, an escape route he hadn't seen before. 'Truth is, yes, I did take the painting, but only because I got wind that he,' he glanced across his shoulder, nodded towards Frank again, 'was bringing Old Bill to the yard' – if Mickey believed it then maybe Georgie would too? – 'and if there's one thing Mickey's always drilling into us, it's never to bring trouble or filth to the yard. On your say-so.' Salocin felt the rope that had been binding his wrists fall away. He tried to stand up but the weight of strong hands pressing down on his shoulders made it impossible. Fearful, he caught sight of his distorted but pitiful reflection in the bright metal of the butchers' knives laid out before him, taunting him. If he could just get an arm free, grab one of the knives, or the cleaver next to it, then maybe – just maybe – he could lash out, cause some damage, which might just give him time to make a run for it?

'Bring his arm round,' Georgie said to one of the men holding Salocin down.

Salocin kicked, struggled, and used every ounce of strength he could draw on to pull away from his captors. But when that proved futile he decided the next best thing was resistance. To do everything in his power, without getting them broke, to keep his hands locked firmly behind him – ironic considering moments ago he had wished they were free. 'Honest to god, Georgie,'

Salocin said, his body rigid, his scalp pricking with fear. 'I don't know what Mickey's plans were for the painting but I know he had every intention of telling you – when the time was right.' Mickey hadn't said any such thing but another one of his famous sayings was "bullshit baffles brains" and right now Salocin's only desire was to get out of there alive. There'd be time enough to fill Mickey in once he'd made his escape.

Georgie, squinting from the smoke rising from the cigarette now hanging from the side of his mouth, shot Frank another sideways glance. And somewhere, in between the grunting, huffing and puffing, as he wrestled with the blokes manhandling him, Salocin heard Ellie's bewildered voice.

'Salocin? Georgie? What's going on?'

'Fuck me, he's strong,' one of the men, red-faced and panting, trying to hold Salocin down, said.

'Want me to punch him again, Georgie?' man mountain asked, his tone monosyllabic.

'Nah, nah, nah, Harry,' Georgie replied. 'I want him to feel this. You hold him down, and Ron,' he pointed to the other, 'you hold his arm behind his back, Charlie you hold his other arm here on the desk. And keep it there!'

'Georgie? Salocin? What the hell is going on?' Ellie shrieked.

Georgie's cronies did as they were told and with the bolt cutters once again in his hand, Georgie hovered above Salocin, his mouth twisted. 'Now, son,' he said, bending Salocin's little finger back and placing the bolt cutters at the base. Salocin shook, uncontrollably, felt bile spurt into his mouth. 'This is for telling me porky pies.' Georgie clamped the cutters around Salocin's finger. 'For fuck sake, Georgie,' Salocin yelled, his voice ringing with desperation. 'You're not seriously going to do this, are you?'

'And the next one will be for thinking you can give my son a good hiding.'

'What!' Salocin exclaimed.

'Stop, Georgie. Please!' Ellie's voice crackled across the loud speaker. 'Whatever it is you're about to do, just STOP!'

'Did you see what he did to her? It ain't right, Georgie,' Salocin's eyes darted towards Frank who, sitting quite still, his face blank, watched his father. Salocin wondered when Frank had first been exposed to such violence, and if it had played some part in his development. 'You gotta be tapped in the head to do what he did to that poor gel,' Salocin roared.

A ripple of quiet stilled the room and too late, Salocin realised that was another thought he should have kept to himself. Georgie frowned, a fleeting look of disappointment flashing across his eyes. He observed Salocin through a series of stilted head movements. His voice, although quiet, was abrasive. 'And why the fuck should I give a shit about some old tart?'

His words were brutal. Salocin, although angry and confused, was once again filled with a renewed sense of panic. *Old tart? Did he actually just say that? Does he actually know what his son has done to my sister-in-law?*

Georgie, never one to waste time, wasn't hanging around. With Salocin's finger gripped between the bolt cutters he pressed down – hard. There was a loud crunching noise followed by a snapping sound. Salocin stared in disbelief as Georgie released the severed finger from the cutters and dropped it onto the desk in front of him. Bloodied and pink, it didn't look like his finger but more like an uncooked chipolata. The pain, immediate, as it shot up his arm, ricocheting off every nerve ending, every fibre – like a ball hitting its targets in a game of pinball – was unbearable. He opened his mouth to scream but no sound was forthcoming. Darkness swirled above him, the shock of it all making him feel nauseous. He could hear Ellie, too, still on the end of the phone. Still yelling. Still demanding to know what the fuck was happening. He could also hear something else, a low guttural sound, something alien, and unnatural, like a wounded animal?

After a few seconds Salocin realised it was coming from him.

ELLIE

Ellie gasped, felt her insides falling away. She had never heard her husband scream before and it was truly terrifying. What the fuck had Georgie done? Distracted by a scuffling sound behind the kitchen door, she looked up. The door crashed opened and Lizzie burst through. Crying, she headed straight for the stairs, immediately followed by Les. Ellie, by now sitting on the floor, crumpled, like a discarded piece of paper, the phone gripped so tight in her hand she could see the whites of her knuckles, made to stand up, run after her, but she was quickly pushed back down again.

'Stay on the fucking phone,' Jeff said.

Fear rose from her chest, forcing bile into her throat. She swallowed it back down, blinked back the tears pricking her eyes and tried to focus on her breathing. Several minutes later Les reappeared at the foot of the stairs carrying a tearful Lizzie.

'Keep them fucking kids quiet,' Jeff warned.

Les took Lizzie back into the kitchen and closed the door behind them.

Where the fuck was Mickey? Ellie thought desperately. She had found a phone box on the way home and called him, told him what had happened to Marie and that angry – furious, in fact – Salocin had gone looking for Frank. Mickey promised he'd sort it. So where the fuck was he? Sniffing, she used the heel of her hand to wipe the tears from her cheeks.

Georgie spoke again. 'Now then, Ellie,' he said. 'The reason your old man is screaming like a little girl is because I just removed one of his fingers.' Ellie took a sharp intake of breath, her hand flying to her mouth, swatting away the images of her husband suffering, in pain, frightened. 'He lied to me about the painting, you see.' She heard a slight whimper, followed by Georgie ordering his cronies to keep Salocin still. Sweat formed under her arms and in the small of her back, moist and cold, it felt strange, like hundreds of little pinpricks. And still there was no sign of Mickey? Was he leaving them to it? Feeding Salocin to the wolves? She hoped not. The best, and the only thing she could do right now was buy Salocin some time, somehow stall Georgie, until, hopefully, Mickey came.

With her mind whirring like the cogs of a clock, she replayed Georgie's confused conversation with Salocin. Had he really called Marie an "old tart?" As stupid as it was, because at the end of the day, Georgie was a gangster, she couldn't help thinking his comments were odd, out of character. What, if anything, did he actually know about what happened to Marie? She wondered if Georgie knew anything at all? Neither he nor Salocin had mentioned her name. What if the "old tart" he'd been referring to wasn't Marie. What if–

Ellie chanced it, asked Georgie if he'd heard what had happened to her sister-in-law. She knew from the silence that followed, Georgie was listening. She also knew that when that silence was broken by the protests of another, namely Frank, calling her a liar, she was certain Georgie had no clue about Marie and, as she had rightly guessed, his reference to some "old tart" had been about someone else – the woman that had saved Marie, perhaps? Frank was silenced and Ellie was urged to continue. Tension crackled across the phone-line and for the first time since this terrible ordeal had begun Ellie sensed a real glimmer of hope. She knew she'd got Georgie's attention so she went for the jugular.

'She was pregnant, too, Georgie,' she said, lowering her voice, her deeply felt sorrow obvious in the softness of her delivery.

'She lost the baby, mind. Doctor reckons – because her injuries were so bad – she'll never be able to have children.' Again silence. 'Course, the police have been sniffing round,' Ellie continued, 'but so far Marie hasn't said a word. Told 'em she doesn't know who did it. She's old school, see Georgie, like you. Proper East Ender. Won't break that code of silence because she knows we look after our own.' Ellie tried not to show it in her voice but she was a mess, her body pulsing with fear. She knew she was taking a risk bad-mouthing Frank but as far as she could see she had nothing to lose, a life without Salocin didn't bear thinking about. She also knew, despite his corrupt lifestyle, there was still some good left in Georgie, had sensed it on the odd occasions they'd met. Georgie was a gentleman gangster who still lived by a set of codes that were fast becoming out-dated.

A deafening bang suddenly interrupted Ellie's thoughts, followed by an ear-splitting scream. She had no idea what the noise was but her ears were filled with a ringing sensation.

'Jesus, Georgie,' she heard someone say. 'Since when was you into guns?'

Ellie put her hand to her chest, held her breath, felt her hearing go sub-aqua. She imagined Salocin lying on the floor, dead, in a pool of his own blood. Stunned, the phone still glued to her ear, she sobbed, silently rocking back and forth like a patient in a lunatic asylum. Even Jeff, who was watching her, threw her a somewhat concerned glance. She felt numb, her world crumbling, her heart closing down. What would she tell the kids? What the fuck would happen to her and the kids? She'd fucked up big time. Her deep-seated desire to find the good in people had meant she'd been wrong about Georgie. *Gentleman gangster – bollocks.*

And then she heard him. Amongst the yelling and confusion she heard the sweetest sound ever – Salocin's voice.

'Fuck me,' was all he said.

Someone had been shot but it wasn't Salocin.

It was Frank. From what Ellie could make out in the chaos, Georgie had shot his own son in the knee.

Ellie would think back to that moment many times over during her life – when she was bathing the kids, hanging out the washing, going for a walk, during Lizzie's graduation, watching Sean's first gig with his first band when they convinced the landlord to let them play at the local pub, when her first grandchild was born – and she liked to think, during that phone conversation with Georgie, she had tapped into something innately good, which, had it never been present in the first place – like with Frank, perhaps – would have led to a very different outcome for her and her family. However, it was also just at that moment that Mickey and Helena turned up. Mickey explained how Frank wanted Mickey out of the way. How he suspected Frank wanted Mickey banged up and how, eventually, he hoped to do the same to Georgie – do whatever was necessary, in fact, to take over Georgie's empire, and how he'd enlisted the help of DI Wiley to do so.

Helena then informed her father that she had been diagnosed with breast cancer, that the outlook was bad and how she, Mickey, and the girls wanted to make the most of what little time they had left together – as a family. She also explained that leaving the girls motherless was one thing but to leave them orphaned was something else entirely.

'Mickey's had enough, Dad,' she said. 'He wants out and I want him out, too. The painting is a gift. A Christmas gift from us to you, to wish you well and thank you, but given on the understanding that you'll give us your blessing and allow us to move on.'

Helena explained that Mickey had deliberately sought the painting for Georgie because of his surname – Wakefield. An obscure but much sought after William Whood, the painting depicted a man with a horse and cart in a field, and as the surname Wakefield, of Anglo-Saxon origin, was believed to have derived from "Waca's field" – the open land belonging to someone named "Waca" – Mickey believed the painting, while both collectable and valuable, was also fitting.

Salocin and Ellie, talking later, had no idea how true Mickey's story was. But what they did know was Mickey had a great mind. A walking, talking encyclopaedia of knowledge who perhaps, under different circumstances, may have been a great actor, a proficient politician, a prodigious barrister. For Mickey Rosenthal had the unerring ability to capture a story, and was, without a doubt, a fascinating, witty but accomplished raconteur. He was also someone who happened to adore his wife and daughters, and like Salocin, he had had enough of his dishonest life.

Georgie still insisted Salocin tell him where the painting was but Ellie insisted Salocin didn't know. She said she had hidden it and she was now the only one who knew of its whereabouts and unless Georgie brought Salocin home to her immediately, he would never see it. She said she was willing to take her chances, and if need be she'd sell the painting, hire the best solicitor, best barrister, money could buy, and Frank would have to take his chances, in court opposite Marie.

Georgie agreed. And twenty minutes later, his Jaguar pulled up on their drive and Salocin, stepped out. His lip was thick and bloodied, his eye swollen, his shirt covered in blood. But, minus a finger, he was alive and in one piece.

'Daddy, Daddy, Daddy,' Lizzie bawled, flinging herself at her father, hugging his legs. 'I did what you said. Turned the lamp on in my bedroom, and you saw it! You saw it and you came back.'

Salocin smiled, although it was more of a wince, and, trying to hide his hand with the missing finger from his daughter's inquisitive eyes, he knelt down beside her, gently kissed her forehead and pulled her into a hug.

Relief surged through Ellie's emotionally battered body. Their ordeal was nearly over. Georgie laughed harder than Ellie thought possible when she showed him where the painting was – namely between two others on the wall of their ransacked living room.

'A wise man once told my husband that if you're going to hide something, it's best to do so in plain sight,' she said.

Georgie placed his hand under her chin, tilted her face towards him, studying her, his eyes bright, his smile razor sharp. 'You've got some guts, young lady,' he said. 'I'll give you that. Remind me a bit of my lovely daughter.' And although there was genuine warmth in his voice, it was also tinged with a noticeable sadness, too.

Later, when Salocin and Ellie sometimes talked about what had happened, Salocin said he reckoned Georgie was weary of his life of crime, too, especially as old-style gangsters like himself were being pushed out by younger, more ruthless mobsters who didn't give a fuck – be that man, woman or child – who they hurt. But at that point he was in too far in, had crossed the line, with no possibility of returning.

Georgie said he'd give them a couple of days then he wanted them out. 'I don't care where you go but you get out of London and you stay out. That goes for your brother and his wife, too,' Georgie warned.

As it was Christmas, Ellie insisted on a month but, as it went, she and Salocin were both so jittery, they were packed up and gone within a couple of weeks. They decided Australia was too far away and instead settled for a small town in the Fens that for a long time felt like the middle of nowhere.

The children quickly forgot about the day the bad men came to their house and Salocin settled into a regular job with a regular income. They used the small profit from the sale of their house to put down on another one, but other than that they had little to no money to start over with. All of Salocin's unopened wage packets had disappeared that day, and whether they lined Georgie's pocket or Les and Jeff's, neither Salocin nor Ellie had any desire to find out. They were together, in one piece, and that was all that mattered. It took a while for them to settle into their new life, to stop looking over their shoulders, and for Marie's scars, both mental and physical, to heal. They missed London, too.

But eventually, in time, they grew to love it.

And besides, there was always Mickey's "debt of gratitude" to call on... if they ever really needed it.

Chapter 33

December 30th
PRESENT DAY – MID MORNING

LIZZIE

I feel exhausted. As if time around us has stopped and I have lived every moment of my mother's story. Astonished, I look at her. 'Mum… you were so brave?'

She shakes her head, laughs. 'Believe me, I wasn't,' she replies. 'But what choice did I have?' She pauses, looks thoughtful. 'They say, don't they, that the memories of the bad, or difficult moments in our lives ease with time, that we forget the pain and suffering associated with them, or at least the memory of it softens? But I tell you this, Lizzie, whenever I think about that time, I can still feel it, still taste the memories, the fear, even to this day. Not to mention the sheer relief I felt when I saw your dad walk through our front door. When Georgie and his cronies eventually left, I had to excuse myself. Leave you and Sean with your dad and lock myself in the bathroom, give in to the shaking that, until then, I'd had to keep at bay. It was so violent, so all-consuming, my knees wouldn't stop knocking.'

She shakes now.

I put my arm around her. Feel her trembling. 'Shush, it's okay Mum. You don't need to say anymore.'

She looks at me, her tired eyes wide, and I see something in them? Relief, maybe? Absolution?

'I do,' she replies. And I realise she *wants* to talk, *needs* to tell me what happened. 'I remember falling to the floor,' she says, 'my legs too weak to hold me, how I lay there, curled up in a ball, crying... for ages. At least, that's how it felt. When I found the strength to pull myself up again, I remember vomiting until there was nothing left, my stomach hollow. Then I stood in front of the mirror above the sink, horrified at the reflection staring back at me. It was as if it was me... but it wasn't... all at the same time? Does that makes sense?'

I nod, squeeze my mother's hand. 'I'm not surprised,' I whisper. 'So what did you do next?'

'I reconstructed myself of course – because that's what we do, isn't it? As mothers? I had two small children who needed me. Not to mention a husband who was minus a finger, some teeth and had a knife wound that needed seeing to.' Mum folds her arms, a slight smile creeping across her face. 'Do you know what your dad said? When I came out of the bathroom?'

'What?'

"About bleedin' time!"

I think of my father, weak from blood loss, exhausted as the adrenalin dissipated from his tired body, the horror of what he came so close to losing present every time he looked at Sean and me, and I thank god for his sense of humour, can't stop the corners of my mouth lifting into a smile.

'And do you know what else he said?'

'Go on, tell me?'

"Ah well. Could have been worse."

I feel my eyebrows shoot into my forehead. 'And, what did you say?'

Mum sniffs. 'I didn't. I just laughed. We both did. Laughed so much it hurt.'

Of course they did. What else was there to do but try to salvage the tiniest bit of humour among the horror? Curiosity gets the better of me. 'So what happened to everyone? Mickey? Georgie? And dare I ask, Frank?'

Mum explains that the incident did Georgie's reputation no harm whatsoever, the consensus being that if he was willing to shoot his own son, what wouldn't he be willing to do? 'As for your Dad and Mickey? Well, they never really saw much of one another again afterwards. Now and again, when enough time had lapsed and your Dad felt it safe to take a train to London, they met a couple of times, chatted over a pint for a few hours. But things were difficult. It was hard, you know, to maintain a friendship after everything that had happened?'

'Yes, of course.'

'Georgie did let Mickey go, though, so he and Helena and the girls could all make the most of what little time Helena had left.'

'She passed away, then? Of cancer?'

Mum sighs. 'Sadly, yes. She hung on for a couple of years, though.'

'And Frank?'

'Well, after his father shot him, he lost a lot of respect. Ended up partially disabled, too. Walked with a permanent limp. Which, thank god, really slowed him down. Drank himself to death in the end, I think. Might be a good idea to ask Laura?'

I arch an eyebrow. 'I intend to. And what was this "debt of honour... debt of gratitude" thing between Dad and Mickey?' I say, waving my hand in the air.

Mum says that Mickey felt indebted to Dad. That thanks to his quick thinking he saved Mickey from going to prison, which in turn helped him persuade Georgie to let him go. 'Plus I think he felt bad about Marie. We all did,' she says, tearful. 'So he came up with this mad idea about "a debt of gratitude". Said any time your Dad, or a family member, found themselves in serious trouble, or in need of help, they were to contact him and he would do whatever he could to help. And believe me, there were times when it would have been easy to call, especially when we were struggling – financially. But your Dad wouldn't do it. Said he'd stolen from Mickey – even though Mickey had stolen the painting – and he didn't deserve Mickey's help.' She rolled her eyes in a way that seemed to say *Men!* 'Your dad said it was the other way round, and that he was indebted to Mickey. He had this mad idea he could help Helena, which was why he insisted on building himself a makeshift laboratory. Your dad had always loved chemistry as a boy, mainly because he liked blowing things up, but he became convinced that his mother had called him Salocin Lemalf, a.k.a. Nicolas Flamel, for a reason. Namely that, like his namesake, he could work out the formula for the elixir of life – which your dad interpreted as a cure for cancer. We both quickly realised he was having a bit of a breakdown, which, with a bit of help, he soon recovered from. The laboratory was then changed to a library, the chemicals he'd ordered, stored high on a shelf out of the way but which–'

'He used as embellishments to the stories he used to make up for Sean and I… and Cassie and Connor, as kids,' I interrupt. Smiling at the memory.

Mum, also smiling, nods. 'Anyway, if not claimed, Mickey said the debt would carry over, even if he were no longer around. We thought about calling it in during that time you were attacked–'

'What do you mean?'

Mum takes another mouthful of tea, then looks at me. 'Well, you were in a coma, and we weren't sure what the outcome would be. Your dad and I wanted to make sure your perpetrator was found, that there would be appropriate justice for his crime, but as it was, we didn't need to. He was caught, convicted and sentenced.'

'And if he hadn't been caught or convicted?'

'Then we would have called in the debt, asked for help.'

'Lawful help?'

Mum's eyes flit towards the ceiling and she lets out a small sigh. 'Where possible, yes. But, as I say, we didn't need to. And then, all this... this awful business with Cassie happened and your Dad made me promise to get you to call the debt in. Especially if it looked like Black would get away with it...' Mum looks out of the kitchen window. I follow her gaze; spot the blackbird flitting between the branches of a tree. She looks at me again, forces a smile. '"It was the best of times, it was the worst of times, it was the age of wisdom, it was the age of foolishness, it was the epoch of belief, it was the epoch of incredulity, it was the season of Light, it was the season of Darkness, it was the spring of hope, it was the winter of despair, we had everything before us, we had nothing before us, we were all going direct to Heaven, we were all going direct the other way..."'

'Dickens?' I ask.

Mum nods. 'The perfect summing of our lives at that time, don't you think?' She lets out a heavy sigh. 'Anyway, there it is. You know it all, now.'

I bite my lip, look down. *Yes. But you don't, Mum.*

Chapter 34

DECEMBER 30TH
PRESENT DAY – EARLY AFTERNOON

LIZZIE

What happens next is a bit of a blur. As if time speeds up and slows down all at once. I leave Mum's, drive home, smile when I pull up on the drive, spot Amra crouched down beside the recycling bin having a sneaky fag, and go inside. Simon greets me in the hallway, tells me about his plans to meet Laura, along with Maisy, and asks me if I mind. 'Of course I don't,' I reply. And I don't. I honestly don't.

Connor is in the kitchen with Robbo, rooting through the freezer in search of something to eat, despite the mountain of leftover food from Christmas Day and Boxing Day still in the fridge. He asks me if it's okay to put a pizza on for him and Robbo to share.

'Of course it is, no need to ask,' I reply, switching the kettle on to make yet another coffee – as if I hadn't had enough already. I watch my son for a few minutes as he chats with his friend, about music, mostly, and wince when they play a video on YouTube. A popular rap song, they inform me. 'One of the best,' Connor insists. Sounds like indefinable 'noise' to me. *Must be getting old.*

And as I continue to watch my son, I think of Dad; find it hard to imagine Connor, who is almost the same age as Dad would have been, married with a baby, and all the responsibility that entails.

Then Simon comes into the room, his face drawn, and I know, straight away, they are here for me. Blood rushes to my head, my breath short, snagging with emotion. Fear tight, coiling in my chest. I shake, which surprises me. It's not like in the movies though, getting arrested. The two plain-clothed police officers that enter the house do so in a blaze of blue light. I cringe, imagining my neighbours' curtains twitching, especially Tabitha's, her poised painted fingernails hovering above her phone screen, ready to tap out a post about my arrest on social media.

They tell me they are arresting me on the suspicion of the murder of Hunter Black, that I do not have to say anything but, that it may harm my defence if I do not mention when questioned something I may later rely on in court. And, anything I do say may be given in evidence. It is at this point I realise someone is behind me, shouting: Connor.

'What? What the hell are you doing?' he yells, his face etched in confusion. 'Si...? What the fuck is this all about?'

'It's okay, Connor. Nothing we can do at the moment,' Simon says, who unlike his stepson, is much calmer, a hint of sad resignation in his eyes.

'Don't say anything,' Simon calls, as they frogmarch me out the door, his voice warm, reassuring but doing little to calm my jangled nerves. 'I'll call Laura.'

And if I didn't want to cry, I would laugh.

Chapter 35

DECEMBER 30TH
PRESENT DAY – MID AFTERNOON

LIZZIE

I stare at the four grey walls surrounding me and shiver. I'm on my own but not alone. I'm being watched. They'll be in to question me soon. But I'll stick to my side of the story. Insist it was self-defence. They've got me though. Bang to rights. Nothing I can do. Well, that's not true. I could do something. Tell the truth for one. But I won't.

I do what I do out of love. It's in the job description. And while I never, for one moment, imagined love would bring me here, to a place full of lies and deceit, I always knew the love for my family was like nothing else in the world. To hurt them is to hurt me, far worse in fact, and to do so leaves me with little or no choice. For when it comes to family, my love knows no law, no benevolence. It challenges everyone and everything, crushing all who stand in its path.

It's funny, though, how we kid ourselves, and one another, about our own moral compass. What we believe ourselves capable and not capable. It's reassuring to think we have limits, convince ourselves there are lines we would never cross, tell ourselves how civilised we are. But like our hearts, civilisation is fragile. The horrors of what we *really* are, underneath, are simply masked by a fine coat of varnish.

Scratch that surface hard enough, throw in the right set of circumstances, and we are all capable of anything.

Even murder.

It wasn't murder though, was it? Manslaughter – maybe? I shake my head. No. Self-defence is what we agreed.

I panic. Look up at the camera in the corner of the room. Wonder who is behind it? Who is looking at me, analysing me. Will they take that shake of my head as an admission to something? Will they study it, along with all my other physical nuances and decide that my body language is giving something away? I know how these things work; I've seen enough of those real-life crime TV programmes. Although, that said, being arrested is nothing like it looks from the comfort of your armchair. It's actually frightening, quite intimidating. I've been patted down, in case I'm carrying something that could cause injury to others or myself; had more fingerprints; a DNA swab, a photo... Which, I suppose, in all fairness, is how it's meant to be. *Fairness? In all fairness? What the fuck am I talking about? What's fair about any of this?* Again I look up at the camera. Wonder if they've heard my thoughts? Which I know is ridiculous? They can't hear my thoughts. Can they?

The door swings open, I stand up and a smartly dressed woman in a navy blue skirt suit enters the room.

'You've got twenty minutes,' a man's voice says behind her.

She introduces herself as Rebecca Adams. 'Your solicitor,' she says. 'Laura sent me.' She waves at me to sit down again, sits opposite me. I wonder, when at home, if she's a Becky or a Becca? She has a briefcase, which she snaps open, takes out a notepad and a pen. 'Now,' she says, clicking her pen with her thumb, flicking open the notepad. 'I need you to tell me as much as you can, as quickly as you can.'

She's young, early thirties I'd say, but there's a resilience about her and I get the impression she's good at what she does, enjoys it. Her shoulder-length blonde hair, scraped back in a neat ponytail, and her make-up, like the rest of her, is neat, minimalistic.

I look up at the camera in the corner of the room. 'What, everything?'

She looks up, follows my gaze. 'Not on,' she says. 'This is a private conversation.'

'Are... are you sure?'

'Quite sure.' There is mild irritation in her voice. 'Now, shall we begin?'

I tell her about the telephone call. It came from an unknown number, while I was out, eating and drinking with my family in a London pub, two days before Christmas. How desperate the caller had sounded, begging for my help. How I then lied to my family, said I needed to meet with my agent, and left them to go to the caller. How, as instructed, I entered the property via a back entrance, overcome by the terrible smell coming from the kitchen which, the closer I got, I realised was coming from a huge bouquet on the side. How I noticed the photos of her, the caller, with men, lying on the edge of the island next to the flowers. Men who looked familiar, in various states of undress, in compromising positions. How I picked them up for a better look, not realising there was a hole in one of the fingers of my glove, unwittingly leaving my print. How, verging on hysteria, she explained what had happened, how he had knocked her around – again. How I examined the bruises on her neck, her upper arms, between her legs, some old, some new. How he had gone off to pick up some "friends". How he said she was to entertain them when he got back. How I said we should call the police. How she begged me not to, how she said he had threatened her, would finish her, and how it was in her interest, and that of some very powerful individuals, not to take her complaints to the authorities. How, legally, she was tied to him, and how if she towed the line he said he would release her from her contract, sooner rather than later. How I said I could help. How she said she needed more time to think about it. How she asked me to leave before he came back, but how she would think about what I had said, and would ring me again, soon.

I tell Rebecca how terrified she was.

When Honey Brown, the singer, hears I've been arrested, she hands herself in. When questioned, her statement confirms everything I have told the police, including how my fingerprint comes to be on some photos found in Black's kitchen.

They then release me without charge.

Honey, on the other hand, is arrested, charged and bailed, as she prepares to go to trial for the unlawful killing of Hunter Black. She is, of course, represented by one of the UK's finest barristers, namely Laura Noble, and the evidence presented, including film footage found in Black's home, plus witness statements given by some of Black's former employees – including his domestic staff – leaves the jurors in little doubt of Black's treatment of Honey, or of the events that took place that evening.

With a unanimous verdict of self-defence, they acquit her. Twelve jurors, despite the prosecution's attempts to sully and vilify Honey's reputation, to pore over her dress sense, her alcohol consumption, her suggestive stage performances and her sexuality, all agree she is not guilty. She agrees, in hindsight, that going to see Black alone, by entering the house via the back entrance as she sometimes did, on the evening of the day in question, had been a mistake. But she says she hoped to plead with Black, ask him – again – if he would consider releasing her from her contract, but, as Black didn't trust anyone, she thought it best to do so by going alone.

What she didn't expect when she arrived was to find him in a drink and drug induced rage because a well-known business friend of his was refusing to play ball – hence the photos, which at that point Honey hadn't seen. And, to add to his already murderous rage, he also, just as Honey entered the house, lifted the gift card from a beautiful bouquet sent earlier that day, which, for some unknown reason seemed to release the most vile, terrible smell about the kitchen. Honey says she tried to get Black to calm down, told him she would try to contact one of the domestics, all of whom had been given time off as Black had plans to fly to America over Christmas.

'Then I saw them, the photos of me, naked with a man who was doing things I had no recollection of – again! I got angry, confronted him and he slapped me, dragged me up the stairs. Told me I'd never get out of my contract until he was ready to let me go. I said I'd go to the papers, take my chances. I didn't mean it of course, I was too scared to do that. But it only seemed to fuel his rage, make him even more angry, and using both hands he grabbed me by the throat and squeezed, until slowly but surely, I felt the life draining away from me.'

She says she knew there was little use trying to pull his hands away because he was too strong, but in a last-ditch attempt to save herself, she lifted her leg and kicked him right between his. Stunned, he released her, staggered back, tripped and fell down the stairs. Shocked, she immediately checked for vital signs and when she found none, simply fled.

She says she knows it was wrong to leave the scene but when she explains to the jurors about the control Black held over her, the threats he had made, the film footage he said he had, how he had convinced her, should anything ever happen to him, that it would be in the best interests of some very powerful individuals if she disappeared, they believe her. However, once she heard of my arrest, she says she knew she had to do the right thing. Especially as she was the one who had phoned me and begged me to go to her at Black's house in the first place.

Throughout the trial, I, along with the other members of my family do everything possible to show Honey our support – even Cassie. It has been a struggle for Cassie to come to terms with this, especially considering Honey's initial betrayal of her.

However, it is amazing just how cathartic, how healing, forgiveness can be. And indeed, just what true friendship can endure and conquer... just look at Ruby and me, Mum and Aunt Marie, Dad and Mickey. Nonetheless, despite her huge heart, her willingness to forgive her friend, there is still a part of Cassie that doesn't understand why I immediately dropped everything that night and went to Honey when she called me. I explain that before that phone call, Honey had been to see me after one of my book signing events in London, had confided in me about Black, told me how sorry she was for what she had done to Cassie. Then I explain how I told Honey to stay in contact, that in the words of my father, there was "more than one way to skin a rat" and if she really wanted help, I may be able to offer her some, via Laura.

There are only a handful of us that know the real reason I went to her that night though. The truth. And for now, for the sake of everyone's safety, everyone's sanity, I'd prefer it to stay that way. Maybe over time, as the scars between Cassie and Honey truly heal, Honey will tell Cassie the truth, or maybe I will? However, I now see why Dad felt obliged to keep a few skeletons in his closet. How sometimes we keep secrets from those we love the most, not because we don't want them to know, but simply because we want to protect them.

Chapter 36

December 23rd – Two Days Before Christmas ...
WHAT REALLY HAPPENED

LIZZIE

The number that flashes up on my phone is not one I know. I never usually accept calls from unknown numbers but as I stare at the screen, feeling my mobile vibrate in my hand, something compels me to answer it. I recognise her voice immediately. She sounds, all things considered, relatively calm, but, as I listen, one of Dad's favourite sayings came to mind, "you can't kid a kidder." There is something in the rise and fall of her voice, the staccato of each word that hits me straight in the solar plexus. She begs me to go to her, to help, and without a second's hesitation, I leave my family and head to the nearest tube station.

Thankfully, only a couple of days before Christmas, the general atmosphere is one of festive good cheer. I convince everyone the caller is Michelle, my agent, asking if I am still about, and if so can I meet her to tie up a few loose ends that we'd forgotten to do earlier that morning. Simon suggests that he, Sean, Connor and Scott have another drink and wait for me at Kings Cross. I say, as I have an open train ticket, they'd be just as well to go without me. 'Less pressure on me to rush back,' I add. Simon looks pissed off – again – but at this moment I don't give a shit.

I know where to go, of course, having been there earlier today, but this time I go to the back entrance, as instructed, and this time I'm not in disguise. I did think, fleetingly, about changing my clothes again, but the urgency in her voice is so profound I can't think straight.

With gloved hands, I push the door open and step in. The smell hits me like a blow to the head. A putrid odour like nothing I have ever smelled before, swirls about me like a tide of sickness. With one hand shielding my mouth and nose with my scarf, the other clutching my stomach, my first instinct is to turn and run. The smell is nauseatingly obscene, makes my eyes water and my stomach heave. Fear pushes me onwards, though, suppressing any urge to throw up.

I step into what appears to be some sort of utility room and call out.

'Hello, it's me, Lizzie. Where are you?'

Heart hammering against my chest, I listen. No reply. The room is dark, with a strip of yellow light seeping through the crack of a partially open door opposite. I fumble forwards, pull the door open and find myself in a huge, brightly lit kitchen. I put my hand up to shield my eyes as they adjust to the light and take in my surroundings. The room itself is breath-taking. High ceilings including a central skylight, a trio of windows at the back, large white surfaces to compliment the dark wood cabinets, two kitchen islands, a six-burner stove, plus a larger-than-life refrigerator – it is everything I imagine the lifestyle of the rich and famous to be. A huge display of boxed flowers, sitting at the end of one island catches my attention, which, the nearer I get, the worse the smell becomes. I also notice some photos beside the flowers. With my gloved hands I pick them up, take a look, find them deeply disturbing.

Taking tentative steps forward, my scarf still pressed against my mouth and nose, I head towards another half-open door, step into what appears to be a hallway.

'Hello?' I call again.

'Lizzie? That you?' comes the faint reply. I see the blood first, a dark, iridescent pool collected around the bottom step of the grand wooden staircase. 'We're up here,' the woman's voice continues. I look up, spot her and another woman. 'Be careful,' she warns.

Chest tightening, I continue ambling forward. The head the blood frames comes into view, attached to a lifeless body. I stop for a moment, take a small inward gasp. Seeing a dead body is nothing new to me. I was lucky enough to be with Dad when he drew his last breath, his pale translucent skin stretched over a frame of jutting bones, a mere shadow on the man I once knew. He was someone I loved though, and he looked at peace once he'd passed away. With his slack jaw hanging open, his dark, startled eyes staring into space, Hunter Black looks every bit as shocked as I feel at seeing my daughter's tormentor laying in a halo of his own blood.

'I can't move, Lizzie,' comes the voice from above again.

I look up. 'Okay, don't worry, I'll come up there, to you.'

Her grey eyes flicker towards my gloved hands. 'Don't touch anything,' she says. 'And mind the blood.'

I kneel beside the body, remove my glove and place my hand above, but not on, Black's mouth, check for any signs of breathing. There are none.

'I've... I've checked,' comes another familiar voice. 'He's definitely dead.'

I climb the grand staircase, the air foetid and heavy, pressing against me, suppressing my ability to breathe. I convince myself, with each step, that I am calm, in control, but fear runs through me like a raging river.

'It was an accident,' Aunt Marie whimpers, as I reach the top of the stairs. 'I didn't mean to ... you know... I... I just wanted to stop him ... push him out of the way.'

Honey sits beside Aunt Marie, legs crossed, holding Aunt Marie's hand, her plump lips encrusted with dry blood. She looks child-like, this woman who had betrayed my daughter, nothing like her promotional photos. Slumped forward, she is staring into space, pinching chunks of plush silver carpet between the fingers of her other hand. Her crumpled white tee shirt, torn at the neck, has splashes of blood on it and the jeans she wears are ripped in several places. Whether that is a fashion statement or something else, though, I can't say. She looks at me, attempts a half-hearted smile then wincing, raises her hand to her lips.

MARIE

Marie looks at her niece, remembers the once fractious baby she helped nurture, the little girl whose eyes lit up every time Marie entered a room, who used to call her Mee-mee, whom she has watched with proud wonder, grow into the woman she is today, with children, and a grandchild of her own. She wonders, like she has on so many occasions, if Lizzie and her daughter, who would have been Lizzie's cousin, would have been close, like she and Ellie. Course, Marie can't be sure the baby she lost was a girl, but a week or so after she suspected she was pregnant, the taste of copper under her tongue was so strong it was as if Marie had been sucking on a penny. Marie's mother had been just the same, only ever having the sickness when she had been carrying Marie's brothers. So Marie was sure her baby had been a girl. Still, she'd been blessed with nieces and nephews. And this one, Lizzie, well, she is extra special. The daughter she never had – couldn't have – whose mother she loves like a sister.

'What... happened?' Lizzie asks. Her voice is so warm, so familiar, Marie immediately feels much calmer, however, her eyes, which dance skittishly between Honey and Marie, say something else entirely. Marie can see the panic and alarm behind them and suddenly she is overcome with guilt. She should never have phoned her niece. What the bleedin' hell was she thinking, bringing her here, dragging her into this mess.

Lizzie needs an explanation and Marie does her level best to give her one.

She starts at the beginning. Tells Lizzie about the cleaning agency she's been working for.

Lizzie frowns. 'You've been working as a cleaner, here, in London?'

Marie nods. 'A very upmarket one.'

'But... why?' Lizzie asks. Confusion etched into her tired face.

Marie continues to explain how she and an old friend she has lately become reacquainted with introduced her to the agency. 'I found her on Facebook, of all places.' Marie adds. 'We used to work together at a clothes shop down the Kings Road when Teddy and I, and your mum and dad, used to live in London.' Lizzie smiles, uses her hand to push her fringe from her eyes like she used to when she was a little girl. 'We met for coffee first, talked about old times. Then it became a regular thing; lunch trips, shopping trips, visits to the theatre. Sometimes I'd stay over at her flat, too. Helped take my mind off Teddy, see?' Marie looks down; feels the tears stinging the back of her eyes, the lump expanding in her throat. 'He doesn't even know who I am anymore, you know, Lizzie? Not these past few months, anyway. And... well... Normally I'd turn to your Mum. But she's still missing Salocin something terrible. And... and...'

Lizzie removes her gloves, places her cold, clammy hands on Marie's. Marie looks up. The corners of Lizzie's mouth lift into a smile. The fine lines around her mouth give her age away but nonetheless it's the same smile Lizzie used to give her aunt as a baby. Lizzie nods as if urging Marie to go on. Marie explains how

Sue, her friend, lives on her own. 'Has done since her husband passed away twenty years ago. She lives comfortably enough, like, but her son lives in Hawaii, so she still works – only part-time, mind – mostly so she can save enough money for the flights to visit him. Besides which, she says she enjoys working, enjoys the company. Anyway, I liked the sound of it; thought I'd like to give it a go, saw it as a bit of a welcome distraction, you know, from Teddy and everything...'

Marie stops talking. Clutches her chest with both hands; starts rocking back and forth. 'Oh gawd, Lizzie. Am I bad for not wanting to see him? To not want to see another bit of my Teddy die every time I visit?' If she was honest, Marie hated visiting her husband. He was now well into the seventh stage of Alzheimer's, which meant he was suffering from very severe cognitive decline. In other words, Teddy, her Teddy, had long gone. No longer able to speak, or communicate, he needed around the clock assistance with everything. And yet, for every day she didn't visit him, she was filled with a devastating sense of betrayal and abandonment. Remembering how, during those first terrible years, after Frank, when she had withdrawn from him, and from the world in general, for a while, Teddy's love and devotion towards her had never once waivered.

Again Lizzie takes one of Marie's hands in hers, and holds it. Reassures her aunt there's nothing wrong with her. There's a slight lilt to her niece's voice though, a note of impatience. Marie can hear the urgency in it.

The sound of a siren forces them all to look up.

'Police,' Honey gasps, her terrified eyes wide with fear.

Alarmed, all three women look towards the stairs. The siren passes and the relief that fills the space between them is overwhelming.

Again Lizzie urges Marie to carry on.

'I asked my friend, Sue, to help me get an interview with the agency. She said the agency preferred older, more reliable staff. People that understand the need for discretion. Most of their clients are rich, see, and more often than not, famous.

Honey looks up, sniffs, shoots Marie a sideways glance, and opens her mouth as if to speak. The only sound she makes, however, is a cross between a snort and a sob. Lizzie asks Honey if she is okay. Offers her some water from the bottle in her bag? Honey shakes her head, looks down again, and grabs another handful of carpet between her fingers.

'God, that smell isn't getting any better, is it?' Lizzie winces, covering her nose with the back of her hand. She turns her concerned face towards the stairs again. Marie follows her gaze, doesn't miss her niece's furtive glance towards the dead body at the bottom of them. Honey notices too, and nudges Marie.

Marie continues to explain how she told the agency she only wanted to work a couple of days a week and how the agency said they'd be in touch if something suitable came up.

'Sue said I could stay with her, at her flat, on the days I worked, if the agency did find me a position. Then, out of the blue, my friend revealed she was planning a six-month visit with her son in Hawaii, asked me if I would keep an eye on her flat, use it as my own if I wanted, and of course I accepted. After all, what are friends for if they can't help each other out once in a while? And then the agency phoned. Offered me some work at a property that was, for the most part, vacant. One of six around the world the family owned, apparently. And, like I'd asked, it was just for a couple of days a week. So I checked where the house was and discovered it was next door to the property of a certain well-known individual.' She points towards the stairs with her chin. 'And well, somehow, after everything Cassie had gone through, it seemed like – fate. Too good an opportunity to miss? So I accepted.'

Lizzie's eyebrows knit together. 'But... what, exactly, did you hope to achieve by working next door to the residence of Hunter Black?'

Marie shrugs. 'I... don't really know. I suppose I just thought, I'd take the job, and see what happened?'

'Right. So how...' Lizzie nods toward Honey '... did you two meet?'

Marie looks at Honey who is staring into space; her dark skin appears sallow, making her seem lifeless, like a shop mannequin. 'I became friendly with Black's gardener, who also tended the garden of the house I cleaned. He had access from one garden to the other via a hidden, specially installed security gate with a keypad and a code only he and the house owners knew. We liked to talk sometimes. His wife has Alzheimer's too, you see? And sometimes, when she was visiting Black, Honey would also come into the garden, for a smoke, start talking to Fred, the gardener, and me.' Honey turns to look at Marie, offers her a half smile. 'She didn't realise who I was at first, did you?'

Honey shakes her head. 'No,' she whispers. Marie looks at her, urges Honey to take a sip of water from the bottle Lizzie is still holding. Marie knows, only too well, how sore Honey's throat must be feeling.

'Of course my first instinct was not to talk to her at all, out of loyalty to Cassie, but...' Honey's sunken eyes film with tears. '... I knew, you see?'

'Knew what?'

'That like Cassie, Honey had been raped. Survivors have a look about 'em, see? Easy to spot, at least, they are to me.' Marie lowers her voice. 'It's something that stays with you. No matter how hard you try and lock it away. It sneaks out again, lingers in the memory, like a bad stain, long after the physical evidence is washed away – and it shows, on people's faces.'

'Sorry, what?' Lizzie says. Her forehead is concertinaed into heavy lines. 'Are you saying what I think you're saying? That you were raped, too?'

Marie nods. 'As vivid to me now as it was all those years ago–'

Lizzie lets out a small gasp, both hands flying to her face to cover her mouth. 'Oh my god,' she mumbles beneath them. 'Why don't I know about this, Aunt Marie? When? By who...?'

Marie's vision blurs. She looks up, stares at the ceiling, notices a cobweb in one of the corners, a yellow stain next to it, wonders what caused it, if there's been a leak?

When she looks down again, she finds Lizzie staring at her, her smile firm, reassuring. 'It's okay. You don't have to tell me.'

Marie swallows the dread rising up from her stomach, shakes her head. 'It's okay. I need to, want to explain... if you'll listen?'

'Of course I will,' Lizzie says softly.

'It happened when I still lived in London. A man, the son of someone your dad worked for.'

'Mickey?'

'No. He worked for Georgie. Anyway, it was bad. Very bad.' Marie looks down again; blinking fast, reminding herself to take a deep breath. 'I got by though, somehow. I was lucky to have a man that loved me, good friends and family too. And gradually, over time, the nightmare of what happened, faded.'

'But... but was he ever arrested? Charged?'

'No. He got away with it. Which was a bitter pill to swallow at times. Nonetheless, I moved on. Learned to live with it, bury it, to a certain extent. And, although Teddy and I couldn't have children of our own, we made the best of it. We doted on you and Sean. You weren't ours, weren't mine.' Marie pauses, and lets her hands fall into her lap, stares at her tummy. 'But you were the next best thing. Then, later there were your children, of course, yours and Sean's, Maisy too, after you met Simon, and life, on the whole, was good. For all of us. Steady, safe, quiet, not everyone's cup of tea, I know, but just what the doctor ordered – for all of us, not just me. There were a few stressful moments, of course. We were all worried to death about you for a while, when Scott left you and the children. But that was nothing compared to later. When you were attacked and we thought we might lose you…'

Marie puts her hand to her mouth, stifles a sob, watches as Lizzie, on the other hand, instinctively raises her hand to her head.

'God I remember that.' Honey says, twisting her mouth to the side, her voice noticeably hoarse. 'Cassie really thought she was going to lose you.'

'But we rallied round, as a family,' Marie continues. 'And eventually, when you came round, I thought, hoped, that would be the last of it. All families have their problems, their mishaps, but what happened to you was particularly bad, so I suppose I thought things would settle down again, get back to normal. But then of course there was Cassie. And when I found out what happened to her, well… let's just say something inside me snapped. I knew I had to do something. Because I know, see, from experience, how much Cassie would need justice, or, or retribution, something… Anything, in fact, that proved she wasn't to blame, that it wasn't her fault. So when this job came up' Marie throws her hands up, 'it felt like it was meant to be.' Lizzie stares at her aunt, blinking slowly. Marie looks at Honey. 'And gradually, over time, Honey confided in me, admitted what was going on with Black. And the two of us became, well, friends.'

Lizzie massages her forehead with her hand. She wears the weary look of a tired, fretful mother alongside the faraway look of a lost little girl. 'Is that why you moved away from London? Because of what happened to you?'

Coy, Marie puts a hand to her head; presses her hair flat

against it. 'Sort of. Your uncle Teddy and I, and your mum and dad, all agreed it would be a good idea to move away from London, make a fresh start.'

'But – I don't understand? Why all four of you? Why did Mum and Dad feel the need to get away too?'

Marie looks at her hands, spins her gold wedding band on her ring finger, and stares at the blue sapphire of the ring on her other hand. 'You'll need to ask Ellie, your mum. I just wanted you to know about me, what was going on in my head. Understand that my helping Honey doesn't mean I was betraying Cassie.'

LIZZIE

For a fleeting moment I struggle with the knowledge of my aunt and Honey as friends, especially when I think of Cassie, how broken she was when Honey betrayed her, siding with Black in exchange for what he could offer her. But as I look at Honey, her sunken eyes, emaciated frame, a mere shadow of the vibrant young woman I had once known, I realise she has more than paid for what she did. I also look at my aunt, remember her face in the black and white photos Mum showed me, a smiling young woman, like Cassie, her whole life ahead of her. Then I think of her afterwards, the photos that followed – her cautious smile, wary eyes. Funny then, how I never noticed that faraway look before? Or is that merely my interpretation now I know better? Growing up, Aunt Marie, along with Uncle Teddy, spoiled Sean and I rotten, but that was just who she was to me – my aunt, ever present, glamorous, and full of cheery resolve. How well she hid her pain, then – or how well I chose not to see it?

Honey continues to explain why she came to the house, alone.

'I was drunk,' she said. 'Heard we'd sold like the god zillionth copy of my latest single and what with all the Christmas goodwill crap, I though it seemed like the right time to talk to Black. I, I just thought…' Her voice cracks, and she falters, a lone tear running down her cheek. Aunt Marie pats her hand and Honey looks at her gratefully. 'Well for some stupid reason, I thought it would be a good idea.' She shakes her head, half laughs. 'It wasn't though, was it? It's all about power with Black. And money. I think that's when the penny finally dropped, you know? When I realised that he'd never let me go. At least, not until he was ready to,' she says sadly.

She explains about the terrible smell in the kitchen, that still fills the rest of the house, how angry Black was about it, how she had phoned Aunt Marie to see if she was next door, if she would come round under the guise of hired help, try to help her calm Black down.

'Wait. You called each other?' I glance between them. 'So, if the police check, they'll make a connection between you both?'

Aunt Marie pulls out a small, nondescript mobile phone from her pocket. It looks nothing like the iPhone I know she has, and Honey follows suit. 'Pay as you go,' Aunt Marie says. 'Disposable.'

'A burner, I think they call them?' Honey adds. 'Just in case, because I'm pretty sure *he*…' She nods towards the bottom of the stairs '…used to monitor my texts and phone messages. So we decided, if we wanted to talk to one another it would be best to use a burner. Chuck it and change it each time we made a call.'

After getting Honey's call, Aunt Marie said she entered the house via the gate between the two gardens – 'I memorised the code one day when Fred was busy chatting, glanced over his shoulder when he was engrossed in whatever it was we were discussing' – and went to find Honey.

In the meantime Honey noticed the photos beside the flowers. 'Ones that showed me and a man, naked,' she said, sobbing.

'Doing things, vile, disgusting things I had no recollection of! And it wasn't the first time that had happened either. I was so angry, I confronted Black, but he slapped me, dragged me up the stairs. Told me I was a worthless nobody. That he had made me what I was, and instead of fucking moaning, I should bow at his feet every day, thanking him. Said I'd never get out of my contract, so I'd better fucking get used to it. I told him I'd go to the papers. Take my chances. I didn't mean it of course; I was too scared to do that. But my threat only made him angrier, more excited. He grabbed me by the throat, like he's done so many times, and squeezed. This time, though, I couldn't breathe. Normally he stops... before it goes too far... but this time he didn't stop. His eyes were bulging, but I swear down he was smiling, like he was enjoying it. Watching the life drain away from me and getting off on it.'

'That's when I went for him,' Aunt Marie says. 'I'd let myself in and found them both upstairs. He was going to kill her. I could see it in his eyes – I've seen that look before, see. So I hit him, hammered on his back with both fists, the little good it did. He barely flinched, barely even noticed I was there – at first. So I threw myself at him, wrapped my arms around his neck and clung on for dear life. He spun round, threw me off like I was nothing more than a nuisance, a pesky housefly. But as he stepped forward, he tripped and lost his balance. So, well, I reached out and, and, I pushed him... ever so gently... and he just... fell.' Aunt Marie looks at me, her lined face drawn, weary, and offers me a smile, which is actually more of a grimace. 'I, we...' she looks at Honey and suddenly they are both children, small girls who don't know what to do. 'I'm sorry, Lizzie. I should never have called you. You need to go and we need to call the police,' she whispers.

'No!' Honey shakes her head like a defiant toddler. 'You'll go to prison, Marie.'

'Not if we say it was self-defence,' I say, seeing it clearly, as if I was writing a chapter in a book. 'That he simply tripped and fell. That I was the one here, with you. Not Marie.'

Aunt Marie opens her mouth to protest but Honey puts her hand up, stops her, looking at her with a fondness, a kindness that speaks of a bond much deeper than I had realised.

'This is my shit and I need to sort it. You wouldn't even be here if it wasn't for me. Either of you,' Honey says, her amber eyes, determined, flitting like fireflies, back and forth between us.

Chapter 37

Present Day

"The strongest of all warriors are these two – Time and Patience."

— Leo Tolstoy, ***War and Peace***

LIZZIE

Honey insisted that both Aunt Marie and I leave. We were not to breathe a word to anyone and she promised, somehow, she would sort it. I believed her too. No longer was she the quivering wreck I discovered when I first arrived at Black's house. Something about her had changed, and she was growing stronger by the minute, like a phoenix rising from the ashes. She told Aunt Marie to go back to the house next door via the gate in the garden, and leave the property at the side entrance as she always did when working there. Then she advised me to leave the same way I arrived, via the back entrance, but to follow the route and roads she suggested as there were less CCTV cameras in place.

It would have been easy to do the right thing, to call the police, but at that moment in time my only concern was Aunt Marie. She was only there because of some misplaced loyalty to me, to Cassie, and to help Honey. But would a jury see it that way? So I agreed with Honey. I found my way back to Kings Cross and waited for Aunt Marie, where together we travelled home.

We received a few strange looks on the train home, of course, because some of the scent from the stink bomb Connor had delivered to Black's house had seeped through to our clothes. So before going home, I went back to Aunt Marie's house, showered, and changed into some of her clothes (thankfully no one was awake when I got home, so there were no suspicious questions as to my recently changed attire). The following morning Aunt Marie burned our foul-smelling clothes in a drum, along with some garden refuse, at the bottom of her garden. Burning her garden refuse was something she did regularly, so no one batted an eyelid or gave it a second thought. Some of the smell still lingered about my person slightly, but I managed to mask it – just – by dousing myself in perfume and blaming the slight whiff on a new organic body wash I was using.

I promised Aunt Marie, that whatever happened, as long as she kept calm, she would not do any time for the death of Hunter Black. I also vowed to myself, that if necessary, I would take the fall. However, by the time I was arrested, several people, including Simon and Laura, knew what had happened. Laura and Honey met, and they hatched a plan. Honey said she would take her chances in court, not least because she wanted to show the world who Hunter Black *really* was, but also because the odds were in her favour. The public liked her. Plus other witnesses, including Black's staff, had started coming forward, giving statements in her defence, including, as it turned out, Amber. Amber – whose boyfriend had attacked me all those years ago, and who had been brave enough to come forward as a witness against him – and her young daughter, had supposedly gone missing some time last year. However, training as an investigative journalist, she had in fact joined Black's staff and had, all this time, been working undercover. There were also rumours circulating about damning film footage found on a collection of USB sticks that had been discovered.

So Honey went to court and was found not guilty. But the media coverage during the trial, as I suspected, was frenzied. It even brought the press to our very quiet little town, which put me out of favour with some. Others, however, like Amra, couldn't have done more to support us. I often came home to find her chasing off nosey journalists or paparazzi, like an angry guard dog – and a Rottweiler at that.

But as the old saying goes though, all publicity is good publicity, and Honey's high profile case and our support of her did nothing to harm our new business venture. In fact it did the complete opposite, found us going from strength to strength.

During that time, Laura also asked to meet me a couple of times, too, socially. So we could get better acquainted, she said. I had my reservations at first but Laura the person was different to Laura the barrister, more relaxed, more at ease than her professional self.

The first time we met was at Clerkenwell. She showed me where her grandfather's scrap metal yard had once been, where my father had worked alongside her father – all long since replaced by offices and loft-living professionals. She also filled in a few gaps, told me how Georgie had passed away during the late 1970s, how her father, Mickey, had never really got over the loss of her mother, Helena.

'He did his best, though,' she said. 'My sisters and I all received the best private education. But it was hard growing up in the shadow of an infamous gangster. That's why he changed his surname, and my sisters and mine, by deedpole to Smyth, so people wouldn't make the link, join the dots, from us to my grandfather, Georgie. It made little difference to how I felt, though, which was always like I never quite belonged, that, to quote Dickens, although born and raised in London, I was 'A Tale of Two Cities.' Looking back, she admitted, she thought she, like my Mum, had postnatal depression. But, 'When Maisy was born, I mistook it for something else, something sinister – madness, or maybe badness, that I was convinced ran through my bloodline. Which is why I felt Maisy was better off without me? Ridiculous, I know, but at the time it seemed plausible. It is also not an excuse. And I have a lot of making up to do, especially to Maisy,' she said, her face fixed in a grimace, a strand of loose hair falling across her face. 'But also to you and Simon.'

She told me her father passed away during the late 1990s. Cancer. But before he did, he told her and her sisters about Salocin, made them promise to keep the "debt of gratitude" should Dad, or any members of his family, contact them. I also asked her about Frank. She said she rarely, if ever, saw him, but when she did, it was always unpleasant, that he gave off an aura, a presence that was bad through and through.

'He was not a nice man,' she said, arching one of her neat eyebrows. 'Used to ask my sisters and me to sit on his knee. We didn't of course, which made him angry. Then again… he was always angry. Always drunk too. He hated being disabled, walking with a limp, so he couldn't get around properly.'

He died some time during the late eighties. Last seen standing on the steps of Wapping Old Stairs to be exact, at the back of a pub, and was washed up a week later, swollen and blued by the water, after supposedly falling in and drowning.

Laura said she didn't go to the funeral and wasn't interested in the circumstances of his death – until recently. 'I suddenly felt the urge to look into it,' she said. 'Mostly out of morbid curiosity. There was one witness, apparently, a homeless man, inebriated, known to the police and apt to make up stories, so his statement was disregarded. He said he saw a woman push Frank into the river. Said Frank had looked up, saw her and laughed – almost as if he knew her – as if he knew what she was about to do, and did nothing to stop her. But the only thing the homeless man could remember about the woman was an unusual blue sapphire ring she wore on her right hand. His statement was never followed up though, his death recorded as an accidental drowning.'

Her words chilled me. And it must have shown on my face

because, taking my hand in hers, she said she had no intention of looking any further into the matter.

'Let sleeping dogs lie, eh?' And she winked.

At the close of Honey's court case we were all there to lend our support, including Cassie and Aunt Marie, even Luke and Eustace turned up. And while Honey, ever the natural born performer spoke to, what appeared to be, several hundred waiting news reporters and paparazzi regarding the verdict, DI Kat Stewart approached us and, shaking her hand, congratulated Laura on her win, said, despite going down as a loss for her and her department, she felt Honey's acquittal was the right verdict. She also introduced herself to Luke, congratulated him on his great music.

'My daughter is a massive fan,' she said grinning, her face flushed. 'She's never managed to get tickets yet to see you though.'

Luke told her about the band's plans to play a charity gig at Wembley with special guest, Honey Brown and DI Stewart VIP tickets on the front row. Beaming like a child, DI Stewart accepted, on the understanding she pay for the said tickets.

'Otherwise, it could be construed as something else,' she explained, a wry smile ironing out the tired creases around her eyes and mouth. 'What with me being a copper and all.'

It was fleeting, but I also noticed how she looked at Aunt Marie, clocked the ring she wore on her right hand. How she and Laura exchanged glances, and how, although it was the tiniest of movements, both women shook their heads.

Chapter 38

FOR BETTER, FOR WORSE

"Time is too slow for those who wait, too swift for those who fear, too long for those who grieve, too short for those who rejoice, but for those who love, time is eternity."

– **Henry Van Dyke**

LIZZIE

Nervous, I check my reflection, again, use my finger to flatten my eyebrow, fiddle with the curled strand of hair brushing the side of my cheek. I catch Cassie watching me, laughing.

'You look beautiful, Mum,' she says.

I swallow, hard. 'You think?'

'Stunning.'

I shake my head, smile. 'And you look, well, breathtaking. Simply breathtaking.'

Cassie winks. Thrusts her foot forward. 'What – even though I'm wearing these?' She hitches up her gown, the dress, with a few alterations, Aunt Marie wore when she married Uncle Teddy, and shows me Natasha's bright white Doc Martins.

I laugh. 'They're perfect, Cassie, just like you.'

Cassie's eyes well up with tears. 'Oh, for god bloody sake,' she says, fanning her face with her hand. 'Don't start me off again. I've only just had my make-up done.'

There's a sharp knock on the door. It's Mum and Aunt Marie. 'Cooee,' Mum says, thrusting her head around the door. 'How's everyone doing?' Both women step into the room, turn towards Cassie and gasp, their fisted hands flying up to cover their mouths. 'Oh Cassie, you look beautiful,' Mum says.

'Yes. Beautiful,' Aunt Marie repeats.

'Thanks.' She gives them a quick twirl. 'And thanks for letting me have your dress, Aunt Marie.' Aunt Marie nods. 'But you weren't supposed to see me yet,' she adds, arching one of her perfectly groomed eyebrows. 'Not until I walk down the aisle.'

Mum waves her hand dismissively. 'Bugger protocol. Couldn't wait,' she says, her eyes glimmering with the promise of tears. 'Grandad would be so proud of you,' she whispers.

Aunt Marie nods her head up and down like an over-enthusiastic toddler. 'Hmm, yes, he would. And Uncle Teddy.'

My eyes flit towards the sash window; a late summer morning sky creeps in behind it, an artist's canvas filled with brushstrokes of yellow and blue, flashes of peach and raspberry. Behind the window, is a tree, where sits a blackbird. I feel the corners of my mouth lift into a smile. *Dad*, I whisper.

Cassie turns away, dabbing the corners of her eyes with a tissue. Regaining her composure, she swings back, arm outstretched, pointing at me. 'What about Mum? Doesn't she look amazing too?'

Mum turns towards me, scrutinising me like a shop mannequin. 'Lovely, my darling girl,' she whispers. 'Just lovely.'

Again, Aunt Marie nods in agreement.

'You think?' I chew the corner of my lip and look down, tugging at the bottom of my cream tailored jacket and using the palms of my hands to press it flat. 'You don't think I should have worn a dress?'

Mum shakes her head. 'No, you were right. The trouser suit is beautiful, fits you perfectly.'

'Very sophisticated,' Aunt Marie adds.

'Thank you. Both of you. For everything.'

'Yes, thank you,' Cassie repeats, flinging her arms about the necks of both women and smothering them in kisses whether or not they want them. 'You are amazing. And you look amazing, too.' She steps back, holding them at arms-length. 'Don't they look amazing, Mum?' she says, full of wide-eyed laughter.

I smile, blink back the tears and nod my head. Mum is wearing a pale blue, knee-length dress, her grey hair, discreetly highlighted, tucked beneath a matching hat, whereas Aunt Marie has chosen a navy blue skirt and matching bolero style jacket, but instead of a hat she is wearing a grey feathered fascinator, perched to the side of her perfectly coiffed hair. 'My heroes,' I reply.

'We're just a couple of silly old women,' Mum says, dismissively. And as if by magic, more tissues appear to stem the flow of tears I fear will be continuous today. 'Oh dear,' Mum adds, sniffing, opening the handbag balanced on her thin wrist, rummaging around inside. 'I, I didn't know which one of you to give this to?' She looks up, her sharp blue eyes now two limpid pools of tears. She thrusts forward a small wooden jewellery box. 'It was the Christmas present your Dad left for me,' she continues, her eyes settling on mine. 'Before he...'

'So I commissioned a couple of replicas,' Aunt Marie intervenes, pulling out a similar looking box from her respective handbag.

Mum looks at Aunt Marie and the tears flow now, regardless of her futile attempt to stop them. 'Oh, Gordon Bennett,' she mutters under her breath. 'Now I need to re-apply my make-up.'

Mum asks that we don't open the boxes until they've left the room. 'I don't think my heart will bear it,' she says, smiling through her tears.

And as she and Aunt Marie scuttle off, Cassie and I look at one another.

'After three?' Cassie suggests.

'Okay. One. Two. Three.'

We flip open the lids to the tiny boxes, which creak like an old wooden door, and peer in. Attached to each gold chain is a small heart-shaped locket. Cassie studies her necklace, fiddles with the clasp until it flips open, then puts her hand to her mouth, gasps. I follow suit, releasing the clasp so that one heart becomes two. On the left half is a tiny photo of Dad, and on the right an inscription, "It's not a life, it's an adventure".

I look up, feel my vision blur, my gaze filming with tears, whereas Cassie, whose speech is barely comprehensible, sobs uncontrollably. I do my best to comfort her; to make my tight, sharp sobs appear controlled, and cogent, but it's pointless, and like Cassie I give in to my tears. When Tabitha returns from her trip to the loo she looks mortified, all her hard work undone by the black streaks of tear-stained mascara now lining both our faces. Thankfully, despite her clucking, Tabitha works quickly to rectify the damage caused by our sobbing, applies her magic for the second time today, then wanders off to join the rest of the congregation.

After the hustle and bustle of a busy morning getting ready, Cassie and I find ourselves alone; mother and daughter wrapped in excited silence. A gentle knock on the door breaks the hush, followed by a warm voice telling us "it's time".

I smile, offer my daughter my arm.

'Why, thank you,' she says, linking arms with me.

I take a deep breath in, then slowly blow it back out again. 'Ready?'

Cassie nods. 'Yep. I think so. You?'

'As we'll ever be, eh?' I take a step forward but Cassie puts her hand out to stop me.

'Do you think Dad is okay about you giving me away? Do you think he understands?'

I stare at her. 'Listen,' I shoot her a look of mock indignation, 'I'm the one that brought you up. Went through all the bad times as well as the good. It stands to reason I should be the one to give you away. Okay?'

Cassie recoils a little, her long lashes flickering, 'What's that supposed to mean?' she replies. 'You're not talking about, about all that shit with Black, are you?'

I stifle a laugh and Cassie, somewhat surprised, asks me what the hell is so funny. I lift my hand, brush my fingers along the soft down of her cheek, stare into her large brown eyes, notice how her cupid's bow of a mouth is now a perfectly painted pout, and trace my finger along the bump in her nose; the one she hates, the one like mine, just like Dad's. I see my daughter the woman but also the many faces of my daughter the girl, a gallery of Cassies, past and present.

'I'm talking about you as a teenager.'

Cassie steps back, laughs, relief flooding her face. 'I thought, for a minute…' She flings her arms around me. 'Love you, Mum,' she mumbles, her voice muffled against my shoulder.

I hold her tight before panic forces me to release her again. I look down. Brush the collar of my cream jacket, relieved to see there isn't a stain. 'Don't want to get make-up on my jacket.'

'Oh shit, yeah. Sorry!' She bends forward for a better look. 'Yep. Nope. It all looks okay,' she confirms.

I use the back of my hand to pretend to mop my brow. 'Phew.'

'I do, though, Mum,' Cassie adds, her tone sombre. 'Love you, I mean. Can't thank you enough for all you've done for me.'

I shrug my shoulders. Tell her it's all part of the service, all part of being a parent. That, for better or worse, whatever happens, she's stuck with me. Cassie, her lip trembling, nods. I wipe the lone tear cascading down her face.

'And anyway,' I say, 'As you're also giving me away, your Dad would have only got in the way.'

Cassie's smile, broad, wrinkles her nose, like it did when she was a little girl. 'Never thought I'd see the day when you and Si would tie the knot,' she says, nudging me. 'A double wedding was a perfect idea. Plus...' She looks down, strokes the gold heart now draped around her neck '...Grandad will walk with us too, now. Won't he?'

EPILOGUE

LIZZIE

The wedding reception went well, full of much-needed laughter and frivolity, surrounded by those we love, family and good friends, which turned out to be reassuringly more than I'd realised. This also comforted me, made me feel safe in the knowledge that should anything happen to me, or any one of us, in fact, we have people, good people, who love and care for us. Dad always said you can never have enough good people looking out for you. And he was right.

It's a cliché but I've discovered time *is* a great healer. When the DJ at our wedding called the happily married couples to the dance floor, our song of choice was 'Everlasting Love'. The same song my father dedicated to my mother; spun her around the kitchen to on countless occasions, during both my childhood and my adult years. The same song, once so painful to listen to after his passing, but after time has worked its magic, makes me smile again. There are still tears of course, always will be, but generally they are happy ones. On the whole I'm grateful to have had such a crazy, obnoxious, kind and loving man in my life. Honoured to have had the privilege to call Salocin Lemalf, Dad.

Connor swore blind he saw him at the wedding, although, having said that, he also confessed to having smoked a bit of weed at the time. 'Honest, though,' he said. 'I'm not making it up.' He asked me if I'd ever seen the Star Wars film, *Return of the Jedi*. If I remembered the scene at the end of the film where everyone is celebrating and Luke Skywalker turns around and sees the ghosts of Anakin Skywalker, Obi-Wan Kenobi and Yoda. 'Well that's kind of how I saw Grandad, Uncle Teddy and...' He trailed off, looked down, and kicked his shoes.

'And... who else did you see?' I asked.

He glanced up again, smiled. 'Freddy,' he replied, through his sheepish grin.

And once again I felt my eyes well up, wondered how the hell that reservoir hadn't yet run dry. Strangely, though, I found the idea of Dad, Uncle Teddy and Freddy, present in the room with us that night, surprisingly comforting. And although I still miss my father's presence, find the gap in my heart, still huge, I count myself lucky to have another good man in my life – Simon. The same man who has loved me unconditionally, for richer and poorer, in sickness and in health, for more years than I care to remember. And who, on our wedding day, promised in front of everyone, to continue doing so. Just as Luke did with Cassie.

If everyone we loved and cared about was at the wedding, that included Honey and Laura. Honey, tall and willowy, her delicate face and razor sharp cheekbones encased in a head of thick, dark hair looked much more like her old self once the trial was behind her. It was a wonderful surprise too, when, unbeknownst to us all, she purchased Sean and Natasha's old cottage in Cornwall. She gutted it and spent several hundred thousand pounds transforming it into both a writer's retreat and a music studio for our music production company, then gifted it to us, as a family by way of thanks for our support. Where possible, we try to use it to help those that come from disadvantaged backgrounds. Cassie, for instance, traced a homeless girl with a guitar she kept seeing around London, and is helping her produce some of her own songs, as well as teaching her about the music industry in general.

And the name of our new business venture? Well, it's ... Adventure Records. I didn't get it at first until Simon, rolling his eyes, a note of impatience in his voice, explained. 'We've called Adventure Records, as in… it's not a life… it's an–'

I cried, of course, once the penny dropped.

Connor dropped a bombshell that night though. Took my hand, towards the end of the evening, asked me to step outside with him to get some fresh air. Even before he spoke I'd guessed my youngest child, my little big man, was leaving me. 'Only for a year,' he said, with feigned nonchalance, 'two at the most.' He explained that he and Robbo had made plans to go travelling. Said they'd saved enough money to last them the first six months, then they planned to find work as they moved around to fund the rest of their backpack tour of the world. Of course, the mother in me, with my maternal instincts firing on all cylinders, didn't want him to go. And if I could have, I would have wrapped him up there and then and kept him with me. However, the person in me, and the writer, willed him to go. To fly the nest, have adventures; take a journey of self-discovery. I gave him my tearful blessing and there beneath the stars, we hugged for a small eternity with me clinging on for dear life to what was left of my son, the boy, before my son, the man, left.

Will he return? I hope so. Only time will tell, I suppose.

And so we have come to the end of this story about my madcap family and this strange adventure we call life. Not that our stories have ended, of course, far from it. They, like time itself, continue evolving, playing out, for better or worse. I'm too old and far too cynical to believe in fairy tales – if I ever did – but after everything I've been through, everything my family has been through, I'll take this.

And always remember… "It's not a life, it's an adventure!"

The End

ACKNOWLEDGMENTS

Firstly, I'd like to thank my editor, Anne Hamilton, whose expertise, passion, and keen eye really helped pulled my story together. Secondly, I'd like to thank fellow writers RC Bridgestock (Bob and Carol), Caroline Mitchell, and Simon Michael who, with their collective knowledge and experience in matters relating to the police force, police procedure, and the law, always replied to, and graciously put up with my emails that often began with the words, "Can I ask you a question? What if...?" Your help has been invaluable. I would also like to thank Michelle Ryles, Natasha Shiels, Gina Kirkham, Tracey Peel-Ridealgh and Patricia Dixon for taking the time to read early drafts of my novel. You are all absolute stars!

Thank you also to my many lovely friends, old and new, some of whom I've met via social media, for your continued love and support of both my books and me – you have often kept me going when, at times, it would have been easier to give up. I'd like to give HUGE thanks, of course, to the many wonderful readers, reviewers and bloggers out there for taking the time to read and review my books, and for spreading the book love. You are all amazing – truly, I mean that. I would also like to thank my lovely children who both tire and inspire me. I love you to the moon and back, and all that mumsy stuff... Thanks also to Steve, my other half who I'm pretty convinced thinks I'm mad (especially when I'm talking to my imaginary friends!) but has always, one hundred per cent, supported my writing. I'd also like to thank Matthew and all at Urbane Publications for your continued belief in my stories.

Finally, last, but by no means least, I'd like to thank my parents. To my dad, ever the raconteur, for filling my head with inspiring, colourful stories, some true, some made up, and my mum, probably my biggest supporter and always my first trusted reader. You are my heroes.

Eva Jordan, born in Kent but living most of her life in a small Cambridgeshire town, describes herself as a lover of words, books, travel and chocolate. She is also partial to the odd glass or two of wine.

Her career has been varied including working within the library service and at a women's refuge. She has had several short stories published and currently writes a monthly column for a local magazine. Eva also works on a voluntary basis for a charity based organisation teaching adults to read. However, storytelling through the art of writing is her passion and as a busy mum and step mum to four children, Eva says she is never short of inspiration!

As well as writing, Eva loves music and film and of course she loves to read. She enjoys stories that force the reader to observe the daily interactions of people with one another set against the social complexities of everyday life, be that through crime, love or comedy.

It is the women in Eva's life, including her mother, daughters and good friends that inspired her to write her debut novel *183 TIMES A YEAR*, a modern day exploration of domestic love, hate, strength and friendship set amongst the thorny realities of today's divided and extended families. This was followed by the bestselling *ALL THE COLOURS IN BETWEEN*.

Testing, testing, one, two teens...

183 TIMES A YEAR

EVA JORDAN

'I really enjoyed this book. It really grasped the nature of mother/daughter relationships very well, in a way that was funny but also at times, touching and poignant.'
Jill's Book Cafe

'*An emotive and beautifully written story of family life.*'
By The Letter Book Reviews